NAHAL TAJADOD

Rumi

The Fire of Love

Translated from the French
by Robert Bononno

THE OVERLOOK PRESS
Woodstock & New York

First published paperback in the United States in 2008 by
The Overlook Press, Peter Mayer Publishers, Inc.
Woodstock & New York

WOODSTOCK:
One Overlook Drive
Woodstock, NY 12498
www.overlookpress.com
[for individual orders, bulk and special sales, contact our Woodstock office]

NEW YORK:
141 Wooster Street
New York, NY 10012

LONDON:
Gerald Duckworth & Co. Ltd.
Greenhill House
90-93 Cowcross Street
London EC1M 6BF

This work has been published with a subsidy from the Centre National du Livre
(French Ministry of Culture).

Cataloging-in-Publication Data is available from the Library of Congress

Book design and type formatting by Bernard Schleifer
Manufactured in the United States of America

US ISBN 978-1-59020-080-3
UK ISBN 978-0-71563-801-9

2 4 6 8 10 9 7 6 5 3 1

To Mahin Djahanbeiglou-Tajadod,
my mother, who, as a part of all beginnings,
was the starting point for this book, and to
my daughter, Kiara Carrière, who is the fruit.

Note

The dialogues and commentary by the principal characters in this book are, for the most part, drawn from their own works.

For Rumi:
Divan-i Shams-i Tabrizi
Masnavi-yi Ma'navi
Fihi mafih

For Shams:
Maqalat-i Shams-i Tabrizi

For Sultan Walad:
Valadn`amah

I have also incorporated information drawn from the biography of Rumi and his entourage, *Manaqib al-`arifin*; written between 1318 and 1353 by Aflaki (Shams al-Din Ahmad Aflaki, d. 1360) at the request of Rumi's grandson.

I was dead, behold I am alive
I was a tear, behold I am laughter
The joy of love arrived
Behold, I am eternal happiness.

Rumi

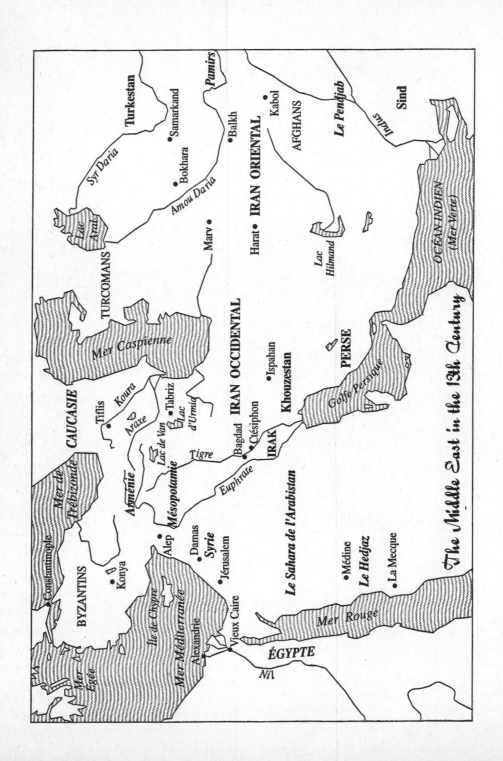

The Middle East in the 13th Century

شمس الدين

The Book of
Shams of Tabriz

The Old Man in the Cold

H E WAS TALL AND VERY THIN, ALMOST SKELETAL, AND WAS bundled into a black felt coat with broad sleeves. His hair, the color of the sky after the rain, stuck out from beneath a boat-shaped hat. He walked quickly, ignoring the city around him—the shops, the inhabitants, the animals— his eyes were those of a visitor, a newcomer. From time to time, he would stop in front of a stall. His gaze wandered across the baskets, the rush, the straw, the reeds. The merchant suggested a wicker winnowing basket, or something similar. The man did not respond. He rarely answered when questioned.

The wind attacked his emaciated face, which crinkled like parchment in contact with fire. He furrowed his brows, trying to adjust to the cold, the brutal cold that had fallen over Konya at the end of autumn that year.

"I am an old man in the cold," he said to the basket maker.

The man continued to present his wares.

"Look at these handles; feel the bottom. No other basket in the city can compare. It could transport a man to heaven."

"I don't need your basket to get to heaven."

When I saw him for the first time, Shams of Tabriz—this was soon after he had met my master, Rumi—he was the same age as I am now, sixty.

But I am the one who is now old and frail. And Shams's saying, "I am an old man in the cold," has become my own. The brazier in the room where I write the story of my master does not warm my tired bones, and of my acquaintances, I am the oldest. The young, eager student of old, the enthusiast of physical exercise and jokes, is now a sage whom others consult. The age of respect has caught up with me. The athlete who split ice on the lake to bathe in the dead of winter now spends his time before the fire. My knees hurt. My hands tremble slightly.

Old and frail, I try to imagine Shams as he was forty years ago. I see him walk quickly away from the basket weaver's shop. I see him walk the streets of Konya, the first city to emerge from the flood, visited by Paul, by the apostle Barnabus and the disciple Timothy, the seat of the first Christian councils, ransacked by the Crusaders, before it became, in the sixth century of the Hegira, the capital of the Seljuk sultans.

The Mongol attacks were unable to extinguish the vitality of this beating heart of commerce, this city populated by Turks, Greeks, Arabs, Indians, Iranians, Franks, Armenians, Uyghurs, Venetians, even Chinese. Every morning, the noise of the water sellers, as they filled their goatskins in the canals outside the city and transported them on the backs of camels, awakened the inhabitants with their cries of fresh water. The launderers, in their continuous comings and goings between the homes of their customers and the river, loaded their mules with musty, soiled laundry and returned with neatly folded piles that were immaculately clean and perfumed. Masons dozed alongside the main crossroads, waiting for the early morning passage of a contractor in search of skilled labor. From the countless work sites—the sultan had been overcome by a frenzy of construction—the noise of pulleys and cords, lifting workers in baskets to the top of the minarets, could be heard until sunset. In the residential quarters, the cries of the rag pickers, who walked the streets calling to the inhabitants, seemed to go on forever. From the courtyards of the schools, the *dabirestan*, could be heard the clamor of children, tirelessly reciting, in their sharp and monotonous voices, verses from the Koran. At night, from the illuminated windows of the asylum, emerged the strange dialogues of a madman, who expressed himself loudly in a language understood by him alone.

In the public baths, clouds of aromatic steam rose from the hot water and, in the caves of the Armenians, the somnolent aroma of old wine, heedless of the clash of Mongol swords. Holding a ladle of water in their hands, female seers revealed, in the pool of liquid, the hidden face of life to their distraught companions.

Foreigners from the west said that Konya was as large as a distant city, located on a fertile plain, on the left bank of a broad river, a city called Cologne. Those from the east compared it to Baghdad or to the even more distant Hampi.

Before arriving in Anatolia, the "Levant," or Anatole, as my Greek friend Thiryanos pronounced it, Shams had but one desire: to meet a true master—a spiritual master. For this reason he moved around constantly. In Tabriz, Iran, his hometown, he had studied with a certain sheikh, known as the Basket Weaver. Everything he knew came from this first guide. Yet, after a while, Shams left him in search of a man who would be able to "see" something in him that the Basket Weaver did not. Nor anyone else for that matter.

Like a wild animal constantly on the run, Shams went from town to town, season after season, looking for his own hunter. This incessant traveling led him to Baghdad, where he met a famous sheikh. The words they exchanged quickly spread to the court of the caliph, the public baths, the inns where the soldiers rested before going out to be decapitated by the Mongols. But Shams was not someone who was patient when dissatisfied. During their only, and very short, meeting, he asked the sheikh what he was doing. The man answered, "I see the moon in the water of the basin."

Shams knew at once that this sheikh was not for him. With an irony that was judged to be trivial, he replied, "Since you don't have a boil on your neck, and since nothing prevents you from lifting your head, why don't you see the moon in the sky?"

With these words he destroyed the sheikh's visionary élan. Then, craving such a man as his own master, the sheikh begged him to remain, calling him the "awakener," the "conductor," the "companion." But he would have none of it. The enigmatic stranger remained impassive. The sheikh sobbed on his shoulder, whispered his sorrow in his ear, tore his clothing, and brutally thrust his naked chest forward for Shams to see. In vain. It was impossible to hold Shams, the "Bird."

Slightly amused by the emotional response of the man whom the dervishes of Baghdad then considered to be "the light of the caliphate," Shams felt he was wasting his time with someone as mediocre as this.

"You are good at nothing. You are unworthy of my company."

Those were Shams's last words before leaving the sheikh and Baghdad. No one knew exactly who he was. He never answered questions about himself. He made his living teaching children theology and the study of the Koran. From time to time, he also worked as a construction worker, a painter, or plasterer. But he did not wish to be seen as a mystic, a professor, or an unskilled worker. He presented himself solely as a foreigner, as someone who was caught up in the movement of the world. Every time he arrived in a new city, he would stay in a caravansary with the crowd of travelers, preferring to pass himself off as a merchant rather than be taken for a holy man or a revered teacher.

Often—for his knowledge, like his instinct, was astonishing—he was asked to stay in a *khaneqah*, a monastery for dervishes, or in a school, surrounded by his peers. He declined the invitation and answered that, being only a stranger, he was obligated to restrict himself to the caravansaries, places of passage. Those who recognized the traveler referred to him as the Bird. Later, it was said that he had traveled around the world before reaching Konya, where Djalal al-din Mohammad Balkhi lived, the man known as Rumi, the Roman, for he had spent the majority of his life in this former province of the Caesars. His disciples called him Mawlana, which means "Our Master." Shams referred to him only by the letter M.

My hand burns to write what I have seen. But I don't want to proceed too quickly. The roads were still dangerous at the time, less well trafficked than they are today, when I write these lines. The sons of Genghis galloped over the land. It was the time when the warrior Tchormaghan set loose his horde of thirty-thousand men to pillage and massacre the inhabitants of the ancient cities, who, rather than defend themselves, seemed to offer themselves as fodder.

Shams's peregrinations depended in large part on the disordered movements of the Mongol armies. At the time, all the lands from the Indus to the strait of Constantinople were threatened. Shams himself was thirty-five when his hometown, Tabriz, was burned by the Mongols. During his travels, he would hear the lamentations of the terrorized population. He often repeated a phrase that was collected, like a seasonal fruit, along the roadsides: "The Mongols arrive, destroy, burn, murder, pillage, and leave."

A story was told to him of how a solitary Mongol horseman arrived in a heavily populated village and killed all the inhabitants, one after the other, without anyone daring to lift a finger. Elsewhere, he was told of how an unarmed barbarian had ordered one of his captives to lie on the ground and not move from the spot. The Mongol quietly went off to find a sword and returned to behead the unfortunate man, who, waiting to die, had not moved an inch.

One day Shams arrived in Damascus. There, he again heard of this strange sense of resignation in the face of the conquerors.

"We were a group of eighteen travelers," someone said to him. "On the road, a Mongol came across our caravan and ordered us to tie ourselves together. All my companions began quietly to attach themselves to one another. I was the only one to refuse the fatal order. I told them we were eighteen against one, but in vain. They continued to bind themselves. Then, all at once, I grabbed my knife and cut the Mongol's throat. The *iltchi*, the Mongol emissary, died on the spot and we fled, leaving behind us our ropes, bonds, and cords. Some of my companions almost seemed to regret that they were still alive."

It was in this same city that, now forty-five years old, he met a young man surrounded by a joyous band of friends, before whom he bowed, then prostrated himself on the ground. He fervently kissed the man's hands and said to him, "Oh, money changer of the world of the senses, take hold of me!" There was no doubt that he used the word "money changer," as if he were exchanging one currency for another.

He had just met the most celebrated student in the city, the young Rumi, as I will call him from now on, who had come to Damascus to complete his studies in philosophy and theology. Far from sharing the euphoria of the stranger, who asked only to be taken hold of, Rumi calmly withdrew his hands, wet with saliva from the suppliant's humid kisses. He bent down and helped the importunate man to his feet. He was barely up when he walked away, leaving the young man to the boisterous admiration of his fellow students. With the insouciance of his age, Rumi attached little importance to that strange encounter. But the other, as he was walking away, understood that the bookish student was not yet "ripe" and that he would have to return. By the other, I mean to say Shams of Tabriz, the Bird.

No, Rumi was not ripe. It would take another fifteen years. Then, one autumn day, as he was leaving the school of the cotton growers, he met, for a second time and quite by accident, Shams, who was leaving the caravansary of the sugar merchants, and his life changed. I will return to this.

It is very difficult for me to put words to paper and simply describe my master, Rumi, the man who entered my life when I was barely twenty, never to leave it again. The man who made his poetry the very expression of love, the most immediate access to God. However, this is my task. The duty I must fulfill at the end of my life. If I do not do this, who will do it in my place?

Djalal al-din Muhammad was his real name. He was born in Balkh, in eastern Iran, in the year 604 of the Hegira (1207 CE). His father bore the title "Sultan of the Wise," for his learning was said to be perfect. However, following a dispute with the official philosopher of the *padeshah*, a disagreement with the inhabitants of the city concerning his surname, and, possibly, fear of the Mongol armies, he was forced to leave the city of his birth in 618, when his son, my future master, was fourteen.

Their voyage was long but fruitful. In Baghdad, father and son met the young, and already famous, philosopher Sohravardi. Before the gates of the capital of the caliphate, the guards asked them, as they did all foreigners, where they came from and where they were going. The Sultan of the Wise, Rumi's father answered, "We come from God, and we go to God." When this answer was reported to Sohravardi, he ran to meet the visitors. He greeted the father respectfully and kissed the knees of his son, the future Rumi, who was on horseback. It is said that my master devoutly preserved, as a souvenir of this meeting—one that may have taken place only in the imagination of certain narrators—a few red hairs from the beard of the illustrious philosopher, which had clung to his clothing when he kissed him.

Later, when he was only thirty-six, Sohravardi was put to death in Aleppo, by the governor of the city, the son of Saladin, who nevertheless claimed to be one of his faithful followers. But the protection of the most powerful of the philosopher's disciples could do nothing against the accusations of blasphemy made by the religious men at court. The philosopher was unable to protect himself from stubbornness and hatred. Between a father who was a sultan and a friend who was a metaphysician, the governor of Aleppo chose the sultan. Brokenhearted, he ordered the execution of his intellectual master.

Along the long road of escape, in Nishapur, the man who would become my master, the son of the Sultan of the Wise, met Attar, the incomparable mystic poet, known as the "Perfumer," for that was his business. Attar offered him a copy of his *Book of Secrets*, a collection of poems that Rumi read constantly, quoted and recited, even though he had himself surpassed, both in form and content, Attar's spiritual and poetic genius. Witnesses of that meeting would have heard the Perfumer say to the Sultan of the Wise, "Soon your son will set fire to the inflamed of the universe." Even if this was not said by Attar, even if it was embellished or invented, nonetheless, Rumi inflamed and still inflames, precisely and literally, the spiritual world, which may be the real world.

It was also reported that when the caravan left Nishapur, Attar, seeing the young man behind his father, said to him, "What a strange spectacle! A sea advances, and an ocean follows behind."

During one of their stops on the slow road of escape, Rumi, at the age of eighteen, married Gohar, the daughter of a prominent inhabitant of the city of Larandeh. I will always remember the name of this city, for my master, in his poetry, praised the unforgettable taste of its fruit, especially the *shaftalou*, a variety of peach.

Gohar gave him two sons. The first was Sultan Walad, of whom Rumi would say that he was the one person who resembled him the most. Sultan Walad became the shadow of his father and assisted him in making all his decisions, however inconsistent or extravagant. Ala, the second son, the bad son, also became the "shadow" of his father, but a dark shadow, filled with resentment and hostility. One day, Ala would cause the departure, the "disappearance," some said the assassination, of his father's "god," Shams of Tabriz.

It was this same Shams who, as I have written, found himself in Konya twenty years later, 26 *Djamadi al-akhar* 642 (October 23, 1244), at the gate of the caravansary of the sugar merchants, looking, like a skilled trader anywhere, for the rarest of goods.

The simultaneous presence of both sons in Rumi's wake seemed to reflect the eternal struggle between good and evil. They resembled the two wings of the angel Gabriel, the wing of light—the right wing—from which perfect nature originated (this was Sultan Walad), and the wing of shadow—the left wing—in other words, the soul that descends to the lower world, personified by Ala.

One day their flight came to an end. The sea ceased to advance and the ocean to follow. At the invitation of Sultan Kay-QubÇd—may God bless his soul!—they made their way to Konya and settled there for a long time, sheltered from the pitiless horsemen of the steppes as well as the incomprehension of an ungrateful people.

And the sea withdrew and the ocean swelled. Rumi began to study his father's philosophy. But the man died when my master was only twenty-four. The young man's grief was magnified by his loss, for he had lost not only his father but the finest teacher. His education would remain incomplete. He would have to wait until another arrived. For a year Rumi waited, and watched.

Like a blade through silk, the Mongols advanced toward the setting sun. The Iranians fled before their armies. Many found refuge in Konya. Some of them reported that they had heard how the famous theoretician of the city of Balkh, Termazi, had suddenly interrupted himself while teaching, sighed, and cried out, "At this very moment, my sheikh, the Sultan of the Wise has left the world of dust for the world of purity. His son asks for me. I must go to Konya to pass along to him the burden my sheikh entrusted to me."

Naturally, in that time of disorder, visions, miracles, strange coincidences, and prophecies were common throughout the world. Whenever these were reported to Rumi, he never sought to discover an element of truth in them. In what order had Termazi said the words, in what manner, at what time? Rumi paid no attention to such things. But he knew, without a fragment of a doubt, that Termazi would arrive and complete his education, which had languished since the disappearance of his father. For his part, Termazi knew that Rumi needed a guide and that it was his duty to go to the grief-stricken son as soon as possible and teach him the meaning of the word "burden," for such teaching is the most precious of gifts.

The old master's arrival in Konya filled Rumi with new desires. Termazi questioned him at length. At the end of the examination, he told him that, in the sciences of religion and certainty, he had exceeded his father by a hundred degrees, but that his father had also mastered the science of speech as well as that of his inner states.

"I now want you to wander in the science of those inner states," ordered his new master. "This has been given to me by your father. Learn it from me and become, outside and inside, his heir, his peer."

Termazi was right. Rumi lacked the other science, that which is learned not by reading philosophical treatises but through meditation and retreat. He surrendered completely to his new guide. Later, his favorite son, Sultan Walad, defined this fusion as follows:

Thus he became his disciple,
Offered him his soul and mind.
Abandoned himself like a dead man.
And as he died before him,
So was he returned to life.
The master transformed his tears
Into a mine of laughter.

Termazi sent his young disciple to Aleppo and Damascus to study. In the main square of the city of Damascus, as he was going to school one day, the young man met, for the first time, a skinny dervish, who begged him to "take hold of him." As I have already mentioned, the encounter was fruitless and Rumi rejoined his friends, while the dervish, Shams of Tabriz, realized that the young man was not yet "ripe" but was still "raw."

Rumi knew this. Upon his return to Konya, he undertook, at Termazi's request, three consecutive retreats of a total duration of a thousand and one days, a number that, based on the numeric value of the letters, symbolizes satisfaction.

At the end of this lengthy trial, he gave Termazi a detailed description of his many mystic visions. In one such vision, he said, "I saw you. You were listening to the teachings of my father. You were in flames and placed both of your feet on the stove and with your hand withdrew the burning embers."

The teacher kissed his student and told him that he now possessed the inner secrets, the arcana of men of truth and the revelations of men of the spirit. His education was over; the "burden" had been given to him. The student had now surpassed the master.

After ten years of residence in Konya, Termazi decided to retire to Caesarea, perhaps realizing that the parched one had need of a stream that flowed from a source that would no longer be his. So he asked his student for permission to leave. This was not granted. The guide was forced to disobey Rumi and left without the approval of the man with whom he was, nevertheless, so intimately connected, "yet unstitched."

On the road to Caesarea his horse became uncontrollable, threw him, and broke his foot. Forced to return to Konya to attend to the injury, he was met by his disciple, who insisted on removing his boots himself. Caressing the broken toes, Rumi asked, "Why do you avoid us?"

"A fierce lion is approaching," answered the old man. "He is lion, and I too am lion. We will not get along."

Termazi's teachings had so deeply penetrated Rumi that he absorbed, through each of his veins, the messages of this first smuggler of truth. And he allowed the old sage, the *pir*, to leave. This time, he was prepared to receive, and perceive, Shams of Tabriz, the lion foretold.

But before the beast strode into Konya, the city made the son of the Sultan of the Wise, then thirty-six years old, his father's legitimate heir. Glory had come to him. People began to call him "Our Master," Mawlana. The school where he taught was never empty. In a single day, four hundred students, among them learned scholars, governors and emirs, and even the sultan in person, attended his classes. Venerated by everyone, Rumi was now considered a pious man, unsurpassable in his learning and his teaching. A peak, a light without equal.

He was of average height, with a thin, hooked nose, large, calm eyes that were slightly lidded; his hair and beard were beginning to turn gray. His upper lip formed two perfect arcs. He walked slowly, withdrawn, always pensive, attentive to the questions that were constantly asked of him in the halls of the school, at the mosque, in the street, in the hamam. He was friendly, of course, but with that slight distance that fame erects around a man who understands its value and the source of its glory. At times the veil of meditation darkened his face, as if he secretly took refuge within himself to search, in the halls of memory, for a distant phrase, an example, a detail he alone knew, a singular comparison, a sudden glimmer.

Those moments were rare. Most often, he spoke freely, on all sorts of subjects, without being asked; and ideas followed one another in his speech without any apparent effort, which stupefied his listeners, for it was as if it had all been written in his head. And this was the man who, later in life, would often invoke, celebrate, and invite silence.

He had the sallow complexion of an invalid and white hands, which he barely moved when speaking, as if his voice, at those moments, had no need of anything else to make itself understood and to convince. He dressed with sober elegance.

He would point to a book and say to his students, "Open it wherever you choose." The student obeyed, read the first two words on a page. Then, Rumi interrupted him and, his eyes half closed, recited the entire page without error. He then commented on what he had said.

Whenever someone annoyed him, he remained calm, even though his comments were sometimes tinged with dogmatism. He often withdrew early from meetings and worked late into the night, reading new books and preparing his classes. Very often, he brought with him a volume of Attar, the mystic poet whom he called his master.

As I write this story, I am reminded of my friend Thiryanos the Greek, the man who, literally, took me by the hand and made me enter the very closed circle of Rumi's initiates. We were the same age, about twenty. We practiced gymnastics and joyfully observed the rules of the community, for which dance would become a higher form of prayer. Even today, old and infirm, I cannot help but relive the endless hours of physical exercise I shared with Thiryanos. As he taught me how to handle a club, he initiated me into the rudiments of Sufism.

For as long as I can remember, Thiryanos always seemed to be going to or returning from the barber. He was excessively hairy and his hair almost seemed to grow before our eyes.

He owed his life to the master's personal intervention. One day Rumi was crossing the market on horseback on his way to his father's grave and slowed to admire some Arab pure bloods being rubbed down, brushed, and combed by their handlers. He detected in the eyes of the draft horses all the fatigue of years past and yet to come; he sniffed the odor of horse manure and dung; he could identify the war horses, the ceremonial horses, and the race horses by the way they whinnied. Suddenly, he heard, in the midst of the *hayahou*, the tumult, the hangmen announce the execution of a young Greek.

"What did he do?" asked Rumi, advancing toward the soldiers.

The soldiers immediately recognized the man whose learning drew the most famous scholars in the civilized world to Konya.

"He's a Greek. He murdered someone," answered the commander.

Rumi got down off his horse and went toward the criminal,

whose frightened face evoked, in its paleness, the snow-covered plain of Konya before the charge of the Mongol horsemen. He rubbed the cold, bony hands of the unfortunate man, which felt like long, twisted worms. Then he covered his shivering body with his own coat. This gesture meant that the Greek was now under his protection, which no one—not the sultan, not the emir, not the vizier—had the authority to withdraw.

The commander immediately sent a report to the sultan, who answered, "Free the prisoner. He belongs to Rumi, who is the supreme judge. That he has intervened in favor of an obscure Greek means little. From me, he could obtain clemency for an entire city."

Obeying the sultan's order, the executioners unbound the prisoner's chains and respectfully turned him over to the men in my master's retinue. Once freed, the Greek prostrated himself before Rumi and kissed the mud attached to his boots.

"What is your name?" asked his savior.

"Thiryanos."

"From now on, your name shall be Ala Thiryanos," said Rumi, who secretly hoped that this man, miraculously saved from death and who now bore the same name as his second son, Ala, would replace the child from whom he was separated by everything except the ties of blood.

Once circumcised and having converted to Islam, under the direction of his master, Thiryanos soon mastered all the subtleties of the science of religion. He shared in his fasting and his prayers, and like his guide, had a fondness for the interpreters of the Koran and the commentators of the Prophet's *hadith*.

One winter day, while Thiryanos was going to the cold, dark oratory of the master's school for the dawn prayer, he found Rumi lying on the ground asleep, in the midst of what appeared to be a pile of spent candles, still prostrate in prayer, his beard and mustache glued to the hexagonal tiles. The Greek convert approached and noticed, on the sleeping face, a few drops of frost stuck to the corners of his eyes. He knew that his master, who had passed the entire night in celebrating the *salat al-layl al tahad-jod*, the "prayer of insomnia," had been crying. He woke him gently and asked his authorization to pour warm water on his face to melt the ice. Rumi acquiesced and accepted the attentions of the young Greek who, in turn, began to cry.

Having become one of Rumi's most faithful companions, Thiryanos accompanied him nearly everywhere. Once, while leaving the mosque of Meram, whose blue cupolas, covered with enameled bricks, defied the summer sky and whose blue faience reminded Rumi of certain mosques in Balkh, his home town, my master and Thiryanos met the philosopher Heydari. At once, the man covered his head with a Yemeni scarf, like women who, at the sight of a man, must veil themselves. I should add that these scarves were then considered to be the softest in the world. And, no doubt, they still are.

Criticized by his own students, the philosopher answered, pointing to Rumi with his finger, "Before the knowledge of this man, all men should cover themselves like women. They should stay in the house and turn the spinning wheel. Compared to him, we must be less than women." He then threw himself at Rumi's feet and burst into tears.

It was Thiryanos who was to teach my master and me Greek. The story of the scarf, for example, was told to me in the language of Alexander.

As for Thiryanos's erudition, it reached such a point that, according to legend, it left the most eminent legal scholars speechless. Having become one of his closest disciples, he followed Rumi in all his spiritual discoveries, even when, misunderstood by his followers, he was forced to confront their hostility. Thiryanos was even forced to appear before the judges, who accused him of claiming that Rumi was God. During the trial, he said that he never claimed Rumi was God, but that he was the creator of God.

"I was an infidel. He offered me gnosis, transformed me into a scholar, gave me knowledge, and helped me appreciate God. I was a man who mouthed God's name; he made me a man who knows God's being!"

Before he died and left me with the sorrowful and implacable certainty that the number of my friends who had perished now exceeded the number who were living, Thiryanos told me of a dream he had had in his first life, when he was still a Christian.

"One night I saw myself in a dream, busy massaging the feet of a man I did not know. The following day, at dawn, after having washed my hands and face, I left my village for the city. Along the road, the man in the dream appeared to me and asked, 'Thiryanos, how are you doing after all the trouble you went through last night?' I fainted from astonishment. When I awoke, the man had disappeared. I only knew the dream was about Rumi on the day he prevented my execution by covering me with his coat. Yes, the man I massaged once in my dreams was indeed Our Master, Rumi, the creator of God."

At the time of the meeting between Shams and Rumi, Thiryanos, the master's two sons, and myself were nearly twenty. Daily exercise had sculpted Thiryanos's body and my own. They contrasted with the frail and tired limbs of the dervishes and pilgrims who surrounded us. Every time I saw Sultan Walad—and even today, forty years later—I could not help but admire the juncture of his brows, which formed, above his nose, a quiver, from which extended two black arrows, now gray. He had his father's lidded eyes and a natural ease that left those who met him with the impression that they had known one another for years. He appeared to be the door through which those who wished to enter the garden of his father had to pass, a door that, depending on circumstances, might be ajar, closed, locked, or wide open. Yes, Sultan Walad was, at that time, the threshold to his father.

Ala, however, was the embodiment of falsehood. His soul reflected his body: ugly, repugnant, deformed. Small in size, beardless and nearsighted, his voice would change during the course of a sentence, moving from a nearly childish and candid timbre to the rough, thick tone of a hoodlum. He could, in one breath, employ sophisticated forms of politeness and the most vulgar insults. Which led to odd results. For example, "Oh, you, before whom the heavens bow, sit your ass on the ground." Yes, I have often heard the son of the great poet express himself in this manner.

From a second marriage, Rumi had two other children, a boy and a girl, who, I believe, will leave few impressions in memory. However, their mother, Kera, was the female part of a story filled with men. Younger than my master, she had to accept, not without difficulty, his metamorphosis following the encounter with Shams. She was forced to admit that her husband had abandoned the prestigious seminars at which one debated repentance, conversion, renunciation, and confidence in God, for dancing, music, and whirling in circles. She also had to accept Rumi's absence, since he was busy exploring the "seven cities of love" at the side of a man who was older than him.

Strangers found her beautiful. Thiryanos could never compliment her enough. However, the Persians, although exposed to her beauty, failed to see it. She claimed that the few Chinese—probably traders—whose path she had crossed at the corner of a street, didn't even look at her, so great was the clash between her physiognomy and their aesthetic ideal. Her face was long, her mouth, which I observed from time to time in spite of the veil, may my master forgive me, was exceedingly wide and her chin rather prominent. When she laughed, her face was covered with wrinkles and creases, which she attributed to her nights of solitude, her nights of doubt. For me she represented—there was no question about it—the mother. In situations where there were complications or difficulties, her presence alone provided tranquility and relief. Rumi loved and respected her until the end of her life. But he was madly jealous and would not even allow her to meet with other women without his authorization. One day, however, she did so. Upon her return, Rumi predicted, almost as if it were a curse, that she would suffer all her life from cold. And since that day, Kera became sensitive to the cold. Even in the middle of the summer, she bundled herself in fox fur. Everyone knew that, in her room, she never moved away from the brazier. Whenever she traveled, she would take a lit candle with her to warm her face.

To complete the circle of close friends, I must now speak of Salah, Salah the goldsmith. He and Rumi first met one Friday in the Abolfazl mosque in Konya, long before the encounter between Rumi and Shams and the upheaval that followed, long before I was accepted among his disciples.

One day, as he was preaching, Rumi heard someone who was uttering a series of terrifying cries. He watched as the man approached his lectern, tore off his turban and freed his hair, and threw himself at his feet. He interrupted his preaching, took the "possessed" man aside, calmed him, made him speak, and offered him a cup of tea with his own hands, a tea that had been imported directly from China by one of his faithful followers, a trader always looking for novelty items.

Rumi and this man, whose name was Salah, had once shared the same teacher and were almost the same age. Salah's father was a fisherman and he himself a goldsmith. That is all Rumi learned, that Friday, of the man who came to him as a corpse, the man who much later, following Shams's disappearance, would replace the irreplaceable for Rumi.

Rumi kept Salah by his side but did not share in his turmoil. Curiously, he preferred the company of this uneducated and almost illiterate individual to the assembly of the wise. I will have occasion to speak again of him.

As for me, it is time that I reveal my name. I am called Hesam. My family is well known. Shortly before the famous encounter between Shams and Rumi, I had lost my father.

I was very young the day he died. A few months earlier, realizing that he was about to leave me, he insisted that I marry into a good family. So, I got married and moved in with my wife in the family home in Faliras, a two hour walk from Konya. My father had barely passed away when all his old companions, with their white beards, wearing pointy toed shoes on their feet and long, oblong hats on their heads, armed with curved daggers with silver handles—the distinctive garb of the chivalric order of the Akhis— prostrated themselves before the adolescent I was at the time and asked that I take the place of the deceased at the head of their *zawiyah*, their hermitage. I, who thought only of building up my muscles, practicing fencing and wrestling, felt that I had more to learn than to teach and refused this responsibility, which was far too heavy even for my broad shoulders.

Shortly after, one of the old men, a lieutenant of the order, brought me to the most famous inhabitant of Konya, Rumi.

At the very moment I threw myself at his feet, he grabbed my hand, squeezed it, then caressed my nascent beard and asked that I let it grow. At once I decided not only to keep the beard but to attend the school of the most eminent of scholars and delight in his presence as often as possible.

My decision encouraged other of my father's friends, of whom their were many, to follow my example. At my initiative the paternal hermitage was closed, its teaching completed by that of Rumi, and my father's inheritance added to the assets of my new teacher.

At the time of the encounter, still very young and occupied, above all, with improving my physical abilities, I spent more time in the apartments of Sultan Walad than in those of his illustrious father. He, quite correctly, considered me one adept among thousands of others, the difference being that I regularly donated, to the great dismay of my father's companions, my rental income to the management of his establishment. Thanks to the intervention of Thiryanos the Greek and the very special friendship that united us—we shared the same interest in athletics—I was finally able to gain access to Rumi's inner circle and emerge from my anonymity among the multitude of students. I enjoyed physical exercise but, above all, I enjoyed writing and jotting down everyday occurrences. For Rumi, and in his footsteps, I would be the pen of the extraordinary, of the unseen, of astonishment, metamorphosis, obliteration. I would also be, but much later, the initiator and scribe of the *Masnavi*, the great work.

We were known as Sufis. Why? I am not sure exactly. Some say that it's because we wear simple garments of *souf*, or wool. But that was not the case with us. In fact, we had decided to practice, within Islam, a particular spiritual path. We sought to acquire not *elm*, or science, but *marefat*, knowledge, the understanding that consists in recognizing that man is incapable of grasping God. For knowledge is what comes to us from others, while understanding is what we acquire ourselves.

Today, old and frail, I can say that the inability to understand is already to understand. Today, having myself become a teacher, I explain to my disciples that, to grasp the different dimensions of Islam, they must imagine a circle whose circumference represents the *shariat*, exoteric religion; the radius is the *tariqat*, esoteric religion; and the center is the *haqiqat*, divine truth. *Shariat* and *tariqat*, the circumference and the radius, reflect the center, each in its own way. We Sufis have chosen *tariqat*, the path that consists in taking a single step outside oneself to arrive at God. It is a slow progression, a passage, a pilgrimage. Moreover, another name for a Sufi is *salek*, which means "pilgrim." Our final goal is to rise within ourselves, starting from the shadowy exterior and working toward the luminous interior, and from the interior toward God. It is deep within himself that the seeker finds God. Concerning this, one of Rumi's verses comes to mind:

> Do not mistake this poor man
> For the seeker of some treasure
> For he is himself the treasure.

As for Rumi, who is and will remain the greatest Sufi of all time, love is the astrolabe of the mysteries of God. It is through love that man tends to return to the source of his being. Along this path, the path of love, we require a teacher, a sage, a *pir*. I also recall a verse from Rumi's *Masnavi*, which I had the honor of writing under his dictation, when he called to me, saying:

> Oh, Hesam, Light of truth!
> Take one or two sheets
> And write further on the nature of the sage.
>
> Choose a sage yourself, for, without him, this voyage
> Is littered with suffering, danger, and fear.
>
> Along the path you have so often traveled
> Guideless, you feel only anxiety within.
>
> Along the path you never perceived
> Do not travel alone, do not deny the guide.

For Rumi, this pilot, this guide, was not his father, the Sultan of the Wise. Nor was it Termazi, who made him travel to Damascus in search of knowledge and forced upon him a thousand and one days of mortification. For Rumi, the *pir*, the sage, was Shams of Tabriz, the old man in the cold, who, in a moment, during an encounter, revealed to him the divine within his being. For me, Hesam, the guide, the *pir*, was none other than Rumi. And, at the time of this writing, I myself am the guide for several thousand Sufis.

Ever since the encounter between Rumi and Shams, our confraternity stood out for its celebration of spiritual dancing, the *sama*, during which the participant achieves a state in which he recognizes a melody previously heard, perceived outside time. Rumi used to say, "Several paths lead to God. I have chosen that of music and dance." He adopted that path after he met Shams. Before Shams, he lived in the shadow of libraries, with the suffering of asceticism, privation, and fasting. With Shams he achieved divinity.

I will always regret my absence when Shams first disappeared. I was unable to be present at their meeting, which was so often narrated, sung, embellished, and commented upon. But I was present when Shams took the hand of Rumi and led him to a cell, where they remained for forty days and forty nights alone.

Suddenly, having seen you . . .

H E CAREFULLY LOCKS THE DOOR TO HIS BEDROOM, USING three padlocks. An unknown man, probably a sugar merchant, leaves the neighboring room and greets him. He answers in a low voice and accompanies him to the courtyard of the caravansary. There, he turns around and returns quickly to make sure the locks are secure. Yet, in that hermetically sealed room, there is nothing but a worn mat, a broken pitcher, and, in place of a pillow, a brick. The door is firmly sealed now, he's sure of it. He carefully rolls the keys in a large handkerchief stained with ink, which he throws over his shoulder like a small bundle.

His age is indeterminate. Some say he is sixty. His name is Mohammad Malekdad but he is known only as "Shams," the Sun. The Bird. He leaves the inn. The sculpted door closes behind him.

"I'm an old man in the cold," Shams repeats, seated, after an icy walk during which neither the basketweaver nor any other merchant had succeeded in selling him anything, before the door to his residence, the caravansary of the sugar merchants.

At this time of day, the passersby are busy. The midday prayer is approaching. Some head for Masdjed Djame, the large mosque. Others, wrapped in shawls and cloaks, holding large wafers of rolled bread under their arm, fresh from the baker's oven, walk more briskly to arrive home before the rice burns and becomes inedible. Women, wrapped in their veils and followed by servants, walk tentatively over the ice, fearing they might slip and fall, disturbing the charm of their passage, which is cloaked in an aroma of rose and musk. And still others, turbaned scholars with ink-stained fingers, make their way to the school to follow the teachings of the teacher who has come from afar, from the ends of the Earth: Rumi, whom everyone calls Mawlana, "Our Master."

Shams observes them. He waits, he is cold. This scene, he says to himself, only God is capable of composing it, like an artist. No painter or poet, no historian or mathematician could have imagined and brought together so many details, with such economy of means, with such naturalness and vitality, such ease, almost nonchalance, and yet so complex.

Shams waits, cold. He looks around.

Then, a man leaves the school of the cotton merchants. He is seated on a mule, surrounded by disciples, who follow him on foot. His complexion is yellow and his body emaciated. His head is covered by a large white turban and he wears a lambskin cloak over a long woolen robe. Fur-lined leather boots protect his feet from the cold, which is biting.

Shams opens his eyes, which are attacked by the wind. Seeing this rider, he recognizes the merchandise he has been looking for. There is no question in his mind. It is the student he met, fifteen years earlier, in the main square of Damascus, the young man who, still too "raw" at the time, had not known how to "seize" him. Today, 26 Djamadi al-akhar, year 642 of the Hegira, he appears ready. He has changed, this man who had disdained Shams's ardent and damp entreaty, "Oh, moneychanger of the world of the senses, seize me!" Now Rumi is ripe. The hoped for encounter can take place. The moment has arrived.

Rumi, on his mule, and followed by his disciples, passes before the threshold of the caravansary of the sugar merchants.

Shams leaps forward and violently pulls the bridle, immobilizing the young rider and his mount.

There is a moment of panic in the face of this violent apparition, but the disciples pull themselves together and attempt to shoo away the old man with his implausible behavior. Some call him a madman. Thiryanos the Greek, wishing to protect his master, brutally shoves Shams and stands between him and the mule. He places his thick back against the animal. Rocking on his mule, Rumi quickly regains his wits. A single gesture of his hand is sufficient to quiet the agitation. There is no danger. Let the stranger speak.

Then, extending his tall, thin silhouette to its full height, Shams asks in a dry voice: "Who is greater, Bayazid or the Prophet?" Rumi knew the words and deeds of the great mystic Bayazid by heart. He had often read, and reread, the passages of the *Memorial of the Saints*, in which Attar referred to this uncommon individual as "the sultan of the initiates," "the argument of the seekers," "the book of endless prayer." Even today, when I consult my master's personal copy, it opens by itself to the ten or so pages devoted to Bayazid, pages that have been worn through constant use.

"For thirty years, I searched for God. Suddenly, I saw: it was he who was searching for me." Rumi often repeated this saying of Bayazid's. Prostrate, he would call upon Bayazid at the end of every prayer and meditate on what the "book of endless prayer" had said some four centuries earlier: "When I left Bayazid, like a snake from its skin, I saw: the lover, the man in love, and love were one. For thirty years I made God my mirror. Now, I am my own mirror."

Sometimes, Rumi would begin a sentence saying, "My example is that of the sea, whose depth is not visible, nor its beginning or end." Very few people knew that this analogy was in fact by Bayazid. And very few knew what followed: "I am the ninth heaven. I am the throne that rests on the ninth heaven. I am Abraham,

Moses, and Mohammad. I am Gabriel and Mikael. I am Israfel and Azrael."

"Who is greater, Bayazid or the Prophet?" Shams asks Rumi. The old man is no longer cold. Now he is indifferent to the wind, indifferent to the embarrassed disciples as well. His eyes await Rumi's response. Later, referring to the scope of this question, Rumi will say that it caused the sky to spread over the ground.

"Mohammad is greater," Rumi says, and he feels what seems like an immense flame leap from his head in the direction of the lowering clouds. "Bayazid's thirst," he continues, "was satisfied by a single drop, proportional to the vase of his understanding. But Mohammad's thirst was immense. He was thirst upon thirst. He was in the thirst. When Bayazid attained the truth, he was immediately saturated and stopped looking any further. But Mohammad, advancing from day to day and hour by hour, increasingly saw the divine lights, majesty, power, and wisdom. That is why he called to God, telling him he would never succeed in knowing him as he deserved."

At that moment, Shams faints. His faint is real. Later, he would say that at that very moment, he did not see Rumi in Rumi; he saw himself. Shams lies on the ground, the other man climbs off his mule, orders his students to pick up the stranger carefully and lead him respectfully—he insists, "very respectfully"—to the school. One of Rumi's sons, Sultan Walad, who is eighteen and particularly close to his father, breaks through the crowd, lifts Shams's head, then his body. Assisted by the others, he heaves the thin, inert frame onto the mule.

The crowd heads for the Master's college, crosses the gateway and enters the square courtyard. Rumi's residence is divided into two parts, the house and the school. In the center of the house, reserved for the family and initiates, are the apartments of the women, the *andarouni*, while the school faces the street. Thinking the bent body of Shams was that of their Master, the students leave their cells, arranged on three sides of the courtyard, and observe the mule and its burden in terror. Some of them leave the covered gallery that abuts the cells and walk down several steps to enter the courtyard to get a better view. Philosophers and jurists abandon the large meeting room, arranged on the fourth side of the courtyard. Government officials, who have come to Rumi for insight into the interpretation of power, stream out of the nearby library, one of the most frequented in the region. Rumor has it that the only real reason that Rumi's father settled in Konya was the temptation to inhale, on shady afternoons, the odor of this *ketab khaneh*, this "house of the book," an offering from the sultan to his illustrious guest.

The women, who have seen neither the mule nor the man on the mule, rush into the inner courtyard planted with trees, now leafless in this cold autumn. The swans gather in a corner of the pond, an immaculate gathering, hurriedly improvised. In the half-empty pond can be seen a useless fountain and several fine cracks that look forward to more temperate weather, however unlikely. Even the flower beds, in the expectation of the customary rotation of the seasons and the arrival of spring, are shaken by this sudden commotion and temporarily appear to upset the inevitable symmetry of the Persian garden. Sultan Walad tries to calm the collective anxiety. No, it is not his father. He is walking a few steps behind the mule. The man who lost consciousness is an unknown, an old dervish apparently. The crowd disperses at once. The robust Thiryanos steps forward, takes Shams in his arms, and carries him to the meeting room, where the doors close on a group of surprised students.

Shams doesn't wake up until fifteen minutes later, when he hears Rumi's voice relating a fable: "A famous Persian merchant was preparing to go to India. Before his departure, he gathered together his entire household—family, slaves, even the domestic animals. Being very generous, he asked them what they would most like to have as a souvenir. Each of them answered differently. Questioned in turn, the parrot said, 'Go to the forest. When you meet my fellow parrots, greet them and ask them on my behalf if it is fair that they live in the trees together while I live in a cage; ask them if it is fair that I die here, far away and alone.' When he arrived in India, the merchant went walking in the forest. There he met a wild parrot and repeated the request made by his pet bird. He had barely finished speaking when the bird began to tremble, fell at his feet, stopped breathing, and died on the spot. Saddened, the merchant greatly regretted what he had said. Upon his return to Persia, he distributed the gifts to his household. When it was the parrot's turn, he told him of the unfortunate death of the wild parrot. As soon as he had finished speaking, the bird in the cage shivered, grew cold, fell to the bottom of the cage, and died. The merchant cried for a long time over the death of his 'bird with the lovely song,' of his 'companion,' his 'confidant.' Then he opened the door of the cage and removed the corpse. With a flurry of its wings, the false corpse flew away and perched on the top of a tree. Terrified, the merchant questioned his bird, who was quite alive, about his strange behavior. The bird replied, 'I simply followed the advice of the wise parrot. By simulating death, he showed me how to escape. The time has finally come for me to be free.' The unhappy merchant had to resign himself to the loss and bid farewell to his former captive."

Shams opens his eyes. He realizes he is in a room with a *korsi*, the long, low and wide table covered with shawls and rugs, beneath which visitors extend their legs, near a brazier. During the winter, the room where the korsi is located served as headquarters. In it the men slept, ate, drank, received guests, studied, talked, grew old, and finally died. Shams's legs are stretched out beneath the korsi. His head rests on Rumi's knees, while Rumi leans against some large cushions covered with rugs.

Rumi, who has for a long while now been waiting for the man to awaken—a man whose name he does not know—sees the stranger's eyelids open. He says to him, as if to conclude the fable of the merchant and the parrot: "For me, freedom is to enter your cage." Then he adds, "I am this suddenly-having-seen-you."

He places his hand on Shams's hair, already gray, and caresses it tenderly. Shams sits up. He sees, around the korsi, a circle of notables, the tops of whose robes—the bottom is hidden by the shawl covering the table—trimmed with garnet satin and embroidered with gold thread and multicolored brocade that matches their turbans, reveal that these men frequent the courts of sultans and the palaces of emirs. One of them holds in his hand a string of ruby beads. For each bead he slips between his fingers, he says one of the ninety-nine names of Allah. Another, who caresses the throat of a nightingale huddled in the hollow of his hand, is the same man to whom Rumi has just related the fable of the merchant and the parrot.

Thiryanos and I are there, as stunned as the others. Does Shams think that we too are pretentious noblemen, in spite of our youth? This is where the extraordinary begins. With a simple gesture.

Shams observes the stupefied eyes of the adepts. They seem to misunderstand the attitude of their guide. I, the most humble among them, only knows how to think. I notice that Thiryanos, my Greek friend, who is at my side, is disturbed. Shams rises and stretches his frame, as thin as the sails of a conquering ship, catches hold of Rumi's hand and leads him toward the door. They leave the room of the korsi. We follow. They skirt the covered gallery and stop before the door of a small room, a cell.

I can hear Shams say to my master, "I have entered fully into your friendship, insolently and audaciously." Rumi recites to Sultan Walad, his devoted son, a few verses of this poem:

On the wheel of dawn appeared a moon
From the wheel it came to stare at me.
Like a falcon that steals a bird while hunting
The moon stole me and ran toward the wheel.

And he adds:
"I was stolen."

The door to the cell closes behind them. They will not leave it for forty days. For forty days they perform *vesal*, the fast for union with the beloved.

Many things were said about that decisive meeting, from which fifty-thousand lines of verse resulted, the crown of mystic literature. Some have said that it took place elsewhere and under other circumstances. A miraculous meeting that some authors have described as artifice, as supernatural. Did Shams simply appear before Rumi, without a word, without asking him any question of a spiritual nature? And did the other fall, like a ripe fruit from a tree?

A biographer of Rumi relates how the unusual meeting took place in the home of the Master, in his library. According to this author, Our Master, surrounded by his disciples, was discussing religious subjects. Shams entered and greeted him, sat on the floor, pointed to the books, and asked, "What is that?" Rumi said to him, "You are ignorant of this." At that very moment, the books and the library caught fire. Seeing the flames, Rumi, according to this author, exclaimed, "What is happening?" And Shams responded, "You too, are ignorant of this!" He then rose to leave, transforming Rumi completely, turning this austere man, who had spent his time until then in a niche of the mosque, into a passionate lover, a wanderer who would go everywhere, anywhere, to celebrate the dance of the spirit.

According to another biographer, the meeting took place near a pool, along whose edge Rumi had been sitting, with several books spread out nearby. Shams approached Our Master and asked him what was in those books. Rumi answered, "It's a lot of noise, you know nothing about it!" Shams took the books and threw them into the water. Rumi then said, with regret, "Oh dervish, what are you doing? Some of those books, which are now impossible to find, were given to me by my father." Shams plunged his hand into the water and pulled out the books one by one. They were not even damp, claimed the narrator. Rumi asked, "What is this secret?" Shams answered, "It is pleasure and ecstasy, you know nothing about it!"

Another hagiographer gives a different version, equally legendary, equally metaphorical, of the meeting and subsequent confusion. According to him, my master, who was on horseback, was questioned by a stranger: "What is the point of such suffering, such mortification, and such knowledge?" And he answered, "To master tradition and religion." Shams replied to him, "The science that does not take you from yourself is worse than ignorance."

All these authors spoke of something extraordinary. Each saw things with his own eyes. But the true circumstances are of no importance here. A birth had been in preparation for years. And I saw it happen. Me, Hesam, I was present when Shams stood up, grasped my master's hand, and led him into that cell. Yes, I was there. I heard Rumi when, just before isolating himself, he said to his favorite son, "I have been stolen." I saw the door close and Sultan Walad prostrate himself before the door.

It is difficult to speak of enthusiasm with simple words. Whether the astonishment of my master, of Our Master, Mawlana, Rumi was the work of books consumed by fire or soaked in water and miraculously restored, or the result of a spiritual dialogue, the encounter was sudden, unexpected, and shocking. An unlikely meeting between an anonymous dervish and an intellectual master, at the end of which the stunned man addressed his agitator in these terms, "I am this suddenly-having-seen-you."

On that afternoon at the end of autumn, we, the disciples, increasingly impatient, hoped he would leave the cell, at least for the hour of class, which that day was devoted to the ascension of the Prophet and the thesis of the *mi`raj*, the ladder, which he identified with man's very being. He did not leave. We said to ourselves that the Master, who loved saying the evening prayer surrounded by his closest disciples, would certainly leave at dusk. He did not leave. Only Sultan Walad, his favorite son, sensed that this retreat was unlike any other. So he sent someone to the andarouni to find his stepmother, Kera, whom Rumi had married two years earlier, his second marriage. She did something quite out of character and entered the gathering of men half veiled, her attitude evoking some imminent disaster, and she questioned them about the identity of the intruder.

"Does anyone know this man?"

No response.

Night came. The faithful gradually dispersed.

Sultan Walad invited Kera to return to her rooms. In spite of her concern, she did as he asked. Before going to bed, I approached the cell on tiptoe. Like all the other cells, it was topped by an enameled cupola, and I put my ear to the door. No noise, not a word. The two men were alone and silent on the other side.

The next day, the faithful, and others, assembled at the school. Some claimed that Shams—they were becoming familiar with the name that Rumi had given him when they met—was a sorcerer, no more or less than a magician. Some students, who had come from Baghdad and the east, from Ferghana, Samarqand, and Delhi, were already upset.

"What's the point of making such a trip to honor a master who vanishes at the sight of an unknown, a good-for-nothing?" With a hypersensitive old man, thought Thiryanos, who, present at the time of their encounter, had observed Shams's behavior.

No one dared enter the closed room. Some recommended that we call to Rumi through the door to remind him of his teaching and family duties. All night long, Kera had refused to sleep, searching in vain for the reason for her husband's isolation. Had she been too demanding, when he only wanted to serve God and his Messenger? Did she no longer arouse his desire? Had she suddenly grown old and worn?

Rumi's younger son, the questionable Ala, a coarse, vulgar young man of seventeen, shouted through the door at the stranger who now shared his father's room. "Who are you to dare soil our saintly home?" Then, in a somewhat lower voice, he added, "Piece of dog shit, cunt snatcher, gelded ass!"

Sultan Walad, the older son, approached his brother and asked him not to make matters worse. Thiryanos and I, seated side by side at one end of the gallery around the cells, observed all this. At times, my Greek friend would remove his turban and readjust his unruly hair. He must have said to himself that, once they had left the cell, he would go to the barber.

Concerning this younger son, I was familiar with his violent temper, which was likely to erupt at any moment. Thiryanos who, in very little time, had managed to become an intimate of the Master and, consequently, learn his deepest secrets, bent forward to tell me that Ala had stolen several precious objects.

"One day," he said, "Sultan Walad, who was looking for a few pieces of misplaced gold, ended up finding them in one of his brother's books!"

I refused to believe it. Such behavior, I felt, could not occur beneath the roof of the Teacher of Teachers, the Glory of Glories, in a house protected by God from the malignant impurity of men. Thiryanos also told me that, since his "adoption" by Rumi, he had experienced the jealousy of other students, who could not understand why a former criminal had suddenly become the current favorite. "They will never perceive Our Master," he added.

I saw the same jealousy at work, this time not toward Thiryanos but toward Shams. From each cell heads emerged, familiar and unfamiliar, plunged in the same bitter curiosity, "Why not me?"

Convinced that this solitude was going to continue, Sultan Walad tried to shoo away the curious. I managed to remain, my discussion with Thiryanos serving as a kind of shield. And I observed. I observed everything.

A bowl filled with pounded garlic, stale, moldy bread, and curdled milk came up from the kitchen on a tray and was placed before the door to the cell. Sultan Walad, increasingly respectful, didn't dare announce to the recluses that a meal had been prepared. He was afraid to interrupt their excitement, perhaps their ecstasy. The devoted son preferred to slip a piece of paper through the crack to encourage them to take refreshments. The door opened and a hand pulled the tray inside.

I saw it, that hand. Yes, I saw it. Was it the hand of my master or that of his "thief"? When asked, Sultan Walad said that he didn't recognize it. Thiryanos, who was near the cell when the hand grabbed the tray, swore to me that it was the hand of a third man. He swore: a third hand. Inside, there were only two, but the legend was already underway.

On the second day, Kera, his wife, again appeared at school, this time appropriately dressed. Her satin veil was made of two pieces: the first was attached to her waist and formed a skirt, the second hid her back, shoulders, and head down to her forehead. The movements of her arms controlled the way the outfit hung and the clinking of her silver bracelets. A small veil of Damascus gauze, coveted by the women of the court, hid her face, which I assumed to be tired and apprehensive. According to Thiryanos, who knew everything, she had not slept a wink for the past two nights. My eyes were drawn to her embroidered silk socks, the latest in fashion, which had arrived with the Mongol conquerors from distant China. When it came to female coquettishness, nothing surprised me. Recently, in Konya, I saw some wealthy Persian women wearing on their gold-encrusted hats—although they were still covered by a veil—several multicolor feathers, reminiscent of the Mongol steppes.

Kera briefly greeted the few men still present, some of whom, including myself, had managed to escape the great exodus ordered by Sultan Walad. She then walked to the cell, sat on the ground, removed her Chinese socks and adjusted her veil. Thiryanos hurriedly spread a rug over the tiles, placed a brazier before her feet and arranged a few cushions around her. Now, comfortably settled in, Kera appeared prepared to sit before the door for some time. A servant brought her some valerian tea, whose aroma I recognized, and a tray of almond paste cakes, prepared especially for the mistress of the household by the *pandjeh tala*, the chef, along with some almond oil and syrup. Kera took a few sips of tea but didn't even bother to look at the pastry. As hungry as I was, I could easily have devoured them all! I was eighteen and had a tremendous appetite.

She leaned against the door of the cell, her ear to the wood.

At noon, while the entire household was getting ready to say one of the five daily prayers, she suddenly changed her position. Still seated, she turned her back completely to the courtyard to look inside the room through the crack in the door. What did she see? I was the only one to see her "see." All the others were busy calling to God. To get a better look, I stood up and walked around the school, losing sight of Rumi's wife for a moment. Having arrived before the main structure of the building, where the cell was located, I found that she had fainted. A bouquet of flowers was lying across her lap.

I went over to her and lifted her head, and had her drink some tea. When she came to, she took the flowers and told me they had been given to her by Our Master in person, who had told her to preserve them with care. I looked at the petals; they were unlike any that grew locally. Kera told me that she had seen Rumi leaning against Shams's knees, both of them silent. That was the first vision she had had of the two men.

"At noon," she continued, "my husband invited Shams to lead the prayer. He refused, saying that no one other than Our Master could do that. My husband obeyed."

At this moment in her story, Kera whispered in my ear, "They were not alone. Six other individuals surrounded them. They disappeared at the end of the prayer, leaving this bouquet of flowers at Our Master's feet."

I didn't know what to say or think. Six other persons? From where? Was Kera trying to confuse me by telling me something she knew nothing about?

Before turning the mistress over to her servants, I asked her to give me a petal, just one. Generously, she offered me several. At once, I left the college and went to a druggist so he might identify the flower. Impossible. Neither the freshness, nor the color, nor the perfume resembled any flower that grew in Konya in autumn.

What was that flower? I spent the entire afternoon asking apothecaries, doctors, herbalists, and makers of ointments and essences. In vain. That evening, sitting in a popular restaurant, I delicately placed the mysterious petals against my copper plate filled with pieces of grilled meat. Armed with long fly swatters, the waiters battled the insects.

An Indian sat down beside me. He looked at my plate and asked me if I would recommend it. I had no idea. There were rumors going around that the cooks, in preparing the dish, had switched the mutton with camel meat, which was forbidden, mixed with various scraps, and colored with saffron and raisin, so that the finished dish would look like real chopped meat. Examining my meatballs to determine their freshness, the Indian noticed the petals and asked me if I had come from Sarandib, on the island of Ceylon. I told him no. He claimed it was the only place where the flower grew.

I became increasingly confused. I spent the rest of the night asking myself a thousand and one questions for which I had no answer. The next day I returned to school and told Thiryanos about my adventure. The Greek was not only familiar with Kera's vision but had, thanks to her, additional information: that morning, when she resumed her place before the cell, her husband came out briefly and recommended that she not show the bouquet to anyone who was not an initiate. And he added, "It is a present brought to you from the 'Poles of India' by the gardeners of the Earthly paradise. This bouquet will heal the dwelling of your soul and the eye of your body."

Kera would keep those extraordinary flowers for as long as she lived. They never wilted and their color never faded.

Later, when Rumi left his retreat, Kera was authorized to give one or two to the sultan's sister, who was stricken with an eye disease.

As for me, I kept my petals with great care. But I never attempted to use them, for fear of finding them ineffective and being disappointed, and for fear, as well, of being cursed by my master, who might have considered me, because of my ignorance, to be a non-initiate, an imposter.

On the fourth day, Sultan Walad had me remain near the cell of the two men to provide them with water for washing—Rumi was fond of the hamam—and of emptying their waste in the ditch in the basement that served as our toilet. A thankless task, some might say, but I saw it as a sign of honor.

Having gotten official approval to spend the entire night a few feet from Rumi and his "thief," I waited for the departure of relatives and friends to spy on what was going on within at my leisure. Later, I would beg my master's forgiveness a thousand times for my indiscretion. But after all, I was not even twenty years old at the time.

That evening, wearing a fur-lined cloak for warmth, I saw Rumi through the crack, leaning against a candelabra as high as he was, reading his father's book from nightfall to dawn. At daybreak, when he questioned Shams on the content of his father's words, his only response was, "Do not read any more! Do not read any more! Do not read any more!" I saw Rumi roughly cast aside the original manuscript of the *Ma`aref*, and then heard his voice ask Shams, "What should I do?"

The household began to wake up. The sound of buckets and pulleys could be heard from the well. The aroma of coconut brioches from the kitchen announced the first meal. I was preparing to leave, equipped with the ewer and copper basin, when I heard Shams's voice repeat the same question: "What should I do?" My master answered with this poem:

When I thirst for you,
Give me no water.

When I am in love with you,
Take away my sleep.

Then he added, "What should I do?" Shams replied, "Do not speak. Do not speak. Do not speak."

Convinced that the silence ordered by Shams could not satisfy my curiosity, I left for a while. When I returned, I learned from Sultan Walad that Rumi was refusing to speak at all. For a long time no word could be heard from within. Finally, one day, Shams himself ordered him to break his silence.

"My father," Sultan Walad revealed, "asked him why. Shams answered that he now required something else. And he asked for a young beauty. Yes, a young woman. My father called me and asked that I bring Kera. Which I did."

His wife was the embodiment of grace. She entered and at once saw that the two men were seated on a sofa placed directly on the rug, and leaning against large velvet cushions. The mattress, drapes, and coverings were carefully rolled up and placed against the wall. Within the coffers of silver-plated copper were piled, pell-mell, the manuscripts of the Sultan of the Wise and an Arab poet. Rumi explained to his wife that he was now forbidden to read the works of his own father and the Arab poet. After her visit, she could remove the books, which now cluttered the room. She was also asked to undergo another ordeal. She had to give herself to Shams if he desired her, if he accepted her as a gift, as a sign of respect from Rumi.

But Shams wanted no part of her.

Sultan Walad told me of Kera's distress. Why had her husband asked that she give herself to this stranger? In the past, Rumi, the Djalal al-din who had existed before Shams arrived, the jealous and possessive Djalal al-din, would not even tolerate her visiting a group of women.

When she left the room, the books under her arms, she asked Sultan Walad to take her place. Claiming she was "the sister of his soul" and that he could not touch her, Shams had demanded, in place of Kera, a young and very handsome boy. At once Rumi sent his wife to get Sultan Walad, "the Joseph of Josephs."

"It was my turn," the devoted son said to me, "to serve as an offering. But Shams wanted nothing to do with me either, even though I was prepared to accept the lowliest task, to shine his shoes, or tie his boots. He did not want me, for he considered me a son."

Shams rejected him just as he had rejected Kera. I was beginning to detect, in Sultan Walad's words, the secret admiration he had for the man from Tabriz. The most faithful of the faithful, he followed his father blindly. He followed him down dangerous and dark paths.

The narrator continued his story, while I decided to take notes, for everything I heard was strange and unpredictable. From then on I was never without my writing desk, a wooden box of sculpted cedar containing a bottle of ink, sharpened reed pens, and rolls of Chinese paper. Today, with a single glance at the old box, all those memories return. I continue.

Sultan Walad told me that Shams then asked for wine. Rumi himself went out, everyone saw him leave the room for a moment, and ordered a slave to go to the Jewish quarter as quickly as possible to buy a pitcher of good wine in his name.

I continued to take notes. When the slave placed the forbidden beverage, whose use is condemned by the Messenger and his God, behind the door to the cell, Shams uttered a cry that everyone heard, and added in a loud voice, "I swear by the First without first and by the Last without last that from the beginning of the world until the destruction of the universe, there never has been and will never be a man like you!"

Sultan Walad then told me, concluding his story, that Shams tore up his clothing and placed his head on his father's, my master

Rumi's, feet. At the same time, in a kind of illumination, I realized that at that moment of his existence, Rumi was capable, if Shams had so ordered, of sacrificing his wife and four children.

I was dead, behold I am alive

FORTY DAYS OF SECLUSION, FORTY DAYS OF WAITING. Winter grew increasingly cold. One evening, the entire courtyard was covered with snow, and we considered putting the low table and brazier, covered with several blankets, into the cell. But this suggestion was rejected. Rumi and Shams wanted to have access to the entire room for other uses. The korsi, in order for it to be effective, would take up too much space. Rumors began to circulate, whispered questions: what was the Master doing that, in spite of the cold, he needed an empty space?

At school, there were no further classes and no more students. A great emptiness, a long wait. The dust and spiders were already beginning to accumulate. A few loyal followers continued to recite the daily prayers under the cynical eye of the gardener, who was busy clearing the snow.

The foreign students gradually began to leave. Since there were no classes, they saw no point in living so far from home and at such financial cost. The Indians left. Those from Herat and Samarqand followed them, then the Arabs. Thiryanos tried to convince the others to wait a while longer. What they were about to see upon the conclusion of the extraordinary retreat would be worth a thousand lessons in philosophy. His plan fell on deaf ears. They only wanted to fill their notebooks with theory. The Greeks left too.

Two weeks had gone by without either of the two men showing the least sign of wishing to rejoin the world. Walking past the
cells that bordered the courtyard, I saw Sultan Walad, standing
and spinning around. I waited for the loyal son to conclude his
strange revolutions before entering the room. He saw me, at once
stopped what he was doing, and told me that he had just seen his
father performing the same dance under Shams's direction.

"A dance?" I asked.

"I paid close attention," he added. "My father was spinning
around, the palm of his right hand open to the sky, and the left hand
facing the ground, as if he were the point and the circle at the same
time. And he turned and turned, without changing his rhythm."

Sultan Walad turned his right hand up and his left hand down
to demonstrate Rumi's posture. But when he tried to spin, he
wobbled and fell.

"I've been trying all morning. But it's hard!"

With his eyes half-closed and his mouth partly open, he
demonstrated other movements, crossed his arms, leaned his head
toward his shoulders. He then explained to me that his father,
before he met Shams, whenever absorbed in meditation and religious fervor, shunned any kind of music, even spiritual. When he
was young, Rumi's mother had tried to initiate her son in music
and dance. But he, being clumsy and skeptical, failed to appreciate
the mystical joy that can be felt from the rhythm of instruments.
He simply shook his hands awkwardly.

"And look at him now! He's spinning!"

This movement, described by Sultan Walad, would later come
to be known as the sama, the spiritual dance, the rotation that
made the dancer the link between heaven and earth, the one
through whom the transmission takes place. Later, Rumi was cred-
ited with this invention and the order he founded: the so-called
whirling dervishes.

The son was dumbstruck, amazed by his father's metamorphosis. Rumi, this pious man who had, until then, known only the

posture of prayer, was dancing, whirling! And me, with my youthful exuberance, I peppered Sultan Walad with questions: what about the meter, the beat, the rhythm of Rumi's movements?

"He matched his steps to some inaudible sound. At times, Shams interrupted and, hanging onto the tall candelabra, also whirled, forming a circle."

The devoted son headed toward a niche incrusted with bits of mirror, where there was an illuminated Koran and a silver lamp. He picked up a rabab. The presence of this lute, next to the Book of God, seemed out of place, offensive. The most uncompromising believers would say: "Profane music has no place here."

"This rabab was given to me by Shams himself," explained Sultan Walad. "He knew I was behind the door. When he had finished spinning around the candelabra, he invited me to enter the cell. It was the second time. Upon entering, I bowed before them. My father, as usual, kissed my hair, reminding me of my childhood and the times he would slip his tongue into my mouth, lick me, and kiss my hair. Shams then said to me, 'Oh, Sultan Walad, you are the only one to enter this doorway, which separates the other world from this one. Take this rabab, go to the governor, and give him back his instrument.'"

Rumi's son was allowed to remain a while longer with them, the rabab in his hand, to preserve in his memory the image of his father who danced, spun, and carefully followed the choreographic instructions of the thin, frail old man, whom he called Shams, the Sun.

Sultan Walad and I examined the unusual instrument, which could only have been introduced into the room after they had begun their retreat. Who would have dared bring an object forbidden by the laws of religion into that holy house? Neither of us knew a musician, singer, or dancer among Rumi's entourage. His disciples, from the emir to the shoemaker, were all strict observers, brought up on the words of the Prophet and the commentary of the exegetes. No dancer. Was it really, as Shams claimed, the instru-

ment of the governor of Konya? This highly placed man, before
their seclusion, had assiduously followed Rumi's classes. Since the
beginning of their retreat, he had shown up several times at the
door of the school to find out if his teacher had left his cell. He was
growing impatient and had little use for the respectful explanations
that Sultan Walad tried to offer. What he wanted, like so many others,
was the presence of the Master, the scope and subtlety of his learning.

For my part I was certain that, during his last visit, the governor wasn't carrying a rabab in his arms. What use would he have
had for it here, in the home of the scholar, that futile and worldly
instrument?

Sultan Walad examined the sound box. The cord vibrated,
and, under Rumi's roof, the very first musical note was heard. I
shivered with fear and delight. Now, we had to act. Shams had
ordered him to return the instrument to its so-called owner. We
went to the governor's residence.

This was the first time I had gone there. A wide alley of
cypress trees led to an interior courtyard. I stopped to admire, on
my left, the famous orange grove. According to rumor, the governor personally ordered his orange trees from China, and, to accli-
matize them, gave them to the most skillful nurseryman in
Khuzestan, before planting them in his garden in Konya. The few
steps that gave access to the main body of the building were bordered with a narrow strip of tulips, which described on the lawn,
verses from the great poet Attar. Their red blossoms spelled out the
following:

In the journey of love
I disappeared in such a way
That I vanished from the sight of both worlds

Do not ask me my name any longer
Nor my trace in these two worlds,
From the leaf both my trace and my name have disappeared

I have disappeared, I have disappeared
I have disappeared, how can one know,
Not having known me, how I disappeared.

The flower beds, alleys, and trees responded with strict symmetry. Only the center pond had no twin. The temperature of the
water was kept warm enough so it would not freeze, and allowed
the aerial dance of the fountain to continue in winter. We passed
beneath an arcade formed by streams of water, which crossed
above the alley and fell to the ground on the opposite side, and not
a drop of water fell upon us. A few peacocks spread their tails and
paraded around to attract our attention from their eternal rivals,
the swans. We entered. A valet led us to a reception room. There,
as we examined the patterns on the rugs, our attention flew, like a
woven bird, from one tree to the next. The smoke from the Indian
incense so profoundly impregnated our clothing that for weeks
Sultan Walad and I continued to exude those distant scents. People
would ask us, "Have you just returned from a voyage?"

Informed of our arrival, the governor appeared without delay.
His beard glistened with brilliant oil from Damascus and around
his eyes could be seen the dark kohl of Isfahan. He wore a coat of
red fox over a long robe of ruby velvet. His turban and multicolor
socks recalled the pattern in the rug. His heeled slippers were cut
from the softest Moroccan leather.

Sultan Walad explained the reason for our presence. The governor took the rabab and examined it carefully. Yes, it was his
instrument. But he did not understand how it had ended up in the
Master's cell, when the day before, in his own music room, virtu-
osi from Samarqand had used it to play the tune known as the
"Chinese Idols."

He led us to the room, the kingdom of hearing, where it was
forbidden to entertain the other senses. An inscription in gold calligraphy asked the visitor to become all ear: "Here, do not eat, do
not drink, do not talk, do not read. Listen."

Ivory stools and sofas placed directly on the rug were the only furniture in the room. There were alcoves in the shape of the musical instruments they housed. One of them, describing the contour of the rabab, was empty. The governor approached the empty niche and placed the instrument inside.

We could not explain such events. We were their victims. Neither the governor, nor Sultan Walad, nor myself had need of magic to believe in the singularity of the challenge that Shams and Rumi had given themselves. For the governor, for the son, and for me, the miracle was their meeting and their persistent union.

When we left the governor, a fan seller, blind like all members of his confraternity, so they could enter the harems without difficulty, insisted that we admire one of his fly swatters, made of woven palm leaves. He also wanted us to buy a broom made of rice straw, lighters to quickly ignite our coals, and rat traps. Since we wanted nothing to do with his matches, traps, or fans, he insisted he could interest us in other things. He possessed a secret, known to him alone.

"Yesterday evening, I saw the man you call Shams enter the governor's palace and leave with a rabab under his arm, the same one you just returned to the governor."

"You saw him?"

"Yes."

"But you're blind!"

"I see what you cannot see. I see with the eye of the heart."

And the man, his eyes covered with a bandana, went on, claiming that once, in Tabriz, just as in Damascus, he had seen Shams enter the courts of the sultans, take their musical instruments, and leave, without anyone daring to stop him. He had "seen," he continued to repeat, he had seen Shams.

And yet he was blind.

It had been a month since the meeting, the union. Not a day went by without the students assembling before the gate of the school. Sultan Walad kept them out of the courtyard to prevent the noise of their discontent from reaching the ears of the recluses. Sometimes an immense lassitude stifled their anger, and they would watch, helplessly, at the remoteness, the deviance of the man who had been their Master and whom they believed they had lost.

In the andarouni, the residential section of the house for the women, Kera began to grow restless. Beautiful and still young, she desired her husband, who now spent his nights with an old man, under their own roof. Every morning, Ala, Sultan Walad's brother, promised he would put an end to the retreat, that he would break the locks and release his father from the grip of the old man from Tabriz. But he did nothing. Paternal authority held him back. Thiryanos and I, thanks to Sultan Walad's friendship, were able to come and go near the cell as we pleased, trying to understand, to the extent possible, the incomprehensible.

During the night that followed the thirty-ninth day, Shams asked Sultan Walad to enter the cell. The old man drew the devoted son into a corner of the room and whispered in his ear.

"I have abandoned the elders. I have chosen the living. Since the Prophet, no one has expressed himself like M [that is how Shams referred to Rumi]. A single coin from him is worth more than a thousand dinars. The one who makes his way to me clings to him. A door was closed. It has been opened by him. I am incapable of knowing M. I say this without guile. I am incapable of knowing M. Each day I discover, in his being and in his actions, something that did not exist before. Try to grasp M. Try to understand him better. Do not be satisfied with his handsome face and beautiful words. There is something more than that. Demand that something from him."

Then Shams remained quiet. Sultan Walad understood that it was time for him to leave them. He was getting ready to go when his father said, "Tomorrow, we will leave here."

Alerted by our friend, about ten of us watched from the courtyard to see when they would come out.

I saw the door open suddenly and the two men appeared, still in this world. Rumi, whose face seemed yellower than customary, allowed the cold rays of the late autumn sun to caress his pupils. Shams, whom I got a close look at for the first time—I had seen him just before they went in and once through the crack in the door—appeared older than I thought.

Everyone bowed down before Our Master. Rumi at once ordered that a bath be prepared. He told me later that what he had missed the most, during those forty days, was the hamam. But before washing his body and bringing his Sun with him into the steam, he took Shams's hand and led him into the interior apartments, where the women lived, where his wife Kera was waiting.

This was a radical change. When he left the hamam, even his clothing was different. He had changed the shape of his turban and wore a new and roomier coat, with broad stripes. Rumi was no longer the man I had seen forty days before. And Sultan Walad, the devoted son, would soon proclaim, concerning his father:

> The sheik-professor became a novice
> Studying every day under the guidance of Shams
>
> The one who was the end became the beginning
> And the one we followed, became the follower.

Everything changed very quickly. There was no more teaching. The school was closed for a long time. Not a single class, not a single prayer. The gardener didn't even bother clearing the snow, which now covered the entire courtyard up to the height of the entrance to the cells, which were now locked.

The books were sold off in front of the gate. The old students would gather to take or buy copies that had been annotated by the Master. We saw before us, in a disorderly mass, the science of Islam in its entirety: *Qovat al-qoloub, Ihya al-oloum al-din, al-Aqani*, and a hundred others. Most of the books were exchanged for musical instruments. Day after day, we were given flutes, drums, and lutes from Balkh, Bokhara, India, or Egypt.

From one day to the next, the library, the most beautiful room in the house, where we once joyfully examined works of medicine, law, and astronomy, was emptied. The recesses that held illuminated manuscripts were emptied of their precious treasures. Candleholders that had been specially installed on the wall to light the lectern without blinding the reader, were moved. The windows, which had been covered with delicate wooden screens to protect the rare books from the sun, were finally opened to the light. Even the rugs were changed. The one that covered the floor, made of a special, tightly woven wool that came from sheep from the Zagros mountains, was rolled up and sent as a gift to the governor. When the room was emptied of all traces of writing, Rumi invited Shams to make himself at home there. In my master's eyes, when Shams entered the room, he instantly filled the place left vacant by the thousands of books.

Rumi's days were now spent learning to play the rabab, guided by young musicians who substituted their gaiety for the morose and pedantic students of the past. The man of prayer, fasting, and preaching, the one who spent dawn to dusk in lengthy incantations to the divine and underwent other forms of abstinence, the scholar who only knew the teachers of law and never tired of reading commentaries of commentaries of a commentary of the Koran, now knew only how to dance, spin around, sing and laugh. Decoding the work of the ancients was apparently a thing of the past. Now was the time for celebration and joy.

One evening, when he was questioned by his wife Kera, Rumi composed this dialogue between Shams and himself, which describes, in its own way, his metamorphosis:

> I was dead, behold I am alive,
> I was a tear, behold I am laughter,
> The joy of love arrived,
> Behold, I am eternal happiness.

He said, "But no, you are not mad,
Unworthy of this house."
I left to go mad,
Behold, see how I am bound.

He said, "But no, you are not drunk,
Go, you are not of this species."
I left and now am drunk,
Behold, I am filled with joy.

He said, "But no, you are not dead,
You are not soiled by joy."
To his face, which gives life,
Behold, I am dead and bowed.

He said, "Oh, yes, you are clever,
Drunk with doubt and thought."
And behold I am ignorant, terrified,
Detached from everything.

He said, "You are a candle,
The one to whom the assembly prays."
Assembly I am not, nor candle,
Behold, I have vanished like smoke.

He said, "You are the sheik, the head,
You are first along the path."
Sheik I am not, nor leader,
Behold, I am your servant.

He said, "You have feathers and wings,
I give you neither wing nor feather."
Desiring his feathers and wings,
Behold, I am without wing or feather.

Kera gave these lines to Sultan Walad, who, in turn, gave them to me. I immediately added them to my notes, to my observations of Our Master's sudden transformation. Bound, drunk, dead, collapsed, detached, dispersed, wingless and featherless: this was Rumi after his meeting with Shams.

And he danced.

Aside from Shams, Rumi met privately only with the musicians. And when the best rabab player in Konya was led into the korsi room, Rumi immediately asked him to improvise something around the idea of the "unexpected." There were only a handful of people present, for Sultan Walad now allowed few visitors inside. He had closed the gates of the school to strangers, the curious, to anyone liable to criticize Rumi, who openly flaunted all of Islam's prohibitions. Shams was there, of course, Thiryanos, myself, and a few others, including the theologian Sharaf, known as much for his ugliness as his cynicism. Also present was Moin Soleyman, the famous director of the town's Koranic school, who later became emir of Konya before being killed and eaten by the Mongols.

The musician began to play. Rumi abandoned himself to the sound of the rabab. He ordered Thiryanos to move the korsi, which he did. Then he stood up, grabbed me by the arm, me, Hesam, and spun around, stamping his foot and reciting improvised poetry. I didn't know what to do. Concentrating as much as I could, I managed to live up to the privilege he had granted me. For the past ten days, Thiryanos and I had, timidly and discretely, started to dance. And now, the Master himself, before the director of the school, the theologian, and Shams, was asking me to share his newfound happiness. I began to turn, first consciously and stiffly, trying hard not to stumble, not to crash into my distinguished partner. Then, little by little, I simply let myself go.

I let my mind wander, I freed myself of my rational mind to become nothing but a mass of dancing particles. I was the sun, the planets, a grain of dust floating in a beam of light, the Kaaba, the pilgrims turning around the Kaaba, a polo ball and the mallet that struck it. I had become love, the lover, and the beloved. An hour, a night, a century, a moment? I couldn't say how much time went by. Maybe it was only dizziness, a brief transition, a state of being outside myself and out of the world, a kind of musical dream.

When the sama was over, Thiryanos and Sultan Walad grabbed me by the hand to "bring me back," as they told me later, and had me sit on the floor. The Master approached and caressed my hair affectionately for a long while. The gesture was without precedent; no one had ever seen him show such tenderness openly. Suddenly, he stopped. His glance had just fallen upon Shams, although I was the only one to notice. I stood up and went to sit in a spot considered inferior to the one occupied by Shams, showing, in this way, that I still considered myself, in spite of the Master's great favor, to be the subordinate of the frail old man. I was not yet twenty, as I have mentioned. I didn't dare believe he had chosen me. And I especially wanted to avoid earning Shams's contempt. For if I lost him, I would also lose Rumi. Which I feared more than anything in the world.

When the rabab player wrapped up his instrument in a cloth of cotton and silk, the school director questioned Rumi about the specificity of the sound of the lute. Rumi replied, "It's the creaking of the door to paradise." More discreet than was customary, the theologian Sharaf asked, "We hear the same sound as you do. But without feeling exalted, without getting excited like you. Without achieving ecstasy as you do. Why?"

"Because, Sharaf," Rumi answered, "we hear the sound of the door to paradise when it opens and you hear it when it closes."

When he went into town, he never left without Shams. Few of the faithful were authorized to join them. I was one of the privileged. Shams himself had taken a liking to me, possibly because I had changed places during the celebration of the sama to demonstrate my inferiority.

A lesson by Our Master, given a few days later, finally resolved this question of the place of honor in a gathering. We had

all been invited by Emir Qaratay to the ceremony for the opening
of the madrasa that bore his name. Hidden behind canvas panels,
the gateway to the Koranic school revealed, for the first time that
day, the extreme beauty of the interlacing of its *muqarnas* and its
sculpted marble columns. Like a garment of stone, verses of the
Koran intertwined with one another, weaving and twisting across
the façade. When they revealed the gateway, I saw my master wipe
away a tear.

Greeted by the emir, we entered a large room surmounted by
a cupola whose drum revealed, in kufic calligraphy, the divine
suras and the names of the first prophets and caliphs. The emir
bowed and, with a friendly wave of his hand describing the size of
the room, invited us to sit down. In sitting on the ground, I had the
impression of diving into the heart of the ocean, for the blue and
turquoise ceramics that covered the walls evoked the sea and the
incessant movement of the waves. The conversation turned to the
place of honor. Where should it be? Along what axis? Everyone
turned to Rumi, who answered, "For the scholars, the summit is
the center of the dais; for the mystics, the summit is the corner of
the room. In the religion of the lovers, the summit is the proxim-
ity to the beloved."

He rose to sit next to Shams, who had decided to sit in a corner, the most ordinary spot, the lowest, the place where people left
their shoes.

Everyone present, lawyers, politicians, scholars, philosophers,
were struck by Rumi's choice. With that gesture he publicly
revealed his attachment to the man from Tabriz. Until then, only
the abandoned students and certain visitors selected by Sultan
Walad had understood the depth of the Master's attachment for
Shams. From now on, the entire city would know.

On another occasion we had gone to the *khaneqah* built by
Nasr, the minister, for a celebration involving an eminent citizen
who had been made a sheik. While the scholars, guides, mystics,
emirs and nobles talked endlessly about the theories and methods

of theology, Shams remained motionless, like a treasure, in a corner. Suddenly, he rose and, moved by anger, cried out, "For how long, astride your saddleless horses, will you run around men's racecourse? For how long will you walk, resting on another's cane? The things you say about the words and gestures of the Prophet, exegesis, and theology, belong to men of another time! You are men of today! Where are your secrets? Where are your words?"

These comments were an illumination for me. I finally began to understand the meaning of my master's lines: "I was dead, behold I am alive." I finally began to understand why, on Shams's order, Rumi had given up all reading, even the work of the celebrated Arab poet, even that of his own father. He now walked without the help of others.

"I was dead, behold I am alive." That day or another I heard Shams say to him, "Slowly, slowly, become a stranger to the crowd. Truth does not accompany the crowd or belong to it. I don't know what can be gotten from it. I don't know what it deprives someone of or what it reproaches them of. You possess the qualities of the prophets, you follow them. The prophets had little to do with other people. They belong to truth, even if, in appearance, the crowd gathers around them."

On that day or another, I no longer recall, Shams asked my master: "If you see me, why see yourself? If you speak of me, why speak about yourself? If you know me and have seen me, why do you speak of illness? If you are with me, why are you with yourself? If you are my friend, how are you your friend?"

Without hesitating, Rumi obeyed Shams's two commands: he separated from the crowd and from himself.

Although at home his son severely limited the number of people who could visit Rumi, when he went out he often had to confront the hostility and denials of the more conservative. My master's reaction depended on his detractors. He rejected some with insults and held off others with anodyne and futile explanations, or sometimes by silence.

One day I accompanied him to the circumcision of the governor's son. The young boy, who was seven years old, was dressed in a mass of rich fabric. Over purple silk pants he wore a tunic with turquoise stripes, closed at the waist with a large brocade belt, which held a dagger whose handle of chiseled gold was alone visible. Emerald bracelets decorated his miniscule white wrist. Pearl earrings hung from his earlobes. His hair was covered with gilt satin, on the front of which an oval jewel gleamed. His eyes were lined with kohl and his lips lightly tinted with red. Seated on a rug decorated with the tree of life, he leaned against a traversin that was three times bigger than his hips. Behind him, a large open bay window looked out onto the sumptuous homes, the blue faience cupolas of the Koranic school of Qaratay and the mosque of Sultan Kay-QubÇd, onto the poplars of the Christian monastery of Plato, where my master had gone on retreat for forty days, and in the far distance, onto the broad surrounding plain, which had been coveted across the centuries by Cimmerians, Lydians, Persians, Greeks, Romans, Christian crusaders, and, more recently, Mongols.

For a moment I had the impression that the color of the sky, a mixture of pink and blue, reflected the garments of the famous son. This thought projected me into the Persia of the king of kings, when the *padeshah* selected his garments, his palaces, his horses, his wives, and his itinerary based on the color of the sky. With his turban, his medals, and opulent outfit, the governor subtlely reflected, by the choice of his silks, the harmony of the room, the clouds over Konya, and his son's clothing. Gold chains decorated the collar and hems of his robe. In his hand he held a string of ruby prayer beads.

The city's leading citizens surrounded the governor. Among them was a great scholar, whose name I will spare you from learning. This was a man who, although he approved of Our Master's behavior, had considerable doubt and many reservations about his more recent practices. In a moment of confusion, he is said to have told his closest acquaintances, "Why should such a learned man, such a king, such a scholar, dance and practice sama? Why does he do what religion prohibits?"

When told of this confusion, Rumi, who rarely justified his actions, waited for the appropriate moment to reassure the scholar. A barber responsible for carrying out the circumcision arrived. The governor took the child and placed him on a low stool. The blade was barely out when the operation was over. The barber cauterized the wound with sieved wood ash. The child's cries were hushed by the congratulations of the adults, the *besmellah*, and the voice that announced, "Now you are a true Muslim!" From outside could be heard the sound of drums and an announcement of the appearance of bear handlers and acrobats. Slaves carried in platters loaded with sweets and syrups. My master approached the child, who now wore a loincloth, and whispered a Koranic prayer in the hollow of his ear. But before leaving the governor, he went over to the scholar and said to him, "Oh sheik, there is one point of doctrine, and I know you have studied it, that authorizes the hungry, thirsty, and dying man to eat what is forbidden. That act, justified by religion and approved by the learned, enables humanity to endure. For some men of God, there exists a situation similar to hunger and thirst, whose remedy can only be found in the sama, the dance, in ecstasy and melodious sounds." And he left the hall humming.

Behold, he is alive.

Water for the thirsty, bread for the hungry

OW, SHAMS WAS ALSO CALLED "THE SUN OF MIDNIGHT" "Water for the Parched," "Bread for the Hungry," and "Healer of the Sick." Ever since the ceremony inaugurating the madrasa of Qaratay, during which my master, sitting by his side, had pointed him out to the citizens of Konya, they all came—scribes, artisans, doctors, soldiers, tailors, princesses, poetesses, courtesans—to see with their own eyes the inexplicable communion between Rumi and the old dervish.

To respond to the keen interest in the new arrival, but more importantly in the uncontested Master, Shams placed Rumi in a closed cell and stood before the door along the gallery, squatting on cushions and buried beneath a pile of blankets. There, he demanded a contribution from those who wished to meet the Master of masters.

"What have you brought? What will you give to see him?"

There were many who paid. Shams asked for more. And more still. He auctioned off his lover. Rumi was for whoever offered the most. And this seemed to greatly amuse Our Master, who burst out laughing when his second son, Ala, grew upset over Shams's behavior, which he was unable to understand.

One day when Rumi was closed in the cell, Shams, before the door, was negotiating the price of the meeting. Finding that he exaggerated, the visitor, furious at his exorbitant demands, said to the insatiable negotiator, "And you, what did you bring that you ask so much of us?"

Gazing into the silver coins, Shams, as he counted the day's take, answered, "I brought myself. Along his path, I offered my head."

Some visitors came not only to meet the Master, but also to see Shams, an object of great curiosity, who was already something of a sensation. One day, two wealthy merchants introduced themselves to me, wrapped in furs, covered with agates, and so perfumed that with the slightest movement it smelled as if someone had just spilled a bottle of floral essences. They wanted to see "Water for the Parched," "Bread for the Hungry," Shams of Tabriz himself. I was preparing to lead them to the former library where Shams now lived, when he burst through the door shouting loudly, "They have to pay first!"

Surprised, the two men thought it was a joke. Pay to see Shams? It was out of the question. When I timidly requested a modest sum for the interview, they called me a thief.

Shams stood in the doorway, taller and skinnier than ever, and in a neutral tone of voice doubled the price. They swore at him, eyeball to eyeball, without the least restraint. In an instant, "Bread for the Hungry" became "Dirt," "Waste," and "Dishonor." Shams bent over, removed his slipper, and threw it in their direction. They ran toward the exit and left immediately. When they had disappeared, he said to me, impassive, "If I don't test those men, they won't know who they are. Did you see how they pretended to be men of faith and devotion? When I—rather gently—tried to put them to the test, did you see their faith? Did you see what my test revealed, how it exposed them before your eyes? Ask the man who claims to be your friend for a dirham and his intelligence evaporates, his breath vanishes. His head and his

feet wander. I challenged them so they could see their own pettiness."

All the same, to demand payment to meet Shams seemed to
me a rather painful task. Still, I had to do it. For he now made me
responsible for determining the price of the interview and of turning the money over to the Master's family and to needy friends. I
decided to watch Shams at work, when, as if it were the most
natural thing in the world, without embarrassment or confusion,
he negotiated the amount for visiting Rumi. I did not have his tem-
perament, his boldness, his cheek. When his "customer" hesitated,
he would get carried away, insult his entourage, become vulgar and
uncouth—before the always amused and admiring eyes of Our
Master—while I tried to calm our guests, settle arguments peace-
fully. However, through the explanations of friends, I came to
consider these taxes an initiatory experience intended to exceed my
comprehension, sweep away convention, and shake up the estab-
lished order.

My first customer came through the door unannounced. It
was the sultan's lieutenant. At his belt he wore two swords of different sizes, whose handles bore the name of the current sultan—may God extend his shadow over our heads!—his father, his
father's father, and the founder of the dynasty. His boots were so
shiny that I could see the outline of my beard in their black
tongues. His walk was noisy and ostentatious as a result, differen-
tiating him from the discreet, muffled sounds of the common folk
with their flat slippers. This was my first attempt and it wasn't just
any old customer! I knew that Shams was watching and listening
behind the door of the former library. I had to succeed. I hurried
to greet our visitor and, after the customary compliments ("may
our eyes grow bright at your sight!") and endless questions about
the health of the sultan, the viziers, the emirs, our guest and his
own family, I informed him, clumsily and hurriedly, of the price of
the interview: ten thousand dirhams. A slave sent by Shams arrived
and whispered in my ear. "Ask him for forty thousand!"

It was a colossal sum. In terror I glanced across to the library where Shams was watching me, and gave him a sign of my power-lessness. He coughed sharply to show his disagreement. I asked the sultan's lieutenant to wait a moment and entered Shams's apart-ment.

"Master," I said, "never will a man, no matter how rich he is, spend so much for a few minutes of conversation. Do you realize that with forty thousand dirham you can restore an entire school, clear a park, build a gymnasium?"

Unperturbed, Shams answered, "That's why I ask so much."

"He'll never pay. He's no fool. He would rather do the restorations himself, in his own name, for his own prestige!"

Shams thought a moment and finally conceded, "Thirty thou-sand. Not a dirham less."

Once again in front of the visitor, I said to him, "For thirty thousand dirham your soul can take nourishment from the sight of Shams. But only for a brief moment."

He accepted! I led him into Shams's apartment and waited for his departure, which I felt to be imminent. Shams never wasted time on long explanations. When he wrote, his sentences were extremely short and sometimes, for me and for the others, incom-prehensible. I closed my eyes an instant. The noise of heels on the tile of the courtyard told me the interview was over.

When he left, the soldier was transformed, drunk, lighthearted. As soon as he saw me, he gave me an additional purse with ten thousand dirhams. For him, the meeting with Shams was worth even more. Apparently, it was priceless.

I went to find Shams to ask him how I should distribute the money. He told me that because of my scruples we had cheated ourselves and could have asked for much, much more. From then on, I had no trouble negotiating the meetings. I offered our star to the highest bidder.

Like a celestial body around the sun, the director of the Koranic school, the future emir of Konya, his wife Gordji, Sultan

Walad, Thiryanos, Salah the goldsmith (whom I'll discuss in due time), and myself all gravitated around my master and Shams. With the passage of time, I felt myself closer to the center, to the heart, of our galaxy.

Gradually, Rumi's other son, Ala, excluded from this dance, began to despise not only Shams but everyone in his father's entourage. Anything that gave us joy and happiness made him angry. Not only did he refuse to participate in any of our samas, but he considered dancing to be the epitome of frivolity. He reviled the musicians because, or so he believed, the sound of their instruments obscured the voice of the muezzin, the call to prayer, the echo of the divine word. Where he felt that Shams's attitude towards money clearly revealed his greed, we, on the contrary, were fascinated, and saw it as a sign of his exceptional character, free from good and evil. To find support, Ala joined the throng of men abandoned by Rumi, those who had formerly attended his classes—now discontinued—enjoyed his availability, and participated in his retreats. Among these men, Rumi's unwanted son sought comfort and, probably, encouragement in publicly denouncing Shams. He met with them in the Koranic schools, the mosques, the bazaar, the hamam, and other places, to castigate the one he called "the man of dishonor," the very man his father said breathed the breath of Christ.

During those meetings, their voices rose up against Shams:

Why has Our Master turned his back on us and allowed himself to be seduced by Shams? We are all famous, the offspring of noble families. We have been seeking truth since childhood. We are the true servants of the voice of the Master and his sincerest followers. We have seen him perform prodigies that no one else has seen. We have heard words of wisdom that no one else has heard. Like falcons, we have captured our prey and offered it to him. We have spread his reputation throughout the world. We have entertained his friends and confounded his enemies. And now we are the ones who are deprived of his face and voice, all because of Shams. What magic has that old man, whose origins are unknown and the source of our misfortune, used to seduce Our Master?

Ala had an anonymous document circulated throughout the city; it bore the title: "How can two birds not of the same species fly and eat together?" The two incompatible birds obviously referring to Rumi and Shams.

With considerable difficulty, I managed to obtain a copy. It read:

> One is an eagle who flies in the sky,
> The other a grounded owl.
>
> One is the sun of the empyrean,
> The other a crumpled bat.
>
> One is the stainless light,
> The other a blind beggar at every door.
>
> One is the moon alongside the Pleiades,
> The other a worm unseen in the mud.
>
> One has the face of Joseph, the sigh of Jesus,
> The other is a wolf, an ass with a bell.
>
> One flies toward the unknown.
> The other, like a dog, lies in the straw.

After examining the document, I hid it in a trunk in my home in Faliras, fearing it might fall into Shams's ink- and saffron-stained hands. It is now before my eyes, worn with reading. The paper has yellowed but the words continue to evoke the hatred and incomprehension of a vicious son. I return it to the trunk and try to call to mind Sultan Walad's uneasiness at the intolerance of the frustrated. Fearing things might get out of hand, he would knit his brows, which met above his nose. His brows, arrows ready to fly, formed the Arabic numeral seven. He said, "They are all thirsty for the blood of Shams. Whenever they see him, they place their hand on their dagger and insult him. All of them hope for his departure or death."

I couldn't say it to Sultan Walad, but I knew that Ala, his own brother, was not unaware of the agitation. Not a day went by without him feeding the anger of the dissatisfied with rumors about Shams and Rumi.

One day I caught sight of Ala in the metalworkers bazaar, seated in the shop of a skilled cutler, a former student of my master, before an array of knives, razors, and scissors. I hid within range of their voices in the shop across the way, where a worker who boasted of knowing the "three hundred and twenty diseases of the horse," was shoeing a dray. To arouse the jealousy of the craftsman, like a child whose toy has been taken away, Ala said to him, "Once my father praised Shams so highly—may a hundred dogs fart in his beard—that I ran at once to report the words to the one he had praised. He responded coldly, 'I am a thousand times more than what he said.'"

Hearing this, I knew that Ala had carefully distorted the sense of Shams's response by failing to relate it exactly and in its entirety. "I swear to God," Shams had said, "I swear to God that I am merely a drop in the ocean of your father's majesty. But I am a thousand times more than what he said."

To further excite the cutler's hatred, Ala added, "I found my father and told him what his friend had said. He said to me, 'Yes, Shams has revealed his greatness, he is a hundred times more than what he claims to be.'"

Then I saw, through the rear legs of the horse being shoed, all the bitterness of the world cover the face of the craftsman. I also saw that he grabbed a knife, whose blade he began to sharpen.

Ala continued, "Quite unusually, my father happened to be present among a group of his former companions. Someone suggested meditating with their heads on their knees. After a certain time, one of them stood up and said 'I can see to the top of the heavens!' Another one said 'My vision stretches beyond the top of the heavens and space! I am contemplating the universe of the void!' A friend added, 'I see beyond the constellations of the bull and the fish! And I see the angels who are their agents!' Upon hearing this, the man of dishonor, without father or mother—may a hundred donkey pricks enter his ass!—in an attempt to ridicule the grotesque celestial evocations of our friends, replied, looking my father right in the eyes, 'As for myself, in everything I see, I see nothing but my weakness!'"

And I, Hesam, hidden in the blacksmith's shop, saw only the blade of the knife. Sharpened and polished, it glittered in the hands of the cutler. Ala interpreted everything incorrectly; his point of view was that of someone who found himself on the outside looking in. Filled with resentment, he was unable to appreciate Shams's duality, when he said, for example, that he was very humble with beggars, very haughty and arrogant with the others.

The danger grew more focused as the days wore on. Shams was no longer able to move around Konya without being insulted. Even the house seemed to have been affected by the turmoil. Everywhere there were whispers, shock, frowns, faces shot through with tremors of anger. I became afraid that the cook, overcome by the general frustration, might try to poison Shams. To avoid adding to the fear and anxiety of the surrounding confusion, I told no one of my own concerns. But at every meal, I ignored all the rules of politeness and grabbed Shams's portion of food and swallowed it at once. After putting away dozens of dishes in this way, I reassured myself: death would not come from the kitchen.

A year had passed since their encounter. Autumn arrived. It was again very cold. Our Master prohibited any commemoration of the event for fear that the Bird, Shams, realizing he had remained too long on the same branch, might suddenly decide to fly away. We obeyed. On 26 *Djamadi al-akhar*, year 643 of the Hegira, there was silence. But in our hearts, each of us celebrated, in his own way, the anniversary of the appearance of "Bread for the hungry," "Water for the thirsty."

I searched for a sign of exaltation on Rumi's sallow face, but in vain. He too refused to display the least feeling on that day, which should have been a day of celebration. The two arcs of his upper lip remained desperately at rest.

I then decided to visit Shams. Without much hope, I entered the former library that often sheltered his solitude, their solitude, his and my master's. Being familiar with the place, I was no longer surprised at the musty odor, so unique to that room—Shams, afraid of drafts, had sealed all the openings. I hesitated a moment in that place, strangely attractive in spite of its confinement. I said to myself that, if the bricks could capture the conversations of those two men, it would surpass all the mystical writings, even those of Attar and Sanai. While examining the room, which jealously guarded its secrets, I found, resting on a low table, a sheet of paper. My curiosity urged me to unroll it. I recognized Shams's handwriting and the odor of the ink, which was still fresh. I read, "What is the arrow? Speech. What is the box? The universe of truth. What is the bow? The power of truth. The arrow is without end. In the box, which is the universe of truth, I have arrows I am unable to release. Those that I release return to the box."

This was the only document written in his hand that day, the anniversary of their encounter. From Shams too there was silence.

It was now the dead of winter. One sunny morning, I accompanied my master into town. My size and strength helped ward off the attentions of the curious. Suddenly, Rumi decided to go to Khan-i-Zia, the caravansary of the minister Zia, where there was a woman named Tavous. This woman was a dancer, who also sang and played the harp. I followed without saying a word. When we entered the courtyard, I was stupefied by the stars, interlacings, and stalactites that decorated each end of the perpendicular axes of the *iwan*.

Like every other caravansary, the Khan-i-Zia had two levels. The lower story held stables, storerooms, workshops, and the dining hall. Having recognized Rumi, the residents, who were eating as he entered, left the dining hall, bowed before him, and asked him to taste their flatbread, which was powdered with sesame seeds and had just come out of the baker's oven. With a wave of his hand, my master refused their invitation, went over to an exterior staircase, and walked upstairs, where there were rooms opening onto a gallery. He stopped opposite Tavous's room. As was generally the case, I busied myself with keeping away the curious, the admirers, and the indiscreet. I was becoming much more proficient at this, just as I was at setting the price of an interview with Shams. Calm was restored.

My master sat on the cold stone tiles and I stood by his side. A moment passed. Suddenly, the door to the room opened. There emerged a whiff of jasmine, followed by a graceful creature whose brows were painted with indigo dye, her eyes underlined with kohl, her teeth rubbed with mother-of-pearl, and her lips tinted red from chewing betel. Behind the nearly transparent satin veil, which she wore negligently on her head, floated dozens of fine strands that fell to the small of her back. Each of her movements was accompanied by the tinkling of colored glass bracelets.

Holding her harp in one hand, which I saw to be white and fine, she approached, bowed before my master, and invited him—the height of audacity—to enter her room. To everyone's astonishment, Rumi accepted. I was the only one who was not surprised. For the past thirteen months, I had repeatedly been shocked, amazed, and unnerved. That the most mystical of men should penetrate the room of a woman of her reputation did not disturb me in the least.

Seeing that I remained outside, busy trying to keep myself warm in the rays of the morning sun, the administrator of the caravansary invited me to come down to the storeroom, which opened onto the courtyard and where samples of merchandise from around the world were stored: glass from Aleppo, spices from Zanzibar, ambergris from India, crystal from Egypt, furs from Azerbaijan, Chinese silk, Iranian cotton. My glance traveled from one article to the next. It was as if by simply touching a Persian fabric, I suddenly found myself there, in Nishapur, in the pharmacy of the perfume maker and poet, Attar. It was as if I were present at his spiritual evolution, on the day when a dervish had shown him that he could, if he wished, fall dead on the spot.

I can see Attar seated in his pharmacy. Suddenly a very poorly dressed man stops before the display and stubbornly examines the products shown. Embarrassed, Attar, tells him, "Don't stand there doing nothing, keep moving, go to your job." The poor man simply answers, "Look how I'm going." He places his turban on the ground, rests his head, and dies.

I observe this from afar. I see the scene again. I am in Attar's shop because of that turban, made of cotton from Khorassan. I can see the man die.

Touching a piece of silk from Suzhou tears me away from Persia and leads me to China, more than five centuries earlier. This time, I can see the royal concubine, Yang Guifei, being murdered. The executioner strangles her with his belt in the presence of the emperor Xuanzong, who, with his broad sleeve, hides his face so he does not have to see the pain on the face of the woman he loves more than anything on Earth.

I am now in the inn at Mawei, surrounded by the imperial guard. Time is running short and they must escape the rebels as soon as possible. In spite of the confusion and haste, the army generals, responsible for the murder of Yang Guifei, appear confident, for they have just eliminated the source of all the trouble, corruption, and questionable appointments. Before leaving the inn, I see the Son of Heaven requisition the silk belt that led his beloved from this world to the next.

I find myself sitting in the office of the administrator of the caravansary. I spontaneously grasp the roll of silk and slip it into my shirt as a souvenir of the murdered concubine. The secret memory of fabric.

Someone brought me some rosewater syrup and almond cakes, and suddenly the sound of the harp could be heard. Everyone grew silent; no one moved. The assistant director and his accountant abandoned their invoices, the grooms their horses, the travelers their packages. The melody was coming from Tavous's room, where my master was listening, the only member of her audience. Soon the musician enhanced her playing by the addition of sung melodies and then, abandoning her instrument, she danced—with movements that were probably extremely graceful— as we guessed by the sound of her ankle bracelets.

I spent the entire morning this way. My master still remained in her room. The odor of grilled food led me to the refectory, where young men were serving roasted meat, yogurt, cakes, and sorbets on large copper platters. I sat down to eat, suspecting that Rumi would not make an appearance for a while. Lunch was served and the noonday prayer celebrated in the *namazgah*, in the center of the courtyard, near the fountain. The siesta passed and still there was no sign of Rumi. Tavous continued to play, sing, and dance. It was almost evening and I was getting ready to send a messenger home so the family wouldn't worry when the music stopped. Rumi appeared, accompanied by the harpist. She held in her hand a piece of muslin, which came from the Master's turban. He had given it to her as a sign of gratitude, a piece of cloth that had brushed his forehead.

He had hardly entered the gate of the caravansary when we caught sight of the sultan's treasurer entering her room, his head covered with a turban of green brocade and wearing a coat of dark blue velvet, with buttons of gold thread on top. Two gleaming swords emphasized his waist. His attentive guards followed behind.

It's easy to imagine what transpired between them. When he saw her, surrounded by the aura of my master's protection, the austere treasurer trembled before a new beauty, more brilliant than before, for her face was now assured, filled with a luminous confidence. He questioned her and learned that Rumi, who no longer saw anyone, had spent the entire day in her company. Shocked, he immediately wanted to marry the woman, who wore, tied around her wrist, the gift from my master, the small strip of muslin cut from his turban. To further grace that hand, he filled it with fifty-thousand dinars—for years that was the story heard throughout the city. After that, he sent Tavous to the bath. He married her the next morning. We were all invited—Rumi, Shams, Salah the goldsmith, Sultan Walad, Thiryanos the Greek, and me, Hesam—to the marriage of the harpist and the sultan's treasurer. How could that fanatic, dogmatic, narrowminded man ask for the hand of the indecent Tavous? The entire city of Konya asked the same question. I was the only one, along with Rumi, who could answer it.

Having spent the day at the caravansary, filled with Tavous's music, it was very late when we arrived at the house. Lanterns illuminated the courtyard and a few candles flickered in Shams's apartment, the one whose door bore the following inscription, written in my master's hand, "the dwelling of the lover of Khezr," indicating that just as the prophet Khezr had initiated Moses, Shams had initiated Rumi.

He entered the room and, bidding me good night, quickly closed the door. I heard him recite these verses to Shams:

I am like a lyre, my head bent in submission.
You, with either hand, strike and caress me.

A week later, four-hundred sixty-eight days after their encounter, Shams left Konya.

Flight of the Idol

URING HIS FINAL DAYS IN THE CITY, THE ACCUSATIONS of his enemies became increasingly serious. The plotters were led by Ala, Rumi's younger son. Until then they had called Shams "an imposter," "a thief of conscience"; now he had become, in their eyes, "an evil sorcerer." They decided to act. Some of them, the most extreme, considered murder. The more moderate wanted to use the law to excommunicate him. Others hoped to make his life impossible and provoke his departure. This last group was successful.

The evening before Shams's departure, his flight, I stopped by to see him, and this time received permission to enter his apartment. Crossing the threshold, I recalled the story of the flight of another bird, told by the poet Attar, in which Bayazid says: "I achieved unity and set myself to observe it. For years on end, I ran through this valley, reflecting as I walked, until I became a bird whose body was unity and whose feather eternity. Then, I flew about the air of 'how.' I said to myself that, having disappeared from other creatures, I should reach the Creator. I then appeared in the valley of divinity. There I drank a bowl that did not quench my thirst for eternity. For thirty thousand years I flew in the atmosphere of the uniqueness of God. For thirty thousand other years I flew in His divinity and for another thirty thousand in His individuality. When ninety thousand years had passed, I saw Bayazid. All that I had seen was myself. After that I crossed four thousand deserts and arrived at the end. When I looked around, I found myself at the first step the prophets take."

In the room, which was quite comfortable, Shams shivered with cold. His long fingers looked purple. I bent down, took his hands and brought them to my lips, trying to warm them with my breath. He spoke to me of different things, then said to me "Now the moment has arrived when I must leave. With every moment, separation. With every moment 'come!' With every moment 'go!'"

I have always been angry with myself for not seeing in those words, which are quite explicit, his clear desire to leave.

The following morning, Rumi found Shams's room empty. He at once sent men to all the caravansarys and all the gates of the city to prevent the Bird from flying away, but their efforts were in vain. Disguised as an anonymous dervish, the man—sought after by the most illustrious of scholars, solicited by the emir and the sultan—succeeded in leaving the city undetected.

For a year, the interior of the house was filled with a compact silence. No more drums, no more vielle, no more dancing, no more music. My master no longer saw anyone, no longer laughed; he avoided the public baths and almost didn't eat. His only connection with life seemed to be the hope that someone would bring him information about Shams, the Vanished: Where was he? What city had he gone to? Who was he seen with?

Any time an unknown visitor requested an audience, Rumi—through the intermediary of one of us—had him questioned about the condition of the roads, the presence of bandits, the comfort of the inns, the security in the cities. Failing to understand why he was being asked so many questions, the unfortunate traveler attempted, in his answers, to be as precise as possible. We always concluded the interview with the following question, which was repeated a hundred times:

"During your travels, did you happen to meet a man about

sixty years old, rather tall and thin, sensitive to the cold, dressed in a black felt hat, gruff and irritable?" The stranger usually answered that his attention had not been particularly drawn to such a man. Grouchy old men, yes, he had seen all sorts; tall, not so tall. And frail ones as well—thin ones, shivering ones—that's all you saw along the roads.

We returned to the Master and provided these explanations to the man who, now, identified himself as "the one who only waits."

"Four-hundred sixty-eight days!" Rumi repeated tirelessly. He had kept an accurate count of the time spent in Shams's company.

During the following months, the plotters, who believed that the flight of the Bird would change his indifference toward them were disappointed. Not only did Rumi not readmit them into his company, but, believing that the real reason for Shams's departure was their contemptible behavior, he chased them from his home and his entourage. For their part, the former students, who had hoped he would resume teaching, again filled the courtyard.

"Clean this place of their filth," my master said to me, adding, "so I don't aim for their shadow."

In Persian, "to aim for someone's shadow" was a harsh threat. It meant that not only did one aim for their actual body but also its shadow, to destroy the totality of their being. I heard this expression dozens of times a day. Rumi, the gentle and flexible, became impatient, angry, became Shams of Tabriz himself.

Ala, the Master's evil son, felt lost. He, too—once Shams was outside the walls of Konya—hoped to rediscover the Rumi of before the dance, the man who surrounded himself with thousands of disciples, the man who prayed day and night. But for a period of time, Ala, too, had to leave: his father refused to look him in the eye any longer.

Time passed slowly. My master celebrated no sama, didn't compose a single verse. A year passed in complete silence. That winter it snowed continually and the enameled cupolas of the madrasa of Konya kept their white covering for many months. For years we had gotten into the habit of making ice for my Master, who was especially fond of fruit sorbets. During those nights of bitter cold, Thiryanos and I, to make the blocks of ice, would let water flow into shallow pools. Since we were the most physically fit of all the disciples, it was our job to break the ice into large chunks with a hatchet and a pick. We would carry the blocks of ice on our broad shoulders—at that time my chest resembled the pillars of the mosques and not the arcades—into the vaulted caves that had been specially prepared for that purpose. One morning, as we were working, a stranger entered the courtyard. He said he was a merchant, originally from Damascus. He was questioned like all the others. And he answered our questions about his possible meeting with a tall, thin, shivering old man by saying that he had seen, on many occasions, in the bazaar of his home town, someone whose appearance corresponded exactly to that of Shams. I at once dropped the block of ice, prepared to let it melt and lose a day's work, and ran to tell the Master. He was posing in the former library for a famous painter of the court. The painter, at the request of Princess Gordji, the sultan's sister and fervent disciple of my master, was trying to paint his portrait so that the painting would become the lady's spiritual companion during her travels.

I didn't want to disturb the concentration of the artist, who, brush in hand, glanced from the model to the paper. With one stroke he drew, with another he added color. Rumi, standing, spoke about the precision of the prophet and painter Mani, who succeeded in drawing, on a sphere the size of an egg, the "habitable quarter," that is, terra firma, together with all its cities, and the "uninhabitable three quarters." Even more sublime, said my master, was Mani's cloak, which was visible on his body but invisible when he took it off.

When the portrait was finished, the artist cast a final glance at Rumi and at his work. To his astonishment, the portrait quite suddenly had lost all resemblance to its model. Disconcerted, he made a second attempt, which he also cast aside. He was obviously having a hard time. With tears in his eyes, he retouched a line, diluted or enhanced a color, and, finally at a loss for what to do, in his despair and uncertainty gave up the idea of starting again. Seeing the painter's frustration, my master recited a poem. I listened while looking at the sketch for the portrait, and it seemed to me that the image of the man who was speaking, perpetually imprecise, continued to take shape and dissolve before my eyes:

> Ah! Without the least color
> And without any sign, I am!
> And when will I be able to see myself
> At last the way I truly am?
>
> You say, "Bring your secrets,
> Speak to me of them, place them in the center,"
> But who can say where the center is
> The center that I am?
>
> When will the stream of my soul
> Remain still?
> I who remain still,
> Streaming soul that I am.
>
> My ocean, it is there
> That he too has drowned.
> What stupor, that ocean
> Without shore, and that I am.
>
> Do not look for me in this world,
> Do not look for me in that world,
> For both are being lost
> In this world, here, that I am.

Like nothingness I am free
Both of loss and of profit.
What strange and unique thing
Without profit or loss am I!

I said, "Breath, you are like
Our essence," and it said to me,
"But what can this essence be
In this visible that I am?"

I said, "Behold that which you are."
He said, "Oh, be silent,
The tongue has not arrived
That can say what I am."

I said, "If the tongue saying
What you are has not arrived,
Behold the one who speaks
Without a word, and that I am."

And I, footless like the moon,
I went toward nothingness.
Behold your servant who runs
Footless, and that I am.

A voice came, which asked,
"But why do you run?
Behold here in this visible
The invisible that I am."

I saw him, Shams of Tabriz,
And thus I have become
The only ocean, the treasure,
And the quarry, also, that I am.

"I saw him, Shams of Tabriz." I couldn't ask for a better response. I repeated the line almost exactly: "A merchant from Damascus saw Shams of Tabriz."

He cast an irritated glance at the spot where I was standing, covered with water, like a puddle of urine. I provided a few explanations about the pieces of ice that must have melted in contact with my skin and infiltrated my clothing. He observed my hands, still bloody from the cold and the effort. Then, with complete serenity, he had me repeat the good news, once, twice, three times . . . "A merchant from Damascus saw Shams of Tabriz." It seemed to me that he wanted the resurrection of joy to last. He then sent me to get the merchant and a few articles of formal clothing to offer him.

I left the room, trailing behind the liquid imprint of my exertion. I returned to the snow-filled court and the bringer of news. Enthusiastic, the man who had never hoped for even a simple interview with Rumi, now found himself being treated as Our Master, Mawlana's benefactor. Rumi ordered the painter to make a portrait of Shams, stressing that no effigy could reproduce the breath that animated his face. The artist set to work at once. The features of the Bird gradually began to materialize in black ink. When he had barely completed his sketch, the merchant shouted, "That's him! I'm sure of it. The man in the Damascus bazaar. That's him!"

At that moment a smile returned to my master's face. I saw our grief transformed into joy. Life again returned to the household. A slave sprinkled the ground with rosewater and lit the lanterns. The kitchens prepared cakes and syrups. The men enlivened their dark clothing, which until then had been characterized by the black of sorrow, with bright colors. Thiryanos and I abandoned our blocks of ice. And after all those months of suffering, I saw Rumi start to write again. We sent trusted men to Damascus to find his lover and give him his letters.

A week later, the first answer from Shams arrived, "I want to make it clear to Our Master that I am occupied with the prayer of blessing and am no longer in contact with any living creature."

For a long time we wondered about the meaning of the message, in the end interpreting it as a sign of return, of loyalty, of an upcoming wedding celebration. The fact that he was "no longer in contact with any living creature" must have reassured Rumi, who, until then, I had not thought capable of jealousy. Musicians crowded into the courtyard of the school, prepared to attack the most joyful melody. Thiryanos, Salah the goldsmith, Sultan Walad, and myself were looking forward to the imminent celebration of the sama. From the andarouni, the women's quarters, the sound of castanets could already be heard.

Rumi picked up his fine pen, and in a single session, wrote a response to Shams's enigmatic message, a poem he allowed me to read. I pressed it to my lips, then to my eyes. After those signs of veneration, I read:

From the moment you went away
I was separated from your gentle honey like wax.

Every evening I burn like a candle
Joined to his flame, deprived of his affection.

When it was separated from your beauty,
My body became a ruin and my breath an owl.

Turn your horse's bridle this way
And fill to the brim the trunk of the elephant of love.

Without you, the sama is no longer practiced.
Joy has been stoned, like Satan.

Without you, not a single *ghazal* has been spoken
Until I received this envoy's visit, a sign of honor.

Afterwards, joyful at hearing your letter,
Five or six ghazal were composed.

You illuminate my night, which is like day,
You are the glory of Damascus, Armenia, and Rome.

Another envoy carried this poem to its recipient, Shams the Bird. Rumi received other letters from Shams.

The exchanges lasted three months. One day, feeling that the duration of the separation had ripened him and that he could now, finally, gather the fruit, Rumi asked the One Who Had Flown to return to Konya. A new expedition made its way to Damascus. It carried but a single poem, which was given to Thiryanos, who was charged with convincing Shams to return.

Go my accomplices, grab my friend and
Bring him to me at last, the idol with fugitive feet.

With sugared song and gilded arguments,
Bring home that fine-faced moon.

If he tells you he will arrive a moment later,
That promise is a ruse, and he deceives you.

His breath is hot. With charms and magic
He knots the water and seals the air.

In Shams's response we found no resistance to the idea of returning. My master at once had his son, Sultan Walad, and twenty of the faithful, go to Damascus to bring back the "idol with fugitive feet." I accompanied the devoted son and his small troop to the gate of the city, one spring day at dawn. The Turkish tribes were taking down their tents and assembling their flocks before leaving for the summer. The barking of the dogs answered the cries of the storks, who rested their wings on their slender legs after returning from a long migration. I recalled that popular saying that describes the stork as a bird that makes its home at the tops of minarets and makes the pilgrimage to Mecca every year dressed, appropriately, in white. My master always said that the stork's cry, *lak lak*, was a sign of the profession of monotheism in Arabic.

After our joyful goodbyes, I had to leave Sultan Walad and his retinue. Watching them as they left for Damascus, I could already imagine their return, bearing the most precious of gifts, Shams of Tabriz.

As the days passed, anticipation of their meeting seemed to improve Rumi's appearance. Beneath his ever-present sallowness could be seen a hint of crimson.

Once again he began to dance. As he often did, he would dance while chewing pieces of ice. His spirit returned. Any occasion provided an opportunity to start whirling. One day, in the middle of the bazaar, he met a Turk who was selling fox skins and shouting, "*Dilkou! Dilkou!*" (fox, fox) in his mother tongue. At once, my master separated from his followers and began to whirl as he hummed, to the same rhythm, "*Del kou, Del kou,*" which in Persian means "Where is the heart? Where is the heart?" Following his movements, adjusted to the refrain, we danced our way back to the school.

Another day, absorbed in the dance, he distributed his clothing to the singers, while continuing to turn, until he was entirely naked. His host, seeing him in this state, ran up to cover him with a robe of scarlet fabric, a lynx fur, and a turban of Egyptian wool. Rumi, however, continued to whirl, without concern for whether he was naked or clothed. When the festivities were over, as he was returning home, he heard, along the road, the sound of the rabab coming from a kind of cabaret run by Armenians. He stopped, gathered the assembled crowd, and began to dance with them. At dawn, he offered them his sumptuous garments and left, nearly naked once more.

At times I would take him in my arms during the sama and cover him with my own coat, for, freeing himself of all his clothing and overcome with joy, he had again begun to dance unclothed. How could we have imagined that we would see this man, the object of our respect, of our veneration, this man, the voice of God, the union of worlds, dance naked before us?

One morning he went to the public baths, where, after having his head shaved, he remained for hours under the jets of cold water. Some of those present, who gathered the cuttings as if they were relics, later claimed that he had remained for three days beneath that glacial cataract. Sometimes he would leave the hamam shortly after entering, simply because he had seen the masseuse chase someone from the bath to attend to him, Rumi.

Once, I found him in the bath, examining his own body with pity. Knowing that I was in the room, he said, "I have never experienced shame in my entire life. I don't know what it is. But today I am ashamed at the sight of my skinny body. My body has spoken to me, my body has turned away from me, my body has complained to me, reproaching me for not giving it a single day of rest."

He had grown terribly thin. Compared to his own, my athletic body seemed to be made out of entirely different material. I remember the first time I had seen him, three years earlier, dressed in a coat the color of milk and wearing a stylishly knotted turban. At the time, his muscles seemed to have been carved in stone. His walk hinted at a flexibility that would soon manifest itself in his dancing. He began to grow weak soon after Shams left and he lost both weight and strength in his anxiety, his not knowing where the old lover had gone to. Even the most delicious food prepared by his wife Kera, olives from India, prunes from Balkh, and apples from Syria couldn't cheer him up. After months of simply letting himself go, he finally became aware of his tortured body, which had become frail, thin, and weak.

Every Thursday evening he visited a group of women, where, surrounded by rose petals and inundated with jasmine water, he whirled until dawn, with the noblewomen of Konya as his musicians and singers. He greeted every tree he passed. Some said they saw the trees bow to him in return. He spoke learnedly to dogs, who surrounded him, yapping and shaking their heads, showing that they understood his insights. He went out of his way to visit the ruins of an old temple and offer a plate of sugared cake to a bitch that had just had a litter. Had he lost his mind? When his boots got stuck in the mud, he took them off and walked barefoot. He would take off his clothes, offering his coat, turban, shirt and shoes to a beggar. He sucked on yellow gooseberries and punished his body, as he told me later in private, impregnating his sweet saliva with that bitter, acrid astringent. He complained of his fame, which he compared to chains of iron, because of all the strangers claiming to be his lovers.

Once again, he called upon his favorite reciter, a hunchback with a very gentle nature, and the great flute player Hamzeh, to accompany him during the sama. Some of his followers would claim, write, and certify that, during one of those ceremonies, while the hunchback, then at the gates of joy, bent deeply over his drum, Our Master, in a transport of ecstasy, rubbed the musician's hump with his hand and ordered him to stand up straight. Healed on the spot of his disgrace, the now upright hunchback returned to his home, where his wife, who did not recognize his profile, refused to open the door to him.

As for Hamzeh the flutist, I, Hesam, myself witnessed an extraordinary event concerning him. One day, we were told that this virtuoso had died suddenly. My master went immediately to the house of the deceased. I followed him. He entered the bedroom where the corpse was lying and remained there alone for a long time. After a while, I heard—and I was not alone—the very distinctive sound of Hamzeh's instrument. In no case could Rumi have been the musician for it required the breathing and skill of a professional. When the music stopped, I heard Rumi's voice, "Now, he is dead."

Who had been playing? I hesitate to say.

Some of the faithful, the same people who loved to gossip, were not satisfied with my account and started a rumor throughout Konya that Rumi had brought the flutist Hamzeh back to life for three days and three nights and during that time, he played the flute for Rumi without stopping.

Again I found him, like before, involved in children's games. One day, for example, he found that his son, Sultan Walad, had grown bitter and bored. Rumi questioned his devoted son about the origin of this lassitude. He was unable to give a reason. Then, my master left and, a moment later, covered from head to toe with a wolf skin, burst into his son's room crying, "Hoo! Hoo!" Upon seeing the Master of Masters gesticulating like a wolf, Sultan Walad was overcome with wild laughter. And I, who was privileged to witness this humorous spectacle, laughed as hard as I could. If I, too, were interested in making up stories, I would say that the wild laughter lasted three days and three nights!

Once more, for long nights he would rest his head against the wall of the school and repeat, "Allah! Allah!" The weavers of legends, always the same individuals, claimed they saw Rumi's mouth open, although his lips were motionless, and heard his prayer rise from within his chest.

He reprimanded those who interrupted the ecstasy he experienced at the sound of the rabab. I heard him scold someone who, in the midst of a concert, came to announce the afternoon prayer. He cried out, "This, too, is a prayer! One requires the service of the visible, the other invites the invisible to the understanding of Truth!"

On those same walls, he wrote, "It is forbidden to deprive oneself of the nourishment of the spirit." In his books, the ones that had escaped the massive sale ordered by Shams, he would jot down lines such as, "The tears of the beloved are the proof of the lover's pleasure" and sing:

> Desire the one who holds you in his desire
> Seek the one who holds you in his quest.

Once again, just as it had been before Shams's departure, he promised some of the faithful that he would spend the night with them, and asked them to get ready to receive him. My friend Seradj the Tatar, who could be recognized by his long mustache, was among them. He prepared his finest evening outfit, a lightweight silk tunic, worn over satin pants, and waited impatiently in the school dormitory. When Rumi finally appeared, he ordered, "Put on your sleeping clothes!"

My friend did this at once, in the hope that his guide would soon join him. However, occupied in endless prayer, Rumi did not join him. Twirling his mustache, my friend begged him, "Oh, sultan of religion, won't you rest for a single moment? Dawn is approaching and I am dying with anticipation of my God."

Rumi answered, "Oh, Seradj, if we go to sleep, who will take care of the sleepers?"

Seradj did not reply. The end of his mustache, after having been twirled for so long, resembled a worn string.

Other friends told me similar stories, where Rumi promised them a solitary night during which, to their immense regret, he did nothing but meditate. I was not among the frustrated companions, nor was Salah the goldsmith, who seemed to be one of the few persons capable of filling Shams's absence.

Another of my close friends related how once he had found the Master alone in the assembly room. The young disciple prostrated himself before him and sat on the floor. Rumi said to him, "Come closer!" Resting on his arms, the young man slid delicately in Rumi's direction. Rumi repeated, "Come closer, come closer!" When they were next to one another, Rumi said to him, "Sit so that your knee touches mine." My friend obeyed. "When I touched him," he told me, "I had goose bumps."

In that posture, Our Master began to speak of Shams of Tabriz until, buried in the depth of his words, the disciple lost consciousness. When he came back to his senses, he heard the Master say to him, reproachfully:

Do not linger like an idler in this bazaar of perfumers.
Sit next to the one who has a provision of sugar.

This friend decided to live in the Master's home, filling himself day and night with the sugar he found there.

Once again Rumi showed his ridicule for those who hoped to practice self-discipline. Accustomed to a comfortable existence, they could not manage to complete the challenge they had set for themselves. Such was the case of a high-level administrator who wanted to go on retreat in the Master's school. Rumi agreed. But after a few days, the recluse, overcome by hunger, could no longer tolerate the harsh conditions of the retreat. He escaped at night and went to a friend's house, where he satisfied his appetite with duck cooked in butter and spicy rice. Satisfied, he returned in secret to his cell.

The next day, as he always did ever since he had received news of Shams, Rumi came to the door of the cell, placed his finger upon it, smelled it, and said, "Now, that's strange. This room is giving off the scent of duck and rice and not the scent of mortification." The unfortunate man threw himself at the Master's feet. "You are the bearer of so many revelations! But why should I isolate myself in a cell where nothing talks to me?"

I did not try to find out how my master had smelled the aroma of duck and rice, which had been eaten in another house the night before. This did not bother me. For me, the essential thing consisted in observing the acts and gestures of a man transformed by love, a teacher of celebrated talent but sometimes lacking in inspiration, who had become an illuminated poet. I listened and watched this being who suddenly embodied metamorphosis, movement, ecstasy, excitement, enthusiasm, transition, breath . . . I watched the most beautiful poem of all time come alive before my eyes.

Once again, having left his solitude, he agreed to participate in the sama, where he preferred the company of ordinary folk to that of philosophers. I will never forget the violence of Rumi's anger toward a man who had risked ridiculing his companions.

"Rumi's loyal followers are strange individuals. Most of them are ordinary people, artisans and courtiers. There are fewer scholars and learned men around him nowadays. Wherever there is a tailor, a cloth maker, or a grocer, he accepts them as one of the faithful." Upon hearing the insult, my master cried out, "Brother of a whore! And you, a man in love with the devil's prick! Wasn't Halladj a cotton carder? And wasn't Aboubakr of Bokhara a weaver? In what way did their trade impair their understanding?" The man who, after the flight of the Bird, spoke little, had rediscovered his former loquacity. As in the past, he often employed his favorite insult, the one used by all the inhabitants of his native Khorassan, "brother of a whore."

Once again, while awaiting Shams's return, the dawn of his Sun, knowing that the other would return, he accepted, as before, the invitation of the greatest notables to dance in their homes. Moin Soleyman, former director of a famous Koranic school, was in the process of becoming one of the most important men in Konya; for this he had placed himself in the service of the Mongols. Of all his former students, Moin Soleyman had been one of the first to most easily assimilate my master's metamorphosis. Upon learning, after the two men had been secluded for forty days, that classes would end, he understood at once, and without regret, that teaching would continue elsewhere, in other forms. So he accepted the ecstatic dance as the first step along this new path. One day he was found spinning around, imitating the endless whirling that had been the fruit of the union between Rumi and Shams. For my part, every time I met him, the harmony of his appearance and his headdress drew my attention. The sobriety of his clothing dissimulated a real sense of aesthetics. He had banned from his wardrobe and his household furnishings all colors except for black, ecru, and white. Even his face reflected those colors exclusively. He had a very black beard and very white skin. A repetitive gesture, however, set him apart. He would often place the first joint of his index finger in his mouth, wet it with his tongue, then hold it up to his nose to sniff it, or so it appeared.

During one of those long winter nights before the return of the Sun, Moin Soleyman had invited Rumi to his home. As was customary, each of the guests placed before him, as a gift, a wax lamp weighing more than three pounds. As usual my master entered last. It was, as he saw it, a mark of respect for the late-comers of less importance, who, after Rumi's entrance, risked not being admitted.

Holding a tiny candle in his hand, he entered, sat on the floor, and, as was customary, placed the diminutive candle before him on the hexagonal black and white tiles. The city's most important men, the viziers, the qadis and muftis, all present, looked at one another with surprise: what was the Master up to now? Clearly, the man was mad. Sensitive to their doubts, Rumi said, "The breath of all those lamps arise from my miserable candle."

With those words, some of the men tilted their head to show their skepticism. He then blew on the small flame, which went out . . . And all the lamps went out with it at the same moment. In complete darkness, there was a murmur of astonishment from the guests. I heard Moin Soleyman wet the first phalanx of his index finger with his tongue. Was it a sign of his lack of comprehension?

I was never able to explain the prodigy. The tellers of tales, as customary, embroidered the event to make it even more miracu-lous. They claimed that, after having extinguished all the lights, Rumi sighed and all the flames came to life again. Then the lamps went out one by one. But the Master's tiny candle continued to illuminate, alone, the black and white home of Moin Soleyman.

With the approaching return of Shams, Rumi's taste for mockery returned. One day, an administrator came to him and told him of the prodigies of a saint.

"Master," he said, "this man of God is capable of transforming pure water into blood! I can bear witness to it; I was present when he did it. What do you think?"

I heard Rumi answer. "It's not transformation, it's a waste!"

Once again, his sarcasm, extinguished by Shams's absence, came to life against his adversaries. One day, as he was passing before the kiosk of a sheikh of great renown called Nasser, he heard the man denigrate him before his students.

"Look at the face of their master, Mawlana, look how dark it is! Look at the path he follows, how it is narrow! I have no idea what his face is or what his path, or what his clothes are like. I see no light in him. None!"

I heard my master call out to him from a distance, very loudly, "And you, you sodomite, how do you choose?"

Neither Nasser nor his disciples dared reply to such violence. And we, and our whole group, continued along our path, following Rumi, who was already talking of other matters. Nasser, the philosopher, the sheikh, the great scholar, ended up living in the worst part of Konya in search of any young hoodlum who would agree, for a fee, to penetrate him. The local gossips said that he had caught the venereal disease of the sheiks. My friends claimed that his passive homosexuality revealed itself at the very moment Rumi insulted him that day. Nevertheless, on certain nights, walking down dark alleys in the less reputable parts of town, I could recognize Nasser's voice as it rose from the shadows, asking, pitiful and needy, "Is there no one who will fuck me?"

Once again Rumi administered remedies, such as poppy syrup, to the lethargic. Some of them, healed from their long, long sleep, but now insomniacs, came to consult my master who, this time, simply rubbed their head. Restored to health, they spoke of their healer as someone who changed suffering into joy, disease into health, ignorance into understanding, an enemy into a brother.

He despised the merchants, who, following a fad that spread during a time when the Mongol threat became increasingly greater, distributed their wealth and aspired to become Sufis. I was present when, in order to escape the entreaties of such merchants, Rumi took a ewer and went to the toilet, where he remained for a long time. Not being a teller of tales, I won't say he stayed there three days and three nights. But he was there for a good long while.

Uneasy, the merchants asked my friend Seradj the Tatar (this was the man who had spent an entire night vainly hoping to sleep with Rumi, and turned his mustache into a shoelace from repeated twisting) to intercede on their behalf. Standing in a corner of the toilet, Rumi, without waiting for Seradj, who had now joined him, to make his request, asked, "Where am I from? And the world, from where? To my nose, the odor of excrement is better than the odor of the things of the world and the inhabitants of this world!"

Again he astonished us with his strange behavior. We questioned him endlessly to find out the reasons. For example, he became infatuated with the obscurest of the obscure, an executioner known for the cruelty with which he carried out his terrible activities. Rumi took a great liking to this man, almost began to venerate him. One day, we found my friend Thiryanos, himself a former criminal saved by my master, completely beside himself. He had just surprised Our Master in the process of honoring the executioner. Of course, the Greek was not the only one to question him about his attitude. Rumi explained to us that one of the victims of this executioner was a saintly man whose greatest desire was to free his soul by leaving the cage of his body. By simply practicing his trade, this executioner had realized the wish of the sage, one of God's chosen.

Once again he took us to the most surprising, the most incongruous, places. One day we entered a caravansary, where a beautiful prostitute was staying, surrounded by a number of equally lovely young women. When Rumi appeared before her, she threw herself at his feet and humbled herself. Then, in a loud voice, so that he would be heard by everyone present, my master compared the debauched woman to Saint Rabia, and her whores to legendary heroines. An important gentleman, who was present at the scene, reproached him for showing those impure beings such courtesy. Pointing to the prostrate woman, he responded, "She, she walks beneath a single color, she appears just as she is, without artifice. You, if you pretend to be a man, do the same as she, cast aside the two colors so that your exterior resembles your interior."

The distinguished gentleman didn't say a word. As for the prostitute, I saw her the next day waiting—she had been there since dawn—for the Master's house to open, so she could enter, like a devout initiate. The night before she had renounced her trade, abandoned her home to thieves, and freed her girls. Now an intimate of the Master, she absorbed his teaching to the point of arousing jealousy among the princesses who claimed to be visionaries.

Once again he appeared before his disciples in Damascus, in Mecca, in forty different places, although he remained in his home, in Konya. Questioned by those who thought they had seen him, he answered, "I am like a fish in the ocean. I raise my head wherever I wish."

Once again he settled questions of law that no jurist had been able to resolve. For example, a thief who had climbed into a tree to gather its fruit was asked by the owner to come down. The thief, refusing to obey, had sworn, "May my wife divorce me if I come down from this tree!"

Three days passed—again, three days and three nights!—but the thief refused to break his oath. Hunger, thirst, the attention of the curious, and the presence of wild animals at night were unable to change his mind. When consulted, my master, sucking his gooseberry, decreed, "Let him go from this tree to another and then he can come down. And if that tree is isolated, have him first climb down onto a horse and then onto the ground."

So it was. And the man agreed.

Once again Rumi teased his wife Kera in public. One time she wanted to know the nature of the inhabitants of paradise. Rumi told her, "They're idiots. If they weren't, how could they be satisfied with paradise and its streams?" After this, he composed a poem, which was given to me by Kera in person:

If in hell I can grasp your hair,
I am ashamed for those who dwell in paradise.
If I am called without you to the prairie of paradise,
The prairie in my heart will feel narrow.

Once again he preached that we must seek the world and God within ourselves. A dervish, who wished to leave this world for the beyond, asked him where he should go to meet God. Rumi answered, "How do you know that God is not here?"

All that is in the universe is not outside you,
Look within for everything you want, for it is you.

Once again he attended spiritual meetings, where everyone expressed their ideas, their theories. To one of the faithful of whom he was especially fond—ever since Shams's departure he no longer refused to see certain adepts—he asked why this one-time favorite had not expressed himself during the meeting. The friend responded, "All the great men were present. I was afraid." Rumi reassured him, "All you had to do was open your mouth. I would have been the one to speak."

On another occasion, Rumi said to a companion who was hesitant to meet Moin Soleyman, the former head of the Koranic school who had become a pawn of the Mongols on the great checkerboard of the world, fearing his own ignorance of mysticism, that once he came face to face with the man, he, the humble and weak companion, would simply have to open his mouth. The words he uttered would be his own, those of Rumi. I was told the meeting took place in Caesarea and that the doubtful friend, after being encouraged by the Master, revealed so many gnostic truths that the man of politics, who wore only ecru, black or white, remained silent, and brought his moistened index finger up to his nose. I believe our Master's promise had revealed in our companion some hidden knowledge, submerged in a mass of doubt, frustration, and obscure humiliation.

Once again, he spoke with his cat, which, sitting on its hind legs, allowed itself to be caressed interminably. When my master began to sigh longingly, the cat imitated him with its plaintive cries.

Once again, he chewed raw garlic with every meal. He danced and sweated so much he caught a cold, then had himself bled and took a steaming hot bath, repeating with conviction that the cold was a remedy against delusion.

Once again, when he was at the hamam, he called for his barber and asked him to cut his mustache and beard very short, just enough so that one would notice the difference between a man and a woman. He said that it was pleasant to wear a long beard, but that while we must wait for the mystic to care for his beard, combing it again and again, the inspired man has time to reach God, with or without a beard.

Once again, he devoted his attention to us, his followers. One day, when all the companions were together in the house, he told us, "Know that there is but a single person in the world, that that person is with you, that it exists for you, works for you, and desires you." And he added, in verse:

I have remained in the prison of the world out of kindness,
Where am I from, and the prison, where is it from? Who have
    I stolen?

Once again, he honored his wife Kera, whom he had abandoned since Shams's departure to spend his time in prayer, mortification, and fasting. He honored her to such an extent that, to escape her husband's awakened appetite, she was often forced to take refuge on the balcony. I know from one of her friends that, before the announcement of Shams's return, during the long period of uncertainty, she constantly complained of Rumi's lack of interest in her and the absence of desire she aroused in him. With the change in the Master, she spoke of him as if he were an angry, drunk lion who, in one night, had penetrated her seventy times.

The tellers of tales would have said it was for three days and three nights. But she said, "In one night! Who would believe it?"

Once again, he took an interest in the smooth operation of the school and the house. He inspected the rooms, especially that of Shams, to see if anything was missing or needed to be changed. During one of his inspections, he told a carpenter, who, in the process of repairing the door to Shams's room, had driven a nail into it, "Our home is the residence of saints, and this room belongs to Shams. The nail you have driven into this door pierces my heart." Upon my master's advice, the carpenter, not wishing to profane the holy place, withdrew.

Shams was going to return.

One day during the month of Moharam, in the year 645 of the Hegira (May 1247), fifteen months after the flight of the Bird, a month after Sultan Walad had left to find him, we received a letter from the faithful son informing us of the arrival of his caravan, with Shams as the passenger of honor.

"I have crossed the deserts without apprehension. The mountains were no more than straw. The shrubbery along the road was like silk. Heat and cold were like sugar and dates. In Damascus I met King Shams in a caravansary, busy playing trictrac with a young man from the land of the Franks. I stood outside the door and observed from afar this mystery of God among men, delaying the reunion our community has dreamed of so ardently. King Shams won every round and systematically demanded money from his young partner, who paid but seemed to get increasingly annoyed. When he threw the dice for the last time and lost again, he rose and slapped his opponent; he slapped our Shams. My twenty companions and I wished to enter the room at once and strike the uncouth stranger who had dared raise his hand to the Sun. We were restrained by the voice of our king who, wishing to prevent others who surrounded the players from doing the same, said to them, 'This child is a pole, but he doesn't understand himself very well. Step away from him.' They excused themselves and left Shams and the young man standing in front of the overturned trictrac board. The stranger began to gather the pieces while Shams bent down to put on his shoes. I entered, followed by my twenty companions. Together we bowed before Shams, the Sun. Visitors, guests, and especially the young stranger, were dumbstruck at such signs of respect for a skinny old dervish, dressed in a turban and robe of inexpensive cloth, little inclined to talk and confusing when he did.

"Shams approached me, kissed me, caressed me with exaggeration and asked for news of my father. I relayed the greetings and prostrations of Our Master, then took his blessed shoes and into them, on behalf of Rumi, poured a bag filled with gold. I added that all the disciples asked forgiveness and regretted their former behavior. They promised that, from now on, they would banish envy and embrace friendship. Shams cast a glance at his shoes filled with dirham and said to me, 'Why does your father want to trick me with gold? His desire alone is sufficient for me.' He agreed to go with us. Stunned, the young Frank uncovered his head, threw down his money, and begged Shams to accept him as a disciple. Shams responded, 'Return to your country, honor your friends with your visit, become their pole, and do not forget us in your prayers.'

The young stranger with blue eyes and blond hair prostrated himself and remained in that position until our departure. When we left the caravansary, I offered my horse to Shams and, out of humility, decided to make the return trip on foot, walking next to his stirrup. We crossed the paved streets of the town and followed the grand bazaar, where we made a brief stop to purchase silks for our wives. In the marketplace every language could be heard. I recognized Turkish, Persian, Arabic, Armenian, Greek, and Indian, but there were many unknown languages as well, which, I was told, included the language of the Iberians, that of the Franks, that of the Saxons. Leading our group toward the gate of Damascus, I saw walls covered with marble of different colors, gardens of pistachio trees and a multitude of fountains and pools. We crossed deserts, rivers, and valleys for an entire month, knowing that our caravan carried, among its merchandise, the mystery of God among men. We will meet tomorrow in Konya."

Later, after their return, I pestered my friend Sultan Walad for news of the reunion with Shams. I continued to take notes on everything that concerned Rumi, and even then wanted to be a witness to those extraordinary events. But Sultan Walad remained intentionally evasive. According to him, the letter contained everything he wished to reveal. He was silent about everything else. I persisted in questioning him. One day, he gave in and said, "Listen, I had a very hard time convincing him to return to Konya. The shoes filled with gold—big mistake. You cannot imagine how much that irritated him. What else can I tell you, except that he told me he liked Syria, where he had gone? Especially Aleppo, which he preferred to every other city, even Konya. He loves the homes, the streets, the moats and crenellations."

I had a hard time imagining Shams of Tabriz appreciating the architecture of a city. But I had complete confidence in Sultan Walad, whose tongue never spoke a single lie. So Shams, the unexpected, the unpredictable, could suddenly see beauty in a building. Sultan Walad also reported Shams's own words, which he spoke as they were returning from Aleppo, "Rumi is the only man who could get me to move from here. Even if someone told me that my father had risen from the grave and wished, before disappearing again, to see me leave this city, I would answer, 'Let him die, I'm not moving from here.' Paradise is Damascus or just above Damascus."

Nonetheless, Shams left paradise to return to Rumi.

"We will meet tomorrow in Konya." Those apparently insignificant words at the bottom of Sultan Walad's letter, turned the house upside-down. The gardener at once went to inspect each flower of each rose bush and carefully adjusted the height of the fountain's jet so that its sound was flawless. The cook struggled to insert mashed garlic into pieces of ice in order to combine in a single food two tastes that the Master enjoyed. The women left the andarouni and went to the public bath, where they washed and did their hair and make-up as if they were one woman, and that single woman belonged to Shams. The musicians tuned their instruments for hours on end. Drums, vielles, and flutes blended with the vocalizations of the singers, rehearsing their voices. The disciples ran to the bazaar to dress in new clothing, as if it were New Year. Some began hastily inspecting the cells to remove anything that was likely to displease Shams.

Thiryanos and I tried to satisfy everyone. Donkeys for carrying the women, ice for the cook, invisible props to straighten the flowers, replacement bells for a frame drum, a collection of poems, including a poem by Attar for a singer who had suddenly forgotten his entire repertory, a certain way of tying a turban for a companion who was always trying to look his best, an alcove for the illuminators. And many other things as well.

As for my master, he secluded himself with Salah the goldsmith for hours on end. In spite of all my activities, I continued to keep an eye on their cell. I continually asked myself what they could have to say to one another, as the Idol with the fugitive feet drew near. Later, I learned, from Rumi himself, that they were preparing a retreat, for Rumi and Shams, in Salah's own house.

The apparent repentance of the skeptics, Shams's former enemies, was not sufficient to liberate Our Master from thoughts of future threats. By planning to withdraw to the goldsmith's home with his dear friend, he was hoping to escape their inquisitive glances, and above all, those of his own son, the suspicious Ala.

That day, which was filled with hope and disorder, I did not see my master's youngest son. Was he at home or had he too decided to seek refuge, to prepare to confront the unbearable return? I never found out. He must have kept to himself, for his former accomplices, the horde of frustrated men, pretended, for the moment at least, to be the most fervent of the fervent, immersed in the collective joy.

That evening, exhausted, before leaving the school I cast a final glance toward the door of the Master's cell, which was slightly ajar. I saw his frail silhouette, his arms and head raised to the sky in a posture of gratitude.

The following day we all arrived earlier than planned. Breakfast was served in advance, the garden was watered at dawn, the morning prayers were said at an unusual hour, the cocks crowed prematurely. Even the sun seemed to rise early. From the gardener to the day star, we all hoped our eagerness would hasten the arrival of Shams of Tabriz.

Around noon, we were told of the arrival of his caravan. The musicians grabbed their instruments and played one of Shams's favorite tunes. The singers recited the verses of Sanayi, Attar, and Rumi, which had been newly composed for the occasion. We stood in a row near the door of the school to welcome, one by one, the man whose absence had so disturbed Our Master, Mawlana.

They arrived.

Shams caught sight of Rumi, dismounted his horse and said to him, "I saw you, alone. You. The others were occupied with something and satisfied with their condition. The spiritual men were busy with their spirit, others with their intelligence, others with their soul. I saw you, you, and no one else. All the companions followed their own desire and left you, alone."

I heard my master answer him as follows:

> They have arrived, my Sun and my Moon,
> They have arrived, my eyes and my hearing,
> My silver face has arrived
> And my gold mine has arrived.
>
> The drunkenness of my head has arrived
> The clarity of my view has arrived.
> And if you desire something else,
> My something else has arrived.
>
> He has arrived, my thief
> And my destroyer of regret,
> The Joseph with the silver face
> Suddenly is at my side.
>
> Today is better than yesterday
> Oh friend everlasting
> And yesterday I got drunk
> When I heard from him.
>
> What I searched for yesterday
> In the light of the torch
> Today, a mass of flowers
> Has appeared on my path.
>
> Why fear death?
> The immortal water is here.
> Why fear blame?
> The shield has come.

The two men embraced and prostrated themselves in the posture of giving thanks, their knees and foreheads pressed against the
ground. Many companions arrived at that moment, when the two
men became one. And I, Hesam, saw my master's shadow and that
of Shams commingle, become one. I assert this. I vouch for it. I
bear witness.

My master, my disciple . . .

T HIS WAS A PERIOD OF CELEBRATION, OF ENDLESS SESSIONS OF the sama, prodigious narratives, affectionate reunions. Peace seemed to have lodged in the school's filbert trees.

In spite of the serenity, my master decided, as planned, to move in with Shams at Salah the goldsmith's house. I was asked to prepare their belongings: some clothing, extra turbans, two or three books by Attar, and a flute.

I began to envy Salah, their host—a sentiment I was unaccustomed to. I hid my resentment as best I could, but never managed to understand why my master had decided to move to that man's miserable shack, where every object reflected his craft as a goldsmith, and not to my house, in the comfort of a real home, filled with books, writings, and gymnastic equipment, like those bows equipped with chains and the small trestles known as *kabadeh* and *takhteh shena*. Of course, Salah had always shown himself to be the most faithful of the faithful, and he was one of those rare individuals capable of attenuating my master's sorrow in Shams's absence. But, with the arrogance and vanity of my youth, I told myself that it was certainly not because of that petty artisan's culture and erudition that my master showed him such affection, far from it. In fact, Salah expressed himself badly and never managed, during discussions, to develop even the shadow of a simple philosophical idea. He spent his days in his shop beating gold. That was all. Yet, he was one of Rumi's favorites.

The move by the two newly rejoined lovers—and it was Rumi and Shams who referred to themselves as lovers—raised a new complaint among the envious. Yet, given my jealousy of Salah, and profoundly upset by my master's choice, I could not blame them entirely. However, our goals were different. The others were jealous of Shams, whom I loved, while I—how unfair is youth!—I was angry with the goldsmith. Years later, after the death of Rumi, his devoted son, Sultan Walad, revealed to me something his father had said about Shams, Salah, and I. One day, when I was not present, he had said to his followers, "Do not speak of Shams before Salah, and do not speak of Salah before Hesam. Although the union, in the heart of their lights, is total and undifferentiated, it is a question of the jealousy of God and we should not provoke it."

Salah's home was much smaller than the Master's, but nothing seemed to disturb the two reunited lovers. This wasn't a real retreat, for they would return to the school, where the rest of us, those in the first circle, witnesses of their life together, absorbed the rarest kind of learning. But when they lived at the goldsmith's, no one, with the exception of Salah—him again!—and Sultan Walad, was allowed to visit them. Walad had other good reasons to go there and did so with considerable persistence. For he looked forward to spending time with the goldsmith's daughter and took increasing pleasure in her presence. The two fathers saw nothing wrong with this. On the contrary, they were looking forward to this union.

Shams's life with Rumi did not resemble their life together after they first met, when they isolated themselves in a cell for forty days and forty nights. Now, they sometimes went out separately. When Shams expressed this desire, my master asked me to accompany him on his walk, for he feared that his Sun might be attacked while he was out. He also feared that his Bird might decide to fly off again.

My presence at his side did not seem to bother Shams. I think he liked me a great deal. And I amused him. He took pleasure in reminding me, teasing me really, about my hesitation and awkwardness when he had ordered me to charge visitors for meetings. For my part, I put him on the same level as my master: the divine level. Could I have envied God from being with himself, from preferring his own company to that of humans? My jealousy was directed elsewhere: it was in their choice of living with Salah the goldsmith and not with me.

And then one day, we were walking in Konya, in the midst of the crowd, wandering through the noise and confusion of the city, sidestepping the donkeys loaded with merchandise for the bazaar, running into veiled women hurrying by, avoiding stray dogs hunting for scraps of meat, catching snippets of the Koran sung by childish voices, passing dervishes in no particular hurry to get anywhere, sometimes tossing a coin into a beggar's extended bowl, amusing ourselves with the satisfied expression of a traveler after a meal at a good caravansary, or the final glance cast toward a mirror in the door of a barbershop by some fop who had been freshly shaved and trimmed.

A Mongol horseman riding at a gallop suddenly rose up before us. The crowd separated, clinging to the walls. Behind his horse rose a cloud of blinding dust. When the invader disappeared at the end of the street, I began to complain, as I rubbed my irritated eyes, about the barbarians, who treated us as if we were invisible. Shams then told me the following story:

"Not long ago in Aleppo, I saw, near the exit of a stall, a terrified crowd trying to get away. I walked forward. They yelled at me, in alarm, 'Don't go in there! There's a dragon who can swallow the universe in a single bite!' This did not scare me. I walked toward an iron door that was wider and taller than anything I had ever seen. It was closed. The lock weighed over three thousand pounds. One of the crowd tried to warn me, 'He's in there, the dragon with seven heads! Do not linger near this door!' My courage was revitalized. I broke the lock and entered. All I saw was an earthworm."

The tale told to me by Shams was limpid. At that time, as today, we lived under the permanent threat of the Mongols. Our sultans ended up as vassals of the great khan of China. Terrorized, subdued, they tried, in spite of everything, to preserve some of their cities, such as Konya, from the Mongols' incendiary appetite. But we found the situation to be precarious. In 1243, a year before Shams appeared to my master, the sultan Kay Khosrow had been defeated by the Mongols. Toqat, Caesarea and many other cities were sacked. The bitterness of these misfortunes hung over all our heads. In every Mongol we saw a rapist, a strangler, a throat cutter, a destroyer. It was impossible for me to imagine our women marrying such men. And yet, they did. When he had finished telling me the story of the dragon, I questioned Shams, knowing that he himself, in his many travels, had experienced the ferocity of the Mongols, but also the terrorized fascination of the mouse before the serpent, the magic fear that the entire world felt at their appearance, which every creature felt within itself. Why did we behave this way? Why, Shams of Tabriz, why? He answered, as we continued our walk:

"The entire universe is contained in a single person. When that person experiences his 'self,' he experiences everything. The Mongol is within you. The Mongol is your own anger." He then told me, with his own particular verve, a few humorous details of his experience among the invaders from the steppes. "We were seven hundred men. Seven Mongols attacked us. They took our clothes, but in return they gave us a superb beating."

Then, without transition, he went from laughter to anger. He began to yell so loudly that I could see the nerves on his neck swell, the veins on his forehead delineate the Arabic numeral eight. He was no longer speaking to me but to someone who once had cried over a brother killed by the occupiers. And Shams criticized the absent mourner.

"Why do you cry? The Mongol with his sword has given your brother eternal life. Should you cry over him, asking 'Why this escape?' The jail has been destroyed by the Mongols and you cry, asking yourself why they have put a hole in the wall. You strike your face and whimper, asking yourself why they have broken the cage and freed the imprisoned bird. Why they have opened a wound and removed the filth, the impurity. You lament, asking yourself why that filth was removed."

Shams's fits of sudden, terrible anger, were primarily directed at Our Master, as if to provoke him, to challenge him.

One day I accompanied them, with other companions, to the house of a celebrated flutist. The purpose of our visit was to hear the sound of a certain flute made from a special kind of rosewood. The weather was beautiful and I felt in Shams, who was always chilly, a certain sense of relaxation due to the mildness of the weather. He bent his back less, which made him appear even taller. Rumi, who was always complaining about his sallow complexion, offered his face to the rays of the sun, hoping, in vain, for a change. Winter and summer, night and day, one could have said that he wore a piece of yellow satin on his face.

Greeted by the musician at the entrance of his house, which was covered like all the others with a roof of red tiles and corbels along the avant-corps, we entered the rectangular courtyard, where cypress trees rose above the walls. Suddenly, Shams stopped. Rumi, without a word, did the same thing. The unfortunate flutist also stood motionless. Why did they stop? I had no idea.

Moments passed, what felt like a long time. Then, Shams began to move forward again. He took the open-air staircase to reach the first floor, where there was a succession of rooms and the music salon. Our Master followed him along with the disciples. In the salon, other musicians were waiting for us; upon our arrival they rose and prostrated themselves. Shams, who had entered first, did not respond to their greeting. And Rumi imitated him. As he was about to step toward his hosts, he suddenly froze. He was about to open his mouth to speak, then his lips closed. Unsettled by this lack of courtesy, the host and his guests reluctantly decided to return to their seats, along low benches that lined the walls pierced with windows, and began to play a piece that evoked separation. A dappled light, created by the wooden latticework along the lower part of the windows and the green glass on top, highlighted the ceiling decorations, which held my gaze.

Right in the middle of the concert, Shams began to laugh wildly. Rumi, seated at his side, did the same thing. Shams stopped at once; his face looked bitter, disenchanted. Rumi also tensed up. I have to admit that, for my part, I was extremely upset, thinking of the musicians' embarrassment before such an unpredictable and disconcerting audience. The concert went on, however, for better or worse. When it concluded, Our Master thanked each of the musicians, as if nothing had happened, and recited verses that also spoke of separation. The musicians, overcome by this belated but sincere attention from the Master, forgot their confusion and told us they had never played so well. We were served a plate of lettuce accompanied with a dressing made of vinegar and mint. After eating, we descended the staircase and crossed the courtyard, where I found, in storage rooms on the ground floor, enormous reeds that were waiting to become flutes. As a form of thanks, Rumi blew into the host's instrument to bless it.

When we returned to the school, Shams allowed his anger to express itself, an anger that was directed fully towards the man who claimed to be his lover. I would never have thought that such comments would one day be directed at Rumi.

"I have to clarify our situation. Our life, together, is based on what? On fraternity and support? On the relation between master and disciple? Between teacher and student? Now, you place my knowledge above your own. If there was only one reason for our separation, that would be it. You teach me nothing! If I had been able to learn something here, in Konya, I would have had no reason to leave for Damascus!" Then, he added, as if he were addressing some invisible interlocutor, "Alone, free, I went everywhere, stopping before whatever shop happened to be there. I can't drag him, the doctor of law, just anywhere! No. I can't bring him wherever I go."

In spite of this outburst, my master remained silent. He listened, submissive. I moved away, wanting to spare my ears those sacrilegious words, but all the same I heard Shams continue his diatribe.

"If I, if I become bitter, you become bitter. If I laugh, you laugh. I don't say hello, you don't say hello. As far as I know you possess a universe of your own, separate from my own, free from my own! You compare my writings to those of others. But I, as far as your writings are concerned, don't even compare them to the Koran! And another thing. When you say, 'write,' why are you so reluctant to do it?"

In response to these accusations, some of which seemed incoherent to me, my master recited for Shams some verses that I consider the most inspired of all the poetry in the world.

You are that light that told Moses:

I am God! I am God! I am God!
My master, my disciple! My pain, my cure!
I say these words openly, "My Shams, my God!"

Later, much later, long after Shams's disappearance, when Rumi had finally become the great poet we know him to be, I heard him compose this ghazal:

You are Noah, you are the spirit.
You are victor and vanquished.
You are the heart that is opened
To the door of secrets for me.

You are the light and the feast,
You are triumphant happiness,
You are the bird on the mountain of Tour,
I am wounded by your beak.

You are the drop and the ocean,
You are kindness and anger,
You are sugar and poison,
Don't torment me any more.

You are the chamber of the sun,
You are the house of Venus,
You are the garden of hope,
Oh friend, let me in.

You are the day and fasting,
You are the fruit of poverty,
You are the water and the pitcher,
Give me water this time.

You are the seed and the trap,
You are the wine and the cup,
You are raw and you are cooked,
Don't leave me so raw.

For Rumi, Shams was all this at once. He was everything, and
the opposite of everything. Sometimes master, sometimes pupil,
one day poison and the next the cure. But, most of all, he was
his God.

"My Shams, my God." . . . Whenever I hear him repeat that
blasphemous line, I run to close the doors of the school so that
none of the uninitiated will report it to the theologians. As interpreted by them, that line could lead Rumi straight to the gallows.
I recall Halladj, who, more than two centuries ago, was martyred
for having dared to say: "*Ana'l-Haq*. I am the Truth." And wasn't
that other philosopher, Sohravardi, the sheik of al-Ishraq, the sheik
of Oriental wisdom, put to death on *5 Radjab* of the year 587 (July
29, 1191), by other doctors of law, who considered his work to be
disrespectful of religion?

Rumi himself had said, "my Shams, my God." I carefully scrutinized all the disciples. Who was the traitor among them, the one likely to denounce the Master with his impious words? Our usual companions were there, but I also caught sight of Ala, the ungrateful son, seated in a corner. From that moment on, I felt the threat against Shams to be real. Shams, who, during his first appearance, had changed Rumi, the learned professor, into an enthusiastic dancer, Shams, who now became a god.

While Rumi continued to recite the poem in which the blasphemous words "my Shams, my God," were repeated again and again, like an incantation, Ala, the superfluous son, rose suddenly and made for the door of the school. I myself opened one of the leaves to let him out, knowing that he was going straight to the doctrinaire theologians to nourish whatever vague hatred for Shams they harbored, and repeat to them, word for word, the incriminating words: "My Shams, my God!"

Once Ala was gone, I approached the cell of the two lovers. My master's voice could not be heard. I looked inside. Shams had taken off his turban, letting his shaggy gray hair fall onto his shoulders. He was getting ready to remove his coat. I heard him say to Rumi, "I want to describe all things to you. But I'm satisfied with telling you those things in secret. Description is unworthy of you. I have been looking for someone of the same material as me, to make him my *qebleh*, to direct my face toward him. For I am growing bored with myself."

With a gentle hand, he caressed Rumi's forehead and continued. "Ever since I met you, books have had no appeal for me. No book is as helpful to me as your forehead." He looked at Rumi for a long time, a very long time. I would even say patiently. Then, finally, he said, "Leave with me. You too, look!"

It was with those same words that Shams ordered Rumi to escape drunkenness, that "unguaranteed drunkenness," as he called it wherever he went; it was with those same words that he ordered him to awaken the creatures and lead them toward Truth.

Yes, I heard Shams say to Rumi, "Oh brother, do not collapse! Leave with me! You too, look!"

When I reported this conversation to my friend Thiryanos the Greek and to an Indian disciple, the man spoke to me of a religion practiced in his homeland, which also taught the renunciation of one's own happiness, of the paradise one had finally earned—he called it "nirvana"—and of one's own drunkenness, to remain with men and lead them to the difficult beatitude, to the "other shore." The Indian added that those beings—all too few—who accepted the sacrifice, who renounced eternity to remain part of the world's furious movement, were called *bodhisattvas*.

For that Indian, Rumi was a bodhisattva.

Summer arrived and my veneration for Shams grew in spite of the confusion in his words, his vulgarity, his improprieties, his madness, his impatience, his prodigies. In spite of them or, rather, because of them.

And in spite of his caprices, as well. He didn't like fruit if it was too cold, right out of the pantry. He ordered us to leave it outside for a long time so it could be eaten at room temperature. But even then he often found something wrong with it: not ripe enough, not juicy, disagreeable, odorless. No matter what we did to prepare his meals according to his multiple requirements, nothing satisfied him. He found the grilled meat to be overcooked or not cooked enough, the rice was too mushy or too dry. I surprised him one day in the process of explaining to the cook that he must never take his eyes off the stove throughout the entire cooking process. "Not for a single instant," he insisted.

In any event, he never finished what was on his plate. When someone offered him syrups, drinks, or cakes, he always asked for half a glass, half a bowl, or half a portion, thus complicating the job of the person who was serving him. And me, whenever I found a half-empty glass of mint syrup, no matter where, I saw the imprint of Shams of Tabriz.

He had a particular fondness for melons. He became maniacal about it. For example, he absolutely insisted that their flesh be firm, the taste sweet, and their scent similar to that of the orchards of Tabriz, his native city. I still don't know why, but I had become the only person who could choose the ones he liked. When someone else offered him one, he would taste a piece, then spit it out on the rug or on someone's coat, or into the water in the pond, or a cup of mint syrup. And he would then denigrate the person who had grown the melon, the person who had sold it, and the person who had bought it. No one dared assume responsibility for such a hazardous job. Except me. I had become the specialist of Shams's melons. I walked along the rows of melons in my garden in Faliras and, with the help of my young wife, picked several melons. I smelled, I probed, I examined the ribs on my fruit, I muttered incantations in order to prevent myself from making the wrong choice, before deciding to harvest several for Shams of Tabriz. At the risk of appearing boastful, I can say that I was rarely wrong. For I was never the recipient of the mouthfuls of fruit he felt, depending on his mood, to be mushy, bitter, and odorless.

One late afternoon during that lovely summer, Shams, Rumi, Thiryanos and a few friends had, as usual, climbed up to the flat roof of Salah the goldsmith's house. To cool the surface, the servants had poured water on it and spread out a large rush carpet. The sun was setting behind the domes of the mosques and illuminated our faces with an ephemeral light. We heard the call of the bird catcher. A flock of doves appeared and landed on the roof of a neighboring house. We could hear nothing other than their cooing. With profound attention, Rumi observed them as they pecked the ground, shifted from leg to leg, coupled, and finally went to sleep. He must have been thinking of Attar's famous *Conference of the Birds*. Do I dare try to paraphrase it in my own words? Thousands of birds, guided by Salomon's hoopoe, one day decide to journey to find their true king, Simorgh. At the end of their travels, after most of the birds had turned back or gotten lost, experienced shock or collapse, only thirty birds succeeded in reaching their king, Simorgh. Thirty, for *si morgh* means "thirty birds." Those thirty birds who had gotten through, the si morgh, were able to look upon the face of their king. When they looked at Simorgh, they saw thirty birds, and when they looked at themselves, the thirty birds saw that they too were the Simorgh. And Attar says, "No one in the world had ever heard anything like it."

Rumi watched the doves on the neighboring roof for a long while, then turned to Shams and, staring at him, recited the following lines:

> Oh, Shams, truth of Tabriz, we are the testicles of your bird,
> We boil, beneath your feathers, until the moment you take flight.

Shams answered, "You, you possess beauty. I possess both beauty and ugliness. You have seen my beauty, but my ugliness, you have not seen. This time, I abandon hypocrisy and practice ugliness so that you see me fully, in my grace and in my ugliness."

Then, no doubt considering the image of a "bubbling up beneath his own feathers," he added: "The one who accepts my words is recognized by the fact that the words of others appear cold and bitter. It is not that he speaks to others, while remaining cold. It is that he does not speak to them at all."

Then, I, Hesam, the young disciple with the athletic physique, dared to intervene in this dialogue between my two gods. "Our Master Rumi," I said, "is only goodness, while Shams bears the mark of goodness and the mark of violence."

Thiryanos considered my comments as an affront to Our Master's lover and told me to keep quiet. Shams took offense and grew angry, as he so often did, not with me, not with what I had said about the mixture of goodness and violence, but against my friend, to whom he heatedly replied:

"You're an idiot Thiryanos! Our Hesam was comparing my attributes to the attributes of God, who possesses both violence and goodness. When he expressed himself, those weren't his words, it wasn't the Koran, they weren't the acts of the prophets, those were my words that came from his mouth. Now, you and those like you, you dream, with your halting intelligence, of becoming, in two days, like the greatest mystics, like Bayazid, Djoneyd, and Shebli! You dream of drinking from their cup. Bunch of fools."

Thiryanos assumed a hangdog expression. And I must say that I, being a fatuous young man, was rather delighted at my friend's discomfort. There was a long silence among the disciples. Then, suddenly, Rumi burst out laughing, realizing that his entourage was cruelly lacking in discernment. And yet, they all wanted to reach their own Simorgh, their true king. He stood up, still laughing, walked down from the roof, laughing, crossed the courtyard, laughing, and threw himself, fully dressed, into the pond filled with goldfish, still laughing.

One evening, also in Salah's house, where Our Master and Shams had taken refuge, a spiritual dance was being celebrated. In the hall, shaped like a loggia, from which one had access to the various rooms, the best flutists, tambour players, and vielle players were gathered. A singer, whose voice was the most beautiful in the entire land, was preparing himself by inhaling a preparation made with incense, an ancient recipe that went back to the time of the magicians of Ahura Mazda, who would inhale such vapors before dawn to awaken the sleeping world with their incantations.

Dozens of lanterns illuminated the courtyard and seemed to invite the water from the tiny pond to shimmer in the light. Frogs, enchanted by the moon, lifted their head towards its disc and croaked in chorus when it disappeared behind the clouds. I looked into the water and followed the dance of a necklace of tadpoles on its pearlescent surface.

Shams and Rumi left, hand in hand. Both were wearing a thin cotton shift of a light-colored fabric. It was the first time I saw Shams in such a cheerful outfit, topped by that hat that we began to refer to as his "crown"—for, didn't it decorate the head of a king? I knew from Salah, who doled out information drop by drop, that on the top of his turban, the words "God is great" were inscribed and that inside, in calligraphic letters, one could read: "In the name of God, the merciful, the beneficent." The front bore the expression, "There is no God without God," and the back, "Mohammed, the Prophet of God."

When they drew near, I threw myself upon the ground at their feet. Of late, my attention had been drawn only to Shams. Without being fully aware of it, a feeling buried deep within me anticipated his disappearance, his concealment, possibly even his death. I told myself that, at all costs, I had to record his words, his gestures, his oaths, his impatience, even his arrogance. One day I heard him say, "I am God's only creature." On another occasion, he said to Salah, "If you remove the Kaaba from the center of the circle, the prostration of a believer will be directed to the one who happens to be opposite him."

The celebration was to take place in a narrow room. Thiryanos, who had just left the barbershop and had a newly trimmed beard, questioned Shams about the secret of the sama. Shams let go of Rumi's hand, sat on a cushion placed on the ground, and began to rub his ankles as if to prepare them for the gyrations of the dance. He then said, in his usual fashion:

"During the sama, the men of God often perceive the divine manifestation and can more easily leave the world of their own existence. The sama pulls them from the other worlds and connects them to the face of truth. There exists a sama that is illicit and prohibited: the one during which a hand is raised without ecstasy. That hand deserves hell, while a hand that is raised in ecstasy achieves paradise. There is an authorized sama: the sama of ascetics and pious men who, during the celebration, give way to tears and tenderness. Finally, there is a sama that is a duty: the sama of beings for whom this practice is like prayer, like bread and water during periods of extreme need. The seven heavens and seven earths, and all the creatures begin to dance at the moment a true believer enters the dance. The dance of men of God resembles a leaf floating on the water: inside is a mountain and outside a piece of straw."

Shams forgot his ankles, pointed to the narrow dais on which the concert was to be held, and added:

"When I was still an adolescent, love ruined my appetite. If someone suggested that I eat, I would refuse all food with a wave of my hand. Sometimes, I would accept a mouthful, but I spit it out at once and hid it in my pocket. Inhabited by that love, one time, when I was practicing the sama, an exalted friend suddenly grabbed me and made me turn like a bird. In his hands I was like a piece of bread greedily seized and torn apart by a young man who had eaten nothing for three days and suddenly finds himself before a plate of food. He made me turn, turn, and turn some more. His two eyes were two pools filled with blood. A voice rang out, 'The adolescent is still raw. Leave him in a corner and let him consume himself from within.' The dancer left me."

Throughout the celebration of the sama that followed, I kept repeating, "The dance of men of God resembles a leaf floating on the water: inside is a mountain and outside a piece of straw."

Bit by bit, I felt that Rumi was growing tired of staying at the goldsmith's, where he saw no one. For, aside from a few visits from his wife Kera, he had completely abandoned his home and began to look forward to renewing his friendships. In spite of the constant presence of Shams and Salah, who began to assume a preponderant role in my master's daily life and heart, everything about his refuge felt uncomfortable to him—the soft mattress, the rundown bathroom, the kitchen odors. On many occasions he smelled the odor of his son, Sultan Walad, which reminded him of his abandoned home. During my visits, he asked me to provide details of the gossip concerning his employees. Had the cook, a husband and father, succeeded in seducing the black Kanizak, the young slave, whose old, handicapped husband had recently died? Was the blind beggar still suspected of working for the information services? Was the gardener still running after the young reader of the Koran, who was enrolled in the neighboring school? But what was far more important than the extramarital affairs of the Kanizak and the cook, was the attachment being formed, day by day, before his eyes, in the retreat he was beginning to tire of, between his son Sultan Walad and Fatima, Salah's daughter, who was twelve years of age.

My master had been in the house of the goldsmith for the past seven months, sheltered from the stares of the insolent. During that time, Sultan Walad had used any pretext to visit. He followed Fatima around from the dawn prayer to the late night prayer. He didn't meditate, he hardly prayed, and rarely did he participate in his father's conversations with Shams. However, he followed the goldsmith's daughter, ten years his junior, wherever she went. In the evening, when we were returning, he avoided any philosophical conversations and spoke only of a technique for chasing gold that had been developed by a North African tribe, which could be used to fashion a necklace of interlinked rings without any solder whatsoever.

Throughout this period of "dissimulation," Rumi, deprived of his followers, chose Fatima as the object of his teaching. I began to grow jealous of this adolescent with long black hair, who appeared unveiled before my master, for the initiation she was receiving was profound. Once I surprised Rumi describing to the girl, who still sucked her thumb, the theophanic function of the mirror. One night when he couldn't sleep, Shams, who was walking in Salah's house, saw Fatima standing, while everyone else was asleep. She answered, quite simply, that at night she remained upright. I know she ate little and rarely spoke. To us she never uttered a word.

Her confidant was none other than Rumi himself. However, she became friends with the daughter of Princess Gordji and Moin Soleyman, the former director of the school and future governor of Konya, the man who licked his index finger. This girl, called Eyn, unlike Fatima, spoke a great deal. She informed her mother that her girlfriend told her, described to her, the appearance of the spiritual residents of the heavens, which are invisible to the profane eye. For a long time, Eyn would draw these celestial beings, surrounded by light and energy, which she showed to her father, who, although one of the most faithful of men, had never seen such apparitions. Fatima's personality intrigued all those who visited, beginning with Sultan Walad. In spite of the difference of age, he was genuinely taken with her. For her part, the discreet and silent Fatima spoke to him at length and often, factors that were interpreted as signs of love. In light of this, Rumi, in agreement with the goldsmith and his wife, agreed that their children would be engaged. She was twelve, he was twenty-two. They would have to wait another four years to get married and legally enjoy the pleasures of the flesh.

At the start of autumn, we celebrated the marriage of Shams to a very beautiful woman, forty years his junior, who had been raised in the same house as Our Master. Her name was Kimia. Ala also desired her.

Although in love with his future wife, Shams did not seem particularly happy about the idea of marriage. We were a hundred times more excited and enthusiastic than he was. Rumi hoped the union would keep the Bird near him. Years later, he told me that, from the first moment they met, he had felt that the duration of their remarkable union would be short.

I had become quite skillful at extorting substantial sums from Rumi's visitors. Given my talent, it was to me that Shams came to find the money to pay for his wedding—how I did so mattered little. I set to work, and my first step was to calculate the donations from the royal family. Always cautious, my master's son explained to me that we shouldn't ask too much of the sultan, or his sister, Princess Gordji. He felt it would be wiser to implore their generosity when the situation was serious, or at least more critical.

How were we going to find money? There was no question of asking anything of Salah, for example. This man of the people continued to practice his trade as a goldsmith and owned no more than a tiny garden, where he spent all his time when he wasn't working. As for asking one of Rumi's other close disciples, Thiryanos, for example, that would have been ridiculous—leaving his "previous existence," as he used to say, his former life as a thief, a criminal, a condemned man, he had shown up with empty hands, more or less destitute. The other followers were also mostly poor. Only one of them had an adequate income: me.

First, I turned to some of my father's former friends, wealthy, generous men who had always shown themselves to be devoted to the paternal confraternity I dissolved after his death. After a lengthy discussion of the potential benefits of their gift, I managed to convince them of opening their wallets slightly.

I then made some very complex calculations to determine the amount I still needed. It was at that moment that Shams came to see me. "Hesam," he said to me, "religion is found where there is money. Give something, become a servant and enter within us."

Why make religion subservient to money? I didn't understand. Was this some new test? It didn't matter. My only desire was to enter deeper within him. The price I had to pay was of no consequence. I sold the furniture in my father's home and our collection of rugs from Isphahan, Indian ivories, Chinese lacquers, and Syrian faience.

"Sell everything! Everything!" I ordered my slaves.

I kept repeating those words until they informed me that, aside from themselves, there was nothing else in the house. With that news I was filled with an immense joy. I could finally set them free and fulfill the Prophet's gesture of emancipation. I said to them, "All of you. For love of Rumi, I give you your freedom." The servants left.

Even though the hermitage was closed, some of my father's former companions from the confraternity had continued to meet there. When they found the house empty and bare, lifeless, they were extremely annoyed. Their anger didn't bother me in the least.

For me, what was most important was my generosity toward Shams. If necessary, I would have sold my beautiful garden in Faliras; and with that money I would have filled Shams's shoes. But that wasn't necessary. The sale of my furnishings and the amount I collected in donations greatly exceeded the expense of the marriage. I decided to give the additional money to Shams. He kept but a single dirham for himself and ordered me to give everything to the poor. However, satisfied with my generosity, he added, "The reckless seek death the way poets seek rhyme, the patient a cure, the prisoner freedom, and the schoolchild Friday afternoon."

I completed his thought myself: "the way lovers seek the gift of self."

Contrary to custom, Shams decided upon a very intimate ceremony. I was made responsible for erecting a tent in the center of the courtyard to welcome the highly select group of guests, and install dozens of braziers for the chilly husband. The sunniest room in the house, the *tab khaneh*, was decorated by Rumi's wife, Kera. That was where the marriage would be celebrated, that was where the sacred texts would be read.

Shams refused to have an imam present, and instead asked Rumi to read the matrimonial verses. All three of them, Rumi, Kimia, and Shams entered the *tab khaneh*. Through the door, which was briefly left ajar, I saw flower petals scattered across the floor, splendid lamps, and clouds of incense. The door closed behind them.

I later learned, through my master himself, that Shams asked Kimia to remove her veil before Rumi at the very moment when he read the sura of union. He told me, not without irony, using the various commonplaces of Persian love poetry, that when the bride removed her veil, he contemplated her hair, which reminded him of the "nocturnal waves on a turbulent lake," her neck, whose "whiteness could be compared to the first snowflake in autumn," and her waist, "which begged to be embraced."

Shams was not the kind of man who shared. His possessiveness had long ago been revealed in his relationship with Our Master. He himself had to approve any visits, excursions, celebrations, or dances. Even the purification in the public bath, which Rumi was so fond of, only took place under his control. And my master indolently allowed him to govern his life.

After the wedding celebration, Kimia, the young bride, moved to the women's apartments, where a private party had been organized by Kera. No men were allowed. The male guests, gathered in the overheated tent, waited patiently for the return of Rumi and Shams. When they arrived, the guests prostrated themselves and wished Shams and Kimia—the union of the "Sun" and the "philosopher's stone"—a long life together. Then we were served a succession of fowl, game, and meat macerated in a base of lemon, basil, and garlic; this was followed by a dizzying variety of cakes baked with orange-flower water, rosewater, and pomegranate juice. When the plates were cleared, incense was burned in the tent to cover the odor of food.

Now the dance could begin. The musicians were asked to play the *daf* and the rabab. Rumi, Shams, and several others, including Salah, Thiryanos, and myself began to dance the sama. There were not many of us but those who were present that night were deeply struck by what they had seen. At the end, Shams, to my astonishment, spoke to me about Salah.

"This goldsmith's words confuse me. I am like a man watching a tightrope walker, determined and fearless, walk across a high rope, who feels his own heart drain of blood."

That evening, for the first time, I saw, through the intermediary of Shams, Salah's other side, the one that only revealed itself in a certain light. The slope that Rumi would have to climb years later.

Naturally, after the marriage, the smallest detail of the couple's life gave rise to entire evenings of gossip across the city. Within the governor's harem, eunuchs and concubines spoke of nothing but Kimia's beauty, the woman who would become the branch on which—and this was Rumi's hope—Shams the Bird would settle and make his nest once and for all.

Curious of everything, as I was at that time, and especially wishing to write down these events, I decided to ask Shams about his marriage. My questions would have to be subtle and prudent. With Shams I had to take as many precautions as possible, for his anger could explode at the smallest impropriety: What sort of love did he feel for Kimia? Did it resemble the love that united him to Rumi? Was it greater? Was it of a different kind? As always, his reaction was totally unpredictable and disconcerting.

"Patience is my specialty," he said. "People learn patience from me. You see how patient I am with Kimia? You think I love her. In reality, I love only God. Some think I am harsh with her because I want to strip her of her possessions. I pardon them and I pardon her. The other day, for example, I went to her house. Her own household was quite surprised and seemed to say to me, 'How did you end up here?' It took me a while to familiarize myself with the walls and rugs. In order to sit down, I had to familiarize myself either with the inhabitants or with the walls and furniture. I heard her say, 'Come meet my husband.' I then saw someone stick his head out on one side, and another person on the other side. And this pleased her. All this to tell you that the patience I show to Kimia is insignificant compared to my real patience. I regret the money I give her. But I give for God. I give because she is teaching me how to play chess. Another example: The other day I saw her sell a *gandoura*, a garment with laces. As soon as clever people see the sun, they sell their winter clothing. But the day it rains, and when it snows, and when the white mountain greets the city, the same people withdraw into a corner and regret having sold their warm clothing. Now, Hesam, summarize everything I have just told you so I know how you are going to tell it."

I condensed his words as best I could. This seemed to please him. But later, reading my notes, I saw that he was right to have me repeat his words. For his words as well seemed to be birds that flew from one branch to another.

In the autumn of that year, which would bring with it the seal

of separation between Shams and Rumi, and which my master compared, in the very first verse of his mystical Koran, the *Masnavi*, to the separation of the flute and the reed, the separation that brought about some fifty-thousand verses of love poetry and symbolized in the hearts of lovers, for centuries to come and perhaps for all eternity, the torment of rupture, of disjunction, of dispersion, I invited Shams for a walk in my garden in Faliras. He was not the kind of man to get excited about the subtleties of the leaves, or the steps that crushed them underfoot, or the movement of the gardener's daughter, who swayed between two trees, or the gardener himself, who complained constantly, as all gardeners do, of the bad weather, or the harmonious migration of the storks. He saw those things with different eyes. For him, the details of the world were lovers and every detail of the universe was in love with a face, to the point of rapture.

Later, when Shams had disappeared, my master wrote of this comprehensive love.

> If the sun was not also in love,
> Light would not rest on its beauty.
>
> And if the earth and mountain were not in love,
> No plant would grow in their hearts.
>
> And if the sea had never known love,
> It would have, in the end, a place to rest.

We crossed alleys of poplars, plane trees, and cypresses. Shams observed, with a certain disdain, the uniform lawn and carefully manicured boxwood shrubbery. He must have been wondering what all the attention to order and uniformity was good for. To prevent his shoes from slipping on the sand covering the pathway, I had ordered the gardener to cover the soil with wicker mats. This also allowed us to sit on the ground, close to the baskets of

iris, narcissus, and wallflower. In spite of my veneration, I experienced a slight sense of bitterness, for he paid no attention to my efforts to entertain him respectfully.

My wife, several months pregnant, introduced herself, kissed Shams's hand, and asked him if he would agree to practice his method of learning the Koran in three months with her future child. His response was evasive. With a sign of the hand, I encouraged my wife to leave us, for fear my guest would grow annoyed.

I felt Shams's body penetrated by a cold that was not yet here, a future cold. He then reminded me of his constant chilliness, and told me how the contact of his skin with metal objects that had been sheltered from the sun sent shivers of cold up and down his spine. After bathing, he went on, it took his skin hours to dry and no towel could absorb the rebellious droplets that, notwithstanding the natural laws of physics, became embedded in his back, especially between his shoulder blades. He then developed an entire theory about the particular texture of his skin, according to which, his sense of touch was unlike anyone else's and the marks left on his fingers by colorants were difficult to remove, so that all he had to do was eat a single mouthful of saffron rice with his fingers, and his index, already penetrated by the color of ink, became forever recognizable from the orange-yellow of the spice.

Suddenly, he thrust out his fingers as proof of his epidermal theory, pointing out that simply having shelled fresh walnuts a month earlier had turned his nails permanently black. I carefully observed his darkened nails, trying to retain in my memory their bony, imperfect contours, the lines on his hand, and his long fingers on which no trace of manual labor could be seen. Yet, I wondered. For during his lengthy travels, during his long search for Rumi, he must have had to earn his living as a laborer. I grabbed his hands and kissed them for a long time, worshiping even his dirty nails, which were blue with cold. A secret voice whispered to me that Shams's immense presence would soon be no more than a long, harsh absence. I could already perceive the day when I would have to accustom myself to the emptiness, the loss. However, a voice in me continued to whisper that this absence would one day become transcendence.

He pulled his hands from my lips and we began to walk again. Then, all at once, he spoke to me of his childhood. This surprised me. I had never heard him express himself so explicitly about his past.

"I was a child. I saw God, I saw the angel, I observed the invisibleness of the upper and lower world, believing that most people saw things as I did. It was much later that I learned that they saw nothing. Before my father I did not reveal the external appearance of my devotion. How could I have revealed to him my interior and its inclinations? He was a kind and generous man. One barely uttered two kind words, and he ejaculated, although he was not in love. The good man is one thing, the lover another."

He grew silent. As always, his words contained enigmas. I tried to reflect on them. He did not even look at my orange or lemon trees loaded with fruit, the pride of my garden. I took advantage of his silence to ask the gardener to bring us some bread cooked on stones and some sheep milk cheese. His voice rose once more. This time, he spoke of my master, as if everything brought his thoughts back to him.

"I was water boiling from within, which bubbled and stank. Suddenly, M's being struck me and the water flowed. Today, it flows delightfully, cool and satisfied."

He returned to his childhood.

"My father was unaware of anything about me. I was a stranger in my own city. My father was a stranger for me. My heart grew wary toward him. I always thought he was going to beat me. He spoke to me tenderly and I thought he was going to strike me, that he would throw me out of the house. I was a child, no one understood how I felt. My father did not know how I felt. One day, he tried to tell me, 'First of all, you're not crazy . . .' I stopped him at once. 'Listen to what I am telling you. You behave toward me like a chicken that hatches duck eggs and raises duck-lings. They grow up. One day they accompany their mother to the edge of a stream. There, they jump into the water. Their mother, who is a chicken, walks to the edge of the stream. But she does not enter the water. Now, Oh my father, I see the ocean become my vessel, my country. That is my condition. If you are mine or if I am yours, dive into that ocean. Otherwise, go stand with the chickens.' My father answered, 'If you behave this way with your friend, how will you behave toward your enemy?'"

We shared the bread and cheese.

I found you alone

SINCE CHILDHOOD, ALA, RUMI'S MALEVOLENT SON, HAD desired Kimia, Shams's young wife. Everyone knew it, beginning with Rumi, who, in spite of this, had offered the young woman to a man his own son hated. Ever since his father's metamorphosis, the cessation of the classes on theology and the incessant dancing, Ala had considered Shams to be an imposter. With Shams gone he had hoped that his shadow would never appear again over the family garden, even if, before his eyes, his father was clearly in pain. He hoped that the pain would pass with time. He could not tolerate the benevolent attitude of his older brother Sultan Walad, who had, ever since the first day, put himself at the service of this stranger whose real name, family, origin, and trade remained unknown, this strange man, who had succeeded in isolating their father, imposing his own desires, prohibiting their religious retreats, banning the great works of the past and, the height of humiliation, making visitors pay dearly simply to see Rumi.

Why, in spite of this, did Sultan Walad continue to support this man, the source of a thousand disorders? Like his father, the older son had lost his mind and, possibly, his heart as well.

Ala had always seen to it that he passed in front of the gallery onto which Kimia's bedroom opened, so he might cast a fleeting glance inside. But when the marriage was announced, Shams forbid him from walking there. "I forbid you from entering this room and importuning me. I have chosen this room for the isolation it affords."

Later, to soften Shams's words, some claimed that he had never threatened the Master's son, even if Ala was culpable and, to some extent, a voyeur. According to these informers, who were capable of sweetening the most bitter statements, Shams supposedly said to Ala. "Oh, light of my eyes, although you possess every internal and external quality, from now on you must enter this apartment with tact." For anyone who knew Shams, those words could never have come from his brash, audacious, and often violent mouth.

The son's hatred for the man he called the imposter had reached its peak. Ala could not go a moment without criticizing, calumniating, or reviling the man.

His enemies, who were everywhere, intrigued and maneuvered. Ala was present at all their meetings, whether they took place in a bazaar, a hamam, a madrasa, or a *khan*. He skillfully stoked their anger and the latent bitterness in them, distorting, even inventing blasphemous words that Shams was said to have uttered, caricaturing his behavior—which was, it is true, quite strange for the narrowminded. In this way he aroused the intolerance of the fanatics, instilling in them the idea of assassinating this unwelcome individual, the intruder his father had gone so far as to identify with God the all-powerful. These vindictive men became increasingly numerous. The Master's former students, to whom the doors of the school had been closed, the writers whose books had been discarded, the wealthy who had been treated with disrespect, and the emirs to whom one no longer bowed, all conspired with Ala against Shams.

One day, around mid-autumn, Ala felt the moment had come to transform these intrigues into a genuine conspiracy. To do this he chose the Davali hamam, famous for its tile work, composed of rectangles of red, yellow, and black stones incrusted in the white marble. He secretly met with the *dalak*, or masseur, who was to be part of the plot, and four men who had ample reason to want to see Shams dead, and knew how to hold their tongue. They met in the circular pool located in the center of the octagonal sauna, their faces masked by humidity, steam, and splotches of water, their bodies covered with a long red and blue towel, where they sat rubbing themselves with dry jujube leaves or soap. The dalak, who saw to it that no one else entered, brushed the sinks, which were fed by pipes carrying hot and cold water, and arranged in alcoves in the walls, as he took part in their concert of accusations, protests, and complaints. One young man, a former student of Rumi whom Shams had evicted and who had just been shaved and had his head polished, in a room halfway between the entrance and the sauna, began to reproach the Master's lack of discernment ever since the imposter had "blinded" him. Ala added to this, saying, "My father has shut himself into a field where the sheep of the devil graze, a circle into which are admitted only criminals like Thiryanos the Greek, illiterates like Salah the goldsmith, brainless wrestlers like Hesam, and, most of all, crooks like Shams."

A bookseller and bookbinder, who had lost his best customer in Rumi, since no one read anything any longer at the school, had just left the central room after having been bled with cupping glasses, as shown by the bandage between his shoulder blades. Filled with rancor, he declared, laughing, "They say that Rumi no longer honors his wife, and that he saves all his passion for Shams. How could someone ignore a woman as beautiful as Kera for a bony old dervish shivering with cold?"

The third conspirator, a magistrate by profession and a man who did not tolerate the "disorder" caused by our dances, after having his armpits and torso shaved, sat on a marble bench, displaying his fatty flesh. This man, who thought of himself as a writer, sententiously declaimed, "One must see Layla with the eyes of Madjnoun."

He was making an allusion to the love story that we all knew by heart. Madjnoun was so in love with Layla that he went mad and began to wander in the desert, becoming a friend of the wild beasts. The caliph Haroun al-Rashid, eager to meet the woman who had stolen Madjnoun's reason, told his ministers "Bring this Layla to me. I want to know why Madjnoun has released into the world such a great passion that his story has become the mirror of all true lovers in the East and West."

The court spent a fortune, employed a thousand stratagems, and finally brought Layla to the caliph. She was led to the seraglio, where, as night fell, at the caliph's order, candles were lit. He arrived and observed her for an hour, then for another hour, without understanding the reason of a now mythical love. He said to himself that he should have her speak and that her speech might possibly reveal on her face the prodigy he was unable to see. He turned to Layla and said, "Is that you, Layla?" She answered, "Yes. I am Layla, but you are not Madjnoun! The eye in Madjnoun's head is not in yours. If you wish to see my beauty, look at me with the eyes of Madjnoun."

By referring to this story, the shaven man obviously wanted to say that to see Shams's beauty, to the point of preferring him to Kera, one needed to see him with Rumi's eyes.

The dalak, who continued to scrub the sinks, stopped for a moment.

"I also work for the grand vizier," he said with a certain vanity. "And I can confirm that up there, in the palace, they are also fed up with Shams. They say that he lacks gratitude for his benefactors, that he is like a cat!"

Ala completed his sentence with a shrug of his shoulders, "A cat who has become God."

The curse had been spoken. This blasphemy, the identification of Shams with God, caused all the shadowy conspirators to speak at once. Now, if the words were to spread through Konya, anyone could take it upon himself to denounce, strike, stone, or even kill the old man who took himself to be the creator or, worse yet, who allowed others to confuse him with God. The other men were silent. In the presence of the abandoned son, they dared not accuse Rumi directly, feeling there were attenuating circumstances: he had been charmed, bewitched, duped, seduced by the man from Tabriz. The Master's only fault was his lassitude. He had to be awakened. They had to prevent his long sleep from becoming weakness, amnesia, permanent absence.

"A cat who has become God!" Ala allowed the expression to make its way behind all those foreheads dripping with sweat, before letting fly his deadliest arrow.

"If this pool could talk, it would redouble your anger toward Shams. Look at this hamam, these cupolas and their windows, these glass panes, these marble benches, and the water that bathes us. They have witnessed the worst crimes that can bind one man to another. Shams and his acolytes led my father here, undressed him, encouraged him to dance naked, to enter this pool filled with undressed men, to brush against their muscles, which moved beneath the water to the rhythm of the drum and the flute. Even the musicians were as naked as earthworms, without even this towel that covers us."

With those words, one of the conspirators, a fanatic theologian, suddenly climbed out of the pool to avoid contact with the impure water, the refuge of forbidden caresses. The others followed him. Ala had succeeded in doing what he had been planning for months. At last his accomplices had decided to take action. They moved to the entranceway, where the heat was less intense. Above it was a gallery whose floor was covered with rugs and straw mats. The dalak circled the room before locking the doors to the street.

The obese magistrate, who had great difficulty putting on his boots, for his enormous stomach prevented him from bending over, was the first to speak, "Let's accuse Shams of a crime, rape, for example, and have him appear before a court."

The young student with the shaved head, busy trying to locate the end of his belt, which had disappeared into a belt hole, answered with a gesture of impotence, "That's pointless. Shams has no fear of justice or dishonor. We must be clever. Offer him, in exchange for his departure, a house, a man or a woman—especially a man!—somewhere beyond our country's borders. And I swear to you that this crook will leave here!"

The bookseller, who was carefully putting on a long black shirt so as not to irritate the scabs caused by the bleeding, offered another suggestion, "I have contacts in the Mongol camp, where I exchange Arab manuscripts for Chinese and Tibetan prints. I can spread the word that Shams is a spy, in the pay of enemies, and that the only reason he is here in the territory conquered by the son of Genghis, is to gather military information. All that is needed is for a single Mongol to become suspicious and he'll lose his head."

Rumi's former student found this solution a bit too radical. While rubbing his body with an essence made from mud collected after the rainy season from the plains of Maharashtra, in India, he came up with an unusual plan.

"We can abduct Shams, blindfold him and take him to some distant city. Without resources he will be unable to leave the place. He won't be able to return."

The fanatic theologian, who was knotting his turban with meticulous coquettishness, found the suggestion to be idiotic. He answered, not without contempt, "If he desires, Shams will always find the means to join Rumi. No! We must turn him against Konya, make it so that he has no other choice than to flee the region of his own accord. That he disappears forever, disgusted. Otherwise things will turn out as they did after his initial departure. Rumi will search for him and have him brought back. He may even go in person to accompany him in triumph, with all the honors due to a king upon his return from a victorious campaign."

Ala remained silent. As usual, he had gotten dressed in haste, away from sight of the others, for he was ashamed of his body. He felt that his accomplices were now ripe. That the time for murder had arrived. For him, the solution was obvious. He spoke, but his voice was so low that the others had to lean forward to hear him.

"We will make use of an intermediary. This man will hire a band of criminals known for their discretion. He will pay them well and will ask them to kill this pain in the ass, Shams. When, where, and how is their business, not ours. We will play no role in this. None of us will know the day, the place, or the manner in which they eliminate him. None of us will be able to stop the wheel of death. Once the work has been completed, the intermediary will disappear. Then, we will piously grieve for Shams, cry for him, mourn him at his burial. None of us will be suspected." And he concluded, in a way typical of him, "From now on I ask that you stop braying like asses and destroying our projects."

Murder! That is what the unloved son was proposing. They all wanted to see Shams dead, but to put those words into practice . . . Objections were raised. How could they place their confidence in an intermediary? And what if he decided to blackmail them for his silence? With a gesture of his hand, the way one would shoo away a fly, Ala swept aside their doubts.

"I have chosen the man in question and he does not know any of you. He is a professional murderer. This is not his first time. And it won't be his last, either. If he talks, if he blackmails us—a hundred pricks up his ass!—it will be the end of his career. And then, he will be the only one to be judged and punished. As for us, for lack of proof, we will be spared. Suspected, possibly. But suspicion is like steam in the hamam, it dissipates whenever the water is changed. That son of a whore, that donkey's ass, knows this. It's his job. He will not expose himself to any risks."

They all nodded. After all, who would accuse those honorable men, a bookseller, a theologian, a diligent student with a shaved head, an obese magistrate, or even an employee of the hamam, of having plotted the assassination of Shams of Tabriz? So like the water in the pool, their words vanished from their memory.

Before leaving, Ala insisted. He asked them one last question. Did they agree to his plan? Their silence and the severity of their expressions answered for them. Yes, they agreed.

The bookseller was the last to leave. He threw a bag filled with leather for his bindings across his back. Behind him, drops of blood, which dripped from his incision—in spite of the surgeon's care—left on the white marble a thin garland of purple spots.

The day after the conspirators' meeting in the hamam, early in the morning, my servant handed me a letter that bore Shams's seal. I opened it at once and read: "Meet me this afternoon at the entrance to the bazaar of the bird catchers. Bring something to write on, for I'm not in the habit of writing. Ever. Since I never write, it stays with me."

I caught sight of him in the midst of the usual crowd of passersby and amateurs. I called to him from a distance, but he couldn't hear me over the sound of the thousands of birds. I walked toward him, bowed, and kissed his rough hands, his nails stained with ink and spices. He appeared to be amazed and observed the cages more than the birds. For my part, I admired the iridescent plumage of the miniscule finches, the gold of the parakeets, the green, yellow, and red of the parrots. I held my nose because of the strong smell of their excrement. The noise they made was deafening and further heightened by the cries of the porters, as they pushed their carts, warning the crowd to step aside and allow them to pass. My attention wavered between a swan and a peacock, and my thought took flight toward the first parliament of birds, described in Attar's poem, when they decide to leave in search of their true king. I thought also of Shams's name, the Bird. Did he identify with one of these birds? No one knew, except perhaps for Rumi, who was his sky.

He stopped suddenly before a stall, greeted the old bird catcher with the white beard as if he were an old friend, and asked me to follow him into the back room. We passed a number of cages made of iron, bamboo, glass, and even one of gold, ordered by the caliph of Baghdad. The cages held rare birds whose song was delicate and whose coloring highly unusual.

As evening approached, the noise from the bazaar gradually gave way to an unexpected quiet. The thousands of birds, a cloth thrown over their cages to encourage them to sleep, slowly grew silent, one by one. That same silence was also felt in the stall where we were gathered. The birds were flying to the kingdom of dreams.

Once his work was over, our elderly host joined us with a bottle of Okbarra wine, one of the famous grapes from our neighbors to the south, and three small pitchers. The wine was said to be the finest in the entire Orient and we began to drink, without remorse. The religious prohibitions against the consumption of alcohol didn't matter to us at all. Besides, it was widely known that the caliph of Baghdad, his cadis, and viziers also gave in to the temptation. I, Hesam, even knew that certain ulemas, having ruled on the fate of a despoiled wife, a soldier who had been raped, or a plagiarized writer, organized weekly drinking parties, during which they exchanged their austere clothing for multicolor robes and strolled the vast corridors of the palace of justice singing, disguised and crowned with flowers.

Drinking without restraint, Shams said to me, "I feel something circling me like an animal that is approaching. I feel I'm being threatened, hunted. I feel heavy and very distant from what defined me, my joyfulness. I feel that M is tired of being forced to stay indoors, for he rarely goes out any longer, at least not in my company. He must be tired of having to constantly justify himself to his family, to frequent only the small circle of devoted disciples, to dance only to muffled music in abandoned caves. I know that if he does all this, it is only to save me, me. But he can't continue like this, I can feel it. One day or another he will want to appear in public with the one he loves, and do so openly, share with him the experience of ecstasy in the sama, and take his breath away, when, far from all fear, he lovingly embraces him. Yes, he will want to close his eyes at night and hear only the breathing of his lover without worrying about the constant threat of footsteps around him, footsteps that spy, that wander. Hesam, he can do none of this with me. I am the only companion marked by the seal of shame, of baseness, and imposture. One day, when he begins to dance for someone else, openly, remember my prediction. Hesam, I have made up my mind, but I will never reveal it to you. Today, I have asked you to meet me so that you would write down some of the things I feel about M."

I wanted to protest and convince him that my master was not tired of him, that no other attachment was as precious, but I dared not tell him. After all, who was I to console Shams of Tabriz?

He emptied his pitcher of wine and continued.

"Oh, Hesam, if I had known that events would take this turn, I would never have left Damascus. If I returned to Konya, I did so only for him. For at that time, my separation from Rumi caused me no suffering, nor did his union bring me any sense of well-being. I owe my well-being to my own nature, and my suffering as well. When they came to get me in Damascus, I was just as before. M has the authorization to sleep between Kimia and me, even if we are unclothed. Sultan Walad, his son, is not just some stranger, he is my own. But his brother must be told to behave with greater humility toward me and not to laugh or talk so much in my presence. M prostrates himself before me, makes me sit by his side, and constantly sings my praises, except when a vision surprises and agitates him. M is something different. Something different. That's what I wanted to say to you. Preserve it well."

As I often did, I wrote it all down, word for word, without trying to order his thoughts, without trying to understand what he was saying or to whom it was addressed. Clarification came later— when it did come—in light of new events, additional information.

Shams grabbed my inkwell, which he looked at as if it were a threatening object, for a single drop of ink, according to him, could stain his finger for a long time. He smelled it, then placed it carefully on the floor, straightened, and continued.

"Even today, if I ordered M to banish his children from Konya, he would do so."

I doubted this. Certainly, Sultan Walad was as attached to Shams as his father. For Shams, he might accept to go away, to wander from city to city. But for Ala, the malicious son, who swore only by the suppression of the "God of his father," this would certainly not be the case. As for my master's two other children, a boy and a girl given to him by Kera, they were too small and were not involved at all in this. I could not imagine that their father, now exhausted by his confinement, the subterfuges, the precautions and dissimulation required by Shams's presence, would have the audacity and the will to drive them from Konya. No doubt, the first few days after the unforgettable encounter—it's been two years already!—he would have been capable, if ordered by Shams, to banish all four of his children. This is what he would have done, offering his favorite son and his young wife to his "heart's thief," so that he might make use of them as he please.

Shams, meanwhile, continued to speak.

"M is the moonlight. The eye is unable to reach the sun of my being but it can reach the moon. The brilliance and luminance of the sun prevent the eye from seeing it. The moon cannot reach the sun but the sun can reach the moon."

I wrote down these words, even though I realized that he had just put himself above Rumi, like the sun above the moon. I also knew that, in their relationship, below and above did not exist. Sometimes one was God and sometimes the other, indefinable, unnamable.

The cooing of the birds grew softer. Only a pair of hoopoes, late-night lovers, continued to coo. While beating his right foot in time with their singing, Shams again changed the subject, at least superficially.

"Within myself I love many people. There is, inside me, great tenderness for them, but I hide it. Once or twice, I have revealed this to them in speech, but they did not appreciate its value. Since then, I make sure that the tenderness inside doesn't grow cold. I have revealed it to Our Master. It has continued to grow, without ever diminishing. Oh, Hesam, I can only silence truth."

As his foot continued to mark the beat, his torso and head began to vibrate to the rhythm of the romance of the hoopoes. The sudden intrusion of three beggars into the bird catcher's stall ended these movements. They had come to beg for food.

"Go find something for them," Shams ordered me. "If you bring them something, your recompense will be worth ten pilgrimages to Mecca."

I left. The bazaar almost seemed to be asleep. No hustle and bustle, no noise. The doors to all the stores had been locked, except those where I could see, through the half-drawn grate, a bird catcher who was counting his silver, lit by a hurricane lamp. I heard the barking of the dogs that accompanied the soldiers on watch, who walked up and down the alleys. The halo of their torches approached. I hurried my steps to avoid them, for I did not know the password, which was required of anyone who was in the bazaar at this late hour, and I wanted to avoid being questioned at all costs. I quickly crossed the bazaar of the soap makers and perfumers, from which, in spite of the lowered grates and locked doors, thousands of scents from other parts of the world filled the night air. In spite of my haste, I could not help seeing the bazaar as a box that held all the odors of the Earth, a map of many scents.

Once out of the maze, I had no trouble finding vendors who sold grilled meats, vegetable fritters, and candied fruit. These were distributed from large wicker baskets lit by lanterns and carried by a mule with a collar of pearls and tiny bells. I purchased chicken kebabs wrapped in pastry. Then I asked the password from the soldiers on watch, who barred access to the bazaar. That way I was able to return without difficulty to the bird catcher's stall.

Shams was dancing. He whirled around, following the beat of the insomniac hoopoes, before the astonished gaze of the beggars with their broken teeth, rheumy eyes, and misshapen bodies. As soon as they saw me, they grabbed my kebabs, muttering their confused thanks, and disappeared into the night out of fear that other beggars, attracted by the odor of the meat, would demand their share.

After they left, Shams interrupted his dancing. He grabbed me, placed his forehead against mine and whispered, "The separation ripens and grows complex. I'm going to ask M. If he says, 'Go,' I'll go."

His breath grazed my lips. He was panting a little. I breathed in those veiled words that foretold his departure. I didn't know what to say. Should I convince him to stay at the risk of his life or, worse, at the risk of tiring my master, who was—after so much dissimulation, so much precaution—forced to live constantly on edge. Should I, on the contrary, allow him to leave without warning my master, prepared to draw upon myself, no doubt forever, Rumi's hatred? No! I was only twenty years old and a simple disciple, and neither of those facts gave me the right to meddle in such a relationship. Aside from the two of them, only God could intervene.

Shams backed away a little. "I entrust Our Master to you," he said. "Don't let him swallow just anything. Do not act sharply or authoritatively toward him. Lower your head and, to deflect any danger from him, beg him to act differently."

What was he talking about? I was unable to understand. Was he afraid that Rumi would commit suicide if he were to leave or abandon him?

That night, in the obscurity of the bird catcher's back room, I was merely Shams's scribe, scrupulously writing down, by the light of a candle, what I would call his predictions. He seemed to me very tired, very anxious as well; his eyes had lost their ordinary brilliance. I closed my notebook and suggested he return to Salah the goldsmith's to sleep. He agreed. But before leaving, he called the bird catcher, who was measuring seed, and kissed him on the forehead.

Outside, in the dark alleys of the bazaar, I questioned Shams about the identity of the bird catcher. Who was he? Had Shams known him for a long time? Was he a sage whose secrets remained unexplored?

Upon hearing these questions, he resumed his customary vivacity and his eyes, once again, began to shine in the dark. He then told me the following story, whose words I engraved in my memory.

One evening, when Shams was returning from the market, he met an old bird catcher who was returning home. He was carrying two cages attached to his shoulders by a stick. With each step, they swung up and down. The man, who was tired, proceeded slowly, his head bent. That day he had sold only two birds. He was bringing back three or four others, who already seemed to be sleeping in the sunset shadows.

Shams decided to walk alongside the man, at least for a while. He had heard the other man say in a low voice, as if he were speaking to his birds, "No, no, you have nothing to complain about . . . No, no. I took you out and I'll take you back . . . I take care of everything. In the morning I feed you sugar and I make sure the water you drink is always fresh. I polish your beak, I smooth your feathers, I clean your cage, I perfume it, I repaint it once a year. Oh, if someone could carry me on their shoulders in a cage like yours! If only someone could give me something to eat and drink every day!"

Then, Shams thought he heard a very weak voice respond to the bird catcher. He came closer, listened closely, and heard one of the birds speaking to the old man in a language that the two men could understand. And the bird said:

"You think we are in a cage, but you are mistaken. Listen: tiny insects are the prisoners of my feathers, of which they are unaware. You yourself live in a cage, your house is a cage, your street, this entire city is a cage . . . Where do you think the bars of your cage end? The entire Earth, our planet, is a cage. The Moon is a cage. The Sun is a cage. The universe itself is a cage, swinging on the shoulders of the infinite."

The old bird catcher answered only with a sigh of lassitude. Shams was not even sure that he had heard anything. A little later, as the shadows began to fill the streets, the merchant began to complain again and wanted to know the fate of the bird. Then, an even weaker voice, that of a bird that was almost asleep, could be heard, although with difficulty. Shams had to move closer to the bird catcher, who could not see him in the darkness, and he heard the voice of the second bird, who said, in a language different from that of the first, but which he could also understand:

"Forget all that, close your mind, for night is here. The bird that spoke to you is you, it is your thought. And you are its cage. You think that this cage exists, but you are wrong. Your thought has very solidly secured its own bars, which you have so much trouble undoing and which you cannot even see. Return home, place what you think are your cages on the ground, stop thinking, eat and sleep. When you are asleep, then all the cages of the world will open and we can resume our conversation. Good night."

"Good night," Shams said to me as he crossed through the doorway of the goldsmith's house.

A short time later, at Rumi's request, a few of us were privileged to be asked to the Djame mosque, which was famous for the way the architect had managed to conceal the weight of the materials with which it had been constructed. The group included Shams, Sultan Walad, Salah the goldsmith, Rumi's confidant, and myself. Rumi insisted we celebrate the dawn prayer there. Shams's presence at his side, in a place frequented by believers from all over, soldiers, artisans, beggars, aristocrats, and clerics, was not without risk. Were someone to denounce him, Shams was likely to be stoned, or stabbed, or have his throat cut. I was afraid that our morning walk in the open air would come to a bad end. It was not unlike the celebration given after the release of a prisoner, or the feast that sometimes precedes an isolation, or separation.

Perhaps this would be the last time they appeared together. I didn't dare consider that possibility. What would Rumi be without Shams? After Shams he would not resume his classes, would no longer be surrounded by a swarm of disciples, would not continue the exegesis of his Koranic books. Without Shams, would he dance alone? Without Shams, would he throw himself, overcome with wild laughter, into the school fountain? Without Shams, would he, in the throes of ecstasy, remove his clothing? Without Shams, would he still love God?

In spite of the early hour, the square before the mosque was already thronged with public writers who had set up their kiosk, sword swallowers with blue eyes and drooping mustaches, story-tellers, jugglers, and street singers. Some, at the approach of my master, prostrated themselves. Others, who did not know him, wondered about the reason for such respect. After all, we did not appear to be men of the court or the army or the clergy.

Before entering the grounds of the mosque, we removed our shoes, sandals, and boots and put them in the numbered receptacles. Along the side a hundred ewers, aligned near the door to the bathroom, invited the faithful to purify themselves.

As we crossed the large portal, whose archway was entirely decorated with stalactites, I heard a voice directed at Shams, "Dogs aren't allowed inside the mosque!"

Furious, I turned around to strike the man who had dared insult Shams. Behind me, a crowd of individuals advanced slowly toward the *sahn*, the interior courtyard. I stopped and watched them one by one to try to identify the profaner. Unsuccessfully. I tried to reassure myself, saying that, aside from me, no one had heard the insult.

From the top of the needle-like minaret, the blind muezzin—because he was blind he could not look down upon the unveiled women in the gardens of the harems—sung the call to the morning prayer. The sun rose shortly after. The time of the service was determined either by an astrolabe or by a hydraulic clock that indicated the hour, the half-hour, and the quarter hour musically during the day and with light at night.

After the ablutions, we said our prayer in the *shabestan*, guided by the imam, who stood before the *mihrab*, the ogival alcove decorated with mosaics and precious woods, the mystical doorway indicating the direction of Mecca. One day a Chinaman, speaking of our religion, told me that the Buddhist temples also had this kind of alcove. A Persian Zoroastrian also claimed that their fire temples, the *atash kadeh*, also had a similar structure. Entering from all sides at once, a uniform light accentuated the serenity of the *shabestan*. The ground, which our foreheads grazed at the moment our prayer became most fervent, seemed like a surface floating in space, a mirror.

The prayer over, the imam returned and saw Rumi among the congregation. He had come to beseech his God in complete anonymity. The imam walked over to him and kissed his hand, without showing the least sign of gratitude toward Shams. The lack of reverence was noticed by everyone present. Rumi's sallow complexion turned even paler at the slight. He quickly moved away from the imam and motioned to us to follow him into a room that led to one of the covered galleries, a room set aside for the preachers to nap in. We moved away from the *shabestan*, but could hear the imam as he climbed the seven steps to the *manbar*— marking each degree of his ascension with the sharp sound of his sword.

When our group was isolated in the *esterahatgah*, a room whose walls were covered with faience, Rumi rested his head on Shams's shoulder and asked that he not let himself be affected by such insults. Shams buried his hand in Rumi's turban and grabbed a few strands of his curly hair, drew them out, stroked them, and said, "In this world, I have nothing to do with people. I have not come for them. The ones who truly show us the path in this world, I point them out, I place my finger on their vein."

He let go of Rumi's head, leaned against the cushions placed on the ground, and told the following story:

"Someone made a vow to travel to Mecca. In the desert, his foot caught in some thorns and was broken. He was unable to follow the caravan. After many hours of solitude and despair, he saw a man approach him, to whom he cried out, 'Save me!' Instantaneously, the man brought him back to the caravan. The pilgrim demanded, 'I beg you in the name of the one God, tell me who you are that you have such power.' The passerby stepped aside, blushed, and said 'Forget your curiosity. You have been saved from danger and are near your goal.' The penitent responded, 'I swear to God that I will not leave you until you give me some explanation.' The man answered, 'I am the one about whom the children read in their books that he shall bear God's curse upon him until the day of allegiance. I am the devil.'"

Shams concluded his story with these words: "I wanted you to know that the man who believes in the devil, and considers him from within his faith, achieves his goal. But the man who observes the Prophet without faith is lost in disdain, just as the imam and the individual at the portal whose words are indecent will be lost."

Salah the goldsmith, who my master began to call "the soul of the mystics," although he was no more than a humble artisan who spoke badly, grabbed the collar of his coat between his thumb and index finger, removed it, folded it in three, and placed it on the ground before Shams. Already, our confraternity had begun to develop a ritual. Salah's gesture was based on the sessions of the sama, during which, overcome by ecstasy, the dancers, Rumi and Shams at the time, removed their clothing and threw it on the ground, a sign of detachment and spiritual liberation. That is why Salah, although there was no music or singing, had "removed his coat." With that gesture he indicated that he was revealing himself, that he was "naked," that he allowed his vices to be seen.

He then kissed the ground that had been touched by Shams's feet, and asked for his protection. Shams, still seated, said to him:

"One day, a child heard me speak. Although he was young, he stepped away from his parents and became increasingly intrigued with me. All day long he rested his head on my knees and his parents were unable to criticize him. From time to time I could hear him say:

> In your street lovers come and go.
> From their eyes blood will flow, and they will go.
> Others still, like wind, will come and go.

I said to him, 'Repeat it! What did you just say?' He answered, 'Nothing.'"

Shams remained silent. He seemed absorbed by the memory of that child who, perhaps, was one of the few, before Rumi, to have understood him. Salah asked, "What became of him?"

Shams answered, "At eighteen, he died. That is why I can only speak to myself or to one in whom I see myself. There are things I could never say. Only a third has been said."

He said this last sentence while staring at Our Master with his clear eyes. For us, it was becoming obvious that this third had only been expressed to Rumi, the man he called the "diver." He referred to himself as a "merchant" and said that he placed a "pearl" between them.

He went on:

"We, we still don't have the ability to speak. There is a seal on our heart. There is a seal on our tongue. There is a seal on our ears."

Because the room was unheated, Shams, who was always chilly, grabbed Salah's coat, unfolded it, and huddled inside it. Only his head emerged from this container of wool, felt, and cotton. From it his right hand emerged, blue with cold, and with his index finger he caressed Rumi's eyebrows. When Shams had first begun to do this, we were all surprised, my master most of all. And then, with time, we began to accustom ourselves to this strange mark of tenderness. But that tenderness could manifest itself in even stranger ways. Shams pressed his face to Rumi's and tickled the interior of his ear with each hair of Rumi's eyebrow. My master did not react. Several times I had heard that he didn't realize the pleasure this gesture gave to Shams.

The skinny index finger continued its caress. Then, Shams said to Rumi, "In your heart I don't see myself as I saw myself before. May God once more make me gentle to your heart. I pray for that and advise my friends to pray for that. I pray because I am unable to give you advice."

It was the first time we saw in Shams, this incandescent Sun, a flame about to go out. He had accustomed us to his imperious domination over Rumi. Now he displayed his vulnerability, his fault. So even Shams of Tabriz could be sensitive to the disaffection of his lover.

And for some time now, according to Shams, Rumi seemed to be searching for some ecstasy other than dancing, other than the metamorphosis that took place when they first met.

Some twenty years later, when I in turn became dear to my master's heart, he mentioned, always in veiled terms, the period before the departure of Shams. He would say to me that his transformation was incomplete, that he required something as important as the arrival of Shams to set free in him something he was still unaware of. Some twenty years later, when, under his dictation, I wrote down the mystical poems that would become the *Masnavi*, he and I, and all the wanderers on the path of love realized what was then missing in him: the poet. He became a poet through a unique and unsettling event—the disappearance of Shams.

I always wanted to believe that my master's disaffection toward Shams, his weariness at having to hide their relationship, his detachment in the face of his demands, for Shams wanted only one thing, which was that Rumi become the lover he had been at the outset, arose from an even greater need. Rumi pushed their relationship to the point of irreversible indifference. And yet, he loved Shams.

During this morning of prayer, Shams demanded a different kind of behavior from Our Master. Perhaps he wanted Rumi to insult the vulgar imam, or kill the man who had called him a dog. Perhaps he hoped that Rumi would set aside his prudence and, risking dishonor, embrace him publicly.

Nothing happened. Our Master remained impassive. He acted as if he hadn't heard the insult by the stranger, or witnessed the imam's contempt. I was unable to explain the reason for his insensitivity. The same question must have certainly preoccupied Shams.

He stopped caressing Rumi's brows and said to him, in his customary style, filled with unusual expressions, forcing us to be extremely attentive:

"I cannot tell you to leave. However, it is my duty, for your own interest, to leave. Separation is a cook. During separation, we ask ourselves: why didn't I do the little the lover asked of me? So little considering the sorrow of separation. Sometimes, I caused discord by not speaking. At other times, I spoke enigmatically and maintained the two sides of my thought, although clarity was needed. What would it have cost me? For you I would make fifty voyages. My voyage is there only to resolve your situation. Otherwise, what difference would it make to me, between Rome and Syria, between Mecca and Istanbul? The difference arises from separation, the separation that cooks, the separation that accomplishes. Now, is it better to be cooked and accomplished in union or in separation? Where is the one who cooks in union and opens his eyes in union? Where is the one who stands outside and wonders when he will finally be able to go inside?"

At the idea of a new separation between his father and Shams, Sultan Walad noted that no one among us would have agreed to it. If Shams had really decided to break with Rumi, we would all interpret the act as his secret, but quite real, desire to harm Rumi.

Smothered in Salah's coat, Shams bent before Our Master, drew his hands from the ocean of fabric that covered them, grabbed his feet, and said, "How could I go against your wishes? I, who fear that in kissing your feet my eyelids will rub against and irritate them."

His voice became a whisper, barely audible. "I found you, alone. I am the friend of the friendless." With a gesture from Our Master, we left the room. What I last saw upon leaving was the image of those two solitudes embracing one another, becoming one.

The autumn of separation moved forward toward the cold. One day, Thiryanos invited me to join him in a competition. Like him, I enjoyed these contests. My devotion for Rumi and Shams had in no way reduced the hours I spent fencing, doing gymnastics, swimming, running. Often, even within the school, I would practice, with empty hands, manipulating imaginary bars and clubs. The spectacle may have seemed ridiculous, but it followed a particular tempo, the one used when athletes performed a series of rhythmic movements. On several occasions Rumi stopped to admire the way my muscles flexed, bent under the imaginary weight. For his part, Shams also acknowledged the value of the human body, which, during the whirling dance, was intended to connect heaven and earth, without ever weakening.

Dressed in short pants, their bodies naked and tattooed, two young fighters struggled in a covered arena before a pubic of undisciplined and noisy admirers. The jury consisted of former champions. As bare as the competitors, their soft, worn torsos still showed signs of old tattoos that were supposed to represent the face of Rostam, the mythical hero of Iran. His thick mustache disappeared in the folds of their stomach.

The fighters came from all the countries of the world. Among them were Mongols, Uyghurs, Tibetans, Iranians, Turks, and Greeks. They all made a good living. According to the rules, they were bound to chastity in order to preserve their strength, but only a small minority seemed to obey the requirement. The majority preferred other forms of physical interaction, preferably with members of their own sex, an interaction during which their hardened muscles flowed into one another, knotted up like stony tendons on a rocky outcrop.

During the fight, as each of the wrestlers tried to pin the

other's shoulders to the ground in victory, Thiryanos and I spoke about our principal concern: the threat to Shams. We watched distractedly a match between a Tibetan and an Uyghur. However, my friend had bet a small sum on the success of one of the wrestlers. I was hardly paying attention to the fight when the Greek told me something that we had suspected for quite some time: Shams's firm and irrevocable intention to leave. Thiryanos repeated to me the exact words that the Bird had said to him: "They are doing all they can to drive me away from him. They will be happy once I'm gone. But this time, I will leave so that no one will find me again, so that no one will be able to provide the slightest information about me. The years will pass by, every trace of me will be lost. They will end up saying I was killed by an enemy."

I nodded, overcome with immense sadness. For me, the wrestling match no longer existed. I was trying to give Thiryanos my analysis of the painful event that was about to take place. Shams's desire for departure hid some dissatisfaction. He felt that Rumi's criticism demanded something more than a relationship that grew increasingly entangled, day by day, in trickery, dissimulation, and camouflage. Hoping for an excess of love that never arrived, Shams, who also had to confront the threat of a plot, quite clearly foresaw a definitive break. I knew him well enough to confirm that the reason he postponed his departure was simply to prevent his lover from experiencing, at least for a little while, the one, true form of suffering, which consists in being cut off from the one you love for all time.

My Greek friend gave a shout of encouragement: the oiled shoulders of his champion grazed the ground. The Uyghur arched his back and managed to resist the Tibetan's assault. Groaning with effort, he raised his back.

Thiryanos sighed with relief. He told me he found my comments quite appropriate. According to him, Shams was no longer the man he had been, the man who boasted of having destroyed Rumi, for, as he used to say in his own way, construction is in destruction. After their encounter, we had all noted the transformation of Our Master, but no one spoke any longer of the love that flowed in Shams's veins. And Shams was the one who insisted that Rumi call him "the lover without guarantee," "the torch for the smuggler," "the inflamer of sleep," "the inundation of the dervish's harvest," "the king at the potters' gate," "the key ring." While Shams continued to demand the openness of their first days, Rumi became increasingly reserved. The instability, as Shams knew, as well as Rumi, arose from a new state, the state of loss, of privation, of eyes that could no longer see the lover and closed to recall his memory.

This time the Uyghur slowly got on top. I don't know why, but at that very instant, I remembered an anecdote that Shams had told me. I wanted to tell it to Thiryanos but I wasn't sure he would pay attention. Besides, could he even hear me in the midst of the crowd's roar?

"One day, Sultan Mahmoud caught sight of the mythical bird, the *homa*, whose shadow brings happiness. He at once ordered his army to arrange themselves beneath the bird. All of them did this, with the exception of his favorite slave Ayaz. Seeing that he was not beneath the bird's shadow, the sultan himself went to find him. He eventually found him curled up beneath his horse. 'Why aren't you under the *homa*'s shadow?' asked the sultan. The slave answered, 'You are my mythical bird! The shadow I seek is your own. Why do you insist that I leave you to seek something else?'"

Of course, I indicated, turning to Thiryanos who was now very excited by the way the match was going, in telling me this fable, Shams was not only speaking to me, but to Rumi. The shadow he sought, and which he had found, was that of Our Master. His bird of happiness could be none other than the one he simply referred to as M.

Contrary to appearances, Thiryanos had paid attention to my story and my commentary. Still focused on the ring where the fight was taking place, he said to me: "The difference between the two lovers derives from the fact that Shams's fulfillment has already occurred but Our Master remains unfulfilled. To complete this love, their separation is needed. They know this and some of us know it as well. You too, Hesam—don't try to hide it—you know it. But can they, inhabited by their mutual attraction, carry out this separation? Who is going to break the bond, draw the border, erect the wall? Which one? Who?"

My friend then began jumping up and down in his seat, his arms raised, adding his own voice to that of the Uyghur's fans. His favorite succeeded in pressing the Tibetan's shoulder to the ground. My friend would collect a small amount from his bet. The Tibetan was on the ground. Winner and loser kissed one another on the forehead and left the ring. The referee rose. His stomach unfolded to reveal a tattoo of a sightless Rostam, whose pupils had been erased with time. To collect his winnings, Thiryanos made his way through the crowd, which began to disperse. I thought of Shams and my master. Which of them would press the other's shoulder to the ground? Did there have to be a winner and a loser?

The following day the noonday sun warmed the autumn air, the autumn of separation. Shams and I went to a public garden, cooled by fountains and artificial springs. After removing our boots, we entered a pavilion shaded by poplars, where food was being served. Several customers were already there. Shams sat down on a bench covered with mats. We ordered roast kid and wine. Shams took a few sips and judged it mediocre, and ate, as always, without enthusiasm. I liked it but as soon as he had given his unflattering assessment, I said to myself that the wine wasn't that good after all. Shams only had to give an opinion on a dish, a drink, a poem, or a book for me to immediately adopt the same point of view, in spite of my internal resistance. If I happened to disagree, I remained persuaded that he was always right and that, in the end, I would end up agreeing with him. I was beaten before I had even started.

"Seeing me," Shams said, "a sheik grows surprised. Another lowers his head. Another prostrates himself without ever rising. Another rolls around on the ground. Another strikes his head with his shoes until his forehead bleeds."

A group of gypsy dancers, or Kolis, came in. These people, with their dark, shiny eyes, had arrived in our land centuries ago from India—from Lahore it was said. They were still treated as strangers here, a bit like Shams in fact, and spoke an unknown language. Yet the horses obeyed them.

They had barely entered when the girls began dancing to some popular tune. To my astonishment I heard Shams hum the well-known words of the song. How was it that Shams, who sometimes grew bored with the Koran, knew such lyrics? I asked myself the question, as well as many others, without ever finding a satisfactory response, although I understood that my fascination fed precisely on such uncertainty. I liked the surprise, the lack of assurance. During my walks with Shams, in the caravansaries, the cabarets, or other public places, on several occasions I was required to distribute money to the itinerant musicians, not to reward them but to get them to stop playing. I saw him, when he couldn't manage to get them to keep quiet, plug his ears before the distraught performers. At such moments, deeply embarrassed, I would try to meet the astonished gazes around me and appease them with a forced smile.

That day, on the contrary, he liked the Kolis. He hummed along with their songs. Since he could not tolerate the slightest breeze, he asked for a blanket, in which he wrapped himself at once and continued, muffled as he was, to follow the dance.

The Kolis were replaced by a singer who could alter his voice and was able to mimic different characters. His story involved a princess who made love to a slave, previously chosen from some disreputable corner of the city, then washed, perfumed, drugged, and led to the royal couch by a horde of female servants. He mimicked the freshness and distinction of the princess as well as the vulgarity and astonishment of a peasant who thought he was living a dream. The performer did not hesitate to use obscenities, which, I knew, greatly pleased Shams, a stubborn opponent of courtesy, convention, simple politeness, and the rigid precepts of ordinary morality.

Seduced by the details, which were really quite vulgar, of the lovemaking between the slave and the princess, Shams continued to drink eagerly. Had he forgotten the severity of his judgment concerning the mediocrity of the wine?

At the moment when the storyteller was miming the princess's penetration in various postures, with a multitude of details ranging from the dark brown color of the captive penis and the pink of the regal vulva, to the active role of the servants, the languorous music, the sighs and heavy breathing, two individuals appeared in the pavilion whom I suspected of belonging to Ala's band.

For a second my heart stopped. In a flash I saw Shams dead. In my mind I saw him, there, at that moment, pierced by enemy knives as his blood mingled with the stream that flowed at the foot of the trees. I saw myself laying out the blessed corpse of my master's lover, covered with deep wounds, and kissing his slender fingers, stained with ink or the green of a fresh nut. I heard the shouting of the crowd crying for help. I restrained the manager, who wanted to stop the bleeding by cauterizing the wounds with a red-hot metal rod, the same one that had been used to grill kabobs. I heard the rustle of the Kolis' skirts as they ran out, fearing someone would accuse them of the murder. In the eyes of the storyteller, I caught the tears of the princess and the confusion of the slave.

One of the supposed assassins approached Shams. I rose to intervene. But the other simply pointed at him with his finger and said to the other customers at the top of his lungs: "Oh, Muslims, a blasphemy is being committed under your very eyes and you do not even react! Look at this man, who bears the name of the divine inscribed in his hat, as he drinks the forbidden drink without remorse."

Shams, still rolled in his blanket, put the wine-filled crock on the ground and said, impassively, "Wine is allowed or forbidden depending on the person who consumes it. If we pour a goatskin of wine into the sea, the wine doesn't transform the sea, it does not disturb it. It is permitted to use that water for washing and for drinking. But a small pool is soiled by a single drop of wine. To be more precise: If I am the one drinking the wine, I am the sea, while if it is someone like yourself, brother of a whore, even barley bread will be forbidden."

The second man approached Shams to strike him. I stood up to my full height. Because of my build and my threatening stare, the man backed away. I followed him to the door as if I were chasing a harmful animal.

His companion, the noisemaker, appeared perplexed and somewhat frightened. He seemed much less dangerous than the other. I amused myself imagining this strict practitioner of the Koranic rules as he wondered whether, in his hands, barley bread really was forbidden. And then, after catching sight of the name of the Prophet and the name of God in Shams's turban, perhaps he saw him as a respectable believer, worthy of imitation? I wasn't far from the truth, for he finally asked Shams, timidly, "What must we do to remain within the law?" Increasingly concealed by his blanket—his inscribed turban and his bony face were barely visible through the wool—Shams answered, "If you have, until now, avoided what is forbidden, from now on you must avoid what is permitted. To each man his sin: for some sin is found in fornication and cunning, for others it is in the absence of the divine presence. For some, the garment of fornication is a contrived garment, for others the contrived garment is that of convention."

Shams had managed to awaken a glimmer in the man who had insulted him. The offender, looking pensive, walked away and disappeared with his companion, who prudently remained behind the door. I settled with the manager, leaving a large tip for the dancers and the storyteller. We had barely escaped the danger. I

motioned to Shams that it was time to leave. The hour had come
to return to his hiding place, to conceal himself from curious eyes,
even in solitude, even without Rumi.

Reluctantly, he removed his blanket, stood, followed me to
the exit and, inadvertently, put on the shoes of another customer.
He often confused his belongings with someone else's. When he
noticed that his feet were not comfortable, he removed them,
searched among the shoes, and finally located his fur-lined boots
and put them on. We were now able to leave the pavilion. I was in
a hurry to return; we had just taken a considerable risk and it was
pointless to take another. But a customer, who had seen Shams try
on his own shoes, made an insulting remark. Shams remained
motionless but sighed, in a nearly inaudible voice, "Let someone
remove this vestment even if it is mine."

To avoid other unexpected encounters, I encouraged him to
walk quickly. But he resisted, dragged his feet. Finally, he said to
me, "My hand can do nothing. My poor heart cannot land just
anywhere. This bird cannot feed on just any seed."

We found ourselves on the shore of a lake across which boats
filled with sightseers were gliding. I had a vision: one of the boats
had just capsized. On board were the storyteller and all his characters, the princess and the slave, joined together even as they
drowned.

I was raw, I was cooked, I was charred

ENTERED MY MASTER'S HOME, WHERE IT WAS NOISIER THAN customary. The servants, in a state of total confusion, were preparing to accompany the women from the women's quarters to the Meram garden. Others were prodding the mules, which the women would be riding, toward the main gate. The women, still in their apartments, were whispering and complaining about the hasty departure. None of them were ready. None of them were prepared to show themselves looking so unkempt before all of Konya, in the magnificent Meram garden, where the city's most eligible bachelors met.

Standing in his apartment, Our Master appeared uncomfortable. I advanced cautiously, removed my shoes before entering the room, and greeted Rumi with the "reverence of the seal," my two arms crossed on my chest, the fingers of my right hand touching the left shoulder, the fingers of my left hand touching my right shoulder, the big toe on my right foot placed on the big toe of the left, and bent forward in a sign of respect. The position of the feet reflects the extreme devotion a cook once had for Rumi. One day, when he went to the outskirts of Konya, it was reported that the cook, seeing his fire go out, let his own foot burn so that the dish intended for Rumi's guests would be ready in time. Noticing that only his left toe was charred, the cook interpreted this as a failure of devotion. He felt he should have let his entire foot burn, in spite of the pain. When Rumi appeared before him, the unfortunate cook hid "the shameful toe" beneath his right foot. Our Master, who noticed everything, pointed to the cook as one of the few true believers on Earth and said that, from then on, the gesture of placing one toe over the other would forever evoke, among his followers, deference, faith, and purity of dedication.

My Master answered my greeting by slipping his left hand over his chest, inside his coat, and placing his right hand on top of it, on the outside. I approached and kissed the hand outside the coat. In return, he placed his lips on my turban. These new rituals, within our small circle, symbolized the escape from this world and the entrance into the other, through the celebration of the sama. The turban, for example, embodied the tombstone, the white garment of the whirling dancers, the Muslim winding sheet. The abandonment of the coat signified the renunciation of material bonds. Turning around and around represented the flight to truth. The palm of the right hand, open toward the sky, revealed the readiness to enter heaven, and that of the left hand, turned toward the ground, the transmission of those benefits to our nurturing mother.

Once the greetings were concluded, Rumi told me that Shams appeared to be furious, for they had argued and Kimia had left the house in the direction of the Meram garden. "That's why I've ordered the women to bring Kimia back as soon as possible. But they're dawdling; they haven't even left yet! Go see how Shams, the Sun, is doing. I'm afraid his anger is bad for his health."

I left. When I reached Shams's apartment, I heard Kimia laughing, and then her husband. Cautiously, out of fear he might surprise me, I looked inside, through the keyhole. They were wrapped in one another's arms and teasing one another. I ran to reassure my master. "Kimia is back and Shams is certainly not angry. They're enjoying themselves, they're laughing."

Rumi didn't see how it was possible for Kimia to be back when the women hadn't even left yet. It couldn't have been her. He asked me to describe her clothing. From what little I had seen, she was wearing a blue skirt and green jacket with very long sleeves. Rumi admitted that was what Kimia was wearing when she put on her veil before running out. Intrigued, he rose. We headed for Shams's apartment, where my master saw, again through the keyhole, the couple making love. He jumped back, but heard Shams's voice encouraging him to enter the room. Which my master did.

What happened next he didn't tell me until years later, long after Shams's departure. Rumi was talking to other Sufis, who were questioning him about the various manifestations of the divine.

"That day, when I entered Shams's bedroom, I found him alone. I could not prevent myself from asking him about Kimia's mysterious appearance and disappearance. He said to me, 'All-powerful God loves me so much that he presents himself to me in the shape I most prefer. Just now, he revealed himself to me as Kimia.'"

Our master cited another example. This was the story of Bayazid, a man very much like Shams, who had seen God embodied as an effeminate man. Realizing that the Sufis, all of whom were accustomed to drink in his words, did not understand him, Rumi was forced to add a commentary.

"In the case of Bayazid, there were two possibilities. Either he saw God in the form of a homosexual or God presented himself to him according to his preference, that is, as a homosexual man."

This God, who sometimes appeared as a beautiful young woman to whom Shams made love and sometimes as a homosexual male trying to please Bayazid, was indeed the God of My Master. It was this God he spoke of.

Nonetheless, during that autumn of separation, the beautiful Kimia continued to disturb Shams's daily life. Neither myself, Thiryanos, or even Sultan Walad ever learned the nature of

Shams's relationship with his wife. He claimed he did not love her, but seemed to enjoy her presence. If, by some misfortune, she happened to leave him, no matter for how long, Shams's cries could be heard throughout the house. I knew from Sultan Walad, who got his information from his stepmother, Kera, who was Kimia's confidante, that Kimia was very much in love with her husband. For his part, Shams claimed, loud and clear, that he had no interest in sentimental attachments. Were we to believe that his outbursts of anger had no other objective? He confirmed this for me, asking that I write down the following: "Write that I, Shams of Tabriz, cause those I love to suffer."

He said this to me a few days after the drama, which some attributed to Kimia's flight to the Meram garden and Shams's unreasonable anger. For she made the trip without his authorization.

It was especially cold that day. And it kept getting colder. Shams was huddled near the brazier, when Kimia entered their apartment, allowing a gust of cold air to enter. She greeted her husband without realizing this irritated him. She removed her boots, shaking the mud off against the bottom of the door, and put on two pairs of socks, one over the other, for she was deathly afraid of catching cold, and went to sit next to Shams.

Shams had been staring at her since she came in. Suddenly, beside himself, he began to yell and swear. She made a sudden movement and turned her head toward him, as surprised as she was terrified. A sharp pain pierced her neck and made her freeze. She was unable to move her head or arms. At once she went over to the korsi to lie down, and waited for Shams to finish his swearing so she could reassure him and explain to him the reason for her absence.

Shams, who was already beginning to regret his behavior, left their bedroom for the cell where he often went to meditate with Rumi. The following day, at dawn, he found Kimia lying on the floor. Exhausted by the pain, paralyzed, she had been unable even to satisfy her thirst. Her mouth open, her eyes closed, her face disfigured, she already resembled a corpse. Shams called to her several times, but in vain. He went over to her, took her pulse, watched her breathing. With difficulty she opened her eyes but was unable to speak. Shams tried to comfort her. She must have been the first to know that the more he loved someone, the more he mistreated them, that his anger was temporary, that he was no longer angry with her and was very attached to her, if only to improve his chess playing. Without her lessons, even the most novice player would have beaten him, he knew this. Kimia gathered all her strength to offer him a last smile, and lost consciousness.

The greatest physicians in Konya succeeded one another at her bedside without being able to revive her. Indian and Chinese decoctions were equally ineffective, as were the amulets and magical prayers. Even the long and silent presence of my master, leaning against the bedroom wall, hand in hand with Shams, could not save her. She died on the third day.

As was customary, her body was taken to the bath of the dead to be washed with water and dried jujube leaves. After three immersions, the women covered the corpse with camphor. At Kera's request, they added some sandalwood oil, amber, and rosewater. Finally, they wrapped the body with a cloth of ecru colored cotton.

The funeral procession was waiting. Once the corpse was purified and placed on the litter, we headed for the cemetery. Rumi and Shams, somewhat apart from the others, walked side by side. I approached to offer Shams, who was always cold, a woolen shawl. He held out his hand, took the wrap and continued speaking. Without paying attention to me, he said, "I have nothing to do with suffering. Suffering comes from existence. My being overflows with joy. Why allow external suffering to penetrate my being? With a response, an insult, I reject it, throw it out of the house."

He covered his shoulders and remained silent. I moved away to join the others and sing with them verses from the Koran. At the moment when the corpse was consigned to the earth, I glanced over at the two men. Their eyes closed, they shook their heads to the same rhythm, as if some inaudible music was guiding their movements and their interior dance.

After Kimia's sudden death, the external threat became even more evident. We had posted a guard at the entrance to the school, asking that he keep the door closed and not to open it until he was sure of the visitor's identity. I prepared a list of names of those he could let in without concern. Should I include the name of Ala, Rumi's own son, or refuse him access to the home of his father, where he lived? Should I allow him to come and go as he pleased, when all the rumors pointed to his treachery and criminal intent? I didn't dare question Sultan Walad about this. After much hesitation, I gave the guard a list on which Ala's name did not appear. By chasing him from his home, I felt I was acting prudently. Between the anger of the unfaithful son and the risk of Shams's assassination, my choice seemed clear, obvious.

On 5 *Shaval* 645 of the Hegira (December 5, 1247), two weeks after Kimia's funeral, Rumi was awaiting the arrival of Shams and some musicians to begin the sama, under his own roof. After seven months of hiding in Salah's house, Rumi had decided to return to his own home and confront the threat directly.

It was snowing outside. We waited for Shams in the very cell where, following their first encounter, Rumi had welcomed the old dervish. He finally arrived, quite amused by the interrogation he had just gone through.

"The guardian, who didn't know me, asked, 'Who are you?' I answered, 'It's difficult. I have to think about it.' Since he did not open the door, I knocked again and introduced myself as follows, 'Once there lived an important man called Adam. I am one of his sons.'"

Thiryanos, who was standing behind the gate, recognized Shams's voice and saw the guard consult his list, looking for the name "Adam." To save time, Thiryanos told the guard, with a nod of his head, to open the door to the "son of Adam," whose name did not appear on the authorized list.

Shams looked pleased, even rejuvenated. His features, ordinarily so tense and drawn, appeared softened. He did not remove his cloak and, as we all expected, commented on the cold. Rumi invited him to sit next to him, grabbing his hands and warming them with his breath. After which, taking up the guard's question, he asked him, "Who are you?"

Shams answered only with silence.

My master repeated the question. "Are you the light of the essence of God? Are you God?" This was followed by more silence. Rumi continued with the following verses:

> I was cautious, familiar
> With my one prayer mat.
> You made me a toy
> That children play with in the street.

More silence. As if the two men were getting ready for a game, Rumi asked, "Are you a magician?" Shams smiled. A smile that transformed itself into laughter. Finally, he said, "It is not a question of magic. This is about the evocation of God."

Things had changed, something new was born with his "Who are you?" It was the first time since the old dervish had appeared suddenly before my master's mule, before fainting, that Rumi had asked him, "Who are you?" The vielle player stopped tuning his instrument; Thiryanos stopped imitating the guard looking for the name of the son of Adam in his notebook. Sultan Walad, who, for some time, thought only of gold castings and the goldsmith's punch, staggered as he entered and nearly fell to the floor. I, Hesam, took out my pen and paper to write down the exact, and again enigmatic, words spoken by Shams of Tabriz. Who was he? Was he finally going to tell us?

In the most ordinary voice, the voice with which he rejected unripe melons, burnt kebabs, and glasses of syrup, he said, "A calligrapher used three styles of writing. The first, legible to him, was not legible to the others. The second was legible to him and to the others. The third was not legible to him or the others. That third form of writing is me."

Rumi asked another question. "How did this bond between us arise?"

So as not to lose a syllable of Shams's response, I pressed my shoulder to his.

"On that day, what was I? A stunted, fragile man. You were young and solid. There was nothing about me that would have caused you to take notice. But you looked at me with subtlety and were overcome with love for me."

Rumi continued. "What did you want of me?"

"I and three others, we are satisfied with what you give us."

"Who are those three other persons?" asked Thiryanos.

"Salah, Hesam, and Baha."

I had just heard my name, my miserable name, spoken from the mouth of Shams, chosen among the men he judged to be worthy! Of us three, Baha, another name for Sultan Walad, represented in my eyes the only being worthy of one day succeeding Our Master. But who could claim to succeed Shams? Rumi's increasingly obvious penchant for Salah, the choice of his residence, the recommendation that he be invited to all the receptions, the incessant exaggeration of his knowledge—which was quite questionable—in no way justified his glorious proposal. How could a goldsmith replace the Sun?

It was impossible and Shams knew it. But he also knew that, one day, sooner or later, Salah would take his place. And he spoke to him with the language of the men of his guild.

"My being is the philosopher's stone one does not allow to come into contact with copper. In my presence copper turns to gold. It is the same for the perfection of the philosopher's stone."

As for me, my position in the school was certainly enviable.

No one, among the first circle of disciples, could claim the same degree of intimacy with Shams. And through that familiarity I attracted Rumi's attention. By including me in a trio that included the Master's own son and the man who, as far as we could tell, attracted Rumi for reasons still unknown to us, Shams had, at least officially, rescued me from anonymity.

His comment, a bright lamp extended toward me in the darkness, suddenly exposed me to the admiring glances of the others. They saw me now through Shams's eyes. I was no longer the sturdy and useful young man, ready to assist whoever asked; the man who jumped up instinctively to retrieve a book mentioned by a disciple as he was talking and kept at the other end of the house; the one who went down to the kitchen to prepare meat and chicken kebabs so that his name would circulate, along with the grilled meats, in the mouth of visitors; the one who ran to the store to buy whole bags of rice, bottles of rosewater, and mint, and returned laden with his shopping so he could show everyone just how useful he could be; the one who hurried to the cemetery, his face covered with tears, to read the prayer of death over a freshly covered grave, before the mourners had even arrived; the one who displayed in his cell the portrait of the masters whose visit he knew to be imminent, who changed the shape of his beard so that it resembled that of this one or the other, who covered himself with a shawl, imported from the high plateaus of central Iran, to distinguish himself from the other young Sufis and who, still trying to please, massaged the flabby feet and arms of the elderly parents of his colleagues; the one who was called to his master's side only to protect him from his enemies by the strength of his two arms.

Before Shams's torch, I became a man to be praised, to be courted. Before Shams's torch, my hair, my beard, the knot in my turban, became objects of fetish. Before Shams's torch I came into the world.

I looked at the man who, without any hesitation, compared himself to the "perfection of the philosopher's stone" and I, who knew him well, detected on his face, in spite of his control of adversity, an immense suffering, one that foretold separation and bitter regret.

Shams was seated next to Rumi and yet everything about him indicated departure and disappearance. Years later, when I questioned my master about what, in the language of mysticism, was referred to as the "occultation of Shams," he insisted that it was necessary, essential. He did not go so far as to say that he wanted it to happen, but I can state that, for him, the true metamorphosis took place after Shams's "flight." Immediately after.

Years later, when I invited my master to comment on his interior transformations, he said "I was raw, I was cooked, I was charred."

Today, I can say that the "cooking" took place after the meeting with Shams and the "charring" after his departure. I also see how the parable of the "three butterflies" told by Attar can be embodied in one and the same man, how poetry can become the true human experience. The first of Rumi's three stations corresponds to the explorations of a butterfly who has left to flutter around a candle in a distant castle to understand the nature of fire. Its quest allows it to feel the heat of the flame, and only this. This is what my master meant when he spoke of being "raw." We know there is a flame, but we maintain a prudent distance. And we return home.

It was a second butterfly that was "cooked" after it approached the candle and allowed one of its wings to burn. About fire, it learned more than the first butterfly, but upon its return the real nature of the flame continued to elude it. In my opinion this was the state Rumi entered after he met Shams. He was no longer the man of the Koranic schools. One of his wings had caught fire and he began to dance.

The "charring" was the culmination of the one-way journey of a third butterfly that, drunk with the flame and overcome with love, cast itself into it, becoming one with it. Attar says that only this charred butterfly knew what fire is but was unable to tell anyone about it. Rumi too experienced the flame but, unlike the butterfly, burnt, ablaze, and consumed by fire, he left us more than fifty-thousand lines of unforgettable poetry.

As I listened to the words that were spoken in the cell where Rumi and Shams had once remained alone for forty days, I listened to the cold of night. Outside, steps could be heard soiling the snow, grimy hands rubbed against one another, toes bent, knives with chased blades hung down from bony hips. Outside, strangers continued to circle the Master's house.

This is what I can tell you about that last moment. From outside a sole, restrained voice interrupted the lengthy dialogue we had been having on Shams's nature. It invited him to come out. It said, "Shams of Tabriz, are you coming?"

He rose at once and, without leaving us the time to urge him to stay, to stop him from committing the irreparable, he said to Rumi, in a serene voice, "They want to kill me."

No one said a word. We were no longer part of the conversation, it was taking place in the prairie of the angels. We were merely the privileged witnesses of a voluntary conflagration. After a lengthy silence, Rumi recited a verse from the Koran, saying that "creation and the commandment belong to God," and added a few words that were the last Shams was to hear from the man whom the prophets themselves regretted was not their contemporary: "It's the best thing to do."

Those are Rumi's exact words.

"It's the best thing to do."

Without waiting, without a final glance at the man he had transformed, the fruit he had ripened, without so much as a gesture or a word of goodbye, Shams adjusted his cloak—Thiryanos would later say that, at that moment, he heard a fluttering of wings—put on his boots, his hat, which we called his crown, and left.

Outside, seven armed men were waiting to kill him. Inside, the echo of Shams's cry. Outside, a few drops of blood.

Inside, the charring began.

I will scatter you

OUTSIDE, THERE WAS NO TRACE OF SHAMS, NO TRACE OF his attackers. Thiryanos and I went out and looked through all of Konya, the taverns, the caravansaries, the hamams, the heated rooms of the bazaar, to see if he was still alive, the man who had suddenly walked out of our lives. "It's the best thing to do." Shams, who was always chilly, would only be found indoors, sheltered from the snow and cold. It was a fruitless search. Where had he gone? "The bird has flown," some said. Others claimed he was dead, that they had seen his attackers throw his body into a well outside the city. Others, but they only came forward later on, would point to Shams as the mythical father of a child conceived from his blood, taken by prowlers the night of his murder.

There was no news the following day or the days after that.

Our Master ordered that the square Arab vielle be modified into a six-corner instrument, explaining that the six angles of his rabab defined the secret of the six corners of the world, and that the *aleph* of the string represented the familiarity of the spirits with the *aleph* of the word *Allah*. However, although he changed his instruments, none were able to help him.

I visited all the cemeteries, even those where they buried fetuses, disfigured prisoners, and heretics, without finding any sign of Shams's body. Thiryanos had all the wells inspected. I even saw him squeeze his solid frame into a small basket and descend along a well shaft, then return holding the bones of crows and pieces of gold from another age.

Sultan Walad, who had not been sleeping, tirelessly looked for an answer to his question, "Why did he let him leave?" He alone was in a position to witness his father's suffering when, twenty-two months earlier, Shams had left for the first time. He alone, when Our Master and Shams were reunited, had seen the two lovers become one. He questioned his father once, twice, three times, a thousand times. He questioned him in silence, in dreams, in prayers, while fasting, during retreats.

One day he received the following explanation:

"At the start of our relationship, Shams constantly begged me to reveal to him a single one of the beings hidden by the veil of my passion. A revelation came: 'Since you insist, what do you offer by way of thanks?' Shams answered, 'My head.' When the union with this beauty was given to him, when he could finally benefit from its company and was noticed by the vision of its grace, he could not go back on his word. He had obligated himself, he had promised his head for my secret. In this matter it was divine predestination that decided. I, I played no part in it."

But he played a great part in it. We all knew it, especially me.

Even today, I can picture Shams's thirst in the presence of Our Master. This man, the ocean, gave water to the thirsty man, but drop by drop. I can still see the confusion, the resignation, then, once more, Shams's anxiety in the face of Rumi's disinterest, the lover who, from beginning to end, had pursued Shams, even his shadow, and who now showed clear signs of detachment. Once, I had seen my master suddenly leave Shams to meet a disciple who had arrived from Damascus. The gesture was unprecedented and, yet, would be repeated. Abandoned in the middle of the city, Shams, who was perfectly familiar with Konya, had lost all sense of direction. He had walked up an alley he was quite familiar with, walked back down, turned around, and repeated his steps until he finally decided not to return home.

Another time I saw my master leave the tanners' bazaar loaded with bound manuscripts. Suddenly, he took his package, gave it to Shams, jumped into a carriage driven by a young Turk, and took off. I watched Shams stagger forward, broken by the cold—always the cold—by the bundle of books, and his companion's abandonment. I made the entire trip on foot behind him, making sure he didn't see me. He appeared to be distraught. He must have said to himself that Rumi was no longer the lover of those first days, those first hours. He must also have hidden his disarray, for, like all those in love, he knew that, along that path, the more he was needed the less he would receive.

As I write these words, I, Hesam, know that a few days before the disappearance, the murder, or the abduction of Shams, my master had composed a poem whose words, in the heart of the future fugitive, would produce greater pain and blood than the daggers of his enemies.

In Salah's home, inside the cell that for seven months had sheltered the intimacy of the two lovers, Thiryanos was present for one of their last meetings.

Shams, who always seemed to be bareheaded because of his habit of covering his head with inappropriate fabrics and shawls, was addressing a small group of people. He said, "He who knows me desires me. He who desires me seeks me out. He who seeks me out finds me. And he who finds me chooses no other but me."

At the time we all thought that Our Master would never choose a lover other than Shams, that his reassuring presence by his side satisfied him. By provoking his departure, Rumi no doubt sought, through absence and loss, the constant, certain, and multiple presence of the lover. For we thought of what we would not have, rather than of what we did. Having overcome mortification in love, Rumi won his wager, to the point that he himself became Shams of Tabriz, to the point of claiming that a hundred thousand Shams were suspended from each of his hairs, to the point of erasing his own identity and titling his collection of poems *The Book of Shams of Tabriz.*

We can remain on the surface of things in our life and see only the froth of our sentiments. We can also, and this is what I am modestly trying to do, descend somewhat lower into the opacity within us.

Given our astonishment at the two men's separation, especially the vexing question of why Our Master allowed the man he loved to leave, we could have responded like anyone else, simply stating that, "He let him leave from boredom, because Shams had lost his charm for him, because Rumi's affection was increasingly being directed elsewhere."

Those reasons are banal. It seems to me there are others, which I've been trying to identify over the course of years.

And this first of all: my master was cooked. He was ready. A great poet was in the process of being born in him, he could feel it. And this beloved mirror, that other self, could only prevent him from blossoming. There was one too many. Rumi couldn't confront all of Shams's substance until Shams himself had disappeared. As hard as their separation was, it was essential. Against the day-to-day forces of affection and admiration, which were repeated daily, with increasing monotony, other forces victoriously came into play, rising from the most obscure parts of his being, forces that demanded that Rumi at last become who he was.

And for this to happen, Shams had to leave. Even if this would lead to suffering, which ordinary men reject with all their strength, incapable as we are of reading all the secrets of pain, love would have to bend before greater needs. Whatever the price. My master had needed his presence once, now he required his absence.

That day, with three or four disciples waiting for the Master's reaction to Shams's comment, "the one who finds me, chooses no other," Rumi had improvised some verses that clearly prefigured the dispersion, the destruction, the loss, the giddiness, the ignorance, and immolation of the man who had dared declare his love for him:

You are overcome with love for me
And I sent you away,
Listen carefully.
I am warning you, build nothing
Because I will destroy you,
Listen carefully.

If you build two hundred houses,
Like the bee and the ant,
I will make you homeless,
I will make you personless,
Listen carefully.

Were you the mountain Qaf,
Like a fast-turning mill,
I would make you enter the wheel
And make you turn,
Listen carefully.

If you were Plato or Loqman
Through your science and majesty,
How quickly I would make you
Ignorant with a single glance,
Listen carefully.

You are like a dead bird
In my hand, at the time of the hunt.
I, the hunter, will make you
Bait for the other birds,
Listen carefully.

The blades of iron do not rest
On your throat, or wound you.
And yet I sacrifice you
As Ishmael was sacrificed,
Listen carefully.

According to Thiryanos, after having "listened carefully" to the poem, Shams added the following line: "If I speak the truth, the entire city will expel me, from the youngest to the oldest, and M with them." Then, he remained silent.

Who, better than he could appreciate the ruins of love.

Even today I am convinced that when Shams left the precincts of the school to confront the calls of the armed conspirators waiting for him outside, he must have felt invincible to their iron blades, for long before the attack of the assailants, who had always been his enemies, he had been sacrificed, like Ishmael, by hands that had loved and caressed him.

In the days that followed, we received no news.

On the fortieth day, Rumi replaced his white turban with one the color of smoke and had a garment made of striped cloth imported from Yemen and India. He wore that garment, an emblem of separation, for the rest of his life. At the time of his death, 5 *Djamadi al-akhar* 672 of the Hegira (December 17, 1273), having collected his last sigh, I removed it myself from his body.

For twenty-six years, that striped garment, which he periodically replaced, reminded him of Shams's absence.

Even today, long after my master's death, every time I see those stripes displayed on the cloth merchant's shelves or on certain pieces of clothing, I can feel my heart pound in my chest, or rather, at a spot above my navel and immediately below my ribcage, a sensation that resembles a muscular contraction, reminiscent of an unhealed wound.

After Shams's departure, my master looked differently at everything that, from near or far, his companion might have known. He went so far as to convene, for closer observation, groups of quite ordinary people—merchants, scribes, civil servants—who were distinguished only by the fact that they had been, at one time, in contact with Shams of Tabriz. He examined every detail of their faces. And he surprised himself in reproducing, on his own face, on the left side, a wrinkle at the corner of his lower lip. This wrinkle was familiar to me, for it was occasionally to be seen on Shams's face. His eyes and ears saw and heard like the eyes and ears of the lost lover. At once the voice of the shoemaker on the street corner, although banal, became, because the idol had once paid attention to it, a talisman, a relic.

My master visited all the places formerly frequented by Shams. Much later, he acknowledged to me that his heart skipped a beat whenever he passed the entrance to a shop he had once entered in Shams's company. His favorite place, the hamam, where he had gone nearly daily with Shams, became a place of worship, where a thousand and one drops of memory flowed. In meetings, when his fervent partisans gathered, he imagined himself being looked at and listened to by Shams. In the streets he walked the way Shams liked to see him walk. He imagined him, not at his side but hidden, invisible, within himself. Yes, my master, ever since the disappearance of Shams of Tabriz, had become his dwelling, his residence. When he remembered Shams's jokes, the very jokes that in the past failed to make him laugh, he would burst out laughing and even forced us to laugh. Like the joke about "removing the white hairs from my beard." Overwhelmed by the number of white hairs that were invading his customer's beard, a barber shaved the man completely, then showed him the packet of hair, saying to him, "You choose, I'm busy."

My master laughed, staring at my beard and the beards of my friends. He repeated the joke and began another, in which a vizier says to a man, "Take these thousand dinars and do not mention a word of what you have just heard." The man grabbed the thousand dinars and went everywhere saying, "You know the vizier's fart? I'm the one who let it out." He told the joke often, among different groups of people, and every time he told it, he farted and laughed.

At times he would answer questions with the same jibes he had heard from the mouth of Shams. Thus, when someone once asked him about the predispositions of a young dervish, he answered by quoting his former lover word for word:

"Someone asked if a man was capable of something. The response was, 'His father was capable.' The man asked again, 'I'm not asking you about his father, I'm asking you about him.' The response was, 'His father was very capable.' The man insisted, 'Do you hear what I'm asking?' The response was, 'It is you who does not hear. I hear quite well. I'm not deaf.' And we never saw the young dervish again."

At a meeting organized by the governor in honor of some Sufis, at the end of the meal, my master related another of Shams's jokes:

"Seven Sufis, together in a house, absorbed in one another, did not touch their food. Disturbed at seeing them fast for several days in a row, their host asked how he could get them to eat. Someone said to him, 'Bring a sufficient quantity of food, empty the house of young and old, don't let anyone enter, and leave your home.' The host prepared food for twenty guests, put his wives and children out of the house, and shooed away the curious. But in spite of his promise to leave, he remained in the house and spied on his guests through a hole. He saw that the Sufis, who thought they were alone, gorged themselves on the food, until one of them, overcome with stomach cramps, stretched out on the ground. The six others continued to stuff themselves. After an hour, a second fell down and remained on the ground, motionless. This continued all the way to the sixth. Upset, the master of the house, the 'God of the house,' as we call him, entered the room and, pretending to be coming in from outside, asked the survivor if there had been sufficient food. 'No, there wasn't, otherwise I would be dead as well.'"

As he told the story, my master stared at the governor's guests, who, wolfing down veal with vinegar and marinated gazelle with garlic and dill, had begun to burp, belch, and pass gas. Being the obvious targets of the story, they, nonetheless, felt themselves obliged to laugh.

On another occasion, seeing his favorite flutist arrive, my master took me aside and told me how, after having pestered Shams with questions about their mysterious relationship, Shams ended up by telling the man that their relationship resembled that of the flutist and his flute. When I went to grab my notebook to write the words that would finally illuminate their relationship, he stopped me, adding: "After having said this, Shams farted. He then grabbed the flute and held it up to his behind, saying 'If you can play better than that, take it and play.'" As he related the story, my master grabbed the instrument of the best flutist in the city and mimicked the gesture made by Shams of Tabriz.

Where was he now? In what caravansary was he staying? To whom did he address his strange smile? Who observed the fold of his lip? Who covered him with wool when the winter chill crept inside through the windows? At night, who responded as he stretched languorously?

There was no answer. No news of Shams. Just the emptiness.

Some friends tried to appease Rumi by reminding him of Shams's misconduct, his immorality, even his debauchery. In vain. For them Our Master had but one response, "The mark of love is that vice seems like skill." Thiryanos was impertinent enough to ask, "Can't a man in love be clairvoyant?" "We cannot prevent this possibility from existing," said Rumi after a few moments of silence.

I, Hesam, seeing that Shams had disappeared once and for all, began to write down everything he said that I had remembered. I began to jot down phrases that seemed to me obscure, in the hope that one day my master himself would help me decipher them. This notebook soon became an inventory, in which one could read the most surprising combinations of words. For example: "And the men of God, hungry." Twenty years later, Rumi added, in his own hand, "Shams was saddened by those Muslims. They killed him with their hunger and devoured him with their desire. While the men of God went hungry."

In it, one could read, pell-mell, "Someone asked: 'Should we pray?' Another responded 'Yes.' The first said 'Ah.' The second said, 'I'll give you the prayer of my entire life if you give me that *Ah!*'"

Or, "This stain inside, what water could cleanse it?" Or, "Let us go now to the places of ill repute and observe those who have strayed. Those women were created by God. Good or bad, let us observe ourselves in them." Or, "Be in the center and alone."

One day, while he was being questioned about mountain or desert retreats, Shams had said that he personally knew an ascetic isolated on a mountain. According to Shams, this man was not human, he was "mountainous." If he were human, he added, he would be one of the intelligent ones, one of the dreamers, and worthy of knowing God. What would such a man do on a mountain? What would be the connection between the man and the stone? Then, he concluded: "Be at the center and alone."

Even today, I can see him narrating and miming the story of the effeminate prince for whose education, his father, the king, had hired a rough, virile, and intrepid man. This man was told by the sovereign to teach his son martial arts, masculine behavior, and the characteristics of heroes. But in vain. In spite of all the exercises for his muscles, the prince continued to play with dolls like a girl. One day, when the chamberlain announced the monarch's presence, the prince immediately covered his head with a scarf and grabbed one of his dolls. The tutor unfolded his turban and covered his head in the same way, grabbed a figurine and stood next to his pupil. The sovereign arrived and asked where the teacher was. The man undid his scarf, prostrated himself, and said, in a woman's voice: "I'm here, the schoolmarm is here."

In telling the story, Shams covered his head with a shawl, which he constantly wore over his shoulder—the cold, always the cold—assumed the frail timbre of a young girl, and walked with a womanly sway. Very few of us were present at those moments, when, through his wit, he outdid all the clowns in the country.

Through Thiryanos, my master learned of the existence of the notebook I was filling with Shams's words. He invited me, more precisely, he ordered me, to read him an episode every day. In this way I was able to get a little closer to him, although, until then, I thought he saw me as nothing more than a young disciple, useful and well-off, with, however, the distinction of having been noticed by Shams.

So every morning, immediately after the dawn prayer, I went to Rumi's bedroom, my notebook under my arm, and read to him, more or less at random, like a prophecy—this is what he wanted— the words of the "disappeared." In his eyes I had grown in stature. My mouth became Shams's mouth. My voice vibrated with the words of his lover. I transmitted improbable, undecipherable messages. I was the voice of the oracle.

Yet when Shams had spoken those words, most of the time my master had been present and heard them. I think that in encouraging me to read them at random, after so many years, in letting his ears hear those words again in another voice, he was deliberately trying to escape his own chimeras and perceive, through a present entity, absence itself.

I will never forget my first reading. He had looked at me strangely. What was going to come out of my mouth? Would the words of Shams, the man he called "the lover without a guarantee," finally show him forgiveness? That day, when, after the ritual salutations, I took the notebook from the inside pocket of my coat and began to read what I had titled *The Sayings of Shams of Tabriz*, my master suddenly prostrated himself at my feet, wishing to honor the once so ordinary words that had become, because of his absence, remarkable, sacred.

In spite of his reticence, I raised my master off the ground and offered him the notebook so he could choose a passage at his leisure. He closed his eyes, caressed the book, smelled it as if it were Shams's himself, opened it to a page, and returned it to me without a word. I felt he was listening to me with all his being.

I read: "A sheikh said to a dervish: 'The caliph has forbidden the sama.' At once the dervish felt a cramp in his chest and became ill. A doctor was called in. He took the man's pulse but could not identify the illness. The dervish died. The doctor opened his grave, split the dead man's chest, and removed the 'cramp,' which resembled an agate. Later, poor and ruined by poverty, he was forced to sell it. Thus, the cramp circulated from hand to hand until it reached the caliph. The caliph made a ring from it, which he always wore on his finger. One day, in fact it was the day of the sama, the caliph noticed that his clothing was covered with blood. He examined his body; there was no wound. He felt the ring and saw the stone glow, catch fire, and bleed. At once he called the successive sellers until he reached the doctor, who told him the story of the dervish."

My master, deeply touched by the story, in which death circulates like a stone, immediately called his favorite *ney* player, a few disciples who were always around him, and his son, and asked the small group to celebrate the sama at once. Hoping that the dance would relieve his father's suffering, Sultan Walad encouraged everyone to be lighthearted and cheerful. We did our best, but it was no use. Everything reminded him of Shams, the absence of Shams: kissing the ground, repeating the incantatory words, listening to the sound of the ney, removing one's coat as a sign of privation and ecstasy, turning, turning, turning, pronouncing the final *hu*, and listening to us chant the concluding *uuuuu* until we were breathless. How many movements, how many revolutions, how many sounds, how many sensations without him. He recalled, as he told me later, their first sama, when their hands touched, joined, clung to one another, loved one another, withdrew, sought each other out, found one another, caressed and kissed. Yes, he remembered how their hands had kissed. He also recalled other sama, from the beginning of their relationship, during which they forgot those present, the precautions, the uncertainty, the furtive and inquisitive glances, so they would obey but a single master: their astonishment at finding one another in the dance. They were still waiting. Until then, Shams had sought Rumi in all the cities he had "flown over" and Rumi languished in the hope of their conflagration. They met and their mutual attraction tore through the moral laws, propriety, family and social etiquette, to become part of another order, one that was cosmic, stellar, chaotic, an order whose rules escaped the miserable and, in any case, relative classifications of mankind.

My master danced, turned, shook his neck, then, feeling that each of his movements sought Shams, he stopped where he was and ordered the musicians to withdraw. Later, he said to me, "The sama without Shams is a prayer without God." However, my reading of the "Sayings of Shams" continued. The following day, I again presented myself before my master, my notebook under my arm, ready to again experience his prostration, his kiss, and his devotion for the old words, once spoken by his lover. Rumi now interpreted them differently. Words that had seemed innocent now suddenly became enigmatic, decipherable by him alone. He constantly remembered their dialogues and analyzed them in a new light. For me alone he recalled a number of Shams's sayings that emphasized the fact that the Bird never remained in the same spot, that he gladly abandoned friends and family to explore another life, beneath other skies. Yes, my master recalled one of the first of Shams's revelations, when the strange dervish explicitly stated that he had had to change his environment several times and create for himself a new entourage. At the time Rumi didn't pay particular attention to the statement. At the time Rumi wondered how Shams, whose behavior was always unexpected and startling, could attract the aversion of his entourage to the point of being forced to leave. How could one reject beauty and true astonishment?

Shams's departure now illuminated those old confidences. Neither love, nor exaltation, nor conflagration had managed to prevent the chilly old man's true nature from revealing itself, of provoking his departure; they had not prevented him from slamming the door and disappearing. He was the one who prevented habits from forming, "the one the ear of the lover cannot contain," he was "the pearl greater than the sea," "the sovereign of genies that spells cannot hold." He was the arsonist burned, the shaker shaken, the breaker broken, the abandoner abandoned.

On 5 *Shaval* 645, the very moment when Shams had crossed the threshold of the room, responding to the invitation to sacrifice himself heard from outside, and no doubt repeating Rumi's last words, "it's the best thing to do," we had witnessed the origin of the separation that engendered the poet. Shams exchanged his life for a poetry yet to be born. His volatile temper predisposed him to leave, his heart lurched between the certainty of reciprocity in love—the foundation of a guaranteed beatitude—and the doubt, most certainly justified, of being abandoned and let out to pasture.

It took only a split second to make his decision: to leave and shut the door on Rumi's hesitation to negotiate, to barter, to sell him in exchange for his well being. Someone other than Shams would have stayed, would have reminded Rumi of his metamorphosis, their quarantine, the first dance, the nights racing by in the presence of the lover, the fear, the practical jokes and shared collusion. Someone other than Shams would have asked to be hidden for a while to save his own life and try to draw out, to extend the cord of love. But Shams was not that other man.

Even today I believe that for Shams this separation seemed inevitable. He was a bird, and a bird never remains on the same branch. I am certain that he knew that Rumi was most attracted to what was ephemeral, uncertain, evanescent in him. The bird doesn't linger but he can be caught. Tied as closely to Rumi as he was, how did Shams resign himself to leaving? Only God knows.

I, Hesam, who had the privilege of accompanying him during his walks in the city, can state that, in the end he reproached Rumi for his coldness and detachment. Like any lover, did he fear a rival? Did he doubt he would ever again be able to captivate his lover? I have no idea. Still, the awareness that he was loved less than before manifested itself in him in the form of a revelation: he would have to leave. Yes, I believe that Shams would have left even without the taunt from the criminals outside. I can also state that such ordinary motives can obviously explain his actions, but notwithstanding the jealousy, regret, and pride, a more important reason led to their separation. And that reason was known to Rumi alone. Rumi was the only one who had seen, yes, seen, Shams's powerful ability to transform the professor into a lover, and the lover into a poet. Until then his mission had not been accomplished. For the poet to be born, there had to be suffering, a break, a cry, a tear. For Rumi that tear was the tear of separation. Yes, in slamming the door, Shams, though humiliated and abandoned, cleared a path to the most bitter aspect of the experience of love, that of separation. When Shams rose to leave, I thought I could detect, on his pale face constantly attacked by the cold, a glimmer of satisfaction. The split would be fruitful. He had seeded Rumi and was not the kind of man to wait around for the harvest.

Years later, when, exhausted from reading and rereading the works of Attar and Sanayi, I asked my master to compose a collection of poems, he unrolled his turban and showed me the first eighteen verses of the *Masnavi*, which begin, quite abruptly, as follows:

Now listen to the flute's lament at being separated from the reed.

Before the flute can sing, it must be cut, it must be separated from the reed. And it must suffer.

I know that the poet was born in my master at the very instant Shams walked out the door of the school never to return. It was a productive departure. Mission accomplished. Some would say a divine mission.

Was he aware that his departure would give birth to Rumi the poet? I am convinced of this and so are many others. From the lover's pain poetry was born. But what became of his own suffering? Who would untangle his hair, warm his hands, make sure the ink didn't stain his fingernails? What would become of the "ember" that had inflamed my master? No one knew where he went. None of our attempts to find him were successful. The friends and disciples who left in search of him returned exhausted and confused. Was my master hoping he would return? Yes, I think so. But part of him, the part that flew over the Prairies of the Angels, demanded the break, the separation, between the flute and the reed, the paper and the tree, the butterfly and the chrysalis, the rain and the cloud. It required the separation of two bodies once united by a magnetic and inexplicable attraction.

If the flute is not separated from the reed, how will the music escape?

I, Hesam, and with me Sultan Walad, Thiryanos, and some others, were convinced that the departure would not only bring out the poetry in Rumi but also the Shams in him. I don't know how else to say it. Shams was never as present in our minds as he was after his departure. From the prayer at dawn to the one at night, his name returned like an inevitable incantation. And with time, we watched as Rumi became Shams.

One day, hoping to distract him, I invited him into my garden in Faliras along with the little group that constituted his immediate circle. He walked around the garden, gathered some fruit, sat by the edge of the stream, rolled up his pants, took off his shoes, and put his feet in the water. The companions sat down around him on the ground. Very quickly, he began to talk of Shams. We were all accustomed to Rumi speaking only of Shams, as soon as he could and for as long as he could. One of the faithful, who had returned from a long trip and regretted not having known Shams, sighed deeply. Our Master asked him, not without surprise:

"Why alas? What alas? Alas for what? Alas from what? What need is there of 'alas' among us?"

The disciple, quite disconcerted, said, "My regret comes from the fact that I was unable to benefit from the luminous presence of

Shams." After a long silence, Rumi ended by saying, "While you were not able to see Shams, I swear to you by my father's soul that you have found the one who, from each of his hairs, has suspended a hundred thousand Shams of Tabriz, the one who is mingled with the comprehension of the secret of his secret."

This identification of Rumi with Shams of Tabriz expressed itself most clearly in the poems my master began to write. As his pseudonym he chose "Silence," but his poetry spoke only of Shams. Shams's name reappeared constantly, while his own name, Djalal al-din Mohammad, remained masked, silent, before finally becoming *Khamoush*, "the Extinguished," "the Voiceless." That is how the greatest Persian poet chose to define himself. When speaking of this incandescent love, he preferred, in place of words, which were useless and deficient, "the silence of the fish." He would say, "I have torn the garment of the word, I have abandoned speech. I have abandoned expression. I have left language." He would say:

> Silence, for, from now on,
> No matter what others may do,
> We will never harmonize
> Poetry and rhyme.

Or:

> Stop your reading,
> Remain silent, be patient,
> You are the one I will read,
> Like the Koran itself.

Or:

> Stop talking and if someone says:
> "Without the word and the sound,
> Speech has no form"—
> Lie.

What was this "form of speech" that existed outside the word and its sound? The greatest poets have sought it, but there are few who have achieved it, even briefly.

We experienced Shams's absence as a presence. Rumi himself used the words "united and separate." It was in the same spirit that, in speaking of the incendiary quality of love, he referred to himself as being "extinguished," "voiceless." I saw that this period of separation was to be important, for we experienced it as a gestation. Not as an end, but as a beginning. The poet was being born before our eyes. Each dawn brought its light and its stream of words, strangely destined, in the ideal of the man who gave them life, to be silenced or extinguished.

Much later, when he granted me the privilege of being his final companion, my master acknowledged to me, "In my country no profession was more contemptible than that of the poet. If I had remained there, I would be living according to their whims, and I would adhere to their demands, working as a teacher, writing books, preaching, practicing asceticism—all things that are external."

He forgot to say that had he remained in that country, in any event, had he not met Shams, he would never have become Rumi.

I continued to write. *The Sayings of Shams* grew longer. I wrote each sentence, torn from forgetfulness or exuberance, in the precious notebook, which became, for my master, the mouth of his lover. In writing it, I questioned men and women, masters and slaves, friends and enemies. In this way I was able to reveal, from the few words spoken by Shams several days before he was publicly insulted, his intention to leave.

Tired of the lack of attention from Rumi—whether deliberate or spontaneous we never found out—torn between the sensation of understanding him completely, of understanding his reaction, and the common desire of every lover to be the center, the light, the current of air, the one without whom life cannot go on, Shams had exposed this dilemma to Thiryanos, a dilemma that, one day or another, like an unknown passerby, knocks at the door of those who are in love:

"For some, arriving is the way out. For others, leaving is the way out. Pay attention and look closely, whether the way out for you is to arrive or to leave."

We know the response. On 5 *Shaval* 645 Shams of Tabriz left. Certainly, he left the school to show himself to the assassins, or to carry out Rumi's wishes—"it's the best thing to do"—but he did so because he wanted to. Yes, Shams of Tabriz wanted to leave. For him leaving was the way out. He had sensed this and, even if the murderers hired by Rumi's youngest son had not shown themselves, even if Our Master had begged him to stay, Shams the Bird, "the breath of the breath of the breath"—and here I enumerate, for my own joy, the litany of the beloved—"the One who enters by the breast, rises from the intellect, and proceeds toward separation," "the burner of water and mud," "the destroyer of line and style," "the best pure wine drawn from secrets," "the flame from the world of light," "the night," "the sound of the oud," "the musk ground with aromatics," "Joseph himself," "the conqueror of rust," "the lamp on Mount Sinai," "the flayer of the flower's garments," "the mine greater than all mines," "the one that before thats," "the Moon on Earth," "the dawn in the middle of the night," "the shield in danger," "the cloud of sweet rain," "the ocean, bearer of pearls," "the torch of smugglers," "the chain of the heartless," "smiling happiness," "the prison companion," "the thief and the guide along the road," "Jesus of all sorrows," "the disturber of patience," "the thief of reason," "the establisher of order," "the drop and the ocean," "kindness and anger," "sugar and poison," "the water and the vase," "the fruit of poverty," "the chamber of the Sun," "the seed and the trap," "the wine and the cup," "the raw and the cooked," "rest and fatigue," "the gracious walker," "the iconoclast," "the healer of lovers," "the reducer of the world," "the now in anxiety," "the torrent that steals," "the king who nourishes love," "the foot and the hand," "the existence of every being," "sight and hearing," "the light of day," "the joy that burns sorrow," "the sugar-bearing cloud," "the flag of the new world," "the heart soiled by blood," "the breath of Noah," "the desire of the spirit," "the health of the sick," "the water flowing in the heart of the stream," "the blindness of others," "the father of new joy," "the piercer of the vein of life," "the ball in which the world is seen," "the joke corrector," "joy in joy," "the cutter of arrows," "the master of the hunt for the world," "the Moon that overflows the sky," "the pearl greater than the sea," "the mountain that surpasses the plain," "the sovereign of genies the bottle cannot contain," "the water of immortality," "the beginning and the end," "the drunken man and the wine steward," "the visible and the hidden," "the splitter of the dawn," would have left.

The separation of Shams and Rumi, just like their union, was told in different languages and in different ways. Each of them reported a portion of the truth, the one he had witnessed or had hoped to witness. I was told that on 5 *Shaval*, Rumi, seeing that Shams had not joined him as he was accustomed to, took the trouble to go and find him at the school. Not finding him there, he ran to the bedroom where Sultan Walad slept and said, "My son, leave your sleep, wake up and get my guide. Once again my breathing has been deprived of the fragrance of his tenderness."

It was reported that on 5 *Shaval*, while Rumi and Shams were alone, a man, in a weak voice, called Shams from outside. Shams rose and said to Our Master that someone was calling him to die. Rumi responded, "It's the best thing to do." Shams left. At once, seven men stabbed him. He screamed so loudly that his assassins fainted. When they came to their senses, there was nothing on the ground but a few drops of blood.

We heard Shams's cry. A cry of pain, of isolation, of exile, of solitude and separation, a cry of departure. For Rumi, a demiurgic cry.

I had read in al-Nadim's *Fihrist* that the prophet and painter Mani believed that salvation was a call, sent from the world of light to the world of shadows, to primordial Man stuck in Matter, a call like a pointed sword, which revealed to primordial Man his luminous origin. For a long time I myself had tried to hear this call in myself. What would a cry of salvation, of creation, a cry that conceived the universe sound like? In vain I questioned the doctors of law. For the Zoroastrian mage, Mani was a heretic (and was consequently cut in two and nailed to one of the gates of Ctesiphon) and for the Muslims his talents were no greater than those of an excellent painter. I did not despair. I knew that Shams, unpredictable and erratic, could and would be capable of making me hear this call. He did so on 5 *Shaval* 645. Yes, within ourselves, we all heard a cry that would, for Rumi, become the cry of creation, of birth, a fertile cry, pregnant with poems. I saw this cry penetrate my master's six hundred sixty-six veins, I saw my master become someone else, I saw the calcination take place before my eyes.

The impassable had just been crossed. Rumi had abandoned Shams. Shams had left of his own free will, whether forced to or offended, I don't know. The demiurgic cry resounded in our ears. His disappearance was part of a prophetic cycle, similar to the occultation of the twelfth imam of the Shiites—the one waiting for the day of anger and pardon. Evaporated, dissolved, disintegrated, undone, Shams was no longer. Shams had penetrated Rumi.

It was his second departure. Today, I know this. And he will never return. This, I already knew, the day of the cry.

Some have said, and even written, that he was murdered in Konya. Murdered by the jealous and the furious, urged on by the ungrateful son of Our Master.

I do not believe this. For I have never seen his corpse. And his ghost has never appeared at night to call for vengeance.

Shams left a second time. And he has never returned. That is all. He went from city to city, changing his name, his words obscure, bullying tepid souls. Maybe, now, he has died, in some place unknown to us all. One evening, someone recognized him. When? In what city? Who was this person? None of that is of any importance. I enjoy rehearsing that scene. The person asks him, "Are you Shams of Tabriz? What do you do?"

"Who are you talking about," Shams answers.

"I'm talking," says the man, "about the insufferable old dervish who managed to enslave the greatest of teachers. I'm talking about Shams of Tabriz, Shams the untamable, Shams the inextricable, Shams the angry one, Shams the shameful one, Shams the insulter, Shams the unfaithful. I'm talking about you."

"I'm not the man you're referring to," said Shams.

"Yes, you are, you and no one else."

"I am not him," said Shams.

"You are."

Shams then lifted his eyes heavenward, lowered them, held his head in his hands, and said to the stranger who had approached him, in a voice that could barely be heard, "I am not Shams of Tabriz because Shams of Tabriz is dead. I saw him dead."

"What did he die of? Was he killed? Killed by whom?" the man said.

Shams spread his hands slightly and answered in a broken voice: "By me. I am the one who killed him. I am the one who killed Shams of Tabriz."

The man took two steps back and stared at the man he took for Shams of Tabriz. Shams—it was him—added, "Naturally, I wasn't alone. We are never alone when we murder someone. Our Master remained enclosed with his beloved. We could no longer tolerate that, we wanted to see him with us, we wanted him to come back. So we cried out, all of us together, 'Shams of Tabriz, come into the street if you are a man!' Several times we called out for him to leave."

"And did he come out," asked the man?

Shams of Tabriz—was it him?—now breathing rapidly, lowered his voice a little more, as if something in him wanted to cry, and said, "At one moment, from inside, we heard Our Master's voice. We heard it clearly. And that voice said, 'Go, we cannot escape our destiny.'"

"Is that what he did?"

"That's what he did. He obeyed his Master. He bowed his head and left. We were all together, waiting for him outside in the street, with clubs and knives. I was one of them. As soon as he come outside, we killed him."

"But why did Shams go out? He knew he was running a risk."

"He left because his Master asked him to leave."

"But his Master loved him! His Master could not have sent him to his death!"

"In love anything is possible," answered Shams. "Even the absence of love."

In silence the stranger looked at the man he took to be Shams of Tabriz. Then, he asked once again:

"And you left?"

"Yes, I left. The others, I don't know about. I don't want to know what the others do. I left, and since that day I have been walking in search of what I lost."

"What did you lose?"

"I don't know."

Shams motioned goodbye to the man, turned around, and left, limping slightly. The light was fading. Soon the old man disappeared.

The Book of
Salah

I am him . . .

IT WAS AT THIS TIME THAT RUMI BEGAN TO CELEBRATE THE sama almost continuously. The exhausted musicians, dancers, and singers would collapse from fatigue and sleep on the floor in the *sama khaneh*, while the sound of the *ney*, now faint as it issued from weary lips, continued to reach their sleep-filled ears. My master continued to whirl, to cry out, to compose poetry. Tireless.

> The sheikh, the great doctor, out of love became a poet,
> And the pious man a wine merchant.
>
> Love became his path, became his religion,
> And everything that was not love was delusion.
>
> Along his path, there was no blasphemy, no Islam,
> Shams of Tabriz became his king of kings.

That is how Sultan Walad described his father's state after Shams's final disappearance.

A day didn't go by without a stranger appearing at the school to provide him with some so-called news about Shams. My master had expressly asked us to admit them; there was no story he wasn't prepared to listen to. Contradictory reports that

sometimes placed Shams in Syria, sometimes in Persia, sometimes even in China. He had been seen with a woman and children, but also in the company of a young man, or alone and
afflicted. Someone claimed to have seen him the night before in
Konya itself, disguised as a rag seller, bartering needles against
old clothing.

"Why didn't you stop him?"

"He disappeared even before I could place my hand on his
shoulder."

Another day, a man arrived, haggard and breathless. He
claimed to have taken the road that separates Damascus from Konya
without stopping, without rest. But the message was worth the
thirst, the hunger, and the fatigue. My master insisted that he first
regain his strength, which the traveler did without having to be
asked twice. We all gathered round, hoping for some information
worthy of our belief. When he had belched loudly, Rumi, confident
that the man's stomach was well filled, authorized him to speak.

"Master, I saw Shams of Tabriz on the large square of Damascus,
the evening of the annual fireworks celebration. Thousands of jugglers, soothsayers, and hawkers ran up and down the streets, illuminated by lanterns. Indian elephants, covered with velvet and lit
with candles paraded to the sound of drums. Acrobats and dancers
juggled with discs of fire. The crowd, excited by the lights, the
noise, the colors, and the music, reacted like so many awestruck
children."

My master stared at the mouth of the bearer of news. He
tried to imagine Shams, dressed in black, frail and sulking, immersed
in that explosion of noise and light. He knew that Shams would
never have been present for the procession of the animals, that he
would never have lifted his eyes to the fireworks, that he had
always had an aversion for crowds and celebrations. Nevertheless,
he was interested in the story, thus revealing his thirst for information. The other man, a professional storyteller, spiced his tale.
He claimed that one of the elephants carried a reliquary in which

was placed, and venerated, one of the hairs of the Prophet. When the elephant passed, the crowd prostrated itself and kissed the ground. Out of carelessness, a six-year old fire dancer caught fire. In order not to interfere with the choreography of flame, part of an ancient tradition, the young dancer's father, who was the master of ceremonies, ordered his son to continue his act, in spite of the pain and the burns. The ritual had to unfold according to plan. Any disruption, any change could be fatal, lead to years of drought, warfare, rivers of blood, and invasions of vultures.

While listening to this, my master thought only of Shams among the troop of jugglers and acrobats. Was he the cause of the young dancer's accident? Did he intentionally push or jostle him? He was capable of it, Rumi knew this. He questioned the storyteller about this. The man from Damascus answered that Shams was always among the crowd. And even if the darkness hid him, he would reappear shortly after, lit by a ray of light from the fireworks.

As he continued his story, my master lowered his voice and asked Thiryanos to bring him some luxurious clothing as compensation for the narrator. It was a while before Thiryanos returned, loaded with garments worthy of the princes from *The Arabian Nights*.

Upon seeing the clothing, I nearly jumped from my seat. What? All that for this man whose words were so unreliable? After all, wasn't I, Hesam, the school's accountant? I was anticipating financial problems: debt, negotiation of the rate of interest, and repayment of the loan by charging high fees for meeting with the Master, a technique that had been refined ever since Shams had been here.

The narrator answered all the questions, piled on increasingly precise details. According to him, Shams appeared exhausted and bewildered. He was alone. At times, he behaved as if he were being hunted and would turn around periodically, as if to make sure that no one he knew was following him. When he noticed the narrator for the second time, Shams took advantage of the darkness to slip away and dissolve in the crowd. With one eye on the garments, the man continued:

"But I, I had recognized him. I followed his movements. Even from a distance I managed to locate him, even hidden behind the enormous mass of the elephant that bore the reliquary, even hidden in the crowd. I could feel his eyes searching for me. But because I am small, I managed to stay hidden."

My master ordered us to unfold the tunics, slippers, and turbans. A pile of embroidered fabric, stitched with gold and silver thread, and satin encrusted with precious stones, was spread out before our eyes.

I had never seen anything like it. Never would a man of our acquaintance ever allow himself to display his wealth in this way. Even the elegant Moin Soleyman, an administrator at the court of the sultan and a great friend of the Mongols, whenever he came to the school, would tone down his white, beige, and black outfits.

With his fingertips the man from Damascus touched the gold threads that decorated the sleeves of the tunic and revealed a flurry of additional details.

"Shams of Tabriz moved forward with the crowd, when suddenly a young man accosted him. Shams turned around and appeared to recognize him. They exchanged several words, whispering into each other's ears. Then Shams drew from his pocket a purse, which he offered him. The man took the purse and for a while held Shams's hand in his own."

My master was very familiar with that slender hand, the fingers stained with ink or saffron, the nails blackened by cold. For a long time, he had held that hand, which rose up, during the sama, to become the cord that connected heaven to Earth. That hand had loved him, caressed him, snatched him from the monotonous world of ordinary sentiment to cast him into the dawn of growth and eternal fecundity. That hand was familiar to all of Rumi's senses. His tongue had explored its taste, his nose had detected its odor, his fingers had touched its nerves. That hand, held by an unknown during a night of celebration in Damascus, was indeed the one that was indistinguishable from my master's hands, when, wrapped one in the other, they affirmed their union.

As tea was served the narrator minutely described Shams's companion. He did not appear to be very young. His hair was graying—he had noticed this in spite of the darkness—and his gait unsteady.

I observed my master. He was no longer with us. He was in Damascus, his gaze fixed on the two joined hands. Who could he have been, that man who had so much trouble walking? Suddenly, he asked Thiryanos to help him undress.

"In front of everyone?" asked the Greek.

"In front of everyone."

Thiryanos removed Rumi's turban, then his coat, then his tunic and pants. His body was firm and muscular, a contrast to his pale yellow complexion.

Naked, or nearly so, my master offered the storyteller from Damascus the embroidered silks along with his own clothes. Thiryanos, for whom Rumi's everyday clothing was worth far more than any gilt vestment, intervened to prevent the unjustified generosity.

"Master, you can see clearly that he's lying. No one has ever been able to find Shams of Tabriz."

I approved of his frankness. As the school's accountant, I could, by selling a piece of the Master's turban to a wealthy adept, earn enough to run the school for a week. I began to calculate what his complete outfit was worth: a small fortune!

My master smiled at Thiryanos, removed his socks, held them out to him, and added, "Everything you see, I have given to this man because he lied. If he had spoken the truth, I would have given him every life I have."

As with all the others, and although he wasn't fooled, he accepted their stories about Shams. For him it was a necessity. As if, along with the air he breathed and the water he drank, at every moment his senses had to experience Shams. The story of the nighttime celebration and the lover's hand joined to that of an unknown, although fabricated, stimulated and excited Rumi. To the point of jealousy. But aside from the pride and resentment, there appeared in him the need to make the other omnipresent, even if it meant he would have to suffer.

My master was venturing into a world he no longer controlled. Why did he torture himself now about a physical contact between Shams and some unknown when he had encouraged this type of behavior when Shams was living in Konya? How many times had he encouraged him to celebrate the sama with others, in order to deflect an attention that was perpetually focused on the two of them? And Shams went through with it. In Rumi's presence he invited young disciples to their ecstatic dances, after which, the sweat-covered bodies remained unclothed. My master felt no animosity at the time. Quite the contrary, he admired Shams's hold over his companions. How many times did Shams describe to Rumi his control over a chubby old man or a young virgin, "one foot in luck," that is to say, "ready for marriage," in Persian. My master never seemed to be affected by this. In fact, those stories amused him. He wanted Shams to please, he wanted him to please men, women, young and old, disciples as well as ministers, the rich as well as the poor. And Shams pleased them or repulsed them. As for my master, he celebrated his admirers and rebuffed his detractors. Why did he now suffer while listening to this fabricated report?

Maybe he wanted to suffer? Maybe, now, he was worthy of it?

My master was obsessed with the idea of going to Damascus and inquiring about Shams, in the secret hope of not finding him. All the rumors placed him in Damascus. Rumi knew, and we did as well, that none of them were reliable. None of the emissaries we had sent out to track the informers had been able to obtain the slightest piece of accurate information. Still, my master persisted in traveling to Damascus. Their first meeting had taken place on the main square of the city, when Shams had cried out to my master, "Oh, money changer of the world of the senses, take hold of me!" And it was in Damascus that Sultan Walad went to find him after their first separation.

Thiryanos, Sultan Walad, and I all knew, with secret certainty, that we would never find him again. Sultan Walad even felt that Shams had been killed and that the man who ordered the murder was none other than his own brother. But how could he acknowledge it? How could he affirm, before a father who paid for false news, that his own son, who carried his blood in his veins, had signed the epilogue of Shams's life. Years later, following a dream in which Shams had showed him the place where his body was hidden, Sultan Walad admitted to me that he had always leaned toward the possibility of murder and the concealment of the body.

To go to Damascus. Neither Thiryanos, nor I, nor even Sultan Walad were capable of dissuading Rumi. Only Salah the goldsmith, who had grown increasingly close to my master, could do so. But he didn't yet feel capable of restraining him.

Accompanied by his son and a few followers, including several musicians, Rumi left for Damascus. It was a pointless, futile trip.

As usual, after my master's departure, we closed the doors of the school and swept the courtyard. It was at that precise moment, with the dust of my master's cell floating in space, that I discovered in the gaze of Salah the languor of Shams's gaze when Rumi was not there. The same languor would slip into my own eyes ten years later, when I myself was deprived of his presence.

From Damascus I received a letter from Sultan Walad. Along the top was a poem by Rumi intended for Shams, describing his hopeless search:

How many times have I looked for you
From one house or one door to another?

And how many times have you escaped
From one corner to another, from one street to another?

Sultan Walad also said that his father's glorification of Shams during the sama captivated all the inhabitants of Damascus, the learned and the illiterate alike, rich and poor, children, adolescents, the elderly. But above all he felt that Rumi saw himself in Shams, that they shouldn't be distinguished from one another.

One day his father had confided in him:
Do not see us as two, for we are but one.
In two, there is doubt; we are without doubt.
Do not think of me as being different than Shams.
Our souls are but one. Go, forget our faces.

Sultan Walad said that the Syrians, who knew nothing of Shams, could not understand how a man worthy of being called a prophet could flare up, shiver, and grow intoxicated over an old, unknown dervish "with neither head nor foot." We found the same incomprehension everywhere. Whether in Konya or Damascus, whether one knew him or not, Shams seemed unworthy of such ardor and provoked nothing but disdain and hostility.

In Konya, things went on as before. Our life depended on the letters sent from Damascus. One day we learned that Rumi and his entourage were preparing to return. Once again we swept the courtyard, watered the flowers, shook out all the rugs in the school as if we were celebrating the new year. But in secret we knew that the Master's return, without Shams, would bring sadness and melancholy.

Even Kera, his wife, who, now that Shams was gone, could finally get her husband back, became depressed. The reunion she hoped for required a radiant partner, not a man who compared himself to a cut reed. Rumi's "empty-handed" return did not presage any joy or passion for the abandoned wife. She too would have to wait.

Among the household only the cats, anticipating the Master's return, abandoned their cushions, blankets, and rugs to clean themselves, to offer their cleansed bodies to the endless caresses whose return they felt to be imminent. For a long time I wondered if Shams's presence hadn't disturbed them, if the urine staining each corner of the wall, even within the very cell into which the two men withdrew, wasn't a sign of their discontent, if the white hair covering the mattress, which clung to Rumi's black pants, tunics, and coats, did not betray an aversion, a secret dispossession.

My master returned and settled at school. He returned intact, almost jovial. His sallow complexion did not seem to have been affected by the trip, or by absence. He danced, turned, went to the hamam, and composed verses as he sung. I now know that the fusion and separation with Shams, the shame of illicit union, the pain of estrangement, the uncertainty of wandering and pursuit had but a subterranean conclusion, that of providing Persian literature with its most beautiful poetry, stripped of all mannerism, verses that pierced our hearts like a sharp knife forever—"the amorous details of the world."

Once again visitors continued to assail us with false news and voyeurs wanted to see with their own eyes the "excitement of love."

According to them, Shams was in Damascus, where he had been hired as a tutor by an influential family. I had a difficult time imagining him being responsible for the education of a young student. It was not his way. He could change the destiny of a child with a few words, a glance, but certainly not by lengthy and patient tutoring. I still remember the story of the boy who was struck, literally struck, by his words, who said he wanted to remain next to him, "motionless as the ground," and who died when he was eighteen years old. He was not yet mature enough to support the burden of Shams. I can still see Shams saying to me, "Once, I had a troop of students. Out of love I told them terrible things. I destroyed their affection." How could this destroyer of affection now bring it into being? A voice whispered to me that the time may have come for a disciple to finally understand that the instruction provided by Shams was an offering and not servitude, diffusion not expansion, that it tasted bitter but ultimately led to freedom, to identity.

My master must have thought the same way. One day he decided to leave for Damascus, again in search of Shams. The same preparations for the trip, the same wagons filled with flutes and drums, the same skeptical companions, the same sad goodbyes: the routine of disillusion.

Sultan Walad had always been convinced that Shams had been murdered by his enemies. But he didn't dare tell his father for fear that this third shock, following their union and separation, might be fatal to him. So he hid the truth. Thiryanos believed that the Bird had flown again, even more so since this last flight would have been caused by his lover. *Kish Kish*, Rumi had said, and the Bird had flown. I saw my master perfectly fulfilled in absence and separation. For him, these comings and goings did not serve to find Shams. They contributed to his own spiritual quest, which was uninterrupted. My master didn't go to Damascus to find Shams. He went there to find him somewhere other than in himself.

So, once more, he left for Damascus. Once again Sultan Walad sent me letters, blackened by his father's poems. Rumi wrote constantly and sent emissaries in search of Shams, who remained as elusive as ever. As always, the notables, ordinary folk, and great thinkers filled Rumi's household and, as always, even though he was no longer teaching, his slightest word became an adage for us. In one of the letters from Sultan Walad, an offhand remark drew my attention. It said that Rumi had chosen a new friend, a certain Hamid, "in whose mirror he perceived the body of affection."

So, in Damascus Rumi sought Shams in the mirror held out to him by a young friend. Of that man, I learned only his name. Sultan Walad never took the trouble to describe him to me. I never knew why my master had chosen him. Only Thiryanos found out the age of the chosen one: for that matter he wasn't all that young, barely a few years younger than Rumi.

In Konya, not a word had been spoken to Salah the goldsmith about this new attachment. The trips to Damascus did not trouble him. He knew that Shams would never appear again, that he had abandoned Rumi as he would the greatest inheritance. In spite of this assurance, which he deeply believed, he remained sensitive, vulnerable even to Rumi's other relationships. Between the two trips to Damascus, he kept an eye on any new encounter, out of fear that loss would bring about another physical, palpable presence, out of fear that someone else would steal the Master's heart. I felt that even I was suspected. I didn't dare risk reading *The Sayings of Shams* except in the presence of Salah. Some passages concerned him, for example, the one in which Shams says that Salah's words confused him.

In Konya, not a word about the man named Hamid. Salah couldn't bear the thought that anyone but himself could be intimate with the Master. To support the man who was to become the favorite, we decided to remain silent about anything concerning Rumi's brief adventure with an inhabitant of Damascus. Later, after Salah's death, during those privileged moments of solitude with Rumi, I finally decided to try to learn more about the man from Damascus. Why had my master, who had left in search of Shams, taken up with someone else? His only response was, "Shams of Tabriz was always nothing more than a pretext."

Once again, silence.

There are territories whose entry is barred to reason. The passage takes place through the beating of the heart, breathlessness, trembling, and stuttering. To walk on that ground, where Shams seemed only a pretext, I know now that I would have needed very different legs and feet.

In Damascus the searches became increasingly pointless. There were fewer and fewer bearers of false news; they had grown tired of repeating that they had met Shams at the corner of a street, in a caravansary, on a bridge or a boat. The lies seemed to grow tired from being endlessly retold, and my master slowly freed himself of the lengthy quest for Shams.

From Damascus, he wrote the following:

A hundred thousand times I have cut short my hope,
Hope of what? Of Shams, trust me in this.

On the same sheet of paper, I recognized the handwriting of Sultan Walad, who added:

In Damascus, he did not see Shams of Tabriz.
Like the moon, he saw him in himself.

He said, "I am him, why continue to search?
I am like him, therefore, speak of me."

Either you look at him or you look at me.
I am him, he is me, seeker.

No doubt I was in search of myself.
Boiling over in a tank like wine juice.

The juice does not boil for someone.
It works at its own betterment.

The return was imminent. I knew it. Once again, we swept the cells, the garden, all the corridors. Once again, the cats became alert and the women, in their lodgings, perhaps hoping for more intimate reunions, returned again to the souk and the hamam. Kera's servant told me that her mistress seemed illuminated. Shams's final disappearance had left every door open. But this was to overlook Salah, the unchangeable disciple, a native of Konya, to whom we had stopped paying attention.

Open wide the doors

HAVE SPOKEN ABOUT RUMI AND WILL CONTINUE TO SPEAK about him as long as I am able to speak. I have spoken about Shams and I will speak further of him. I have spoken about myself, as briefly as possible, and I will speak further of myself. I have spoken about Thiryanos and I will speak further of him. There is another I must now describe to complete the circle of close friends. That man is Salah the goldsmith.

In the beginning Rumi and Salah shared the same guide, Termazi. They were the same age and both hoped that a spark would ignite them. For Salah the flame was none other than Rumi, who—while preaching about Termazi, the vanished guide—saw, with the eyes of his heart, Salah burst into flame. He witnessed this combustion, and knew that the inflamed man would be his. As for his own conflagration, he had to wait a while longer—to wait until he met Shams.

For a long time I wondered, and others with me, how a speech about Termazi, spoken by Rumi and heard by dozens of the faithful, had been able to pierce the soul of a man so deeply that he would forget all propriety and burst into flame. The same question was asked about Shams and Rumi. How could such anodyne words, exchanged between a shivering old dervish and a learned professor, so alter Rumi and then Shams, Persian literature, and, in the end, the soul of an entire people? I cannot answer this. But it is obvious, at least to me, that God, on such occasions, for a few moments, had made the decision to become incarnate. What did Rumi and Shams see on that distant 26 *Djamadi al-akhar* 642? God himself or the lover? I am unable to answer that. But I am deeply convinced that he saw the flame that was going to consume him.

For Salah the goldsmith, the same perception occurred that Friday, at the Abolfazl mosque, while Rumi was preaching. He heard the words he spoke with his irradiated eyes, his charred flesh. An ember had fallen upon him.

Since that day, Salah never left my master's entourage and seemed to be patiently waiting for the moment when Rumi, emptied of Shams, would finally direct his gaze upon him. That hour was approaching. All of us could feel it.

Everyone agreed that Salah expressed himself poorly. He spent his days in his shop in the bazaar, behind his balance, weighing the gold he would then beat into shape. His gaze, wherever it fell, saw only the glimmer, the reflection of metal and gemstones. His ears heard only the hammering of silver and gold. How, under such conditions, could he have learned to argue? How, born of a father who was a fisherman, could he have been able to master grammar? His sentences were nothing but a torrent of errors. Yet Our Master forbid anyone from pointing them out and correcting them. Later, when he made Salah one of his companions, choosing to speak like him, he would turn those grammatical mistakes into the most sophisticated means of expression. Then the entire city, imitating the Master, began speaking incorrectly. Having been exposed since childhood to educated men, I found myself, on several occasions, distorting certain words just like Salah.

One time, Shams of Tabriz had said to me, "That goldsmith's words confuse me."

He too, like Rumi, saw in Salah a being above the uniformity of vocabulary and the aesthetics of language. Salah was the "ring of keys that had come to open wide the doors." He himself paid little heed to his incorrect use of words, even more so since, sheltered under Rumi's wing, he soon saw that he was being imitated by the elite of the city.

With the announcement of Rumi's return, Salah went to his own home, where he had earlier hidden the two lovers, and removed any trace of Shams. His coats, his scarves, his head coverings and slippers were stored in trunks and sent to the countryside. His chess set was given to the family of his former wife, the young Kimia, who, during her short married life, had been overcome, "checkmated," by Shams. His writings, given to Thiryanos, eventually wound up in my hands. In this way I was able to complete my notes. During those moments of confusion, prior to the second return from Damascus, Salah was the only one to prepare for what came after Shams. No doubt he felt the successor was within him, finally ready to replace the Bird.

My master returned. The dance sessions resumed and joy, which had been chased from the house like a harmful insect, again returned. At times I could hear the hysterical laughter of the women from their apartments within. Thiryanos himself noticed, through the transparency of the veil, Kera's plucked eyebrows, her curved lashes, and her eyes darkened with kohl.

Shams the tormented, Shams the irascible and the confused, gave way to Salah, calm and serene. We never learned when or how the reconciliation took place. But I can say that the union with Salah was not sudden or accidental. It happened effortlessly, without appearing in any way extraordinary. No library thrown into the water and withdrawn intact, no books suddenly devoured by flame and recreated by some prodigy.

Sultan Walad justified the transition from Shams to Salah this way:

The friend remains the same although the garment is another.
He will tear the old garment and it will appear again.

The wine remains the same although the bottle changes.
See the joy with which he strikes the head of the wine steward!

Let's not speak of resurrection, but of perfect union.
From that churning, a howling sea appeared.

In this way Salah appeared after the charring and burning. His stillness resembled the flow of a quiet river devoid of thoughts of broken bridges, uprooted trees, or twisted carcasses carried away by the current. Yes, Salah could be thought of as a calm body of water. Water after fire, Salah after Shams, and as their names indicated, "Conformity" after the "Sun."

Among the first circle of the faithful, Thiryanos adopted Salah with his eyes closed. My Greek friend's devotion to Our Master was greater than any personal choice, any sense of free will. From the moment Rumi's gaze fell upon someone, the chosen one immediately became the favorite of Thiryanos. Consequently, he had no hesitation in following Salah. My own acceptance was somewhat more hesitant, but the future dissipated my trivial and furtive resistance. For, upon Salah's death, as I have already noted, the man who was to replace those calm waters was me, Hesam.

As for Sultan Walad, his reaction was reasonable. According to the devoted son, Salah was balm for the wounded, speech for the dumb, a glimmer of light for the blind. He would calm his father, following so much anguish and suffering, and he felt that this was of inestimable value. Besides, it was Sultan Walad who assumed the responsibility of explaining to Kera that the inoffensive Salah was going to replace Shams and that she had nothing to fear.

What did he mean to the women? Approval? Satisfaction? I'm still wondering. What did they say of these transitions from one man to another? I have no idea. But I never heard any of them say that, as woman is made for man, man is made for woman and for her alone. The Christians, I believe, claim this.

But about these matters, we haven't received the same lessons from God.

Our Master continued to compose poems about Shams and cried his name as he whirled around. But the one who massaged his feet and dried his sweat at the end of the dance was now called Salah. Rumi's invocations resembled a prayer addressed to a divinity or, possibly, himself. As for me, I sometimes wondered where Shams really was: did he exist anywhere but within Rumi? Did he continue to shiver at the slightest breeze? Did he continue to blacken his fingers with ink? Did he still bargain with visitors wanting to meet Rumi? *The Sayings of Shams of Tabriz* has remained unfinished for a long time. No one reports his words to me—and I myself, in exploring the layers of memory, have already reported all his words, all his "sayings."

The era of Shams was fading away, it was becoming the past.

One day in spring, when the buds, the birds, and the sky proclaimed the end of the cold season, my master gathered us together in his cell, which had been completely transformed since the appearance of Salah. The books withdrawn by Shams resumed their place in the room and the alcoves, formerly sealed, resumed their previous use. The brazier that had been filled with coal summer and winter in order to warm the ever chilly Shams, had been stored in the basement. Cushions, placed against the wall provided visitors with a previously banished comfort.

On that day, my master, holding Salah's hand, told us he was appointing him the sheik of our brotherhood, to be our guide, teacher, and model. As he instructed, we were to follow a man who was practically illiterate, who, when saying "affected," said *moftala* instead of *mobtala*, and referred to a "key" as a *qolf* instead of a *qofl*. Nonetheless, we acquiesced, already perceiving that the resistance and animosity would come from outside, from all those in the bazaar who considered the goldsmith to be their equal, an artisan like the others, and from the grammarians who could not tolerate being overshadowed by a man who was ignorant.

On that day, his hand in Salah's, my master said, "In my head there is no ambition to be the first. I do not know a single bird that can share my flight. I rejoice in myself. I want no one. In my wake, a visitor is as undesirable as a fly. Go in search of Salah, demand union from your soul. If you are king, submit to him. Otherwise, by doubting him, you are monsters."

As a sign of submission, Sultan Walad was the first to kiss Salah's hand, still impregnated with his father's sweat. After that, he questioned Our Master:

"Do you love Salah because he wanders in your lights?"

Rumi responded:

"I love him for reasons of attraction, relationship. Yellow amber attracts straw because of the bond that unites them. That same amber doesn't attract anything else, for there is no bond. The same is true for a small camel that runs after its mangy mother. If someone brings it a fine Arab horse, worth a thousand dinar, and says to the little camel, 'Run after this horse instead of following your mother,' he won't run after or follow the horse. No bond unites the camel and the horse. Salah attracts me because of the bond that unites us."

That bond, very different from the one that united Shams to Rumi, grew stronger day by day. Rumi seemed reconciled to tranquility, a sentiment that had been banned when Shams was around. It was a healing process. His serenity was transmitted to us and we blessed Salah, the benefactor, the conciliator.

Given the many trips of the women to the hamam, the bazaar, and the public parks, activities that had been abandoned when Shams was present, I deduced that the good humor had even affected the women's quarters and that Salah, from without, did what he could to please them. He himself was married, the father of two girls—one of whom, as I have mentioned, was very fond of Sultan Walad—and he understood, far better than Shams, the demands of married life. In spite of the bond that united the two men, they had to continue to respect their wives. Contempt, disdain, inattentiveness, and distance had been Kera's daily fare whenever she knew that her husband was with Shams, "the Lover without a guarantee." She was not angry with him for she realized that their relationship was inevitable and, perhaps, even indispensable. When a flood is unleashed, why should a simple little fish fight the flow? She immersed herself in the water until the storm dissipated, until Salah.

I questioned Sultan Walad constantly about the relationship between my master and Salah, his future father-in-law. Realizing that my approach was not one of curiosity but would be written down, for the purpose of archiving the life of the man who, we already knew, would deeply affect so many hearts and minds, he provided me with a wealth of information.

For example, I learned that Salah had told Rumi that in his eyes, before their union, the light had been hidden and he was unaware of it. It was Rumi who had opened his eyes and suddenly the light "bubbled like the sea."

Various references to this "light" seen by Salah were made. He himself spoke openly about the phenomenon, which I was able to witness for myself on one occasion. As he was going to his shop, seated on a mule, he suddenly turned around to face me and, after mentioning something about a bookseller in Konya who was open only two days a week, he said to me, "Here, before my eyes the sea of white light."

I walked forward and tried to make out the waves and ebb and flow of light in the depths of his eyes. There was no sign of a sea of white light. In his iris I saw myself and myself alone. He began talking again about the bookseller who sold only to collectors, then stopped and added, as if it were quite natural, "I see the sea of blue light, the sea of green light, and the see of yellow light. I now see the sea of light the color of smoke."

He stopped, closed his eyes, opened them again, and said, "Oh, Hesam, the sea of black light is now tumultuous."

He stopped again, then added that a certain Aziz had in his

bookstore more than a million volumes and had just acquired a very rare copy of Attar's *Conference of the Birds* for an amount that Salah found exorbitant. After another pause he said that according to Aziz himself, fifteen other manuscripts of *The Conference of the Birds* adorned his shop, one of which was in the poet's handwriting.

I didn't learn anything more about the tumult of the black sea.

The ten years that Salah spent with Rumi were punctuated by events that were less remarkable, surprising, and violent than the twenty-three months shared with Shams. Even today I wonder how a union that lasted barely two years was able to change so much—Rumi's life and our own, and the great river of Persian poetry.

One day, however, I was accompanying my master to the bazaar. The sun lit his yellow complexion and I had the impression that each ray of light that penetrated his skin struggled against his perpetual sallowness. He rarely left his cell and was especially fond of enclosed spaces, like the hamam. The city's doctors, most of them his disciples, suggested that he get some air, walk around, but it was a waste of time. He only left the darkness and humidity of the baths to return to the sama room—enclosed, sealed, and cloaked in shadow.

That morning, within the precincts of the bazaar, we crossed the coppersmith's quarter, strewn with basins, ewers, and copper casseroles, and that of the armourers, where bows and arrows, crossbows, swords, lances, and sabers of various shapes were manufactured. I was unable to detect, in my master's eyes, the slightest interest in this arsenal. On the other hand, he slowed his pace in front of the shops of the makers of styluses and needles. He seemed to take an interest in the process of standardizing weights, in the tempering and dimension of the eye of each needle.

We were not far from the bazaar of the jewelers and goldsmiths, where Salah worked, when Rumi abandoned the needles, stood in the central alley, and suddenly, exalted by the tap-tap of the goldsmiths, began to turn. Right there, in the middle of the bazaar.

At that moment, Salah appeared, shouting and screaming, shoving through the crowd surrounding the dancer. He threw himself at Rumi's feet, and placed his lips on the blessed toes. He then fainted. He simply lost consciousness. Later, he acknowledged to Sultan Walad that an inspiration of the invisible world had told him to leave his workshop at that very moment, for Rumi, not far from there, was caught up in the whirl of the dance.

From the elevated floor of the surgical instruments shop, I saw my master kiss Salah's hair and face, caress him, then draw him into the dance. Unable to sustain Rumi's rhythm, Salah left the circle and told him he did not have the endurance necessary to accompany him in the sama.

Physical discipline and hardship had seriously weakened the constitution of the man, who, for many years, had demanded of his body nothing more than the continual movement of his arm and his hand in beating gold. He ran to his workshop and ordered his workers to hammer without interruption until Rumi stopped dancing. They were to continue hammering, even if the sheets of gold broke into pieces and fell apart. His employees tried to remind him that too much hammering would ruin the gold. But it was in vain. For Salah the only thing that mattered was Rumi whirling. And that whirling, begun at noon, did not end until the celebration of the afternoon prayer.

Afterwards Rumi went to get Salah, whose clothes, which he had torn apart in his stupor, hung in strips about him. They left the bazaar.

I came down from my platform and attempted to scatter the crowd and protect the two men from any unwanted curiosity. Slowly, the admirers dispersed. The sound of the prayer accompanied the closing of the shops and the evacuation of the bazaar. An apprentice locked the door of Salah's shop. I approached him and asked, "What happened to the beaten gold?"

He told me that none of the leaves of gold had been damaged and that, for a few moments, it had seemed to him that their tools were covered with gold. He then placed the key in his pocket, walked away, and disappeared as night fell.

The next day, when I questioned Sultan Walad about the conclusion of that prodigy-filled day, he told me, word for word, that Rumi introduced Salah to the same forms of love and the same favors he had once lavished on Shams of Tabriz. My heart suddenly collapsed. Probably from jealousy, or envy, I'm not really sure. But I also feared the anger and animosity of an entire city that, just as when Shams was present, did not want to see its guide give himself to a single man; a sentiment that was aggravated by the fact that, in this case, the man was an ordinary citizen, someone just like them.

Later that same day, I heard Sultan Walad's words deformed and watered down by one of our own companions. In his mouth the "forms of love" simply became "friendship." Yes, they were already attempting, under the Master's roof and during his lifetime, to moderate and cleanse his actions.

I have often heard it said that "love is divine." I asked everywhere what this meant—personally, I'm not really in a position to know. I'm not so sure that God loves men and, since he is alone and one, I don't really see how he could love. Besides, no one is asking him. At times, however, I have the impression that he loved Rumi and Shams, even Salah.

Sometimes I say to myself that, in that expression, which has been so overused by poets, the word "love" should be understood in its purely physical sense. As if we were to say "sex is divine." The Greeks believed this and apparently so did the Indians, who remain attached to beliefs that are absurd but in which there are glimmers of truth, for they say that the gods are jealous of men because of the physical pleasure that we alone experience. Jealous of men, and even more so of women, for the woman's pleasure, so the Indians claim, along with the Greeks, is greater than any other joy in the three worlds.

Maybe that is why men of worth, after their death, are

received in paradise by young women, who are amazingly beautiful and virgins for all eternity. As if the pleasure of sex was the
supreme recompense for a life of piety and goodness. When, putting
aside these thoughts—to which I know there is no straightforward
answer—I think of Our Master and the extraordinary upheaval
that affected him when he met Shams of Tabriz, I feel that physical pleasure had to play a part.

I am fully aware that certain minds, for whom physical union
is vulgar, contemptible, and probably dangerous—a feeling that is
particularly widespread among the Christians, who have forgotten
that the prophet Jesus, whom they wanted to turn into a god, had
a "beloved disciple" and never got married—consider the act of
love between Shams and Rumi, and between Salah and Rumi, as
inconceivable. They claim this must be viewed as a metaphor, that
this loving union is not physical in nature but amicable, spiritual,
and so on.

I do not share their opinion. I was close to Rumi during those
years; I saw him sing, dance, sweat, cry with joy, remove his
clothes in public and toss them aside, suddenly allow words from
another world to erupt from his lips, and I say that he was a man
with a body, physical, material, and that his true greatness must
also be sought there.

He had managed to transcend the duality between mind and
body, he had unified life, thought, and feeling, he had discovered
the pure source, from which nothing can be rejected or vilified.
Yes, he was a "pot" for Shams's "candle," and that candle lost
nothing of its light. Yes, he was a body that penetrated, and was
penetrated in turn, without experiencing shame or fear, only the
divine joy of existing in totality. And that is just as true for his
relationships with men as it is for those with women. He separated
nothing, excluded no one. Nothing was high, nothing was low.
Nothing was dirty, nothing was clean. When there was pleasure—and he experienced it with Shams, as the fire from the sky
inflames a harvest, and he experienced it with Salah, as the water

from the river drags with it a blade of grass—he accepted it as the greatest blessing. He said, yes, love is divine, and those words assumed an obvious force when they passed between his open lips. He even said that the pleasure we receive, we are obligated to transmit, otherwise it will become our pain and remorse. He said that the pleasure of the body enriches the mind like rain that buries itself within the earth. He said this, he said that, he said a thousand things that I regret not having written down on paper, for my pen is very weak compared to his. I am left only with persistent impressions, very sharp but disorderly, which I have difficulty putting in order.

Besides, do they need to be ordered? I don't think so. Loved by Shams, moved by Shams, possessed by Shams, embraced by Salah, Our Master was a magnificent song in which heaven and earth were revealed, far above complements or reproaches. He had forgotten to be merely a man. He had transcended his own condition. He was the unity of beings.

I do not see why I should dissimulate or tone down the nature of his relationship with Salah, in which he himself saw nothing shameful. Our teaching invited us to comment on what needed commentary and remain silent on what needed to remain silent. But Rumi never tried to classify his love affairs in such an esoteric category, where transmission occurred by means of a vehicle other than language. Far from hiding his affection for Shams, and now Salah, he made it the fulcrum, the axis of our brotherhood. Anyone who refused to acknowledge it was excluded. I acknowledged it and even, years later, will in turn be the principal beneficiary.

At times it seemed to me that God loved Salah, that he was curious about him. I have said it often enough, Salah, the little goldsmith from the Konya bazaar, possessed none of Shams's unchecked idiosyncrasies. Ridiculed for his mistakes in pronunciation and grammar, Salah never grew angry at his detractors. During those ten years of familiarity, I never once saw him angry.

He seemed to be the personification of serenity and stability, the very thing my master, free of the storm of Shams, had need of. In spite of his job, one of the most common, his lack of refinement, and his placidity, so unlike Shams's outbursts and convulsions, it seemed to me that Salah, yes Salah, was loved by God. And it was precisely because he was loved by God that Rumi chose him. In this sense, my master seduced the man whose suitor was God.

It was a winter day. The snow filled my slippers with every step, and the fragile roof of the latrines, where I was headed, nearly bent beneath its weight. As I approached, I heard swearing coming from one of the urinals. I recognized Salah's voice. I held my ear against the whitewashed partition to find out who all this vehemence was directed at. What a surprise! Salah was complaining to the lord of not leaving him in peace even in an impure place. I deliberately did not transcribe all the mistakes of his speech, but in substance Salah said:

"Here, Oh God, I am ashamed of your presence. I know people who burn with love for you and exhaust themselves in retreats, day and night, in physical ordeals, prayer, and sleeplessness so they might be worthy of your concern. But you don't take them into account, you don't resolve their problems, you don't even bother yourself with them for half an hour. And me, you never leave me alone! Not even here! Your pure lights visit me even in the latrine."

Then he was silent. Salah, as he was defecating in the toilet, felt himself in the presence of a superior being whom he identified as God himself. I'm certain he did not realize he was being watched and was actually addressing an invisible presence.

I walked away quietly, remembering the day Rumi had surprised Shams and his wife Kimia in the throes of lovemaking in their bedroom, and, almost simultaneously, had discovered Shams, alone, in the same room. Shams's explanation, as my master reported it, was that all-powerful God loved him so much that he presented himself to him in the form he preferred most, here, as Kimia. Therefore, my master had seen, seen with his own eyes,

God rubbing against Shams, licking his toes, kissing his lips, running his fingers through his hair, absorbing his breath, swallowing his saliva. Yes, Rumi had seen God in the form of a woman in love.

I had just heard Salah swear at God, ask him, like a hunted and harassed lover, for some small space of freedom where he could finally feel alone. That day I understood why Rumi had replaced Shams so quickly. I understood why my master had gone so far as to say to his son, shortly before:

Shams, of whom I spoke so often
Has returned to us, why continue to sleep?

He changed his clothes, and then returned
To display his beauty and advance in glory.

The wine of the soul that you drink from the bowl
Is it not the same wine that flows into the cup?

Cup, bowl, goblet are only recipients.
Only he who knows the wine is worthy of being a man.

Sultan Walad made the following comment about the poem:
"The superior and protective beings are like recipients, and the contemplation of truth, knowledge, and love are like wine."

Years later, I finally understood that after the cup and the bowl, Shams and Salah, the goblet could only be me, when I became the vessel from which Rumi drank, once again, the wine of love.

Careful to avoid being seen, I let Salah leave the latrine and went in after him. Then, I left, crossed the courtyard, my feet buried in the snow and my soul satisfied at having finally been able to remove one of the innumerable veils that interfered with Rumi's passion for Salah. I headed toward my master's cell. The two men were looking at one another intently. Sensing I was on the threshold, Rumi invited me to enter the room and said, while continuing to stare at the goldsmith:

"Observe, in Salah's face, the essence of the king contemplating truth. Behold the guide of the world of the soul, the king of the land of not-where."

I observed, and saw in him the successor of Shams, the domicile of God, the one who changes a drop into a pearl, the smuggler who transforms the trodden dust into gold, the reviver of the tired heart, the donor of the purified soul, the savior from death and extinction, the conductor to the throne of the eternal king, the enlightenment of all secrets, the ascension of earth to the sky . . . and more.

All became clear. In Salah, the beater of gold, the fisherman's son, this simple inhabitant of Konya, owner of a modest goldsmith's shop, I distinctly saw the sheikh of sheikhs, the guardian of God on earth, the axis of time, the Messiah of souls, the spirit of the mystics, the king of the Sufi saints, the guardian of hearts, the Orient of lights, the God of the seekers of emotion, and, as his name so aptly indicated, "the appropriateness of devotion."

I know, thanks to certain Indian disciples, that a similar vision, recited like a universal litany, like a rosary of words encircling the world, was once granted by a divine hero. His name means "black," and I have never been able to remember it. Before the beginning of a great battle, he appeared to his best friend. This man saw him as millions of men throwing themselves into his mouth, he saw him as death and life, as silence, as the element on which everything rests, like pearls on a thread, like the perfume of the earth, the heat of the fire, appearance and disappearance, the luster of brilliant things, and even the deception of the deceiver.

I know that such litanies, which multiply the analogies, the definitions, the praise, are repetitive because the object they have chosen to celebrate cannot be captured by any collection of words or phrases. The words run after the mystery without ever catching up to it.

To my master, who never took his eyes off Salah, I said this, and only this, "I see the one in the other; I see Shams in Salah; I see nothing else."

It seemed to me that everything had been said.

I left the room, shaking my snow-covered slippers against the doorjamb. Outside, the cold that Shams had so feared, no longer concerned me. Shams was in Rumi and now in Salah. He was "within."

I said to myself that the calm, the serenity, and the availability of Salah had been needed so that an ordinary man, like myself, might have access to the beyond, to that brief moment when we feel touched by grace. Shams, in spite of his incandescence, or because of it, gave us no respite. With him, the "lover without a guarantee," we never felt sure, never felt sheltered. In contrast, Salah allowed us to appreciate mystic behavior at length, at our leisure.

So when I described to Sultan Walad my extraordinary vision of the goldsmith, he told me that he had experienced almost the same sensations when, at his father's request, he "bent his head in submission" before Salah and became, for the remainder of his life, his disciple. I asked him to describe to me that moment. He answered:

"It was as if I was drunk. My body and soul were engulfed in light. I did not experience this as a loss but as unlimited perfection. My soul, a small miserable drop, became an ocean. My heart traveled from the bottom to the top. My thoughts developed with time. My spirit took shape. At that moment I saw the prophets in human form, with their heads, their hands, and their feet. I began to speak to them of the mysteries. I was awakened and spoke to them with my tongue, my face. Oh, Hesam, what I saw that day, others will see but a miniscule part of, like a mirage, in a dream."

I realized that Sultan Walad had also seen. And Thiryanos as well.

But others, those who conspired to drive Shams away, the jealous, the narrow-minded, at first temporarily reassured by the absence of the man they considered to be the source of all their troubles, found in Salah a new target. As for Ala, the bad son, he was driven from the house by his father and never spoken of again until his death.

Once more tongues began to wag and the lies began to flow. Those who had reproached Shams for his anonymity, his avidity, his acrimony, his impatience, his unpredictability, now condemned Salah for his lack of education and modest origins. How could the Master of masters fall in love with some ordinary inhabitant of Konya whom everyone had watched grow up? They remembered the time when, still a child, he helped his father with the net, and the day when, with the help of a loan from a bank, he set himself up as a gold worker in the bazaar. His detractors, the same as before, went so far as to find out the name of the bank and the terms of the loan. How could Rumi order his son to follow a man who owed money to the Jews and who had succeeded, after endless negotiation, in getting the interest rate lowered by one percent? The gossips also said that Salah, advised by those same Jews, regularly sent his money, the little he earned, to India, to Delhi, where, ever since the Mongol threat, the capital from all the exiles and travelers in that part of the world was sent.

Already, the slanderers were accusing the Master, who had dissolved in Salah like "sugar in milk." They said: "Rumi sees only Salah. He doesn't take his eyes off his face and is interested in nothing but him. Night and day he prostrates himself before him. Everything he owns is for him. He covers him in gold, silver, and beautiful clothes. . . . a fortune, which the other sends to his account in Delhi. This Salah is worse than Shams. At least he knew how to speak and write and the proper expressions. This one has grown up among us, does not know writing, or grammar, or proper pronunciation. He is incapable of answering the simplest question. Yes, we're beginning to miss Shams of Tabriz."

Others even went so far as to say, "At least the other came from Tabriz. He wasn't from Konya, wasn't one of us."

Salah, who continued to return daily to his shop, saw fewer and fewer customers. His lender revealed the reduction of the interest rate and his gardener quit, tired of picking up the garbage thrown by passersby. On the streets of his own city, he was shoved, insulted, humiliated, and treated like someone who once mingled with the animals and now looked down upon the famous.

He knew his fellow citizens like the back of his hand and was not frightened by their spitefulness. Unlike Shams, he did not get angry. He ignored the hostile gestures and attempted to maintain his happiness and peace of mind. In fact, I heard Salah, a man who never dared attempt display such prowess, quote some wonderful verses by Khayyam:

Hell is a spark of our pointless suffering.
Paradise is a moment of our calm.

The universe is a glance from our past life.
Jayhun[1] is a trace of our purified tear.

He never gave in to pointless suffering. He never nourished his own nightmares. And I can confirm that, while my master burned in Shams's absence, it was only the "calm" of Salah that brought him back to us, to poetry, to dance, to life. Otherwise, like all incandescence, his would have been a voyage of no return.

Although Salah appeared confident, the rest of us feared the violence. As with Shams, the uncertainty, the pretense, the secrecy, the lies, the closed doors and spying, in spite of Salah's claims to the contrary, occupied our daily lives.

One summer evening, when the blue, saffron, and white mosquito nets decorated the terrace and the odor of *kiara*, the rarest of Japanese incense, quieted our minds, Thiryanos picked up a flute and played a melody to which Rumi, a few days earlier, had improvised these lines:

---

1. A river in Central Asia.

Who is it, in the middle of the night, who has come like
    moonlight?
It is the prophet of love who from the place of prayer has come.

He has brought a flame, which burns sleep.
From the place where the king of kings of the sleepless is
    found, he has come.

A ring of keys is held beneath the very arms of love,
And it is to open wide the doors that he has come.

The porter came to tell us that an unknown man, breathless, was asking expressly to see the Master. His message couldn't wait or be revealed to anyone else. He was admitted. The man who entered the room was short, chubby, about sixty years old, and limped slightly. He expressed himself in halting Persian and seemed to be wary of those present. His gaze ran from one point to another, suddenly his voice grew silent and his nails sought to penetrate his flesh. After the customary prostrations, he began to speak:

"Master, I cannot stay long. I would be risking my life if someone were to denounce me. I have just enough time to tell you that the life of Sheikh Salah is in danger, that there is a conspiracy against him, a group of plotters has decided to abduct him, sequester him, torture and kill him."

He had barely finished speaking when Salah burst out laughing, shocking those present. In a lively voice, without a trace of fear, he said, "The blind who have begun to plot against me, do not realize they cannot act against the will of God. No one, if God is my protector, will succeed in killing me or drowning me in blood. You think that in this world I am a worthless man, but in reality what bursts from my heart becomes an ocean. If my king, my master, keeps me inside, why would I go outside, why would I show myself at the door?"

That last phrase reminded me of Shams's departure and

Rumi's authorization for him to leave the house, even though he might find him dead on the other side of the walls. It was clear that Salah was alluding to that consent. Like Shams, he knew he was loved, but he also knew, unlike Shams, that he was indispensable. While the departure of the first seemed imperative to Rumi, the constant presence of the second calmed and comforted him.

Temporarily distracted by these thoughts, it was with some difficulty that I was able to come back to the thread of what Salah was saying.

"I am the mirror in which Rumi sees his own face. How could he, who is in love with his own beauty, do otherwise than to choose himself? Between us there is no duality, for we are one."

I heard, in Salah's mouth, the same words once spoken by Rumi about Shams. Before my eyes, love, the lover, and the beloved became confused, became one in a whirlwind of words.

Our informer excused himself and asked if there was an exit other than the main gate. We showed him to a hidden door in the basement, which connected the kitchen to an alley that ran uphill.

In spite of Salah's assurance, Rumi ordered me to take steps to ensure our security. From one day to the next, we implemented the same procedures we had used for Shams: we checked the identity of everyone who entered, refused visits, stopped holding meetings, restricted our own comings and goings. Salah agreed to Rumi's decision. By general consensus it was more prudent to avoid danger than to provoke it, even if we felt protected by all-powerful God.

In the goldsmith's bazaar, no one whirled. No reprimand addressed to the Creator could be heard in the public latrines. Nowhere in the city did one encounter the spiritual guide who spoke hesitantly and mispronounced his words.

This ended up by tiring the conspirators. In the city it was said that the plotters had grown calm, had "cooled off." The invisible wall we had imposed upon ourselves now worked against them, hounded them in turn. Whenever they were seen in the street, they appeared worried, tired, thin and desperate. There was even a rumor to the effect that many of them had begun to lose sleep.

One day, the former conspirators, and a number of other inhabitants of Konya assembled before the entrance to the school. The crowd appeared to be troubled. Their heads lowered, tears in their eyes, their voices trembling, they begged the Master's pardon and again proclaimed their submission to him. This went on for hours. Rumi had no visible reaction. Even Thiryanos, the unrepentant of the disciples, the man who maintained an implacable hatred toward the envious, softened a bit. I saw a few sparse tears cross his bony face, covered by a thin black beard on which the white hairs were still rare.

While mentally counting his white hairs, two at the left corner of his lip, one on his chin, I asked him why he had given in. He said to me, "The solitude of those men has liquefied like wax the stone of my heart."

My master opened his arms to them. They prostrated themselves and remained on the ground for a considerable time. Later, one of them told me that at that very moment, they felt the barriers come down and their sorrow vanish at once. They felt they were growing wings and feathers. They felt they were being born again as infants. They saw the world of the soul, they saw themselves dematerialized, they saw wisdom bubble up in their chest, intelligence replace ignorance. From shadow they became light, from mourning they became celebration, from the dark night they became the brilliant moon and from scrub brush a rose garden.

Salah helped them up one by one, the longtime companions, who were brought up practically in the same street, near the shore of the same lake. He had never felt his life to be in danger. The danger could not come from those men. He told them that.

They let themselves be kissed by him and went their ways. The God who questioned Salah even in the latrine had, among other things, ensured him of Rumi's love and his own. Yes, a simple goldsmith from the Konya bazaar knew he was loved by God and his greatest poet.

Our children are our hearts walking on the earth

FOLLOWING THE RECONCILIATION BETWEEN RUMI, SALAH, and the people of Konya, we were finally able to make preparations for the wedding of Sultan Walad and Fatima, Salah's daughter.

We had been anticipating this marriage for a long time, ever since the day Rumi and Shams had taken refuge in Salah's house and Sultan Walad had been able to visit Fatima, who was still an adolescent but already a visionary. The wait had been long. The girl's age was the main reason, but also the disappearance of Shams and the grief that had affected our brotherhood.

For a while now those in the school spoke with increasing frequency about the marriage. I first met Fatima in her father's house, during Rumi's retreat with Shams. I wanted to escape the animosity of the envious, the curious, and the narrowminded. She was twelve, an age when young girls could still walk in the courtyard, run in the corridors, and play in the street without criticism from the precepts of our religion. We observed a young, barely veiled creature make her way through the house, torn between a girl who still sucked her thumb and a devotee, who was already strolling along celestial pathways. I recall that she ate very little, at most once a day. Shams had seen her remain standing for an entire night.

We felt that the child born of the union of Sultan Walad and Fatima, mixing the blood of Rumi and Salah in its veins, would embody a love that I can only qualify as divine. As for the inhabitants of Konya, perhaps they saw in the marriage between the son of the Master and the daughter of one of their citizens, the union of Rumi with the city.

As for me, Hesam the accountant, I was responsible for getting the money together for the celebrations: preparing the ceremony, assembling the trousseau, planning for future gifts. This time, experience came to my assistance and I had no difficulty in putting together a decent amount. Kera, my master's wife, used all her skills as well. For more than a month the best cloth merchants in the region, whose trunks were filled with brocades, silks, and veils, thronged our school. Makeup artists, hairdressers, and masseuses set up shop in the interior apartments, whose door banged continuously from the constant coming and going, allowing us to catch a glimpse of the charm of female life. From within we heard the sounds of the daf and the rabab. Sometimes we even heard Kera's voice, humming her husband's poems.

On that blessed autumn day, Sultan Walad was twenty six and his wife sixteen. Shams had been gone for four years.

The day of the celebration, I took Sultan Walad to the hamam, where he was washed, massaged, oiled, perfumed, and shaved. Dressed in new clothes and sitting on a richly harnessed horse, he arrived at the school, where dozens of friends greeted him with hurrahs. Barely inside the gate, he crossed the main gallery, thronged with important guests, and entered the room where, once before, Shams had wed Kimia. It was a small, quiet room. Inside, his father, Salah, and Fatima were waiting. The marriage verses were recited by Rumi. This too reminded me of the other wedding.

Then, Rumi held out his right hand, the palm open to the sky. On top of this Fatima placed her own hand, then Sultan Walad his, then Salah, whose hand sealed the union.

A tent had been set up in the courtyard for the guests. Ministers, governors, and administrators showed by their presence that they approved of the union, as well as the union of Rumi and Salah.

Sultan Walad greeted them and asked them to take their places on the sofas arranged around the tent. Then the servants entered and set a small table before each guest, covered with a tablecloth of embroidered linen on which was a porcelain plate and a silver knife. They first served a cold appetizer of gazelle marinated in vinegar, whose preparation Kera had personally supervised. After this was served lamb, partridges, and a house specialty, breast of veal cooked with marrow and egg yolks. For dessert there was a cake of almond paste and pomegranate seeds. I saw to it that even the humblest guest—for there were not only notables present—had finished his food before ordering the servants to bring in basins, ewers, towels of fine cloth, and flasks of rosewater. The guests were then able to wash and perfume their hands.

Once the meal had been served, Rumi and Salah introduced themselves. For the first time in a very long while, I saw on my master's face a mark, not of sorrow or pain, but of joy, lightheartedness, and relaxation. Salah, as always, appeared impassive and placid.

When I gave the order the musicians, singers, and reciters entered the tent and, almost at once, the sama began, its principal participants being Rumi and Salah. The celebration lasted all night. As he whirled, I saw and heard my master chant these lines to the glory of the dance of the world:

Blessed be our feasts and our weddings in the world.
God has sewn for us these feasts and these weddings.

Venus loved the moon, the sugar loved the parrot.
Let us celebrate the weddings of our handsome king each
    evening.

To begin, this evening, so cool, you make your way to the
    wedding ceremony.
You become the son-in-law of the good, as you are good,
    ornament of the city.

You walk gaily in our street, you walk with grace toward us.
Quickly, you jump across our stream, you, our stream and
    seeker.

Cruel you can be, but I cannot. Demand fidelity.
Place the foot of conquest on our blood purifying breath.

Dance mystics, dance! You who are just, spin around!
Around the fortune of the king of the world, the breath-giving
    king.

Drum around my neck! In the wedding chamber, flowers and
    jonquils.

For tonight the drum will be our most beautiful creation.

Later, my master would tell me that on that night he had the
impression that in paradise the archangels had also begun to
dance. He added that Fatima, his daughter-in-law, had seen what
he, Rumi, had felt. Yes, she had seen the houris play the kettle-
drums and, seeing the celebrations, rejoice. He would also say that
the grace felt that evening was the same that accompanied the
meeting of Adam and Eve, Jacob and Joseph, the guest and the
cupbearer.

The period following the wedding was peaceful. It was nothing like what had happened after Shams's marriage. In fact, where
was Shams?

Rumi would say that he had become Shams, that Shams was
none other than himself. He sung this night and day, so much so

that we often grew tired of hearing it. I watched him as he whirled, his eyes half-closed and his body covered with sweat, utter the name of Shams like a divine incantation, thousands of times.

Still, although he had merged with my master, where was Shams really? When we stopped looking for him and closed the door to the false informers, I felt something deep within my heart tighten, as if we had officially lost all hope of ever seeing him again.

It's possible Rumi saw Shams in himself. He said so, loud and clear, in all his ghazal, and that is why he apparently chose a different man, a different love, with such ease. But I, Hesam, where could I see him? I missed Shams. And the gentle, the imperturbable—except when he railed against God in the latrines—the serene Salah could hardly satisfy the loss.

The arrival of Fatima, who was immediately installed in the interior apartments, was like a pleasant awakening in our certainly peaceful but somewhat somnolent lives. She upset our rules and our complacency. We never saw her eat or sleep or gossip. It was said her food was celestial, that her mattress stretched across the firmament, and that she spoke with those from another world. Eyn, the daughter of the disciple Moin Soleyman, the Mongol stooge, and Princess Gordji, whom Fatima continued to visit, exhausted herself talking about her miracles. Fatima was the one who tore the veil, she was the filter through which one could see all things. And Eyn was not the sort to deny celestial visions.

Ever since the marriage, the poor, orphans, and widows had besieged the school. A day didn't go by without her opening the door to the needy and stuffing them with fine food or covering them with, occasionally luxurious, clothing. Thus fed and clothed, they became so unrecognizable that, when they left, other beggars, taking them to be well off, harassed them in turn in search of a few dirham. This happened daily. A throng of real poor pursued a throng of fake rich, and the poor, after a brief stop at the school, temporarily became as rich as the others. They too, in turn, had to fend off the outstretched hands of the ever-present beggars.

My master, who, upon Shams's orders, had stopped all teaching, now isolated himself with Fatima, resuming the training he had interrupted. Every day I saw her enter my master's room, sometimes even toward nightfall. She would stay there for hours, dancing, playing the rabab, and talking about the I who is not the Self. The rest of us, former disciples, would have liked to benefit from the initiation, even for a short while. But we knew that the doors that opened before her were closed to us forever. I heard rumors to the effect that Kera, who had gradually learned to control her jealousy toward the men who frequented her husband but could not tolerate any female competitor, had reprimanded him sharply about his relationship with Fatima. Thiryanos even heard Kera shouting, crying, and lamenting, then screaming again before growing calm, after a long talk by the Master. Thiryanos, drawing closer, managed to hear Rumi's answer to his wife, "Oh, Kera, Fatima is a part of me. Our children are our hearts who walk upon the earth."

The following day, when Rumi left that part of the house known as the *andarouni*, the women's apartments, to return to the *birouni*, reserved for the men, we searched his face for signs of fatigue, the same signs we had seen a few years earlier when, following some inattention toward Kera, he had to honor her, as she herself claimed, seventy times in a single night. Although the figure seemed to us exaggerated, the fatigue and overwork on his face indicated, just like that distant morning, a night of intense activity.

Once Kera's threat had passed, my master had to settle a difference between Sultan Walad and his wife. Fatima sometimes took advantage of her popularity among the poor and her special place in Rumi's heart. She went wherever she pleased throughout the house and paid no attention to whether or not her veil protected her completely from the gaze of strangers. Addressing a man, she would look him straight in the eyes, without any of the reserve shown by the other women, who turned slightly to the right and lowered their eyelids. On the contrary, Fatima opened her eyes wide. She gave the impression that she dominated our bearded confraternity, which she deigned address with her eyes and her words.

On several occasions I surprised Sultan Walad in the process of criticizing his wife, of reminding her of propriety and humility. It was a complete waste of time. She continued to wear her veil negligently and gaze boldly at those who addressed her. The couple even argued in public. Once, at a meeting, Sultan Walad raised his voice and, Fatima, much to the shock of everyone present, did the same. It was the first time a woman's cry—cutting, strident, sharp, sustained—pierced that assembly of men, and for a long time afterward it resonated in their ears, which had been deafened by the lengthy and profound muteness characteristic of women.

Fatima's cry dispersed the disciples, chased the husband away, stunned the wives huddled outside the walls, and impressed my master. Far from blaming her, he advanced toward her, caressed her hair, and said, "Be what you are. I know that at no time, at no moment, would you elicit passion, or jealousy, or need for the surveillance unfaithfulness demands."

Her hair was so black it appeared blue. Upon her neck she wore thick coral necklaces. Her rings covered the entire length of a finger. When she moved, her bare feet, stained with henna below the ankle, lovingly caressed the ground. She evoked a standard gloriously raised above the gates of a conquered city, on the roof of the palace where the king resides, on the mast of a warship. How could one demand of a banner that it hide or withdraw from sight?

That imperious flag demanded a thousand amazed glances. Unfurled, it floated and danced upon improbable heights. Sultan Walad, the solid base, seemed to ignore the proud movement of that standard and the haughty Fatima considered herself, in her husband's hands, like a bird that has been captured with great difficulty and quickly abandoned.

To settle their disagreement, my master, a stubborn admirer

of the young woman, dictated a letter to me for his own son:

"I am sending you these recommendations concerning our young princess, the clarity of our hearts and our vision, and of the entire universe as well. She has been given to you on deposit for a very difficult trial. The divine spirits, who watch over their children, are keeping an eye on her. It is your duty to honor her as you did during your wedding night and to treat her as you did the day you saw her for the first time, still a child, seated on a horse, seeming to ignore the whole world and probably the Creator himself. Understand that during the hunt that takes place with the net of the heart and soul, your quarry has not yet been captured. Understand that, along this path, you must tirelessly search, run, beat the bushes, flush out, advance, drive out, advance again, track down, search once more."

I gave Sultan Walad the letter, which defined the position of the hunter and the prey. For a while, Fatima, although sensing she was within her husband's coils, was convinced she had also escaped his grasp. Captured yet free.

The reconciliation was short lived. Sultan Walad again began to demand that his wife submit completely to the rules, that she be discreet, and conceal herself beneath a veil, while Fatima spent hours discussing with Rumi the problem of the divine verb articulated in human speech. Obviously, the prey and the hunter did not share the same territory. They argued again, and again my master felt obligated to intervene. I can see him locked in a room for an entire day, writing a letter to the woman he considered the most brilliant of his students, his own daughter-in-law, Fatima.

Years later I was careful to copy the letter in which he stated to the young woman that her sorrow hurt him ten times more than his own. He wrote:

"If my son continues to torment you, I will tear my heart from him, I will not answer for his safety, he will be banned from my grave. You worry about gossip. But you should know that the sea is not soiled by the dog's mouth, that sweet bread does not depreciate in the presence of a fly. Know too that I will never accept the tears, the excuses, the oaths and arguments of those who criticize you. In return, I expect that you tell me everything, for you are the victim. Tell me everything so that I can, to the extent possible, come to your aid. You are, in the world, the temple of God's safety."

The couple was reconciled. However, like us, for years Our Master continued to listen to Sultan Walad complain about his wife, about the "clarity of her heart and her vision." He accused her of fickleness, of indifference, of infidelity, and of attempts at seduction. For years Rumi defended his "princess whose nature was pure, the very essence of patience and tenderness."

The marriage between Rumi's son and Salah's daughter sealed their union. I often saw my master refer to Salah's two daughters as "his right eye" and "his left eye." Fatima, the right eye, gave birth to a son, who embodied the special love that existed between the two grandfathers. Every time my master picked up the child, his thoughts inevitably turned to Salah.

Hediyeh, the left eye, the younger sister, had reached the age when she was beginning to attract the opposite sex. Nezam, the calligrapher, fell in love and wanted to marry her. I was the first in whom he confided his still secret desire. For a long time he had been planning to marry Hediyeh, whom he met at the school. However, she was not yet ripe enough for marriage.

For quite some time I felt that Nezam was troubled by some secret torment. This could even be seen in his art. The line of his brush revealed a buried anxiety and the shape of his letters, like birds or wild animals, lacked weight and bearing. Eventually, I asked what was bothering him: his health, his finances, the Mongol yoke that weighed on us all? No, nothing like that. I became increasingly inquisitive and, contrary to all the rules of etiquette, questioned him about his love life. He broke down. He told me that for years he had been in love with Hediyeh. Her age—she was too young for anyone to ask her hand in marriage—had, until then, reassured him, allowing him to view their possible future together through rose-colored glasses. But of late, Hediyeh showed all the symptoms of a girl ready to respond to the matrimonial verses. She flirted, she blushed. That was the real reason for the sudden collapse of the characters from Nezam's pen. I reassured him at once and promised to ask Sultan Walad if his love was reciprocated, if my master's left eye was eager to gaze graciously upon the face of the famous calligrapher.

It was not long before he had an answer. It came in the form of a drawing of a nightingale whose beak traced the word of acceptance. The lines drawn by Nezam returned to their former firmness and serenity. A single thing bothered us, Sultan Walad and myself: Salah's financial inability to prepare a decent trousseau for the girl. Already, for the marriage of Sultan Walad and Fatima, Rumi's family had closed its eyes to his insolvency and accepted the resourceless bride as a celestial offering. But Nezam was not Rumi's son. The entrance of an impoverished Hediyeh into a traditional home could threaten its future well-being.

Sultan Walad and I decided to ask for the Master's help. After listening to our concerns, he ordered me to contact the governess of the sultan's daughters, a woman named Ousta. This was done.

Ousta, an educated woman, soon showed up at the school. She did not even wait for the official escort; she came on foot, breathlessly, hurriedly, for Rumi's order had a sense of urgency for her. My master let her catch her breath, then said to her, "Go see Princess Gordji for me and tell her that I am counting on her to assemble Hediyeh's trousseau. For this, her highness can ask the help of the wives of the emirs and their daughters, and encourage them to make donations. The gift will guarantee them Salah's favor and protection."

Ousta agreed and, removing her gold and emerald bracelet, shaped like an elephant's trunk, she placed it before Rumi as the first stone of the trousseau. Upon her return she refused to enter the royal coach, which had finally arrived at the school. She ran through the streets of Konya, a basket around her neck, shouting,

"Something for God!"

When she reached the gates of the palace, her basket was already half full with pieces of gold and silver. But this was not enough. She headed directly for the apartments of the sultan's sister and told her of Rumi's request. Princess Gordji thanked God for providing her with such a wonderful opportunity to display her generosity. She ordered her treasurers to open the coffers where the most valuable garments were kept and had them remove, in lots of five, various articles of clothing.

Another was told to choose, from among the court's jewels, ornaments that evoked the bride's innocence. The maid stood an hour before the treasures, then presented the princess with twenty pairs of earrings decorated with diamonds, twenty rings of emerald and ruby, bonnets made of fabric woven with gold, veils of silver thread, and bracelets of precious stones, so heavy that a woman could barely wear them. Princess Gordji spread them before her on a white tablecloth and looked at them for a long time. Each object bore a memory. One of the veils reminded her of her engagement to Moin Soleyman, the Mongols' liege. She wore it proudly that day, the way a fox displays its silvery fur, and yet had but one desire, that her husband remove the veil, along with all the other garments that hid her soft, ardent body, filled with a thousand desires.

The diamond earrings had been a young girl's treasure. When still an adolescent, she had discovered her mother's jewelry box and insisted that she give her some of the jewels, which, according to rumor, were priceless. Her mother gave in to the demand, although out of place, of an overly insistent, overly curious young girl. Later, upon her mother's death, when she was given the entire contents of the box, she replaced the earrings in the empty compartments and remembered, not without remorse, her earlier stubbornness.

The bonnets were from Mongolia and brought back memories of the visit of a female shaman, who had come from the steppes. In offering her the strange headwear, she revealed to her that the bonnets were shaped the way they were, long and high, to carry snakes. She herself never traveled unless one of the snakes was placed beneath her high bonnet and wrapped itself in the maze of her thick hair. Princess Gordji wanted to test the shaman's claims, but in her absence, to avoid any ridicule. She was brought a snake, one that was not venomous, which she placed in her hair beneath a bonnet made of gold thread. With this on her head, she walked for a long time and spoke as normally as possible to her entourage, without revealing to them that with every movement of the snake, her entire body began to vibrate, awakening—to her great surprise—all her senses. New and irresistible sensations. After removing the headpiece and releasing the snake, her fingers helped satisfy a desire whose urgency had grown insistent.

Princess Gordji inspected the jewelry, wanted to remove several pieces, but those memories, joyful or sad, prevented her from choosing. How could she abandon what she had worn for her engagement, give up the bonnet that had been the origin of so many pleasures? How could she forget the affront to her mother when she had insisted on having the earrings, and the tender consent of the woman in suddenly abandoning the jewels?

With a broad, conclusive sweep of her arm, she ordered that all the jewels be given to Hediyeh. Before the astonished eyes of the servants, Ousta the governess picked up a large part of the jewels of the sultan's court. In gathering them, she wondered about the fate of those rings and those clothes, which from a princess's jewelry box or the remoteness of the steppes would now take their place in the modest armoire of the wife of a calligrapher from Konya.

Hediyeh's trousseau grew by the hour. The most influential women of the city filled the halls of the interior palace. Before their arrival, as Princess Gordji rummaged through her memories, the eunuchs had been busy spreading rose petals and jasmine branches across the carpets, covering the sofas with soft cushions and filling the incense burners with lengths of aloe or pieces of ambergris.

In the courtyard, shaded by plane trees and elms, the visitors, carrying bags of various sizes, descended from their litters and, dragging with them their veils, which tried to rival the shades of autumn, entered, with their indolent, nonchalant gait, the interior of the palace. The stone building, dominated by a tower, whose fortifications were decorated with jasper and whose walls with gilt arabesques, was located in the center of a group of buildings: a residence, baths, kitchens, and gazebos.

One of the donors wore a veil of green velvet and her walk resembled the gentle agitation of a cypress shaken by the wind. Barely inside the palace interior, she removed her veil and her gem-encrusted slippers. She held out her diaphanous hands to the black, Mongol, and Turkish servants so they might spray them with rose-water from Isfahan, Shiraz, and Samarkand. She crossed the long corridor leading to the reception hall. There, she folded her veil and slipped it into a silk shawl, handed to her by the slaves at the entrance. She sat down alongside other important women on the sofas and, without delay, removed from her bag, which was heavier than all the others, a clanking mass of gold bowls, plates, and kitchen utensils.

One of the other women related to her the latest fable making the rounds in Konya, the story of a well that was said to have sheltered the twelfth imam of the Shiites since his disappearance. Rumor had it that the well could arrange the marriage of young women if they made a vow of submission to the hidden imam and spent forty nights, nights of doubt, solitude, and anxiety, near the dark cavity. While relating the story, the woman in question inspected with an inquisitive eye the offerings of her neighbor and compared them to her own: sheets, coverlets, and precious fabrics spread across the floor and spilled onto the rug.

A Mongol princess whose hair, plaited with threads of gold, caressed the ground, arrived with a pair of chandeliers, platters, and a chamber pot of solid silver. She was tall, and her broad shoulders impressed the other women. As soon as she had entered, they all asked the question that had been on their minds: was it true that, in crossing Iran by horse from east to west, from one burning town to the next, she had never been separated from the eagle of the great Khan, on whose right shoulder it perched? She responded amicably in her halting Persian, displaying a smile of gold teeth. On one of her incisors Princess Gordji could make out a cross. She questioned the woman about it. The mother of the Mongol donor was, in fact, Christian, more specifically, a Nestorian. As she licked the incised cross with the tip of her tongue, she revealed that she never traveled without her portable church tent, in which she could celebrate the office and pray whenever she wished.

A black slave brought a platter covered with appetizers: walnuts, almonds, figs, prunes, dried apricots. After prostrating herself before the mistress of the house, she asked if she too might participate in their blessed generosity and garnish the trousseau of the Master of masters' left eye with the only ornament she possessed: a toe ring given to her by her mother before she left her home and the sky of her village for good. The princess brought her hand near the curly hair of the slave, whose head still touched the floor in a position of humility, and gave her permission to donate her ring. She covered the black woman's hair, which beneath the caress of her hand felt like a dense forest, with a cloth of embroidered gold that rasped whenever it moved. The negress raised her head, and the reflection of the precious metal on her dark face dazzled all the women present.

Ousta, the governess, took the pieces that would be used for the trousseau of Salah's daughter, had them loaded on mules from the royal stable and sent them to Rumi's school, where I was to receive the treasure. As far back as my memory goes, I can recall nothing like it. Even my mother, who had lived with wealth, could not have imagined such abundance.

Rumi himself came to inspect the trousseau. Astonished, he

ordered that it be divided in two. Salah's elder daughter, the one he referred to as his right eye, had been content to marry Sultan Walad without the shadow of a dowry. Knowing Fatima's character, he wished, by this gesture, to avoid a conflict within the family. I noticed Sultan Walad smile. His father's order had just saved him from hours of criticism and conflict.

The other half crossed, on the backs of those same mules, the narrow streets of Konya to adorn the calligrapher's modest home. A stunned Nezam filled the cubbyholes of his workshop with the most beautiful jewels of silver and gold. When he placed the clothing and the tall bonnets in the old trunk in which he had formerly kept his precious writing instruments, his hand grazed the cold, stiff body of a snake, which he had temporarily mistaken for a reed.

The serpent was waiting to fill the tall bonnet of the bride. This was, among the ancestral practices of the steppes, part of the lengthy apprenticeship toward pleasure.

Thus the wedding between Nezam the calligrapher and Hediyeh—Salah's younger daughter and Our Master, Rumi's left eye—took place. And then . . .

And then Salah's mother died one day in spring when the streets were filled with the heady scent of acacia blossoms and the shadows of the porters pierced the long, straight alleyways.

As if she were a sister, Kera, the wife, took care of the funeral ceremony. It was she, not the family of the deceased, who placed the body, covered with a sheet, on a silk-covered litter. Four men chosen by her carried it to the mosque. She hired the best singers to walk before the procession. And, in an unusual gesture, she herself left the house for the first time since Rumi had blamed her for a superficial outing and the old curse had made her chronically sensitive to the cold, wrapped in black fox fur even in the middle of summer. Walking at the head of the mourners, she displayed to the entire city her devotion to Salah's family, and silenced, simply by her presence, the pettiness of tenacious jealousy.

A crowd joined the procession as it made its way through the city. When, preceded by cries and lamentations, the hired mourners arrived, with their blackened faces and thin hair, Kera asked them to be quiet. For a few dirham she obtained their silence. Obviously, silence cost more than noise. When they arrived at the portal of the mosque, the singers stopped and the body was placed, by the four men with long beards and pallid faces, before the mihrab. Having remained with the women in the courtyard of the mosque, Kera murmured the orison for the dead. After this, Rumi stood by the feet of the deceased and recited the funeral prayer. In his mouth even the divine words bent to his rhythm and I secretly feared he would begin to dance, there, before the corpse, intoxicated by the words of the Koran. Custom required that the prayer be recited by a descendant from the male line. Absent such a successor, the ritual fell to a linear descendent. Today, for the first time, in spite of the presence of the son of the deceased, a friend recited the divine word. This too came as a surprise.

When the religious ceremony was over, Kera, at the head of the procession of women, accompanied the corpse to the hamam and recommended that the attendants wash the dried flesh as carefully as the skin of a young bride. Washed three times with water and jujube leaves, powdered with camphor, its armpits shaven, covered with a cotton loincloth and wrapped in two sheets, the body was put back on the litter to be carried to the cemetery. There, the gravediggers placed the cadaver on the ground, its face turned toward Mecca and an unbaked brick beneath its head. When the grave had been covered over, they placed upon it a roof of bricks that rested on four pillars, a gift of Salah's brotherhood.

After returning to the school, Kera ordered that the doors be opened and that a feast be prepared. Food was distributed to the poor at the other end of the city, while in the reception hall the guests chanted, along with the singers, selected verses from the Koran.

During this time, the cemetery grew dark and the visitors

stepped quickly among the graves. Rumi and Salah, motionless above the brick roof, watched the circumvolutions of an earthworm that slowly, and with difficulty, burrowed into the fresh dirt and began the long work of physical decomposition.

When they had lost sight of the worm, Rumi said to Salah, "Come, let's go."

Salah bowed and, without moving, said to his master, "She has many claims on me. I want to protect her against the terrors of the grave and her fear of the angels of death. Because of her fear of the grave, I ask you that she not be left alone. I ask that she be accompanied by the houris. After that, I will leave."

An hour passed. The two men remained motionless. Then, Salah smiled, looked at Rumi and said to him, "Now, I can return."

There, in the grave, the deceased was no longer alone.

Dance on the way to my grave

THE SULTAN EZ AL-DIN HAS BEEN ON THE THRONE A SHORT time and his minister, Esfahani, has benefited from the immense privilege of assiduously frequenting Our Master. He often told the sultan of the spiritual benefits of those meetings, without managing to affect his deeper sensibility. The sultan, a skeptic, asked for proof. The minister argued, but in vain.

One day, while Ez al-Din was hunting in the plain of Konya, he saw a small snake crawling by the edge of a lake. Unseen by his retinue, he grabbed the snake and placed it in a small gold box, a present from the emperor of Constantinople, which he always carried with him. Upon his return to the camp and once inside the royal tent, where the most precious fabrics decorated furnishings adorned with gold and precious stones, he gathered ministers, nobles, and philosophers. He questioned them about the content of the box, which was carefully closed.

"Look carefully at this box. It was given to me by the Christian emperor of Constantinople to acknowledge the authenticity of our religion. He specifically asked me, 'If your wise men correctly identify the content of this box, I will know that your religion is the true one.' Now, discuss, think, meditate, interrogate the stars or whoever you wish, but tell me what is in this box."

After closely examining the box, which they weighed and

sniffed at, some of the men went off by themselves to think, others formed committees and debated in groups. The administrators consulted the archives. The ministers went to the prisons and questioned their former colleagues, holding a towel over their nose so as to avoid the foul odor of the filthy, lice-ridden bodies of the inmates. But the elderly prisoners knew nothing of the content of the gold box. The astrologers unrolled their maps. The sky itself was questioned but failed to provide any answers. The seers aligned their frogs and practiced divination with them, a novelty that had come to them from China: the croaking frogs corresponded to the vowels and the tadpoles to consonants. This too resulted in failure for no comprehensible word was supplied. The frogs were silent about the snakes.

As everyone was getting ready to celebrate the afternoon prayer, Minister Esfahani asked for an audience with the sultan and invited him to visit Rumi so he might unravel the mystery.

Riders on fast horses came to inform us of the august visit.

Panicked at the idea of the royal intrusion, we ran around trying to make preparations to welcome the sultan with splendor and solemnity. Our Master was the only one to remain perfectly serene. As for Salah, he was still in the bazaar, in the process of closing his shop, as he did every evening. At dusk the royal cortege finally arrived at the school.

We showed the monarch into the *sama khaneh*. This was the first time I had had the opportunity to observe the sultan close up. He wore his official garments, a tunic of scarlet silk, closed with emerald, ruby, and diamond buttons. In his hand he held the box with its indecipherable secret as if it were a scepter or an imperial eagle.

Salah, upon his return from the bazaar, entered the room. Our Master invited him to sit next to him. It had been a long time since any of us were surprised that the goldsmith had been given this place of honor. He bowed before the sultan, then sat silently next to Rumi.

Pointing to the gold box, the sovereign asked Our Master what it contained. Rumi turned to Salah and said, "Let our Sheikh explain the mystery of the box." Without hesitating for a moment, Salah again bowed to the sovereign and said to him:

"Oh, sultan of Islam, why do you go about accompanied by a small snake? Why do you force this unfortunate animal to undergo such pointless imprisonment? I know, Oh sultan, that the real reason for your visit is to test my master. But he, he knows the contents of the heaven's coffers, the distant regions of our planet, the hidden thoughts of creation, and the secret of divine enigmas. Why should he be concerned with your box and your snake?"

At that moment I saw the sultan uncover his head and become a disciple of the most obscure of his subjects, a humble goldsmith from the Konya bazaar.

My master ordered his musicians to begin the sama. At the first sound he rose and drew his lover into the whirl of the dance. The sovereign and his retinue waited until the end of the ceremony to return to the palace. In leaving, Ez al-Din, the Shadow of God on Earth, leaned toward his minister and said, "If his disciples have such power, what greatness must there be in his life, his intelligence, and his mystery?"

The minister did not respond. It had been a long time since we had tried to explain certain arcana and were silent about the perception of the supernatural. There were no words to express the inexpressible.

At the corner of a small street timidly lit by the glow of dawn, the sultan opened the box and let the snake out. The snake, after some hesitation, resumed its customary movement. On the ground, the twists and turns of its body traced the name "Rumi."

In the year 654 of the Hegira (1256), the Mongol general Baydu attacked Anatolia. His troops laid siege to Konya and the inhabitants of the city, familiar with Mongol tactics, anticipated the worst forms of death, and feared they would be raped, strangled, burned alive, hacked apart, cut into pieces, devoured. Everyone imagined death in their own way. The situation seemed hopeless. In the bazaar, people stopped haggling over the price of merchandise. In the hamam, no one supervised the cleanliness of the baths. Everywhere, the flowers, neglected by the gardeners, began to fade. The students deserted the schools. The muezzins forgot to announce the prayer. Children refused to suckle at their mother's breast, and thieves returned their plunder to its grateful owners. Mice barked, dogs meowed. A woman gave birth to a turtle. A Turk suddenly began speaking Chinese. Stains disappeared from clothing. Fish jumped out of the river. Cows began eating meat. A banker went to the bazaar, bought some brocade, and began to sew.

From the other side of the ramparts the Mongol conquerors prepared for the assault. No one doubted that victory, like an abandoned lover, would run to their arms. But we also knew that the Mongols were never content simply to conquer an enemy. For them, the real war began after the battle, behind the front, within the cities. They waged war only to pillage.

In the school, however, all seemed calm. I never found my master questioning Salah, who, because of his profession, was more aware of current events and the Mongol threat. Naturally, the price of gold had risen dramatically. But that as well never entered into the discussions of the lovers.

During those dark days, a crowd of citizens came to the school. They came to ask the Master how they might escape the sinister fate the Mongols had in store for them.

Rumi left his cell, put on his slippers, adjusted his turban, which had come undone from his incessant whirling, and addressed the crowd gathered in the courtyard, from the height of the gallery that ran along the cells.

At once I drew from my gathered sleeve paper and pen to write down his words:

"Do not be afraid. For you are the gift of God to Sheik Salah. As for the city, the destruction and the Mongol swords won't trouble it until the hour of resurrection. Whoever attacks Konya cannot escape the wounds we inflict on them. Know too that as long as the earth of Konya holds my father's blessed remains, this land is protected against all calamities. Yes, this city will be one of the most famous in the world and our descendants will live here in safety for all time."

He then returned to his cell, took off his slippers, removed his turban, picked up his cat and caressed it for a long time, unknotted its fur, and said to Salah, "Those people believe that destruction, death, annihilation, disarray, and fear are the work of the Mongols. But they are ignorant of the truth."

I then saw my master rise, place his arms on the wall for support, roll his head from side to side, and sing the following verses, in which the universe and man, when on fire, are but one.

If it escapes, the lover's breath, and strikes the universe of fire,
That universe without origin, it will dissolve into particles.

The entire universe becomes sea, out of fear that the sea will
    turn to nothing.
Neither man nor humanity remain when man is struck.

A pillar of smoke rising to the sky, neither people nor angel remain,
And from that smoke suddenly he strikes the great roof with fire.

The moment when the sky is rent: neither being nor place remains,
A movement in the universe strikes mourning with celebration.

Sometimes it is fire that takes the water, sometimes the water
    that devours fire,
From the sea of nothingness the waves strike the black or the white.

The sun becomes infinitely small in the light of mankind's breath.
Expect nothing from the uninitiated, where the initiate is so humble.

Mars has lost virility, Jupiter's book is on fire,
No more majesty for the Moon, and its joy beats a melancholy
    rhythm.

Mercury falls in the mud, Saturn is wrapped in flames,
Venus has lost its bile and beats a joyful rhythm.

There is no rainbow, no sky, there is no wine, no cup,
No pleasure or joy, and the balm is struck by no wound.

Water will make no patterns, the wind no longer sweep,
The garden will not shout: joy to you; cloud of April: not a drop.

There is no pain, no cure, no enemy, no witness,
No flute, no rhythm, no lyre beating the sharps and flats.

All causes are annihilated, the wine steward serves himself,
The breath says, "Oh my great God!" and the heart says, "Oh
    God who knows!"

I watched my master whirl to the rhythm of the ghazal, one
of the most beautiful he had composed until then. At the same
time, I observed Salah and realized that the real threat came not
from the Mongol hordes screaming beneath our walls but from the
breath of the lover, which would dissolve the universe into particles and suppress men and angels, indistinguishably, as they lead
themselves toward nothingness.

Season followed season. Konya was spared by the Mongols
because it represented God's gift to Sheik Salah. Once again winter spread across the land of Anatolia, its cloak immaculate and
cold, the kind of cold that once pierced Sham's flesh—the man who
blackened his nails and bent his back—and now entered through
the cracks in the windows of the rooms of the school, all the way
to Salah's bedside.

Illness was killing the goldsmith. We all knew it. While awaiting death he had only one visitor, Rumi.

My master spent an entire night with the dying man, sharing
prodigies and strange secrets with him. At dawn, when he left him,
exhausted and in despair, the room already marked by death, I
waited for him in the long gallery that led to his bedroom, a bowl

in my hand. He took a few sips of tea, then grasped my fingers, which, in comparison to those of the dying man, must have felt on fire to him. He then looked at me with gratitude. During such moments, words were pointless.

The gallery was short and I knew our steps were numbered: no more than three and the door to his bedroom would be before us. I realized that after fifteen years of day-to-day familiarity, I still desired, passionately prayed, that our arrival would be delayed, that the three steps would stretch into four, or even five or six, that the all-powerful God I had served throughout my life would amuse himself in fulfilling my wish.

I counted one, two, three, and the implacable door blocked my path. My master entered his cell and I walked down to the courtyard to leave the school and return to my home and my family.

Along the way I recalled the ten years that Salah and Rumi had spent together. One was leaving and the other simply accepted the fate, which like the autumn wind, had struck Salah, "the wandering Cypress."

Ten years earlier I recorded the departure of Shams during another night of cold and snow, after a series of affronts forced upon him by the Master.

While walking in the snow I could still hear Shams's voice shivering with cold during those dreadful days when Rumi, deliberately provoking their separation, was preparing his own conflagration.

"It is indeed you, yes you M, who said that I am disagreeable, that I am bad-tempered. Suffering gushes forth from me, for you have made my soul your country. The soul is seduced if it encounters the desire to embrace, kiss, and caress, presented in the form of a poem. Within me are signs of absolution. Soon I will fall on the other side and will drown in absolution. The signs are there. Yes, I see them, they are there."

And a few days before his disappearance, Shams said to me, "Winter is coming. Shams needs a coat."

I don't recall having bought him the coat he asked for. My main concern for the entire period before his departure had been to protect him from aggression, to make sure he never walked out of the gates of the school alone. Yes, his coat was worn but I was thinking only of avoiding unpleasant encounters. Is he still cold today? Why, suddenly, does my former negligence in getting him a new coat torment me, as I walk along the snow-covered road to my house? Salah was dying and I was reproaching myself for a former slight toward Shams, who may or may not have still been alive. As I walked, I recalled Shams's departure and Sultan Walad's announcement, "Suddenly, he has gotten away from us." I remember Thiryanos adding, "Yes, suddenly he's disappeared." And I, who felt the house empty of his presence, heard Rumi hum:

> He lit us like a candle; where has he gone?
> Where has he gone without us?
> Every day my heart trembles like a leaf:
> Alone, at midnight, the thief of the heart, where has he gone?
> Like a madman I wander through the desert:
> In that desert, the stag, where has he gone?
> He is with us, even if he is with others.
> Since he is not here, where has he gone?

Salah was dying, and that night as I walked I saw, as if lightning had suddenly set the dark sky on fire, only memories of my master's first encounter. My feet plunged into the snow, I crossed Konya's dark streets and passed old cats indifferent to my presence, caused dogs to bark, and heard the voice of Shams saying to Rumi, "I made a pact with joy. My pact is that joy is mine."

The howling of the icy wind, the wind that prevented Shams from straying outside the school during winter, did not prevent me from hearing my master's approval:

If you are in love, abandon sorrow;
Behold the wedding feast and abandon mourning.

I could hear him say:

The flower's destiny is laughter.
What can we do if it has no tears?
Because of him, jonquils and flowers
Grow in my awakened heart.

My heart is the house of joy.
What can I do if I am not sad?
I flee all that is morose in the world,
I resent hatred.

At that moment Salah was dying. I was told that before passing away he reminded Rumi that when he, under the influence of Shams, had decided to stop teaching, to stop calling upon God, the only being who succeeded in getting him to give a final sermon was not the sultan, or the vizier, or his beloved son, but the offspring of a simple fisherman from the village of Kamelah, who had become a goldsmith in the Konya bazaar, Salah himself. He then added:

"Cover my corpse with all sorts of drums, the *dohol*, the *kous*, and the daf. Go to my grave gaily, drunk, and clapping your hands. Go to my grave dancing."

He then closed his eyes and traveled from the "world of forms to the nowhere of spirits."

With his own mouth Rumi received Salah's last breath. With his foot he struck the beat of a song of mourning and recited the following poem, where each verse concludes with the word "cry":

In your absence the earth and sky cried.
Sitting in blood, reason and spirit cried.

Sad, I don't have the strength to speak.
To describe how all of these have cried.

You were a hundred universes and not a single being.
Yesterday I saw the other world for this world, cry.

Gone from sight, sight has pursued you.
The soul, following sight, tears of blood did cry.

Oh, King Salah, you have gone, swift sea eagle, good-luck charm,
Flown like an arrow, the bow has begun to cry.

Over you not just anyone can cry,
That someone must know, over great souls how to cry.

When, that same night, I was urgently called to the school, the musicians were still gathered around the Master, who sobbed and danced. In spite of the sound of the drums and other instruments announcing the *besharat*, the good news, no one, among those who had been called expressly by Rumi, dared begin dancing. Then, sensing our hesitation, he grabbed my hand, then that of Sultan Walad, then that of Thiryanos, and drew us into a mad, interminable dance. We danced until daybreak, until the first glimmer of the day star caressed the face of the man my master had called, for the past ten years, "the Orient of light."

On 1 *Moharam* 657 (December 29, 1258), as the snowflakes slowly covered the velvet covered stretcher borne by the city's dignitaries, my master, his head uncovered in mourning, followed the funeral procession and the eight groups of reciters. As they walked, he practiced the sama and turned. Beneath his feet, the trodden snow formed spheres, globes, and circles. The group of mourners slowly rid itself of its expensive coverings, offering the clothing and turbans to the beggars scattered here and there throughout the procession.

In the mausoleum, near the tomb of Rumi's father, a burial vault awaited the corpse. The beating of the drums and the voices of the reciters covered the whispers of my master, who chanted the funeral verses. The litter bearers, members of the corporation of goldsmiths, those who, during Salah's lifetime, had never missed an opportunity to denigrate him, now prostrated themselves on his grave stone and asked absolution.

An adept of the Master, the new sultan, Rokn al-Din (1257-1266) was represented by the nobles of his court and the highest military authorities. Among them was an officer I recognized, in spite of his look of sorrow and sense of reserve. Yes, it was him. The man who had come to express the condolences of his sultan and pretend to appear saddened by Salah's death, was the same man who, years earlier, had humiliated and demeaned him, and had wanted to see him dead.

The Book of

Hesam

Find the measure of words

I T IS NOW TIME TO SPEAK ABOUT MYSELF—NOT THE EASIEST thing to do. Salah's death wiped away Shams's disappearance. No one, except the Master, mentioned that distant month of cold and frost, when, by uttering that simple phrase—"it's the best thing to do"—Rumi handed Shams over to his enemies' knives. I am certain, today, as I write these lines, that Shams of Tabriz was not murdered that evening. Was he wounded, jostled, or simply admonished? We'll never know. Ten years have gone by and we still don't know where he is, who he is with, or what crazy ideas continue to torment him.

At the time of Salah's burial, as the drums pounded, I thought of Shams, of his sparse beard, his frail, weak body, his animated walk, his hot breath, his sharp words, his self-confidence, even his high-handedness. He appeared and disappeared with the rhythm of the drums. I saw Shams when he was silent, impenetrable, magnanimous, but also when he was troubled, angry, abrupt; the man who could stay seated for hours on end without saying a word, but who suddenly would begin talking and prevent anyone from getting a word in. The man who spoke in enigmas left such a strong impression on us that we constantly wondered where he really came from, what part of the divine vibrated within him. The sound of the daf revealed to me a Shams who esteemed science but found no benefit in the search for truth, who refused to recognize the Sufi rites, such as shaving the head, the invocation of the divine name, and solitary retreats. Yet, at the same time, he was the man who tirelessly repeated to me that mystic exploration requires a teacher, a guide, a pir. The drum continued to beat and I saw, fleetingly, the man who could tolerate only obedience and submission from his friends, whom he treated cruelly.

I recall his words, shortly before he left Rumi and Konya, "Nothing will come from our friends. They have made no effort. It would be better if we were to go, as soon as possible, to the other world in order to prepare levels for their use, so that their punishments there might be eased."

Salah's body, wrapped in a white sheet, was covered with dirt. The different drums united to lead us toward ecstasy. The Master's voice chanted the suras of death, accompanied the circular movements of the dance. And I, Hesam, suddenly asked myself why Rumi never once pronounced Shams's real name: Mohammad, son of Ali, son of Malekdad of Tabriz. Yes, as the Turkish masons arranged the bricks around the corpse, I heard the Master's voice questioning Shams, years before, about his identity:

"Shams of Tabriz! Tell me who you are!"

And Shams answered, "I am God. I am God. I am God."

The tears in the eyes of Sultan Walad on that day of mourning did not prevent me from suddenly understanding the poetic gifts of my master when, wishing to use the word "God" in a ghazal to describe Shams, he found he was short one or two feet in a line. As if obeying his order, God's qualities helped complete the rhyme. I remembered, although he never once called him by his true name, some of the titles given to him, a list that would be inexhaustible: "The breath of the breath of breaths, the king of kings, the secret of truth, the index of God, love without end, the messenger of nowhere, the light of the Prophet, the jewel of joy, the pure spirit, the fire of love, the painter of China, the summary of being, the summit of the invisible, the perception of truths, the shelter of the world of discovery." I have already enumerated some of those glorious titles, which serve as a litany of Shams. I could cite many more.

For Rumi, his lover was the sun that for six centuries, from the disappearance of the Prophet to the appearance of Shams, had soaked the world of spirits in wine. His place was inside the grotto of revelation, while truth remained outside, the guardian of its secrets. To find that Shams, body and spirit had to be transcended, the veil of love had to be slashed, the two hundred stations had to be navigated. In my mind I ran through those many stations as the last mourners left the mausoleum of Rumi's father. A guard blew out the last candle lighting the room. The tomb, concealed behind a pile of percussion instruments, disappeared before our eyes.

What can explain the fact that, shortly after Salah's death, the man who replaced him, the man who, according to his instructions, became the guide for the community, and embodied Rumi's love was none other than me, Hesam, son of Mohammad, son of Hassan, the modest narrator of this work?

Yes, shortly after Salah's death, Rumi called me into the very room where he had once withdrawn for forty days and forty nights with Shams, the forbidden room, the room that drew the curiosity of those who, like me, had remained outside, alert to the smallest sound, the least sign of a presence. He suddenly asked me to cross the threshold of revelation and the arcane.

I crossed knowing that behind that old wooden door, splintered and dark, other worlds awaited—the world of secrets, the world of light, the world of spirits, of souls, the world of material bodies, the world of the mystery of mysteries, of phenomena, of creation, the world of the imperative, the world of the deity, the world of the visible domain, the world of sovereignty.

I felt that, behind that creaking door, the veils would fall and the vision, the true vision, the vision of the heart, would be granted to me.

I entered the doorway. I saw my master seated as usual, leaning against a pile of cushions, lit by a number of candles, and surrounded by musical instruments, his cat asleep on his lap.

I penetrated that familiar room as if I had never seen it before. I had known my master for a dozen years. I had seen Shams appear and disappear. I had known that Shams coupled with God. I had also seen the poet come to life in Rumi before my eyes. I had heard Salah curse God in the latrine. For a long time, I had recorded these upheavals, as an observer, a listener, never one of the elect.

As I entered the room I suddenly forgot my fear and uncertainty. I forgot that, for twelve years, my most profound desire had been to cross this threshold one day and find myself exactly where I was. Everything seemed to be welcoming, accessible, manageable. I could hope that my master was going to love me intensely. I even felt that God, yes God, would visit me, as he had done for Shams and for Salah.

I am unable to tell you whether it was hot or cold that day. But I know that the candles appeared as bright as a thousand suns. A single flame gave birth to dozens of halos, and the room, so small, so dark, seemed to be inundated with light, and gigantic. I could see no difference between my master and myself. The self no longer existed. I knew that this feeling of peacefulness and impassivity would be short lived but even that didn't disturb me.

After a few moments—even time had dissipated—Rumi spoke the following lines:

> Cloud of gentle rain, come!
> Drunkenness of friends, come!
> You, the king of fakers, come!
> Those who are drunk salute you.
>
> Astonish, wipe away pain,
> Destroy, and offer treasures,
> Find the measure of words,
> Those who are drunk salute you.

You have astounded the city;
It knows everything and nothing.
Because of you the heart is lucid.
Those who are drunk salute you.

I was able to complete each verse, even before the first stanza
had ended. The words intended for me exited his holy mouth and
it seemed to me that it was I who was speaking. Even that did not
surprise me.

Then, my master turned his face aside, addressed an invisible
listener, and continued:

Tell the moon-faced prince
And tell this talismanic eye,
Go, tell the beneficent king:
Those who are drunk salute you.

Tell this rebellious prince,
Tell this worry, this anxiety,
Tell this green cypress:
Those who are drunk salute you.

Tell this peerless breath,
Tell this trap for Madjnoun,
Tell this hidden pearl:
Those who are drunk salute you.

Tell the flame to repent,
Tell the tailor of my *kherqeh*[2],
Tell the light of my journey:
Those who are drunk salute you.

Tell the candle of the Koran,
Tell the feast of sacrifice,
Tell the pride of paradise:
Those who are drunk salute you.

---

2. A garment worn by dervishes.

Then, once again, he looked at me and continued:

Oh, king Hesam,
Pride of the prophets,
You who initiate breath!
Those who are drunk salute you.

In love I was most visible,
More deceitful than all the others,
Happier than those who stole my heart!
Those who are drunk salute you.

Behold this spiritual unrest,
And the rising waters of the flood,
Behold the divine sun!
Those who are drunk salute you.

I threw myself at his feet. His cat woke up, or pretended to, climbed down from his lap, stretched, yawned and arched its back, and with a delicate swipe of its paw, opened the door, against which it rubbed itself and walked out. I was alone with the Master of masters to observe the unrest of the spirit. I felt my hand become one with his, my hair mingle with his clothes, my breath lose itself in his mouth, my toenails bury themselves in his socks. That evening, my master Djalal al-Din Mohammad, whom Shams simply called M, made love to me.

In the morning I left the room. I saw Thiryanos, my long-time friend, leaning against the wall of the gallery. Our eyes met. We were the same age, about thirty, we both enjoyed physical exercise, and for twelve years we had both breathed the exalted air of the school. Seeing me leave that room, he knew immediately that I was someone else. Between us, not a word was exchanged and, yet, all had been said.

I knew that from now on I would have to confront the bitterness and resentment of those who were in league against Shams and Salah, those who suspected Shams's origins, that "nameless dervish without a name or a sign," and humiliated Salah by reminding him that he came from a family of fishermen. In that sense I knew that those who preached "poverty" night and day, the kind that is acquired after intense effort, those dervishes who claimed that the true king was the one who overcame his desires, had nothing to reproach me for. My father, Mohammad Akhi, master of a chivalric brotherhood, was universally esteemed during his lifetime. His properties and furnishings, which I quickly sold after his death to marry Shams and Kimia, still helped maintain our school. For those dervishes who praised poverty but humiliated ordinary folk, I had come from the world of wealth. They wouldn't attack me from that point of view.

But in Thiryanos, I detected a new deference in his attitude. Out of his past as a thief and criminal, he had retained a particular vocabulary, which I sometimes experienced. The words he used came from a world of men, where love was never intended for wives but for prostitutes, where a woman was called a "house," where a contract was made by leaving a hair from one's mustache on deposit, where men who thought nothing of stabbing one another broke down in tears at the sight of a dying pigeon.

During those twelve years of friendship, Thiryanos had initiated me in their way of life, took me to their gymnasiums. He had taught me their gestures and their language. When we were alone, we often expressed ourselves in this way.

That day, when I discovered a more attentive Thiryanos, I at first thought that, to abolish the distance, I would dredge up a word from those unsavory slums. I held myself back. His esteem was sincere and I had a duty to respect it. That same day, others, including Sultan Walad, although without direct orders from the Master, came and prostrated themselves at my feet. Yes, I saw my master's son, the grandson of the Sultan of the wise, kneel down and kiss my feet.

Had I changed? Was I touched by the grace of God? I couldn't say. But I felt that I had just been born, that I too loved all the

details of the world, that I was now pure compassion. A smile
never left my lips and yet I was able to perceive the Earth's suffering whenever a leaf fell.

Without leaving the school, my master gathered his principal
disciples and told them that I was now his lieutenant. He said:

> As the sun fled far from that dark night,
> Change occurred when the lamp arrived.

> Behind the cloud the moon is hidden,
> Who but the star will give light?

Of the three lieutenants, which is the most eminent, asked one
of our companions? Rumi answered:

> Oh, traveling companion,
> Shams was the sun and Salah the moon.

> King Hesam, the sword of truth, is the star.
> He has united with the sovereign.

> View them as one and the same being,
> For each will help you reach God.

> No matter which you prefer,
> You will succeed and die no more.

> Submit to him,
> Agree to pluck your feathers.

He then placed his hand on my head, and added:

> From now on you are caliph and lieutenant.
> For in this circle, there is no duality.

Sultan Walad rose and also showed his submission by saying:

> My father made this man sit in the place of the other.

On his head he poured light upon light.

In one night, in one day, chosen to explore the ways of love, I had suddenly become sheik, pir, caliph, guide, master, the bearer of love, that individual, that parcel, that atom from which love would spread over the immense world, limitless, unrestrained, indiscriminate, a love defined only by itself.

My friends looked at me through Rumi's eyes, in which I could read the passion he felt for me and, passing through me, his love for the entire universe.

Later, my master brought me to the attention of the city and the court. In this, he repeated, although differently, what he had done many years earlier, when, on the day the Koranic school of Qaratay was inaugurated, as we argued about protocol and the places of honor, he went and sat down in the least desirable corner, the one where the guests left their shoes and where Shams of Tabriz was sitting.

Moin Soleyman, former director of the Koranic school and husband of Princess Gordji, had become Emir Parvaneh, and ruled over the entire sultanate in place of the monarchs. In spite of his power, he always remained a fervent disciple of Our Master. That day, he had organized a gathering in his palace that brought together the most distinguished inhabitants of Konya, one of whom, obviously, was Rumi. I was not invited and took advantage of that rare moment of leisure to remain in my garden and teach horticulture to my children. Emissaries from the emir appeared at the end of the alley. They came over to me and asked me to accompany them at once to the palace. Along the way they told me that Our Master, since the beginning of the reunion, had been looking weak. So the emir thought of summoning me to comfort his guide, who, in my absence, had said only the following:

Speech is like milk in the breast of the breath.
Unless there is someone to draw it in, it does not flow agreeably.

Having arrived at the palace, the emir kissed my hand and, holding a candle in his left hand—the index finger of his right hand moving constantly between his mouth and his nose—led me to Rumi. Upon seeing me, he jumped up and addressed me in these terms, "It is you, my soul, my faith, my light, my master, the beloved of truth, the lover of the prophets!"

Dumbstruck, I left the assembly and withdrew to be by myself. Seeing me sitting in the courtyard, a place hierarchically situated below the *talar*, the reception hall, Our Master came down the steps and took a seat beside me. By doing so he transformed a subaltern corner into a place of honor. I heard the envious whisper, "Why does such a man sit in an inferior place, when everyone's position is assigned according to rank?"

I thought I was the only one to have heard those bitter words, when Rumi, pointing to me, answered them, "Hesam is a torch. If he desires elevation, it is not for himself but so the others can benefit from his light. In other words, wherever a torch is found, below or above, he is a torch."

That evening, the dignitaries of Konya looked at me, Hesam, the same way they had once looked at Shams—with envy, hate, curiosity, admiration, and respect—while Our Master had, quite publicly, left the place of honor to sit near his friend.

Listen to the cry of the flute

LIFE RESUMED ITS FORMER COURSE AT THE SCHOOL, WITH A single difference—I was sitting in Salah's place, I was sitting in Shams of Tabriz's place. Time passed without interruption and yet my surprise at my own situation remained. Thousands of questions ran through my mind without my being able to answer the one, true question: "Why me?"

Slowly, with time, always time, I stopped deafening myself with questions and let myself enjoy the holy presence of the Master. As before, I continued to write down his poems, to note his prodigies and daily routines. I tried to use simple words to express the extraordinary metamorphosis of a remarkable being without hiding his human condition, without hiding his sexual tastes, his exaggerated enthusiasm for raw garlic, which he added to bitter milk curd and ate with stale, moldy bread before celebrating the sama, his ability to remain for days in the hamam under streams of cold water or submerged in hot tubs, his cult of silence. In his poems he made increasingly frequent use of the word *khamoush*—silence—to refer to himself, a sort of pseudonym.

I wrote everything down, noted everything. This included the observation that Rumi constantly celebrated hunger and compared an empty stomach to the flute that, in spite of itself, utters cries of desire.

I have to mention his cat, his countless flutes and drums, the crowd of devotees whom we dispersed with false promises, the sultan Rokn al-Din who, like a docile child, submitted to his orders and called him "my master and father," Moin Soleyman, the faithful among the faithful, whom I had surprised prostrate before Rumi, although he had become the most powerful man in the sultanate, and, finally, the city of Konya, spared by the Mongols because it represented the gift of God to Salah the deceased goldsmith.

One night, as I again read, by the light of several candles, the *Conference of the Birds*, my master came to join me. His complexion was as sallow as ever but, since Salah's death, his face also bore traces of suffering for the departed friend. Thiryanos said he had become Salah's double. Fatima, his step-daughter, during one of her frequent nights of insomnia, mistook him for her own father, uttered a cry of terror, and fainted.

With his sallow complexion and his face, which looked like a portrait of Salah, Rumi sat by my side, although no flame was able to animate his skin. At the very moment when his knee brushed mine, I had the most terrifying thought: What terrible grief would Persian literature experience if Rumi died without leaving a single work behind?

My master saw all, understood all. He asked me, very naturally, what was bothering me. I didn't want to upset him but, at the same time, I knew he wouldn't allow the conversation to drift, for "the opportunity passes as swiftly as the clouds."

I bent toward him and said, "Collections of poems have multiplied and their lights have spread across land and sea from East to West. But the words of all the poets would be wiped away by another voice, the one expressed in a book, composed like Sanai's *Divine Book*, but using the meters of Attar's *Conference of the Birds*. If that book existed, it would remain with humanity forever, it would become the accomplice of the breath of lovers. It would reach the summit of compassion and grace."

I had just expressed my deepest desire, like the desire of a childless woman who asks a man to inseminate her. I referred to the meter of the *Conference of the Birds*, of the contents of Sanai's book, although I felt, with my entire being, the torment of a woman, a woman hungry for a child. I spoke to him, I heard my voice pronounce sensible words and, at the same time, filled with anxiety, I sensed his refusal. It was the same apprehension a childless woman feels waiting for the man's response.

I had barely finished speaking when my master raised his arm and drew from the end of his blessed turban a sheaf of papers, which he held out to me. Surprised, I took it and began to read. As I have already remarked—but I want to repeat it—I discovered, written in his own hand, eighteen verses composed according to the meter of the *Conference of the Birds*, whose meaning summarized for me the mysteries of parts and wholes. Realizing that I suddenly held in my hands the very sap of mystical literature, and realizing that those verses would soon be our Koranic verses, I read and reread the first line:

Listen to the cry of the flute as it is separated from the reed.

Rumi had just inseminated me. I experienced the joy of a pregnant woman. I brought the papers to my lips, then my eyes, and kneeled before him. He forced me to rise. He felt the shiver that ran down my spine. No exercise had so deeply affected my body, trained though it was in archery, fencing, wrestling, and clubs, as much as this. To appease me, he placed his hands on my stomach. At once I felt my master flow into my veins and calm my shaking. He had become my blood. Then he said, "Even before you thought of making this request, even before nature demanded it, an order from the visible and invisible world had slipped the thought of composing such a collection into my heart. Now, come, fly on the peaks of your inspiration, fly toward the ascension of truths, imitating the Prophet, and reveal his true intent. For the intentions of our heart cause our intelligence to vibrate and lead our mind to find the words we need."

He stopped for a moment, then continued.

"If you write, I'll compose."

I wanted nothing more. That was my true intent. My life was now inscribed among the lives of the elect. Did I deserve such a privilege? I didn't know. I stopped asking myself questions. I became my master's pen, I would transmit the essence of love.

Once again my body trembled. Rumi's hands, still resting on my stomach, were of no help to me. I felt like a fertilized woman, but this time I was not just any woman, I was Mary into whom the divine breath passed.

I again prostrated myself and kissed Rumi's hands and arms. My tears fell upon his elbow, which I was especially fond of, for I had often held on to it when I was exhausted from the sama.

In that state of prostration, my head buried in my knees, I heard him compose a poem that I learned by heart. It was intended for me:

Oh light of truth, Oh sword of faith,
Because of you the *Masnavi* will surpass the moon.

Oh hoped-for spirit whose noble ambition
has caused this *Masnavi* to appear God alone knows from
    where.

The Masnavi, you carry within you
Continuously, you pull it where you will.

The Masnavi, flowing, attracting, invisible,
But invisible to the fool who has no eyes.

As you were the source of the Masnavi,
If it grows, it is you who has made it so.

We were going to call the work the *Masnavi*, which simply means a poem composed of couplets. From that day on, and until his death, Rumi was constantly creating. Whether he was dancing, bathing, moving or still, he composed and I wrote, quickly. Once, he spoke from nightfall until dawn, without stopping, without realizing that the quills were breaking under the pressure of my fingers, because I was writing so fast.

He often asked me to read the poems to him. When the first volume was complete, after having corrected the words and adjusted the prosody, I read the entire collection to him. This time I was a mother proudly displaying her child.

When I finished reading, I heard him say to me, "Feed the child of the soul."

In 1260, as he did every year, my master left for the hot springs. In mourning because of my wife's death, I decided, this one time, not to accompany him and to remain in Konya to look after my children. But I knew how his trip and his stay would turn out, since I had accompanied him the previous years. He was gone from Konya for more than six weeks. Whenever he left a great celebration was held. For the occasion, the road itself was transformed into a sama hall throughout its length, where the mountains and vegetation replaced the walls of the room. All along the road the faithful danced, the musicians, on foot or on horseback, struck their drums, and the singers recited poems. In the middle of that extraordinary convoy, the Master composed ghazals or completed his *Fihi Ma Fih*.

However, that year, his stay extended beyond the customary fifty days. I began to grow impatient when suddenly, one evening, I had the strange sensation that he would return the next day. I had no doubt about the accuracy of my intuition. I was certain. I had the school cleaned, perfumed the cells, bought a supply of garlic, and sent the women to the baths. I asked his close friends to accompany me to the caravansary of Rouzbeh to welcome the Master.

In the morning an immense procession formed. Big and small, young women and old dervishes, soldiers and poets lined up, each of them holding a welcome gift in their hand. We left Konya and, after several hours' travel, reached the caravansary. As soon as we arrived, I had a tent for Rumi set up in a field. Then, we waited. The hours passed. Nothing happened. Everything was calm. Goats grazed in the pasture, farmers gathered cotton. The only incident to occur during that lengthy wait was the appearance of a flock of geese who were chasing a student. I finally began to wonder if it was reasonable to lead hundreds of companions so far from the city on the basis of my intuition alone.

Gripped by doubt, I jumped on a horse and galloped over the countryside, along the road I assumed to be the one Rumi would take. At times a voice within reassured me. I had never acted capriciously. In the school I had always had the serious job of serving as accountant, scribe, and secretary. I was a long, long way from Shams's mood swings and Salah's eccentricities. God had never shown himself to me in the form of my wife and he had never provoked my anger in the latrine. This presage about my master's arrival, which had come to me the night before, could only correspond to reality. After one or two hours on horseback, I returned to the caravansary of Rouzbeh.

There, I saw Rumi's tent inhabited by his holy presence. There he was. My shout was certainly one of joy but also one of relief, and, especially, of satisfaction. I suddenly realized that I, the copyist, the writer, the treasurer, could also receive messages from the invisible.

He walked out of the tent and I first noticed his eyes underlined with very black kohl. It took me no more than a moment to notice that he looked very well and was much less sallow than usual. I got down from my horse and threw myself at his feet. He was barefoot. His arms seemed ready to embrace me.

I cannot say how long we remained wrapped in each other's arms. After a while I felt his bare feet, at rest on the damp grass, shiver, and I freed myself. Together we entered the tent whose decoration I had personally managed. The light from the candles lit the cushions, the blankets, the rugs, and some musical instruments lying on the ground.

I sat facing him in silence. I then clearly heard, with the ear of intelligence, the bird of my soul—if I can call it that—in the cage of my chest, cooing in the presence of my master's spirit. The voice of Rumi's spirit entered my soul and stole my intelligence, preventing me from speaking. I recalled a passage from the *Masnavi*, composed one morning as my master was rubbing his teeth with a mixture of mother-of-pearl, egg shells, and crushed charcoal:

The melody of the song that escapes the pure body,
At every moment, reaches the sensitive ear.

It follows a path unknown to humans,
It is not of the world that forms inhabit.

The companions do not hear it. He, he hears it.
Happy is the soul that gives itself to the invisible.

I too began to give myself over to the invisible. I had had a premonition about my master's arrival although there had been no news about him and I heard his voice without a single word being exchanged between us. I was present at the birth of the "sensitive ear."

The writing of the *Masnavi* continued, in spite of an interruption of two years following my wife's death. When she was alive, I rarely noticed her presence. Dead, her absence became unbearable. I had married her and ignored her. During our marriage, I spent most of my time with the Master. For I knew that what he had allowed me to experience, the immense privilege of following in the wake of the man whom the angels themselves were jealous of, provided a different kind of grandeur than my married life. Everything that astonished me, transformed me, intoxicated me, took place in the company of Rumi, in the school or elsewhere. Nothing like that happened in the garden of Faliras where I lived, surrounded by my family. In the garden, aside from Rumi's visits, life followed its usual course. My wife's death disturbed the tedious ritual of ordinary life. I realized then, although too late, that I loved her.

After her death, I began to question Fatima, Sultan Walad's wife, and even Kera, my master's own wife. I wanted to know how they supported their husbands' remoteness, their constant unavailability. After all these years neither woman had grown accustomed. Fatima had immersed herself in study and, to draw Sultan Walad's attention, she created, almost continuously, opportunities for conflict. Kera, whom I had great respect for, but toward whom I felt equally guilty, for I had deprived her of her husband, was more assured. In the beginning, when Shams was around, she reprimanded her husband and demanded a kind of compensation, insisting he pay greater attention to her. In fact, I recalled how, after a period of abandonment, she had held on to Rumi the way a starving animal clutches its prey, and had forced him to honor her more than seventy times in a single night—I have mentioned this before but I repeat it here because the number seems so exaggerated.

Over time she realized that Djalal al-Din Mohammad Rumi held himself above marriage and infidelity, that the man, whom she reproached for his lack of concern, spoke with God himself.

For two years I mourned for my wife, two years during which I tried to cut myself off from the Master to give my dead wife the time I had deprived her of while alive. Rumi understood this need and temporarily stopped writing the *Masnavi*.

One day, upon awakening, I felt detached from the thought that had connected me to my wife. I hadn't forgotten her, but the feeling of heaviness and numbness had disappeared. Over the next few nights I felt that my mind was no longer tormented by her, that I could wake up and drink a glass of water or urinate without brooding over her words, without imitating her gestures. I was finally free of her.

When we returned to writing the *Masnavi* and our former habits—chewing garlic, spending hours in the bath, talking to the trees, dancing to the point of ecstasy—Rumi composed the following lines as a prologue to the second volume:

> For a certain time the *Masnavi* was delayed,
> It takes time for blood to become milk.
>
> As long as a new child has not come into the world,
> Blood does not turn into sweet milk; listen.
>
> Like Hesam, the Light of truth
> Has turned away from the sky, has turned his bridle,
>
> Having ascended to the high truths,
> In the absence of his spring, the buds were silent.
>
> But when he came from the sea to the shore,
> Melody enclosed the *Masnavi*.

While I had felt overwhelmed by my feeling of clumsiness toward my wife, Rumi placed me at the pinnacle of heaven, "ascended to the high truths." I wrote down the lines and saw that, he too, considered the *Masnavi* as the child I had longed for. He compared my period of mourning to the time needed to transform blood into milk.

Once again, I wrote while Rumi danced, washed, walked, or dozed. At times he would transpose into his poems the questions I asked him, whether he spoke of his hunger, his travels, or everyday events. So I would always be ready to write, I had asked the best leather worker in Konya to make me a large leather wallet, more flexible than my old wood box, into which I placed sheets of paper, bottles of ink, and reeds.

One night I dreamt of Balal, the Prophet's muezzin, who was

wearing the Koran on his head, and of the Prophet himself, who carried the *Masnavi* on his breast. As soon as I awoke I asked the Master about this. He said to me:

"The Koran is a splendid wife, with a graceful forehead, decorated with jewels, free of defects, but veiled and masked. That wife only removes her veil when she discovers the capital of faith free of crowds. The *Masnavi* is a thief of the spiritual heart. It resembles a finished garden. It resembles a digestible dish prepared for men whose hearts are clear, for lovers whose livers are on fire. Happy the breath adorned with the vision of that invisible beauty. Hesam, the one who wants to understand The *Masnavi*, wander in its appearances and obtain the secrets of its secrets, must have great faith, be stable in love, genuinely sincere, peaceful in his heart, extremely intelligent. He must also master the sciences. But even without those accessories, if he is, in spite of all, a true lover, his love will serve him as a guide."

On that day I understood that love was the key that would open the *Masnavi*.

Once, during winter, he came to my home in Faliras and asked me to prepare a room for him where he could spend a few days without being disturbed. I put him in a bright room, whose walls were pierced with wide bays that looked out over the garden. It is the same room I find myself in today, twenty years later, the reed in my hand, a frail old writer trying to make the dead speak.

Rumi entered and ordered us to cover the doors and windows. He then added, making sure I heard him, "And no food."

I sent the cook away and used a large piece of canvas to cover the room's broad bay windows.

This went on for ten days and nights. Rumi left at dawn on the eleventh day, sallower and thinner than ever before, and immediately asked for some paper made in Baghdad. From my pocket I withdrew a few sheets. He took several steps to unstiffen his legs, turned his face to the rays of the sun, swallowed some bread seasoned with poppy seeds, and drank a few sips of tea. Then, while walking back and forth, he composed verses in Arabic and Persian. I wrote without really understanding what he was saying. At times, it seemed that his ideas were intended for a world that was not ours, that they grazed the untouchable. When he stopped, I asked him for his approval to read them aloud. We were on the terrace, facing the old trees covered with snow. I heard my own voice pronounce words that were intact, primordial, original, words before which even the snowflakes seemed to bend.

When I had finished reading, Rumi led me to the kitchen and ordered the oven to be lit. This was done. He then took the sheets blackened with the letters I had written and tossed them one by one into the flames. He then looked at the hungry fire and said, "Having come from the invisible, those words return to the invisible, without defect."

For good luck I wanted to preserve one or two of the pages. He stopped me and said that the virginity of those mysteries was not suited to the ears of the best in the land. Only the souls of the chosen could hear the words, which were their spiritual nourishment.

And as he left the kitchen, he grabbed a large clove of raw garlic and composed the following poem as he chewed:

Your nature is that of God when you enter a heart.
You reveal the brilliance of Mount Sinai through your heart.

Your nature is that of the lamp, entering the house at night.
And the entire house is lit by the glow of that light.

Your nature is that of wine in whatever group you happen to be.
From your handsome face two thousand outbursts and rebellions
    burst forth.

When joy is hampered by fear, when desire has flown,
What flowers will grow, and plants, from your welcome shower!

When the world is sorrowful, when joy is dead,
You, from the invisible, what other worlds do you open!

This appeal comes to you from the restless,
For, otherwise, how would that dark mud experience grace?

My speech nourishes the angels but if I remain without speech,
The hungry angel says to me, "Speak, why do you remain
    silent?"

He completed his ghazal and asked me to accompany him to
the Zirva hamam. There, he plunged into a pool of boiling water,
where he stayed a very long time. Rumor, or legend, has it that he
didn't return to the school for seven days. During his absence, I
reread the manuscript of the *Masnavi*, surrounded by hungry angels.

That same year (1262), my master's son, Ala, whose jealousy
of Shams was such that he persecuted and attacked him, died of a
disease at the age of thirty six. As he had been chased from the
house following Shams's disappearance, Rumi did not go to his
funeral and deprived him of the prayer of the dead. Except for
Sultan Walad, no one accompanied the deceased to the mausoleum, where his grandfather, the Sultan of the wise, lay. A sinister end for an ignominious man.

It was my habit to go, once a day, to the graves of the Sultan
of the wise and Salah. Because of my lingering love for Shams, ever
since Ala's death, I had avoided looking at his tombstone, fearing
that compassion would cause me to read the prayer of the dead. I
wanted the soul that had so tormented Shams to wander in chaos
and anguish for all eternity.

One day, however, after I had read the litany of the *verd-e
vaqt*, the prayer of the dead, over the two graves, I happened to
glance, inadvertently, at the grave of the banished son. For a second I thought I saw the angels of punishment tie Ala's hands and
feet with heavy chains and lead him away, thus bound. I saw that

he was crying and whimpering, and lamenting terribly. My heart caught fire and I heard myself implore God to obtain his absolution. Then, I saw the same angels untie Ala, leaving him where he was, and disappear.

A week later, my master went to the family mausoleum. I went with him and helped him light the *espand*, the incense against the evil eye, wash the graves, and sprinkle them with rosewater. He recited the litany of the "corpse," then asked me for ink and a sharp pen. Until then he had never composed anything in a place marked by death. I handed him my writing case. He took it, approached Ala's grave, for which he had had only disdain and contempt until then, and wrote on the stone, covered with a layer of plaster:

> Oh generous one, if you accept only the good,
> Where will the evil man moan or cry?

I approached and read the lines, and understood that the idea of pardon had also affected the Master. Ala would be forgiven. Without my asking, Rumi said to me, "I saw, in the invisible world, that my God, Shams of Tabriz, had made peace with him. Yes, Shams pardoned him and intervened on his behalf. Now Ala is one of those we mourn for, one of those protected by divine mercy."

In spite of his wickedness, Ala had obtained eternal peace because of Shams. The man who haunted his nights, who made him sweat with rage, the man he wanted to torture, wound, and kill, had, in the other world, interceded on his behalf and obtained his forgiveness.

I left the grave site listening to my master humming:

> The merchandise no one wanted,
> Has been bought because of this charitable man.

I looked away toward the graves of the Sultan of the wise and Salah the goldsmith, covered with musical instruments, twisted turbans, and flower petals. I thought about the wonderful fate offered to those men of God. I stood alone in the middle of the mausoleum and suddenly felt that my master would one day rest on the place where I was standing. I tried to imagine what would become of him after his death. The morbid thought of his disappearance invaded me. What would become of me without him? Would my child, the *Masnavi*, have reached maturity? I closed the eyes that saw, there before me, the burial ceremony, and recalled our meeting twenty-two years earlier. In mourning after my father's death, I had discovered Rumi when he was already involved with Shams. At the very moment I had thrown myself at his feet, he had grabbed my hand and squeezed it. He then caressed my thin beard and asked that I let it grow.

No diary will ever record that meeting, no biography will bear witness to that caress, which in a moment had so transformed my life.

marry Salah's daughter to Nezam the calligrapher, it was to her that we turned our outstretched hands. This too, I have related.

However, to illustrate the generosity of this noble woman, I cannot leave out the story of the ruby and the architect's dream.

An architect by the name of Badr, very much in vogue ever since the construction of the Koranic school, the madrasa of Qaratay, joined us in my house in Faliras to celebrate the sama. For that purpose I had renovated a few of the cells into a *sama khaneh*, or dance hall.

Our brotherhood began, as any order, by adopting certain rituals. Even dancing and whirling, which were supposed to lead to ecstasy and liberation, did not escape the regulations. So when I had wanted to construct the sama *khaneh*, Thiryanos, who had just come from having his hair cut and trimming his beard, forced me to follow each and every code. We had to erect an octagonal balustrade in the center of the room, install a mihrab, the niche indicating the direction of Mecca, on the back wall, and a *manbar*, a pulpit, on the right side of the same wall, facing the entrance door. This was done.

On the day the famous architect arrived, there were eighteen of us celebrating the sama. Ever since what I refer to as my insemination by the first eighteen verses of the *Masnavi*, that number has come to symbolize our community. To celebrate the sama according to the rules, we took our places in the room. A dervish lit the lamps and spread, before the mihrab, a red sheepskin, an allegorical image for Shams of Tabriz, on which my master sat. The musicians and singers arrived with their instruments: ney, daf, and rabab. They settled in along the northern wall, facing the mihrab.

On our heads we wore a *sikke* and were dressed in long white *tanoureh*. For us dervishes, who were beginning to be known as "whirlers," the hat represented the grave stone and its whiteness the winding sheet. Over the *tanoureh* we wore a black coat, the thick, heavy *kherqeh*.

The sama began with a reading of verses from the Koran and

I am your intimate being

I HAVE NOT YET DESCRIBED THE OBEDIENCE OF THE SULTAN'S court toward my master. Not a day went by that an emir, a governor, or a noblewoman didn't show up at the school. Rumi did not meet them all, but for them the simple fact of finding themselves close to the Master felt like a form of purification.

Princess Gordji, the daughter and sister of sultans and wife of Moin Soleyman, prime minister and emir of Konya, never missed an audience with Rumi. I often saw her show up at the school, disguised as a commoner, accompanied by a single servant. My master allowed her to share his solitude. She would remain with him for hours on end, after which, the imperial guard, a security detail of soldiers, and government emissaries appeared to escort her back to the palace.

Out of fear of being too far from the Master, she had decided not to leave Konya. Once, forced to travel to Caesarea, she ordered the greatest painter in the sultanate to make a portrait of Rumi, which would serve as her spiritual companion during her travels. I have already related the story. I don't know what happened to the portrait.

The princess supported us financially. When we wanted to

prayers to the Prophet and his family. Then, the drums and flute began, the same flute that, in Rumi's poetry, is the symbol of separation.

We then rose and walked around the room three times, from right to left. Each revolution symbolized the four paths of our holy religion: the exoteric path of *sharia*, the esoteric path of *tariqa*, the gnostic path of *marifa*, and *haqiqa*, the path of union.

We then removed our black coats to reveal our long white garments, a sign of liberation from material possessions and the rebirth of the spirit. Preceded by the *samazen*, the leader of the dance, our arms crossed, we approached the Master and placed our lips on his right hand and received, as a sign of approval, his kiss on the *sikke* we wore on our heads.

We then began to turn, the palm of our right hand open to the sky, a sign of welcome to divine beneficence, the palm of our left hand turned toward the ground, evoking the offering of that same beneficence to the creatures of the Earth. When Rumi entered the dance, in the center of the circle, we were nothing but motion. We were only him. I heard him chant:

The wheel of the sky tells me I am weak in the face of your
    dance,
I say to it: through this point I become a compass.

After an hour, Rumi stopped the dance. The music stopped. He sat on the ground. We returned to our places, making sure we did not turn our backs on him and put our coats back on. Before leaving the sama khaneh, my master pronounced the divine name *hu* until he was out of breath. Together, musicians, singers, and dervishes, we expelled the final "u" until our lungs felt they were going to burst.

Outside, the dervishes went their separate ways. Exhausted by the sama, the architect fell asleep on the ground, along with our other friends. He awoke suddenly, holding a ruby in his left hand.

Stunned, he let out a cry, ran to the Master, and begged his forgive-ness. The ruby was Rumi's answer to the incredulity of the dreamer. For, in his dream, the architect had doubted the miraculous power of the Master, which led to his confusion upon awakening and his plea for absolution.

I never learned where the ruby really came from. But it was later given to the princess. Upon Rumi's advice, the architect went to the palace and offered the stone to the great lady. In exchange, she showered the donor and his companions with gifts.

Still, I remained confused and continued to wonder about the provenance of the gem. My master reminded me of an anecdote from the *Masnavi*, where a dervish changes the branches of a tree into gold. Not only had I not forgotten but I recalled the exact cir-cumstances of its composition. We were in the countryside, busy planting saffron bulbs in rows. Rumi said to me:

"All my stories, just as my descriptions of other persons, in fact describe the situation of our friends. Although our predeces-sors made use of alchemy to transform matter, I find that the true alchemy, the alchemy that truly astonishes, is the one that changes the understanding and the intellect."

In his eyes the ruby the architect held in his left hand repre-sented nothing as long as his intellect and his understanding had not been transformed.

The princess's brother, Sultan Rokn al-Din, had risen to the throne a year before Salah's death through the intervention of the Mongol general Baidjou, who, after crushing a rebellion near Konya, had freed him from prison and placed him at the head of the ruling house. At the same time, the emir Moin Soleyman, the princess's husband, was appointed prime minister.

My master's attitude toward these events was always unex-pected. Naturally, he was pleased with Moin's appointment to a high position in government, for he was his fervent disciple. He was also pleased with the spiritual submission shown to him by successive sultans. During the period of union with Salah, the sultan Ez al-Din had, on several occasions, shown his consideration. But the visit of a sultan or the subordination of an emir did not really impress him. His admiration was fed by other streams.

From the first day of his rule, Sultan Rokn al-Din displayed extreme humility before the Master. He publicly called him "my father" and ignored none of his requests. However, after several years, influenced by a group of courtiers who studied with an old ascetic by the name of Sheikh Baba, he slowly turned away from Rumi, ultimately submitting himself fully to his new guide.

That day, the sultan had called us to come celebrate the sama in the building of the metalworkers, those who made copper vessels. I accompanied my master, as always. Rumor had it that without me he would never go outside and that, even if he did, he didn't talk, didn't laugh, and never danced. On that day, therefore, he was supposed to go out, laugh, speak, and dance. And for that reason I accompanied him.

As always, he presented himself last out of respect for anyone of lesser importance who might arrive late. Having arrived before him, I saw an old man, small, thin and frail. He was dressed in a dark blue *qaba* of rough fabric that fell just below his knees and was secured at the waist by a belt of rough canvas. The color was dark enough to conceal any dirt. The contrast between his appearance and that of the sultan, whose clothes were embroidered with threads of gold and silver, and strewn with gemstones, drew our attention. The fame of the old man, the ascetic known as Sheikh Baba, was widespread. The story of his mortifications was known to everyone in Konya.

The entire assembly showed him great respect. The courtiers prostrated themselves before him and invited him to sit at the place of honor. The sultan himself left his throne and sat next to him on a simple stool. Before my eyes I saw all the signs of subordination of a sultan to his sheikh without realizing that the devotion of Rokn al-Din, like a bird that flies away, had left Rumi's branches and settled in Baba's. This was obvious to my master for, when he entered, he greeted the sultan and withdrew to a corner. Reciters read the Koran. Afterward, Rokn al-Din addressed Rumi in these terms: "Let the Master and the great wise men know that, from today, I will serve Sheikh Baba. I have chosen him as my father and he has accepted me as his son."

Everyone present congratulated the ascetic. It was in the midst of this praise that I heard my master's voice shout out, "If the sultan has made Sheikh Baba his father, well, then, I will choose another son."

He rose and left the metalworkers building barefoot. The applause stopped.

As my master was leaving, I turned to look at the sultan. At that moment I had the sudden, shocking vision of the sultan without a head, decapitated. I was still haunted by this image when my friends surrounded me and asked me to find Rumi and bring him back. It was pointless. I knew he wouldn't return. As we spoke my master must have been flying over the Prairie of the angels. The participants dispersed. Some went to look for Rumi, others accompanied the old ascetic, the sultan's new father, to his very humble home.

Days passed without the sultan's choice casting a shadow, no matter how slight, on our behavior. The students did not leave the school and we were forced to turn away candidates for the sama.

One day the sultan appeared. His face, generally made up and clean shaven, showed traces of rebellious hairs and the signs of a sleepless night. Toward Rumi he displayed an almost excessive show of respect by prostrating himself before everyone. Then the two of them withdrew into an isolated room. The sultan remained there for a short time and left, looking downcast and uncertain.

I immediately went to Rumi and asked him the reason for the sultan's visit. Called to Aksaray by the emirs to form an alliance with the Mongols, Rokn al-Din wanted to know if he should go. In response Rumi simply said to him, "It's better if you don't go."

However, Rokn al-Din did go. When he arrived in Aksaray,

the plotters led him to an isolated spot where only the mad and the insane passed from time to time. There they strangled him as he cried out, "Rumi! Rumi!"

At the same moment, we were in the *sama khaneh*, busy celebrating the spiritual dance. Suddenly, my master interrupted his revolutions, put his two index fingers in his ears, and ordered that flutes and other instruments customarily used to celebrate good news be brought in. This was done. He placed the ends of the flutes in his ears, cried out, then composed the following poem as he turned around and around:

Didn't I tell you, "Don't go, for I am your intimate being?"
In this mirage of nothingness, I am the source of life.

I may forgive you and let you wander for a hundred thousand years.
In the end, you will return to me, for I am your finality.

Didn't I tell you, "Do not be satisfied with the goals of this world."
For I am the one who orchestrates the world of your satisfaction.

Didn't I tell you, "I am the ocean and you are a fish?"
Do not end up dry for I am the sea of qualities.

Didn't I tell you, "Do not fall into a trap like the birds."
Come, for I am the strength of flight, the feather and feet.

Didn't I tell you, "You are being robbed, you are being chilled."
For I am the fire, the throbbing and warmth of your desire.

Didn't I tell you, "You are said to possess vile traits?"
Until you forget that I am the source of your traits.

If you are the light of the heart, know where the road to the
    house lies.
If you have the quality of God, know that I am the God of
    your house.

When the dance stopped, he tossed his coat into the prayer niche and said: "Let us now celebrate the prayer of the corpse."

We obeyed him without understanding the reason for the mysterious behavior. Sultan Walad was given the responsibility of explaining the situation. But even before he questioned his father, Rumi said, "They were in the process of strangling poor Rokn al-Din and, in that state, he called out my name. I could not intervene against divine fate. But nor did I want his voice to reach my ears and disturb me. I deliberately placed the end of the flute in my ears so I would not hear his cries."

In this way we learned of the sultan's death. The court learned of it from the blood-covered soldiers who entered the prime minister's palace to tell princess Gordji that she should now wear mourning for her brother. The noblewoman never learned that the one who ordered the murder was none other than her own husband, Moin Soleyman, my master's faithful disciple.

Unlike Shams and Salah, the antipathy of the envious did not manifest itself in the form of plots or attempts on my life. It appeared in the form of the aggressive features of a man named Akhi Ahmad, who wanted to sabotage my appointment to head the khaneqah of Ziya.

The administrator of the royal estate, a man named Tadj, had decided to turn over control of the khaneqah to me, for it had been unmanaged since the death of the former administrator. I wasn't especially looking for this type of responsibility. So, my first reaction was to consult my master and express to him my concerns: the inevitable separation, my absence and the inevitable halt in composing the *Masnavi*. In spite of my arguments, which I found convincing, he encouraged me to obtain the position and devote myself to it body and soul.

Several days later, a magnificent ceremony, organized by Tadj, brought together all of the city's luminaries to celebrate the event. I asked Rumi not to go, knowing that he would be bored and would transmit his boredom to me. Once again he surprised me.

He insisted on going. Generally, we did not host such functions or attend such meetings. Our practices were again disrupted.

The day of my appointment, I went early to the khaneqah of Ziya. I stood a long time before the imposing tree that dominated the courtyard and greeted it, as Rumi would often greet trees. The sun was barely in the sky and cast a weak light on the mausoleum where the different masters of the brotherhood were buried. I opened the wooden door, which creaked a little. The light entered the cold room with me and lit the inscriptions on an old grave. I wiped away the dust that hid half of the deceased's name and discovered that it was a woman, something rare, possibly unique. I remembered the stories concerning the life of the great mystic of Rabia, like the one in which the Kaaba came to meet her in the middle of the desert, and she cried out, "What do I have to do with the Kaaba? What I need is the master of the Kaaba!" She took a different path and didn't even bother to look at the holy place that had moved itself for her.

In reading the prayer to the dead over the grave of the unknown woman lying at my feet, I wondered if she wasn't connected by a bond to the woman who had gone before her and whose fame had been known for centuries.

On the other side of the building, a fountain of white stone, surrounded by walls, served for ablutions. I performed my religious purification and entered the main room of the khaneqah, which was lit by lanterns and supported by a large number of columns. On a throne I saw my name, Hesam Hassan Tchalapi, son of Mohammad, son of Hassan, sewn with gold thread on black fabric. I heard footsteps. This was the guardian of the khaneqah, who had come to give me the ritual costume: a white garment that fell from the neck and was larger from the waist down, a white vest, a black belt tied on the left side, and a conical felt headpiece the color of honey. Thus attired, I waited for the arrival of the others.

The first to arrive were some friends of my father, whose

names I had completely forgotten. Upon his death, when I had dissolved his brotherhood and sold everything in the house, down to the last stick of furniture, to pay for Shams and Kimia's wedding, his friends criticized me. Now, the management of the khaneqah, and not just any khaneqah but the khaneqah of Ziya the minister, had been turned over to me. Now they returned, willingly or not, trying to find, or recall, similarities between my illustrious father and myself. They all knew about my friendship with Rumi but some of them, out of jealousy, feigned ignorance. Others, out of curiosity, wanted only unusual details about daily life at the school; still others tried, through an obvious show of indifference, not to reveal their enthusiasm.

There also arrived all sorts of visionaries, mystics, dervishes, Sufis, ascetics, hermits, anchorites, and loners. Men of the court came as well, including Tadj, my employer.

My master arrived last. I hurried over to him to prostrate myself at his feet. He held me back and, removing my prayer rug from his shoulder, he spread it on the throne, where I was to take my place. These signs served to increase my spiritual rank before the assembled. At the time I was barely thirty-five years old. I was hoping to encourage the Master to complete the *Masnavi*, to assist Sultan Walad in writing down the *Fihi Ma Fih*, to finish compiling the *Sayings of Shams*, and to use all my skills to maintain my master's love for me. At the time I never thought about a time after Rumi. But Rumi, he thought about it. That is why he encouraged me to become the head of the khaneqah, why he refused to allow me to prostrate myself before him, why he carried my prayer rug on his shoulder. With these signs he publicly appointed me, but without saying so, his successor.

Reciters arrived and read verses from the Koran. Afterwards, Tadj had me sit on the throne. I obeyed, trying to avoid Rumi's eyes. Deep in my heart I felt that he was the only man who deserved the seat. When, at Tadj's request, I prepared myself to lead the prayer, a man by the name of Akhi Ahmad, about whom

Thiryanos had already warned me, rose suddenly, pushed me, and said, "My brothers and I do not accept you as our sheikh."

At once, the khaneqah, a place of meditation and withdrawal, was turned into a battlefield. The brotherhood, ordinarily peaceful and easy going, quickly pulled out their knives and challenged the critics. Akhi Ahmad's band, better equipped, had sabers and swords. The men began shouting, blood flowed, and I thought only of protecting my master from some anonymous blade. Because of my physical strength, I managed, without harm and in a few movements, to separate Rumi from the brawl and lead him to a platform that overlooked the room.

I waited for him to say something. But he kept silent and watched the fight, not without a certain amusement. Finally, when the oldest brawlers collapsed from exhaustion and the cleverest looked for a way to stop fighting, he said to them, "In looking at you I see men who destroy their homes with their own hands."

Then, from the platform and so that everyone could see, he placed his hand on my head and composed the following, which was directed at me:

Your love came last, but will be greater than the first,
For God himself has said that the last shall be first.

Looking at the spectacle at his feet, which in no way resembled a dignified gathering, where dervishes with bloody faces mixed with recumbent visionaries, a knife in their hand and their hair in disorder, he added, "Remember the Prophet of Islam. Was he not the last messenger; did he not say he was the last who would be first? In the same way Sheikh Hesam is the last who will be first in my heart, in your hearts, as in the entire universe."

He then descended the platform, leaning on my shoulder, and walked out, as always when he was angry, barefoot. I went with him and left Thiryanos with the job of calming the assembly.

Informed of the brawl started by Akhi Ahmad, the sultan

called his minister of justice and ordered him to judge and execute the accused as soon as possible. Akhi Ahmad's life was saved only through the personal intervention of Rumi, who pleaded for his life.

He came to the school to thank the master, but was asked to go away. Rumi refused to see him and said, "He's not one of us."

From that day on Akhi Ahmad was abandoned by everyone, even the worst degenerates. When the companions saw him on a street corner, they changed sides, sometimes even direction. Ordinary men walked faster, shouting, "Do not touch him! Do not touch him!" and avoided any contact with the pariah.

Later, Tadj organized a new coronation ceremony, after which I officially became the prior of the monastery of Ziya. Later, while I was still engaged in writing the *Masnavi* under the Master's dictation, I was also entrusted with the management of another khaneqah, that of Lala. Once again, Rumi forced me to accept the responsibility. He was not present at the ceremony but congratulated me warmly. In this sense of urgency, I felt that he wanted to make sure my future was stable and comfortable. The man of separation, abandonment, sudden shocks and uncertainties, now worried about my old age. That too is strange.

Abandonment

AFTER FIFTEEN YEARS TOGETHER, I HAD ACCOMPLISHED MY mission: to write, read, correct, and complete the *Masnavi*. When Rumi composed the last poem of the sixth volume— a dialogue between a mother who tells her son, terrified by his dark thoughts, to overcome them by attacking them head on—I did not feel we had completed our work.

We were in the caravansary of the sugar merchants, where twenty nine years earlier, the encounter—I should say, the collision—between Shams and Rumi took place. We were looking at the various forms of sugar, crystallized, in bricks, liquid, when my master completed the final poem of the *Masnavi* with these lines:

In my heart, joyful speech is that
Which from heart to heart finds its opening.

He spoke the word "opening" and said to me, "It's finished."
Suddenly, fifteen years of enthusiasm, passion, intoxication, delirium, and exaltation were over. Our child had been born with the word "listen" and was going to escape with the word "opening." Our child was the voice of love. Engendered by a cry of separation,

he recommended, after fifteen years of wandering and setbacks, that we choose the opening of the heart.

I felt as much bitterness as joy. I was proud of having been able to complete our efforts, to have seen our child grow up. But the completion of the *Masnavi* also pointed to my inactivity, my uselessness. For a long time I had asked myself about the nature of Rumi's love for me. I found the answer in the conception of the *Masnavi*. And I realized that the end of the great poem marked the conclusion of our history and our separation.

I was right to be afraid. For shortly after the conclusion of the poem, Rumi called Sultan Walad, Thiryanos, Moin Soleyman, Princess Gordji, Kera, Fatima, and myself together.

It was very cold. Snow covered the courtyard, and the biting wind in Konya penetrated the house through the cracks in the old doors. While removing my slippers to enter the room, I remembered the hundreds of times I had done so to attend meetings here. One of them would have been enough for an entire life to blossom, to burst open.

Having crossed the threshold, I suddenly began to sweat profusely. What if he was going to announce our separation?

He arrived. We prostrated ourselves. He ordered us to rise. Then, at the very moment my eyes met his, I felt that my anxiety of being rejected was nothing but a wisp of straw compared to the weight of what he was going to tell us. His skin sallower than ever, his hands trembling slightly and his voice shaky, he said:

"Do not fear my departure. You will remain with me in all circumstances. Think of me and I will show myself to you. Whatever garment I wear, I will belong to you always and will fill your thoughts with secret meanings."

He stopped a moment, then continued.

"My life is a benefit for you. My death as well will be a benefit for you."

Princess Gordji burst into tears. Fatima cried out for the second and last time in her life—the first had been on the day of the assembly when she had cried out against the anger of her husband, Sultan Walad. The emir, Moin Soleyman, banged his head so hard against the wall that he began to bleed. Sultan Walad scratched his face. Thiryanos suddenly began speaking Greek. Kera threw off her veil, tore her clothing, and revealed her flesh. She said, "Oh light of the universe! Oh breath of mankind! Oh secret of this breath! To whom shall we turn? Where are you going?"

Rumi answered, "I shall not remain outside your circle."

Her flesh still visible to our eyes, she continued. "Will someone other than you appear?"

Rumi removed his turban, unknotted it, and delicately covered Kera's body, saying, "If he appears, it will still be me! In the universe, I have two attachments: one to you and the other to my body. When, through the favor of the unique King, I shall be stripped of this body you see here, the other will remain for you."

In my confusion, I decided to negotiate with God, to offer ten years of my life to delay Rumi's death, if only for a few months. That God that Salah cursed, that Shams embraced, that Rumi held in his mouth could also, I was certain, grant me this relief. But it was not to be.

Before closing the meeting, my master placed his forehead against each of ours and remained that way a long time. When he touched Thiryanos's forehead, he was still speaking Greek.

I was about to leave the room when Rumi ordered me to accompany him to his bedroom.

There, he wrapped himself in a blanket and spoke to me of the time we had spent together. He told the story of the grammarian who had fallen into a well. A dervish tried to rescue him by using sentences whose grammar was incorrect. My master asked me if I still remembered the ending of the story. I hadn't forgotten. The grammarian, from the bottom of the well, corrected the dervish's mistakes. The dervish, annoyed, left the grammarian in the well and shouted, "Stay there then until I correct my grammar!"

He also spoke of the day when he had felt that the prophet Khezr, whom he called "my brother," deprived him of his conversation because he was taking too much time with his grooming and winding his turban. That too I hadn't forgotten. Ever since the incident, my master no longer wound his own turban. He gave this responsibility to his companions, who placed it on his head.

It was slowly becoming night. Behind the door the sultanate's most distinguished doctors were gathered. They waited in vain. My master's death was not one that medicine could address or correct. Those men, whom the emir had taken from the hospitals and the bedsides of other invalids, were sent away. From behind the door, crying could be heard, objects were broken, footsteps faded quickly away. In the room Rumi slowly fell asleep, his head on my knees.

I heard him recite, in a weak voice, strange litanies:

"Oh great God! I am prepared for any terror, any burden, any sorrow, any delight, any marvel, any sin, any calamity, any obedience, any disobedience. Oh great God! Place a light in my heart, a light in my grave, a light in my ears, a light in my eyes, a light in my hair, a light in my skin, a light in my flesh, a light in my blood, a light in my bones, a light before me, a light behind me, a light beneath me, a light above me, a light to my right, a light to my left. Oh light of light! Make me light."

He wasn't surprised to see me writing. For fifteen years I had written down everything he had said.

He concluded his lengthy litany and sat up. He remained like that, leaning against me, wrapped in his shawl. As he went to change his position, I thought I saw a young man appear, whose beauty nearly caused me to lose consciousness. In love stories I had read where the lovers seemed to faint on nearly every page. I would never have thought that a simple vision could shake me up like this. My master welcomed the young man with great courtesy and asked me to remove his sleeping clothes. I helped him undress. Then, seeing that neither the Master nor the handsome intruder were moving, I advanced toward him and asked him who he was, why he was here. He answered:

"I am death. I have come at the order of the Most High to learn the will of the Master."

I then heard Rumi's voice say to him:

Advance! Advance! Oh my breath!
Oh messenger from the court of my Sultan!

He then added, calmly, "Carry out the order that was given you."

The apparition disappeared.

I had just seen the angel of death. The doors of the other world, the world where Rumi, Shams, and Salah were with God, the world where thoughts took shape, those doors, so ardently desired, had just opened before me.

My master put his clothes back on and asked me for a basin filled with water, where he soaked his feet. Silently, I wiped his forehead and chest as he murmured poems I have tried to learn by heart:

The friend bore a cup filled with poison
And yet we drank, for it was offered by his hand.

We are, from within, far above the sky.
Matter places us below the earth.

Through our qualities we will arise.
And yet we have the appearance of the dead.

From outside, I heard the family and the disciples crying loudly. Rumi told me to ask them to be quiet. "Tell them I understand them, but what good does it do to scream so loud?" He then said to me, "My friends pull me from this side, and Shams calls from the other. I must go."

I continued to wipe his face with gestures that were involuntary, ancestral. I was in pain but didn't cry. My master was dying before my eyes. With his breath, he whispered, "Place my corpse above the other graves, for I will be the first to rise."

I was about to leave to carry out his wishes when Sultan Walad, he too broken by sorrow, entered the room. Rumi caressed him for a long while then asked him to go and rest. Sultan Walad left. On the doorsill, I asked him to change the arrangement of the graves inside the mausoleum.

Rumi fell asleep, his feet still in the basin. I gently caressed his eyebrows and the tendons on his hands.

When he awoke, he asked me to come closer, to place my face against his, my lip against his, my eye against his, and said to me:

Place my head on the pillow; go, leave me alone,
Leave me, for I am ruined, a nightwalker, wounded.

Alone in the night until day with the wave of desire,
If you wish, come and pardon; if you wish, make me suffer.

Leave me for fear that you too might fall into despair,
Choose the right path and leave the path that leads to despair.

He remained silent a moment, then began breathing faster. He turned his head away. His voice returned, weaker now, as if it had one last thing to say to me:

I am there, water in my sight, crawling in the corner of sorrow.
Upon the water of my sight, erect a hundred mills.

The stubborn one who exterminates us has a heart of granite.
If he kills, no one will say to him: "Remember the price
    of blood."

Fidelity is not forced for the king of pretty faces.
Lover with the sallow face, be patient, be faithful.

Aside from death, a pain for which there is no cure.
So how could I say: find a cure for this pain?

Yesterday evening in the street of love, dreaming, I saw
    an old sage.
He motioned to me with his hand: Decide and come with us.

If a dragon appears on the road, love is like an emerald.
With the light of that emerald, go and chase the dragon.

This was the last poem of Rumi's life. Death took him while
he was still speaking. It was 5 *Jamadi al-akhar*, 672 (Sunday,
December 17, 1273).

I placed my mouth on his and breathed in his last breath. I
undressed him, removing the mourning clothes he had worn since
Shams's disappearance, and dressed him in ordinary clothing. I
then opened the door and let the companions enter the room.

The emir kneeled before Rumi's body and stayed that way for
many hours. Behind him, standing, silent and serene, his wife,
Princess Gordji, observed the dead man. I was seated, my back to
the wall, and tried, with an effort that tore me apart, to acknowledge
that Rumi was no more. I told myself that, as soon as possible, we
should carry out the ceremonies, select the location for the grave,
arrange him as he had asked me, above the other graves, perform
the funeral rights, and then I no longer knew what to do. For a second I thought of asking him.

Death assured me that I would have no further response.

In the morning, we called an imam, respected by all, who proceeded to wash the corpse. Spontaneously, the companions sat on
the ground. When the imam poured water over the corpse, which
was lying on a litter, we drank every drop that flowed over the body.

Suddenly, the imam cried out and let his head fall on that of the Master. Later, he told me that at the moment he was washing his chest, Rumi had moved.

Thiryanos ran to the barber. He then met the funeral attendants. I was wandering around the courtyard when my Greek friend suggested that I not look at the body, which was being carried out of the house on a covered litter. I kept my eyes closed and imagined my master celebrating the sama and spinning until he was dizzy. By the gate, Thiryanos and Sultan Walad stood by as the procession passed. Later, I learned that at the exact moment when Thiryanos saw the Master's body, clothed in winding sheets, take its place in the carriage, he simply said, "Our Master is leaving."

I understood that death was a departure.

I opened my eyes and saw the two men approach me. We embraced one another. I understood that death was a reunion.

Each of us had something to do. As the school's accountant, I had to see to it that the burial expenses were paid. Sultan Walad had to take care of the matter of succession. Thiryanos was to inform the foreign disciples of his death. I understood that death was also responsibility.

When the purification was over, a procession, preceded by seven oxen, accompanied the corpse to the mausoleum of Rumi's father, the Sultan of the wise, where Salah was buried. In the street, men, women, scholars, Sufis, artisans, commoners and government officials, Greeks, Iranians, Turks and Romans, Christians and Jews surrounded the procession. Monks, a copy of the Bible in their hand, chanted verses from the Psalms, the Pentateuch, and the Gospels; the rabbis advanced as they read from the Torah.

The emir called the bishop and the chief rabbi, who were also present, to ask them the reason for such enthusiasm. They answered, "We have understood the truth of Moses, the truth of Jesus, and the truth of all the prophets from his teaching. We have seen in him what we have read about in books about the behavior of our prophets. We consider him to be the Moses and Jesus of our time."

A Jew added, "Rumi is the sun of truths. All creatures love the sun."

A Christian priest said, "Rumi is like bread. No one can do without bread. Have you ever seen a hungry man avoid bread? Oh, emir, you are far from knowing what he really was." The emir remained silent.

Readers of the Koran read the funeral verses. The muezzins called out the prayer of resurrection. Twenty groups of singers recited the songs of death, which had been composed by Rumi himself. Musicians beat the *naqarreh*, or kettle drum, and blew the *sorna*. Six times, the litter, seized by the crowd, was reduced to pieces.

It was almost night when the procession reached the mausoleum. Sheikh Sadr, named by Rumi when he was alive, waited to pronounce the funeral prayer. In the room, filled with the crowd, there was barely room to breathe. I greeted the sheikh. He reminded me of his last meeting with Rumi, when Rumi, refusing any other medication, had agreed to take only what Sadr recommended. While swallowing the syrup, he told him that, from then on, between the lover and the beloved, there remained nothing but a garment woven of poems, and that the light would rejoin the light.

I hadn't forgotten. I too remembered that on that day Rumi had refused all the bottles I offered him.

Sadr waited for the noise to die down before beginning.

"There has been but one sheikh in the world. He is gone. Now the thread of the meeting will be broken, the clasp on the necklace of thought will be lost. Now, the organization of business will languish, the people's discipline decline. Now, there will remain no further trace of fraternity or pleasure, the throne of the fortune of sultans and emirs will be trampled upon by the Mongols, treasures and heads will be carried off, the schools and khaneqah shall be transformed into inns, benediction will vanish, the shadow of tyranny will fall upon the world and the universe will come undone."

The sheikh burst into tears. Those who heard his speech cried, while from outside we heard a loud, shout of sorrow.

I found myself next to Sultan Walad and Kera, when she told me in a low voice that she had just seen her husband floating in the air, his wings open wide, as if to protect us.

My friend Seradj, the man who, years earlier, had waited all night to visit with Rumi, approached and told me, while twisting his long mustache, "I have just spoken to the Master. I questioned him about the world in which he is and he said to me, 'I am not recognized in the other world any more than I was in this one.'"

I heard nothing, saw nothing.

When the corpse was placed in the tomb, I caressed my master's eyebrows for the last time. I kissed the meeting point of his brows to preserve the roughness of his hair on my lips for all time.

I placed my head on his heart and heard it beating. I kissed his forehead and quoted Shams, who had one day said, "The extinguished lamp will ignite the illumined lamp and leave."

Then his body was buried and his turban placed on the stone.

I waited for the mausoleum to empty out. It took hours before all the lights were extinguished and I could leave.

Inside the school the Master's cat refused to eat or drink and allowed itself to die after a week. Malakeh, Rumi and Kera's daughter, found the cat's body, washed it, wrapped it in a white sheet and buried it beneath the Master's tomb.

Every time I go to the grave, I recall something Shams said, "On a grave, someone had written, 'Life is no more than an hour.'" My life has lasted only an hour but I spent it with Rumi.

Epilogue

Shams of Tabriz, you have known love and not reason

IT TOOK ME FOUR YEARS TO WRITE THIS BOOK. DURING THAT time, my mother died and, after ten years of trying, I gave birth to a daughter. I named her after Rumi's grandmother—Kiara. The book was interrupted by periods of mourning, birth, and nurture.

My husband, who is also a writer and works constantly, often criticized me for these interruptions. I answered him by quoting a line from Rumi that begins: "For a certain time the *Masnavi* was delayed" (the *Masnavi* being the poet's greatest work and the greatest in Persian literature). The second half of the verse, I admit, escaped me at the time, and I forgot about it. It even seemed to me somewhat enigmatic. In fact, I had simply forgotten it. At the time I was breast feeding my daughter and my days were divided into three-hour periods that corresponded to her feeding times. One day, I opened the second volume of the *Masnavi* and read the opening lines:

For a certain time the *Masnavi* was delayed,
It takes time for blood to become milk.

"For blood to become milk." The words were addressed to me. I closed the *Masnavi*. I placed the book against my lips and my eyes—as is done with the Koran—and felt that I had made the right decision, that Rumi was with me.

This book is closely associated with the memory of my mother, Mahin Djahanbeiglou-Tajadod. When she was pregnant with me, she took courses in Persian literature at the University of Tehran. Even after she had obtained her doctorate, she regularly attended the seminar given by Badi al-Zaman Forouzanfar, the great Rumi specialist. She went every Thursday morning until the death of the famous professor put an end to his unique teaching.

When my mother, my husband, and I were working on a translation of a hundred poems from the *Divan of Shams of Tabriz*, her deep knowledge of Rumi's poetry was based on her attendance at Forouzanfar's seminar. Whenever we encountered problems, when her old notes were no longer adequate, she would call her friend in Tehran, Mohammad Reza Shafi'I Kadkani, the best of Forouzanfar's students, who would always have an answer for her.

Today, Professor Shafi'I Kadkani has replaced his teacher in the literature department at the University of Tehran. Once, during a class—this was after the creation of the Islamic Republic of Iran—a time when his seminar was attended not only by his own students but by other professors, auditors, and hundreds of people "thirsting" for knowledge of Sufism, he said, "God made a mistake in creating Rumi."

I did not want to write a scholarly treatise on Rumi's life, for, in spite of my academic background, I have never found that approach—complete, precise, in depth, implacable—to contain any trace of beauty or feeling.

I was enrolled in the École Pratique des Hautes Études working on my doctoral dissertation, which involved the study of an eighth-century Chinese Manichean text. One day, when the teacher had finally succeeded in deciphering, not without difficulty, a

Manichean manuscript written in Coptic, he asked what I thought
of it. I answered spontaneously that I found it "beautiful." The five
or six other students in the room glared at me. Within the walls of
academe, use of the word has been forbidden.

Later, I was constantly confronted by the same problem.
Beauty had to be sought outside the university. That is why I decided to tell this story by writing it in the first person. This did not,
however, free me of the need for scientific rigor. In *Rumi: The Fire
of Love* all the phrases exchanged by the characters are words
actually spoken by them. I have invented nothing, satisfying
myself, rather, with creating situations for my characters. I have
kept an annotated version with all the textual references.

So, this is not a scholarly biography. Had I wanted to write
one, I would have used formal names and titles: Djalal al-din
Mohammad Balkhi, also known as Khodavandgar ("lord"),
Khamoush ("extinguished," "silent"), Mowlavi, and later, Rumi.

If this were a scholarly biography, I would have provided an
exhaustive list of his works without limiting myself to the *Masnavi*
and the *Divan of Shams of Tabriz*. I would have added that the
Masnavi is a poetic form in which the verse lines, within a given
poem, adhere to the same meter and flat rhyme scheme, providing
us with the total number of couplets in Rumi's Masnavi: 26,000. I
would have written about his quatrains, his *Fihi Ma Fih*, collected
by his son, Sultan Walad, and presented as a series of interviews
with his followers, and especially with the powerful Seljuk minister Moin al-din Soleyman, of the *Makateb* ("Epistles"), and
Madjales-e sabaeh, his sermons. I would have mentioned his con-
temporaries, the great poet Saadi, as well as Fakhr al-din Eraqi, a
student of Sohravardi and an inhabitant of Konya. He is the one
who said about Rumi, "He came into the world a stranger, he was
a stranger, and he left a stranger." I might also have mentioned the
name of Safi al-din Hendi, the great theologian and his single-
minded goal: to ban the sound of the rabab, with which the
dervishes celebrated the sama. Rumi said of him that it was easier

to convert a thousand Christian unbelievers to Islam than to attrib-
ute purity to Safi al-din, for the scroll of his soul had become, like
the color of a child's homework, dark and obscure. I would also
have listed the names and dates of the Seljuk sultans of Asia
Minor: 'AlÇ' ad-D¥n Kay-QubÇd (617-634H/1219-1236), who
invited Rumi's father, Baha Walad, to Konya and wanted to house
him in his own home, and the brothers Izz ad-Din Kay Ka'us (643-
655H/1245-1257) and Rokn al-Din Kilij Arslan IV (655-
664H/1257-1266), both of whom were disciples of Rumi and
showed him unqualified respect. To conclude, I could have dis-
cussed his children, three sons and a daughter: Baha al-din
Mohammad, known as Sultan Walad (632-712H /1225-1314), Ala
al-din Mohammad (624-660H /1226-1262), Mozafar al-din Amir
Alam (†676H /1278), and Malakeh Khatoun (†703H/1305). And
so on.

I wrote in the first person—masculine—putting myself in the
place of the third man to play an important role in Rumi's life,
Hesam, or, more specifically, Hesam al-din Tchalapi Hassan ibn
Mohammad ibn Hassan, because of a line I had read in his biography, written after his death between 1318 and 1353, a simple
line from a fourteenth-century text—today's Persian has hardly
changed since then. That line was addressed directly to me and
required no commentary, and could easily do without an appara-
tus or exegesis of any kind.

One simple sentence. In Persian it reads: *va Mowlana eshq
bazi ba ou mikard*,[3] "And Mowlana (Rumi) with him (Hesam)
made love."

Before Hesam, there was Salah, and before Salah, the very
famous Shams, the Sun, the ember. But never had a line of such
clarity explained their relationship—mystical, esoteric, emblem-
atic—in such a simply human way. During my reading, I had gathered information on their spiritual retreats, their nights of solitude,

---

3. Aflaqu, *Manaqeb al-arefin*, II, 737.

their desires—even physical—without any clear indication that would have allowed me to describe those famous nights and observe the "lovers" directly.

"And Rumi with Hesam made love." That line allowed me to identify with Hesam, to be Hesam, and to feel as he did the experience of physical love in the first person, masculine singular. It allowed me to enter the cells, the hamams, the shops in the bazaar, and the caravansarys frequented by Rumi and the others. It also demanded that I search and try to understand how and why all this had been possible. That "I," that first person masculine, could not but know.

Why does Rumi suddenly say to Shams, to the man he loves most in the world, that he should leave, exposing him to death? Why this sudden separation? Why, from that moment on, do we witness the birth of one of the world's greatest poets? What role does love play in the pain of separation and creation?

The "I" I had chosen forced me to find an answer.

My husband suggested, however, that I retain a contemporary point of view, which would have allowed me to observe those "mythical" events, the foundation of Persian literature, more objectively. But it was too late. The "I" had already set off on the trail of Rumi, trying to discover how a poet was born of love.